MURDER AT THE KENNEDY CENTER

MARGARET TRUMAN

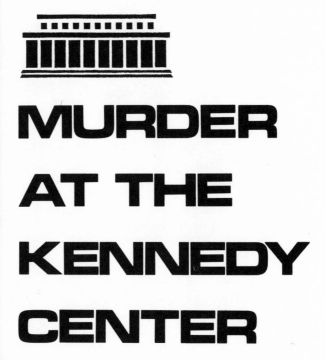

MURDER AT THE KENNEDY CENTER

RANDOM HOUSE
NEW YORK

Library of Congress Cataloging-in-Publication Data

Truman, Margaret
Murder at the Kennedy Center / by Margaret Truman.
p.   cm.
ISBN 0-394-57602-0
I. Title
PS3570.R82M754   1989
813'.54—dc20   88-43204

Manufactured in the United States of America

98765432

FIRST EDITION

Book design by Carole Lowenstein

For Aimee Elizabeth Daniel
with love
from Gammy

MURDER AT THE KENNEDY CENTER

ONE

MOMENTS AGO, she'd been angry and filled with the bravado such anger generates. She'd threatened, the volume of her voice kept low, the intensity high-pitched.

Now, she saw it. It was a revolver. Not a big one. There was a toylike quality to it.

"Don't be ridiculous," she said, her voice cracking, a tentative laugh behind the words indicating the fear that gripped her body. "No, please, don't do this. We can . . ."

The gun was thrust forward, its short barrel ramming sufficiently hard into the softness of her belly to move her back a step.

"Oh, no."

She saw the finger squeeze the trigger. Her flesh muffled the report. The bullet penetrated her, taking with it muscle and nerve, bone and skin. It tore through her back, slower and wider than when it had entered.

She was driven backward, her beautiful eyes open wide and fixed on the last sight they would ever see, the face of her murderer.

TWO

WELL, Leslie, how does it sound to you?"

The wife of Senator Kenneth Ewald smiled at Ed Farmer, her husband's campaign manager, an aide who seldom smiled himself. "Everything sounds wonderful, Ed. We all think we know about show biz, but I had no idea how much was involved in putting together an event like this. Ken will be delighted."

"That's because it's a one-time event; everything has to be invented or imported for the occasion," Farmer said in his characteristically flat tone. "There are very few genuine experts. It's like a presidential campaign."

The others in the Kennedy Center's George Rogers Clark Room agreed that everything seemed to have been covered; everything and everyone was in place or would be. From above, ceramic birds and animals looked down on them as if holding a meeting of their own, or judging this one.

The Marshall Boehm family had donated the room to the Center, including the collection of ceramic wildlife, and it was a popular tourist stop; there had been more than 85 million visitors to the handsome, sprawling arts complex since its dedication in 1971. The Clark–Boehm Room was seldom used for meetings, but a socialite on the committee who liked little animal and bird sculptures had pulled strings.

"It's a shame that Mac Smith couldn't be at this final meeting," Mrs. Ewald said, "after everything he's done to help us get this started and on track, and keep us legal. But his teaching comes first. It certainly looks as if it'll be worth the time and talent and money of everyone here, and we've certainly stocked the pond with celebrities."

"Boris," Farmer said, "have you any final comments?"

Seated at the opposite end of the table was a menacing man with a shaven head, hooked nose, and absolutely black eyes like moles in his head. Boris Trenka was the Kennedy Center's artistic director.

Trenka, who'd defected to the United States ten years earlier, after many years as artistic director of Russia's Bolshoi, said in a low voice thick with an accent, "This is a *television* production. I know nothing of television."

Farmer sighed. That was all he had heard from Trenka since they began to work on a musical gala to advance the presidential candidacy and the coffers of Ken Ewald, senator from California.

"I don't think we should adjourn until Georges returns," said one of Trenka's aides.

Another aide remarked, "I suppose he's still having trouble working out Sammy's transportation. There was a foul-up."

"I don't think we need to be concerned about the travel arrangements or the lives of the rich and famous," Farmer said. "That's Georges's job."

"I should hope it's not ours," said Trenka haughtily.

Farmer ignored him and looked at an attractive young woman seated to his left. "The stars will get here. Anything we've neglected to cover, Andrea?"

Andrea Feldman had worked with Ewald for a little over a year. Because a great deal of her five feet nine inches was in her legs, she didn't appear to be tall when seated. She had thick black hair that hung loosely to her shoulders, and a face surprisingly fair considering the dusky color of her hair and striking eyes. She wore a smartly tailored gray suit and white blouse with a simple collar, and her makeup was so expertly applied as to be undiscernible. Her nails were without polish, and the only jewelry she wore was a simple gold band on the ring finger of her right hand. She smiled. "No, Ed, I think that covers it. With all the high-priced talent around here, I can't imagine anything going wrong."

The door opened, and Georges Abbatiello entered the room. A veteran director of TV music specials, including the previous year's Grammy Awards, he was a short, slight man with thinning hair, a perpetual look of harassment, and hands in constant flight, small birds hovering around a feeder—or a meeting. "Sorry I'm late," he said, "but there's been a misunderstanding with Sammy's people." He plopped in a chair next to Trenka and said, "Sammy is marvelous, just dances through these problems, you know, the old soft shoe." He looked at Trenka. "Have I missed anything?"

Trenka said, "I think not. There is little to miss."

"Oh, there is something else," Andrea Feldman said, holding a finger in the air. "Miss Gateaux's manager wants us to put her on later in the program."

Abbatiello stood, hands moving. "That's ridiculous, impossible."

"Why?" Farmer asked.

"Why?" Abbatiello said in a voice that had risen to fly with his hands. "You don't just arbitrarily change the order of guest appearances. We've choreographed this down to the last second. The final version of the script is being typed at this moment. The orchestra has rehearsed everything in order. No, tell Ms. Gateaux's manager that one thing we don't need now is a diva's temperament." He sat down, elaborately weary.

"Why did you wait until now to bring this up, Andrea?" Farmer asked.

"I talked to her manager just an hour before the meeting and made a note to bring it up, only it got lost in the shuffle. She wasn't demanding it—was very nice, actually."

"I think it's ridiculous to have her on the program anyway," an Ewald media consultant said. "The senator, as everyone knows, is a jazz lover. He knows nothing from opera, so why have an opera singer? Opera doesn't pull in many votes."

"Jazz pulls even fewer. Are we really going to debate this now?" Farmer asked.

"I disagree," said Trenka, the first hint of amusement in his voice all day. "At least we will have some serious music represented."

"This whole conversation is academic," Farmer said, closing the briefcase in front of him to make the point that he was about to leave. "Roseanna Gateaux has been invited to participate, and she will. The senator likes jazz but was especially pleased when she agreed to appear on his behalf, and that's that." Farmer, a slender young man with rimless glasses, a hairline that had started its rapid rise in law school, and a fondness for colorful wide-striped shirts, bow ties, and penny loafers, had been with Ewald since the senator's early days in California as a national political figure.

"What do you think, Mrs. Ewald?" Andrea Feldman asked.

Leslie Ewald smiled. "I think I share Mr. Trenka's appreciation for having opera represented in the musical fare. I happen to particularly enjoy opera, and Ken loves jazz. One doesn't preclude the other. I think it's nice that both will be heard. Maybe we should include some rap music, too." There were a few smiles.

Farmer stood. "And," he said, "let's not go changing performance schedules at this late date. The show is tomorrow, and there's enough for this committee to do to make sure the parties and such go well. Thank you all very much, ladies and gentlemen, for taking yet more time this afternoon." To Andrea, he added, "Call Ms. Gateaux's manager, tell him to convey to her that we love her, that it is too late to make changes, that her part of the show is prime time, before audience fatigue sets in and before we lose part of the TV audience to a very popular network comedy that cuts in before we're finished. She's an artist, she'll understand."

Farmer and Leslie Ewald were the first to leave the room. As they led two Secret Service agents into the upper lobby outside the opera house, Farmer growled, "Stars. Spare me."

"I know, Ed, but it is wonderful that all these artists have agreed to appear on Ken's behalf tomorrow night. The jazz lineup alone reads like a Who's Who, and also having performers like Sammy Davis, Jr., and Joan Baez is really an incredible affirmation of their belief in him."

"More like a belief in having someone in the White House who appreciates them. Some of these performers aren't exactly what you'd call left-wing Democrats. Once they saw Ken pick up a head of steam in the primaries, they seemed to have forgotten the impurity of his ideology." He laughed scornfully. "Like all the other committee frauds."

Ewald had come in fourth in the Iowa caucus in February, third in the New Hampshire primary the same month. There was talk of dropping out. Then he took sixteen of the nineteen states on "Super Tuesday," March 8. That was when Perry, Bradley, Cuomo, Gore, Nunn, and Alexander called it quits, leaving only Ewald and Jody Backus in the remaining pro forma races.

Farmer and Leslie Ewald crossed the sprawling main lobby and passed through the Hall of Nations, the flags of all countries currently maintaining diplomatic relations with the United States lining the soaring white marble-veneer walls above them. Farmer helped Leslie on with her raincoat and opened the door to the outside, where her limousine waited. "Ride?" she asked.

"No, thanks. I'm going over to the office." The senator's private campaign office was across the street in the Watergate Office Building.

Leslie extended her hand. Farmer took it. She said, "It's going to work, isn't it?"

"The show tomorrow night?"

"No, the campaign. He's going to become president."

Farmer released her hand. "Let's just say things are looking good, but you never know. The last primary can't hurt him, and then the convention will be the coronation. As candidate. Unless something happens that throws everything off—which would open up the convention as it hasn't been opened for years."

She stared at him; he was never optimistic, which, she often thought, was unusual for the campaign manager of a man running for the White House. But every time she had those thoughts, she reminded herself that Ed was right, that in the rough-and-tumble, right-and-left, right-or-wrong democracy called the United States, there should be no celebrating until the final ballot had been cast on November 8, and until the Electoral College had pronounced its verdict.

She said, "Thanks for everything, Ed. The gala is going to be wonderful. What a send-off to the convention, what a boost. I may even find it gala and relax and enjoy myself."

"When you think about boosts and lift-offs, remember NASA and the *Challenger* astronauts," Farmer cautioned darkly.

Without another word, Leslie Ewald got into her limousine.

NOT far from Kennedy Center, in George Washington University's Lerner Hall, Mackensie Smith peered over his lectern at the students in his crowded class on advanced criminal procedures. He was a craggy, fine-looking man in heavy horn-rimmed glasses.

"I think that does it for today," he said, running his fingers over stubble on his cheeks, which seemed to reappear in minutes no matter how many times he shaved. "Aside from the cases you've been assigned to analyze by the next time we meet, I have an additional assignment for you." He smiled as assorted groans welled up. "I expect you to watch the musical salute to Senator Ewald tomorrow night."

A young man named Crouse said, "Professor Smith, I thought the classroom was not to be used for political purposes." The other students laughed along with him.

"And this classroom isn't," Smith said, closing his portfolio of lecture notes. "All I'm suggesting is that you take an hour out of your busy schedules and enjoy some good music. I expect well-rounded attorneys to graduate from this university."

"Professor Smith," a young woman called.

"Yes, Ms. Riley?"

"When Senator Ewald is elected president, will you be his attorney general?"

Smith sighed; he was tired of the subject. "If Senator Ewald becomes the next president of the United States, he will undoubtedly choose someone for that post who wants it. That rules me out. Watch the show. You'll be quizzed on it."

He went down H Street to Twenty-second, took a left to G, stopped in at DJ's Fast Break for a sandwich to go, and slowed to a leisurely walk in the direction of his home on Twenty-fifth. The sky was over-cast, and mist that threatened to degenerate into drizzle gave the air a thick quality. It was early June but felt like April, which, Smith reminded himself, was better than feeling like August in Washington, D.C. He pulled the collar of his raincoat up closer to his neck and thought of that question he'd been asked so many times since Ken Ewald seemed almost assured of his party's nomination.

Mac Smith and Ken Ewald went back a long time together. Their relationship wasn't intensely political. Smith had never been much interested in partisan politics, but certain issues, certain causes, had always been dear to him, and he approved of Ewald's stance on them.

They'd first met when Ewald had begun to push, vigorously and at great political risk, for legislation on gun control, particularly handguns. Smith, at the time, was one of Washington's most respected attorneys, especially in criminal law, and had been asked to testify at hearings held by Ewald's committee. Shortly after Mac Smith's appearance, he received a call from Ewald inviting him to a dinner party at the senator's home. That began a limited friendship that had deepened over the years. It wasn't that they spent much time together; their busy individual lives precluded that. But there were other parties, issues, occasional plane trips together, and Smith found himself not only the senator's friend, but an unofficial legal—and, at times, personal—adviser to Ewald and his family.

Issues beyond gun control drew Smith to Ken Ewald. The current president, Walter Manning, had little interest in the arts, and his administration reflected it. Ewald, on the other hand, was the leading Senate voice in support of all things cultural, and every writer and artist, every musician and theatrical performing-arts group in the country, knew that any slice of the Federal pie designated for them was the direct result of these years of Ewald's unfailing championing of their cause.

From Smith's perspective, Ewald was a well-balanced politician. As a freshman in Congress, he'd vigorously opposed the war, yet was a staunch supporter of maintaining military superiority over the Soviets. He'd called for the return of a WPA in which all able-bodied welfare recipients would work, or undergo training while collecting assistance, except the mentally ill, homeless, and AIDS victims. He had his faults, of course, but Smith had few reservations about supporting the man in his run for the White House, especially after the reign of Walter Manning.

Smith turned the corner at Twenty-fifth and headed for home, his narrow, two-story taupe brick house with trim, shutters, and front door painted Federal blue. Attorney general? he thought. It brought a smile to his face. He had thought of many things he might be interested in doing with the rest of his life, but being directly involved in executive-branch politics was not on the list.

He opened the door and entered the place that had been his home for the past seven years. Rufus greeted him with unwelcome enthusiasm. "Stay down," Smith said, pushing on the blue Great Dane's huge head. When Rufus stood on his hind legs, he looked his master in the eye.

Smith answered the ringing phone in his study, making sure to put his sandwich on top of the refrigerator, out of Rufus's reach.

"Mac, it's Leslie."

"Hello, Leslie, how are you?"

"Tired but happy. I just came from the final meeting on the show and party. It's going to be lovely, Mac. I'm so excited."

"Splendid. I assume Ken shares your enthusiasm."

"I think so, although I haven't seen him enough to find out. I'll be glad when the last of the primaries is over, the convention is behind us, and . . ."

Smith laughed. "And you're choosing drapes for the Oval Office."

"I don't dare say it. Bad luck to say such things. At least that's what gloomy Ed Farmer would say."

"Somehow, Leslie, I don't think luck will have much to do with it."

"I just wanted to tell you how well the meeting went, and to thank you again for your help."

"I didn't do much."

"More than you think. It's always comforting to have the clear-headed wisdom of Mackensie Smith on tap. I've got a last-minute idea Boris and Georges won't like. Have to run, Mac. See you tomorrow. Don't forget to shave and wear a clean shirt."

THREE

KEN EWALD, senior U.S. senator from California, stood alone in the anteroom behind the president's box in the Kennedy Center's opera house. Chairs upholstered in a white, green, and red floral pattern surrounded a glass-topped coffee table. The carpet was the color of ripe cherries. Small paintings dotted pale green walls.

He walked to where the seal hung next to the door and removed it from its hook. His fingers traced the raised wording: SEAL OF THE PRESIDENT OF THE UNITED STATES. The letters were in blue, the background gold. An eagle dominated the center, its breast a shield of red, white, and blue. The seal was always on the wall, unless the president and his party were attending an event in the opera house. When that happened, it was hung in front of the box for the audience to see. Tickets to the box were part of the president's patronage—to give, if he wished to share them. Otherwise, the box stood empty during performances.

Ewald opened the door and stepped into the box. Below were twenty-three hundred empty seats. The party to kick off that night's musical gala was in progress onstage. Ewald had been down there moments before. Bored, he'd wandered up to the box. The lead Secret Service agent assigned to him for the night, Robert Jeroldson, remained outside in the foyer on Ewald's instructions.

He looked down at the stage where Leslie, their son, Paul, and daughter-in-law, Janet, stood with some of the celebrities who would perform that night. His physical distance from them at that moment was symbolic; never before had he and Leslie worked so closely together, yet he knew the inherent pressures of seeking the presidency created tremendous and understandable pressures on her, and on their marriage. A politician's wife—she garnered more votes than any platform could.

He surveyed the stage for other familiar faces. They certainly were there, some pleasing, others representing necessary evils. He looked around the empty box and wondered at those who'd occupied the White House in the past. Some had spent considerable time in this presidential box. Others, like the sitting president, Republican Walter Manning, had been openly without interest in the artistic events that gave life to the nation's cultural center.

He looked down at the seal in his hands and was suddenly overwhelmed at the significance of the office it represented. The decision to run for president had not come easily to him. He'd spent countless hours of private debate over whether he was indeed qualified to lead a nation that not only was the most powerful on earth, but meant so much to him. He knew he was up to the task as far as experience and insight into the workings of government went. Years in Congress—first in the House, then in the Senate—had given him a broad and deep understanding of how things worked, how things got done. But was that enough? Did he want it badly enough, was there enough of the proverbial fire in his belly to carry into the job itself?

He thought back to when Eugene McCarthy had sought the presidency. McCarthy had been on a television talk show. The host—Ewald couldn't remember who it was—commented that certain critics of McCarthy claimed he did not want to be president bad enough, to which McCarthy replied, in his urbane manner, "No one should want to be president *that* bad." McCarthy had gone on to say during that interview that he thought every president should take off one day a week to read poetry, or to listen to music. Ewald had smiled at that comment; it represented, to some extent, his own feelings, even though he knew the suggestion was impractical.

He also thought back to Ronald Reagan, the only president who seemed to come out of the White House looking better and almost younger than when he'd entered. Days off to read poetry and listen to music (or to watch old western movies)? Perhaps. It really didn't matter. The fact was, Ken Ewald *did* want to be president of the United States, because he felt the things he believed in were good for the country, would take it from a White House mortgaged to big business, oil, and the furthest right of military interests, and return it to a White House in which people mattered more than machines and money.

He went back to the anteroom and hung the seal on the wall. Critics said that he was naive in some of his plans involving social welfare. There were his own dark moments when he thought they might be right, that the only way to govern America was to be hard-nosed, isolated, ruthless. Maybe. But even in those small hours, he told himself that he was not without his own hard edges, his own recognition that to govern effectively *was* to compromise, to allow pragmatism to take the edge off dreams. He was ready to do that. His dreams would be accommodated in the larger context of being president. First, you had to win. You had to *be* there if any part of any dream was to be realized.

By the time he returned to the stage, the party had gained momentum.

Ewald was delighted to see Paul. His son's successful import-export business had kept him in the Far East for two weeks, and there had been a question whether he would make it back in time for this salute to his father. Ewald had to smile as he thought of the telephone conversation they'd had a few days ago. Paul had called from Hong Kong, and after some talk about how well the campaign was going, he'd concluded with, "Dad, you know I'll be there if I have to rent a Chinese junk and row it all the way back myself." Ewald often told his friends that if you were only going to have one child, you were lucky to have one like Paul.

His daughter-in-law was another story. Small and slender, lips abstemious and poorly defined on a pinched face, Janet was a moody young woman—at least when Ewald was around her, which, he was grateful, wasn't often. What his handsome, successful son saw in her was beyond him, although he'd settled long ago on her superior bosom, surprising for such an otherwise meager frame.

Ed Farmer joined him. Ewald grinned, nodded, and said, "She's a beautiful woman, isn't she?," referring not to Janet but to Roseanna Gateaux, surrounded by a group of admirers off to the side of the sixty-four-feet-deep stage, a stage almost as large as the Metropolitan Opera House at New York's Lincoln Center, or Russia's Bolshoi.

His campaign manager said nothing.

"Just lusting in my heart," Ewald said, his smile expanding at the corners of his mouth. That smile, and the form it took, was part of the boyishness that balanced the crags and lines in his tan face. Soft, curly brown hair helped, too. He was forty-six, one of the youngest presidential candidates since John Kennedy.

Farmer looked meaningfully in the direction of a Washington columnist, stationed nearby behind a glass of champagne. "Keep those lines to yourself until after you're president . . . *Senator*," Farmer said sharply. "Come on, we need photos."

Ewald watched Roseanna Gateaux move gracefully to where a pianist, bassist, and violinist recruited from the National Symphony played show tunes, their melodies floating harmlessly up into a canyon of lights, pipe battens, grids, fly lines, and counterweight pulleys.

"Let's do some photos," Farmer repeated.

"Now?"

"Yes. How often are all of you together? We'll pose you with some of the stars, then do the family." Farmer gripped Ewald's arm and guided him to where his family stood with a few of the artists who would appear later that night. Ewald extended his hand to the pianist Oscar Peterson. "I've been collecting your records ever since they came out of Canada on ten-inch discs," Ewald said.

Peterson shook Ewald's hand and smiled. "That's nice to hear, Senator Ewald. You're talking about a long time ago."

"Yes, I know," Ewald said. "I was turned on to jazz in my early teens. I remember very well the first two records I ever heard. Really heard, that is. One featured you—it might have been your first recording—the other was a Dixieland album led by Muggsy Spanier."

"That's an eclectic beginning," said Peterson, considered among the greatest pianists in the history of jazz. Leslie Ewald joined them.

Ewald turned next to Sarah Vaughan. "I've been a fan of yours for almost as long, Ms. Vaughan. I still say the record you cut for Emarcy when you were nineteen—the one with Clifford Brown, Herbie Mann, and Jimmy Jones—is the finest jazz vocal album ever recorded. My wife will testify to the fact that it's played loud and often in our house."

She thanked him. "How nice it will be to have a president of the United States who appreciates American music."

Ewald laughed. "More than just appreciates it. Devoted to it is more like it. I plan to have regular jazz concerts at the White House."

"Provided you get the nomination and are elected, Ken," Leslie

Ewald said. His smile never broke, but there was a fleeting anger in his eyes as he looked at her.

Peterson graciously excused himself.

Sarah Vaughan turned to Ewald and said, "I understand one of your favorite songs is 'Lover Man.' "

"That's right."

"I'll be singing it tonight just for you."

"Wonderful! I can't wait."

The singer walked away to join trumpeter Ruby Braff, bassist Ron Carter, and drummer Mel Lewis, who were laughing at a joke one of them had told.

Farmer had collared the campaign photographer and set up shots of Ewald and family with some of the jazz musicians. When they were through, Ewald turned to his son. "I'm very happy you could make it back, Paul. This whole thing wouldn't have meant nearly as much without you."

"Well, I have to admit that rowing that junk took something out of me, but here I am." They both laughed. Ewald turned to his daughter-in-law and asked how she was.

"Just fine," Janet replied. To Paul, she said, "Let's go."

"They want a picture of us, son."

Paul looked at his wife. "Two more minutes, Janet. I want my picture taken with the next president of the United States."

Janet tugged Paul's arm. "Please."

"Take the picture," Leslie Ewald said to the photographer. She moved close to her husband; Janet was at Ewald's other side.

"Big, happy smiles on everyone," Farmer said. "This is a gala."

Ewald put his arm around his wife and smiled, exposing a solid set of white teeth. Leslie's smile matched his in intensity and attractiveness. As the photographer tripped the shutter and the strobe went off, Paul turned to look at his father. His expression was one of sincere admiration. Janet Ewald, her delicate clasped hands a fig leaf below her waist, managed to look as though she suffered only minor pain.

After a dozen more shots had been taken of the family, Ken and Leslie posed together, just the two of them. Having their pictures taken obviously caused them no discomfort. Every shot was quick, smooth— candidate and wife at a celebrity cocktail party at the national arts center named after John F. Kennedy, whom Ewald frequently quoted in his speeches. He was a "Kennedy man," part of the cosmetic as well as ideological legacy, cut from the same political cloth, tailored and barbered to heighten the effect, and every bit as handsome and charming. After eight years of a conservative administration, the country seemed ready for a return to Camelot. Ewald felt confident that in the general election in November he could defeat the current vice-president of the United States, Raymond Thornton, the obvious Republican nominee.

For a time, he'd been less confident about the Democratic Convention in July in San Francisco, where he would have to bring in enough delegates to defeat his chief opponent for the nomination, southern senator Joseph "Jody" Backus, the leader of the conservative wing of the Democratic party, preferably by the second ballot, after the favorite sons—and daughters—and such.

Backus had started strong in the early primaries, but had fallen behind. Still, the party had changed dramatically as the nation shifted into a more conservative stance. Liberal Democratic beliefs had been denigrated again. There were still some powerful Democrats who were convinced that a candidate like Ken Ewald, with his well-documented commitment to the sort of social programs that seemed to scream of big government expenditures, was anathema to the majority of the electorate, Republican and Democrat alike. It needn't be that way—not all progress and programs required billions. But Jody Backus, even though the numbers coming out of the primaries had placed him behind Ewald in Democratic voter preference, retained considerable clout within the party. Now, with the latest changes in regulations, you could win the primary battle—and lose the war.

Yes, Ken Ewald was confident he could defeat Raymond Thornton in November. But first he would have to work down to the wire to ensure his nomination in July. Tonight's televised gala from the Kennedy Center would help.

Gerry Fielding, a congresswoman from northern California and an ally, walked up, smiling. "What are you going to do for an inaugural gala, Ken," she said, "with this big production number tonight for a mere candidacy? Remember, for one event Bush had Sinatra and Baryshnikov and Arnold Schwarzenegger."

Ewald said, "We're doing *The Messiah* and I'm singing the title role."

A white-jacketed waiter carrying leftover hors d'oeuvres passed the Ewalds. The senator picked a *spanakopita* from the silver tray and popped the phyllo pastry filled with spinach and cheese into his mouth. Leslie started talking with other people, freeing him to wander away, Farmer at his side, Agent Jeroldson maintaining his usual watchful but discreet distance behind. Ewald stopped to exchange banalities with friends ("Looks like campaigning agrees with you, Senator"; "Your wife looks as lovely as ever, Ken—and you seem to be holding up, too, ha-ha"), or to be gracious to strangers who wished him well in his pursuit of the nomination ("No, Jody Backus and I work closely to-gether in the Senate. It's just that we see things a little different sometimes").

He left the theater, stood on the landing, and looked out over the red-carpeted grand foyer, longer than two football fields ("You can lay the Washington Monument in it and still have room to spare," the tour guides all said). Eighteen Swedish crystal Orefors chandeliers, each weighing a ton, cast uncertain light over the expanse. Ewald saw through floor-to-ceiling windows that a jet aircraft, its whine snuffed out by the building's impressive soundproofing, was making its ap-proach to National Airport, just across the Potomac.

He started down the stairs when a "Good evening, Senator" stopped him.

Ewald turned to face Mackensie Smith.

"Be back in a minute," Farmer said.

"Hello, Mac." Ewald extended his hand.

"You look bored," Smith said.

Ewald laughed. "I can't be bored at my own party, can I? Even if it's just another excuse for photo opportunities. I think the bash after the show will be a hell of a lot pleasanter. I assume you know, Mac, how much I appreciate your efforts in helping to put this night to-gether."

Smith shrugged. "I always wanted to rub shoulders with the stars. Now, I'm getting my chance."

"And?"

"It was less exciting than my mother told me it would be. You should be in your element tonight, Ken. Lots of good jazz to be heard."

"Yes, I love it. Of course, you'll have your addiction to opera satisfied, too."

"That's true, although as with any addiction, the craving only grows stronger after each 'fix.' How's Leslie?"

"Fine. Under some strain, but still comes up smiling."

Smith was two years Ewald's senior. His body was cubelike, not fat but square, solid; he'd been a star linebacker at the University of West Virginia. Ewald's tall, slender physique was more that of a basketball player; indeed, he'd been enough of a court performer at Stanford to make the Pacific Coast all-star team, second string, with the "second string" usually omitted from biographies prepared by his office.

Smith had shaved just before coming to the party, but a heavy five o'clock shadow said he hadn't. His head was covered with a close crop of salt-and-pepper hair. His eyes were the color of Granny Smith apples. The nose was prominent, his chin jutting and strong. He looked at Secret Service agent Jeroldson and said to Ewald, "I could never get used to that." When Ewald didn't respond, Smith added, "Spending my life being watched."

Ewald had been distracted by a couple who'd carried their drinks to the grand foyer and stood gazing up at the seven-feet-tall, three-thousand-pound bronze Robert Berks bust of President Kennedy. He gave his attention back to Smith. "I agree, Mac. Having these guys sleep with me is the only reason I ever considered not running."

Smith smiled and looked down at his empty glass. "Think I'll get a refill before the show starts."

"That's three hours away. You must be getting desperate. Where's Ann?" Ewald asked. Annabel Reed had been Smith's companion for a number of years.

"Out of town, Ken. The irony of it. Here I am involved with my first and last television extravaganza, and she picks tonight to be away on business. She'll be watching at her hotel. See you later. And—break a leg."

Ed Farmer, the rest of the Ewald family in tow, came to where the candidate stood alone. "Time to go to the hotel, Senator," Farmer said.

It was now six o'clock; the performance would begin promptly at nine. They'd taken a suite at the Watergate across the street rather than have to return home to kill time.

"Okay," Ewald said. Then, almost to himself, he added, "I wish he'd change his mind."

"Who?" Farmer and Leslie asked in concert.

"Mac Smith. He'd be a tremendous asset to us."

"He already has been," Leslie said.

"I know, I know," Ewald said as they walked down the stairs to the foyer. "I was surprised he agreed to get involved at all, considering his disdain for vulgar politics. Maybe it will give him a taste of campaign excitement and he'll decide to get more active with us. He'd make a hell of an adviser on drugs and other crimes. And a great attorney general."

FOUR

IN ANOTHER SUITE at the Watergate, Sammy Davis, Jr., was playing Pac-Man. The electronic game traveled with him wherever he went. A quart bottle of strawberry soda with a straw was at his side; half a case of it sat in a corner of the living room.

"I know how last-minute this is, Sammy," Georges Abbatiello said from where he sat on a leather barstool, "but I really would like to accommodate Mrs. Ewald. She's a nice lady. She called me a half hour ago and asked if you and Roseanna Gateaux would do a duet. She remembers seeing you do one at some benefit in Vegas a year or two ago. She said she was reluctant to ask because Roseanna had requested a last-minute change in the schedule and we turned her down, but then she figured nothing ventured, nothing gained. Would you be willing to come on again and do a duet with Roseanna? We'll find time by shortening up on the jam sessions."

"Hey, man, happy to. The lady's a gas." He continued to play the game.

Abbatiello smiled. He knew Davis's reputation was that of easy cooperation, but he didn't expect him to be *this* easy.

Things had begun to fall apart in the last hours leading up to the telecast, and Georges and his staff were in a mad scramble to straighten them out. He was used to dealing with the quibbles of performing artists, but most of the problems were coming from the political side—politicians insisting they be onstage when Ewald and his family made an appearance, security people questioning arrangements they should have thought of days before, big egos clashing with bigger egos and lesser significance. He was glad he'd earned his ulcer in show business rather than the political arena. As he'd said to his wife a few minutes before, this was his first and last contribution to politics—*anybody's* politics.

Davis lost the round. "I'll beat this sucker yet," he said, laughed loudly, and joined Abbatiello at the bar. "You want a soda?"

"No, thanks, Sammy." Abbatiello checked his watch. "Give me a fast rundown of how the duet goes—timing and such. And the sheets. We need the lead sheets for the orchestra." Davis's musical director, who'd been dozing in a large leather chair, came to life and worked with Abbatiello on the changes.

At precisely nine o'clock, with the opera house filled with Ewald supporters and friends of supporters out for a pleasant evening—and maybe to be seen—the curtain rose, the orchestra launched into a spirited, jazz-flavored arrangement of "California, Here I Come," and the musical gala in honor of Senator Kenneth Ewald began.

As it turned out, the impromptu duet between Sammy Davis, Jr., and Roseanna Gateaux was the hit of the evening. They romped through a medley of old and familiar songs like "Baby, It's Cold Outside" and "A Bushel and a Peck," the elegant and beautiful diva the perfect foil for the talented, manic, and considerably shorter Davis. Host David Letterman delighted the largely Democratic audience with barbed one-liners about the current administration, who was manning the Manning, etc., and roasts of the Republican party in general, and Joan Baez quietly transported those old enough to remember the 1960s back to that quaint period.

The finale was to be a jam session featuring all the jazz musicians who'd appeared in smaller groups. Just before Letterman announced that they would play Ellington's "Take the A Train," Ewald and his family were brought onstage. A restriction imposed by the Kennedy Center management was that there would be no overt political speech-making during the evening. Ewald, who had no intention of violating that, simply said, "The kind of artistic and creative energy displayed here tonight is symbolic of what this great nation has always spawned . . . in its excellence and diversity and community." He turned and looked at his family, smiled broadly, and went on, "And all of us thank each and every person who has made this night so memorable. We are deeply grateful." Then, on cue, he turned to the assembled musicians and said, "Okay, they said I could count this one off." He tapped his foot and counted, "One, two, one, two, three, four." Oscar Peterson began the intro, and the Ewalds were led from the stage to take their seats again in the front row.

that, and always natural. And in a nation that thought itself suspicious of oratory, what a wonderful—and critical—ability that was for anyone seeking office . . . seeking success in any endeavor, for that matter. This night, Ewald almost threatened to burst with honest enthusiasm, and when he'd finished his brief talk, the applause was twice as loud as when he'd been announced.

Suddenly, a detonation of Vesuvius fountains and Catherine wheels sprayed broad strokes of lacquered, multicolored light—greens and reds and yellows—across the black sky, the vividness of the colors dissipating as they trickled down the canvas to the horizon. All eyes turned in the direction of the fireworks; "ooohs" and "aaahs" blended with the snap, crackle, and pop of the display.

The sky show lasted ten minutes. As the last traces of sulfurous smoke wafted toward the party and the applause by a few overzealous souls continued, the band began playing, the dancers flocked to the floor, the portable bars were surrounded once again, and the party moved back into high gear. Washingtonians were often ready to party, Smith thought, for what they did by day was no party. *For* the party, perhaps, but no fiesta.

He waited until he felt it was appropriate for him to leave—a few minutes before midnight on his watch—and sought out those to whom he should say good-bye. He started toward the Ewalds, but they were busy. He thought of Andrea Feldman, but saw that she was in a shadowed area of the terrace talking with a man who looked like Ed Farmer, and although Smith could not hear what they were saying, their faces and body language suggested that theirs was not a pleasant chat. He found a few others he was looking for, then left the Kennedy Center, enjoying the pristine night that had displaced the wet weather of the previous day.

As soon as he entered his Foggy Bottom home ten minutes later, he threw off his raincoat and called Annabel at her New York hotel.

"It was a wonderful show, Mac," she said. "I loved every minute of it."

"Thanks. From a pragmatic point of view, everything worked, everyone seemed to be happy with it, we'll pay the bills, make some money, advance the candidacy, and I'm glad it's over. As little as I had to do with it, it still took too much of my time. How are things with you?"

"Fine. My dinner with the investors went well. Damn, Mac, I am sorry I couldn't be there, but you know that—"

"Annie, when you have serious investors from Europe who tell you the only time they can meet is for dinner one evening, you don't beg off because you have a party to go to. Of course I understand. I'm just glad it went well. When are you coming home?"

"I'm shooting for the noon shuttle. I'll go directly to the gallery."

"I'll call you there."

"Call me every minute. I miss you, Mac."

"I miss you, too, although I have to admit that what I missed most was not being able to do the funky chicken with you."

"Mac, are you . . . ?" She started to laugh, wished him a good night's sleep, and they ended the conversation.

Eleven o'clock was Smith's usual bedtime. This night, however, he found himself wide awake, and picked up where he'd left off reading Edmund Wilson's *The Thirties*. He finished a series of entries on the famous Scribner's editor Max Perkins, and looked at the Regulator clock in his study. It was almost four in the morning. Smith marked his place with a bookmark and said to Rufus, "Come on, it isn't often you get to be walked at this hour."

He put on a George Washington University windbreaker, slipped the choke chain over Rufus's head, and they went out to the street. It was a beautiful night—or morning; Smith breathed deeply, and a smile crossed his face. He was one of those people who was profoundly affected by the weather—hating the hot and humid summers, growling about the icy winters that sent inexperienced D.C. drivers sliding into each other with frightening regularity, and loving times like this, feeling good and doubly alive because of them. "Come on, Rufus, let's move and get some air in our lungs."

There was no such thing as a brisk walk with Rufus. The Dane was too interested in stopping to smell territorial markers left by previous visitors. They meandered, stopping-and-going, in the direction of the Kennedy Center, where only hours earlier there had been so much activity, so much gaiety. Now, everything was still. Lights from the Center shone brightly in the black night.

They had to wait at a corner as a D.C. cab careened past them viciously. "Dumb bastard," Smith snarled as he watched the red tail-lights disappear around another corner, but decided nothing must spoil his mood. He looked left and right, then set off at a trot across the broad avenue separating the Center from where they'd stood.

The man and the dog slowed to a walk and went up the ramp leading to the Center's front entrance. Smith had never walked Rufus there before, but, then again, he had never been out quite this late with his best friend before.

There was little for the nosy canine to investigate on the ramp. They stopped to look down over the Potomac for a few minutes, then turned and retraced their steps back in the direction of the house, walking this time on the far side of the fountain.

Smith hesitated in front of a massive horizontal relief that was the centerpiece of a small, parklike area, the relief called "War and Peace." A plaque on it read AMERICA 1965–1971—DONATED BY THE GOVERN-MENT OF THE FEDERAL REPUBLIC OF GERMANY. Funny, Smith thought, how much of the Kennedy Center had been given by other govern-ments, other nations. The intimate Terrace Theater had been a gift of Japan; the huge chandelier in the opera house was from the people of Austria; marble lining the grand halls came from the citizens of Italy; paintings from Peru; meeting rooms through the generosity of Africa and Israel; sculpture from Great Britain—foreign tributes everywhere to the American arts center that had been conceived by President Eisenhower, nurtured by Lyndon Johnson, and eventually designated as the only memorial in the nation's capital to the slain John F. Kennedy. Smith had taken the tour of Kennedy Center more than once, and had been privy to many of its inner dimensions at meetings and social events. No matter how many critics had taken aim at Edward Durell Stone's long, horizontal architectural approach, Smith was glad it was there, and that he lived near it. It was, in effect, the centerpiece of his neighborhood, and he always felt particular pride in what it symbolized.

Funny, too, how a structure so full of life a few hours earlier could be so devoid of it now.

"Come on," he said, yanking at Rufus's leash. Rufus balked; because of his size and strength, when the dog balked, he almost always pre-vailed. The Dane pulled hard as he tried to go behind the relief to where a small cluster of wooden benches provided seating in the midst of carefully tended shrubs, bushes, and small trees.

"No, come on, Rufus, we don't want to go back there."

Rufus kept up the pressure on his leash; Smith finally gave up and went with him. Once behind the relief, Smith tried to see what the Dane would wet down, or what had captured the dog's attention. A half-moon provided some illumination. The first thing Smith saw was a long, colorful feather on the ground. Rufus sniffed it and continued pressing into the shrubbery. "Hey, Rufus, what are you . . . ?"

Then he saw what the dog was after, a silk-stockinged female foot. A shoe with a medium heel rested close to it. *"Damn,"* Smith muttered as he shortened the leash and moved closer, fearing to interrupt something private. Now, the length of a shapely leg was visible, and then the woman, her skirt hiked up her thighs. Rufus, as though understanding what was at stake, stopped pulling and stood at attention, a low growl coming from his throat.

Smith pushed aside a low branch. He saw what he sensed was the full body, and knew immediately who it was by the exotic feather belt around her waist. "Good God," he whispered as he stepped over her legs. Andrea Feldman's arresting eyes were wide open—but gone to glass. Her mouth was open as well. Blood had oozed from her chest through the fabric of her dress. Her purse was on the ground; it had opened and its contents bled into the dirt, too.

Smith crouched and took her wrist. Then he looked at the debris of her death. Lipstick. A small makeup mirror. A pen. And a key, obviously from a hotel. Smith read the writing on the large red plastic tag attached to it: BUCCANEER MOTEL, ROSSLYN, VIRGINIA. The numeral 6 was also imprinted on the tag.

He led Rufus to the front of the relief, looked for someone, saw no one, and quickly ran, the dog leading the way, to the house, where he burst into the living room, thumbed through his phone book until he found the number he wanted, and dialed.

A deep, sleepy voice answered.

"Joe, Mac Smith. I'm sorry to wake you, but there's been a terrible accident. Maybe a murder."

Joe Riga, chief of detectives of Washington's MPD, was now awake. "Where? Who?"

"A young woman named Andrea Feldman, who worked on Ken Ewald's staff. I was walking my dog near the Kennedy Center and found the body."

"Why didn't you call—?"

"Nine-one-one? Joe, I don't know what this means, but I have to . . . well, there could be ramifications. Considerable ramifications. If you want me to call nine-one-one, I will, but . . ."

"No, Mac, sorry I even suggested it. I understand. Where's the woman, the body? You sure she's dead? Okay, forget that last."

"Behind the large relief across the fountain from the Kennedy Center, in front. She's in the bushes."

"I'm on my way."

"Fine, I'll meet you there—and Joe . . . I would appreciate it if we could keep this quiet for a few hours."

"We can keep it quiet until I see the body and call it in. I can't do more than that. It probably won't keep for long anyhow. You know this town."

"Sure do. And thanks."

"You can make a positive ID on her, Mac?" Riga asked as they stood over the body.

"Yes. Her name is Andrea Feldman."

Riga handed Smith the flashlight he carried, squatted, took the chin between his thumb and index finger, and gently moved her jaw back and forth. "Still slack," he said. He slid his hand down the top of her dress and nestled it in her armpit. "Didn't happen long ago," he said as he removed his hand and stood. "Still some warmth. I'll call it in."

"Joe, maybe you can do one favor, a legal one."

"What?"

"Let me get hold of Ewald and tell him what's happened before the identification is announced. All I need is an hour, or even a few minutes."

"No problem." Riga called in for backup and a forensic unit to come to the scene. "Identity of victim uncertain," he said into his radio.

Smith thanked him and returned home, where he dialed the Ewald house.

A sleepy Leslie answered.

"Leslie, it's Mac Smith. Sorry to be calling at this hour, but this is important. Is Ken there?"

"Yes. Why?"

"Leslie, Andrea Feldman has been murdered."

There was silence on the other end of the line.

"I was walking Rufus and discovered her about an hour ago. Someone shot her outside the Kennedy Center, across from the main entrance."

"Mac, this is dreadful. Who could have done such a thing? Where is her family?"

"I have no idea, but I thought Ken ought to know right away."

"Of course." She turned away from the mouthpiece and murmured. Ewald came on the line. "Mac, could you come here right away?" he asked.

"Of course, but . . ."

"Please, Mac, come now."

"Sure. Anybody there to make some coffee at this hour?"

"Of course. This is unbelievable. She was at the party. She was alive. I'm shocked."

"So was I. Hot, black, and strong. I'm on my way."

FIVE

THE STATELY two-story redbrick Ewald home was on the upper reaches of Twenty-eighth Street in Georgetown; behind it, Oak Hill Cemetery. The house sat on a rise of land, giving its occupants a view of the Dumbarton Oaks mansion and gardens.

Smith pulled up in his blue Chevy Caprice and told one of two uniformed security guards that he was expected. The guard used an intercom to confirm it, and pushed a button that caused black iron gates to open electronically. Smith pulled into the circular driveway and was about to knock on the front door when Leslie Ewald opened it.

"Hello, Leslie."

"Hello, Mac." She looked past him to the front gate. Smith observed her closely. The flesh around her eyes was spongy, like putty that has been rubbed with a thumb covered with pencil lead. Lines he hadn't noticed earlier in the evening seemed suddenly to have exploded at the corners of her mouth. She bit her lip, realized he was looking at her—realized he was there. "I'm sorry, Mac, please forgive me. I hate having to . . ."

She looked at the gate again. Smith, too, looked.

"We've always had one guard. Now, there are two. Ed Farmer had the extra sent over as soon as we told him about Ms. Feldman. They're going to install an electrified fence around the property—like one of those things that fries bugs." She looked up at the portico roof. "Cameras, too. God, how I hate it all!"

"Beefing up security might be wise," Smith said, "considering Andrea Feldman was a close working member of the staff. The media people and others will be all over you when it comes out."

"Yes, I suppose you're right."

"Let's go inside," Smith said.

She ignored him and pointed to her left. Parked on the road at the corner of the property was a small white car.

"Who's that?" he asked.

"Press. They were at police headquarters. I suppose we'll end up being surrounded."

As she entered the foyer, she started to cry. Smith followed and shut the door behind them. She looked at him with round, moist eyes that were spilling tears down her cheeks. Her body heaved, and she threw herself against him. He wrapped his big arms about her thin shoulders and held her for a time, saying softly, "Easy, easy. It's terrible that Andrea Feldman has died but . . ."

"You don't understand, Mac."

"I assume I will quickly."

"Yes, very quickly." She regained her composure, even forced a smile. "I haven't fallen apart in years." She took his hand. "Come, Ken and Ed Farmer are in the study."

As she opened the door, Farmer came through it, followed closely by Ewald. "Mac, good to see you, thanks for being here," Ewald said, putting his hand on Smith's shoulder. "Back in a minute."

Leslie looked as if she might cry again, so Smith asked if he could have a drink before the coffee. "It's been hours since the party." He really didn't want one, but his strategy worked. She now had something to do. She quickly departed, leaving him alone in the paneled room.

He'd been there before on dozens of occasions, yet for reasons he couldn't identify, it was strangely new to him at this moment.

Two walls were taken up with floor-to-ceiling bookcases. A third wall contained cases with glass doors that housed Ewald's extensive collection of antique guns—a strange hobby, Smith often thought, for someone perpetually at war with the NRA. "They're beautiful to look at, and they have great historic meaning. Shooting them is another matter," Ewald always said when questioned about it. Smith had always found Ewald somewhat enigmatic—predictable in a few unappealing ways, persuasively attractive in others. A human being.

Leslie returned carrying a scotch on the rocks for him, a balloon glass containing a dark liquid for her, partly consumed. "Did I get it right, Mac, scotch?"

"Yes, might as well stay with it. What are you drinking?" To keep her talking.

"Brandy and port. When Ken and I were in Scotland a few years ago, we took a particularly rough boat trip to the Orkney Islands. My stomach was queasy, and I asked the bartender for some blackberry brandy. He insisted a combination of port and brandy was more effective. He was right. I've felt like throwing up ever since we got your phone call, but this settled my stomach right down."

When they were seated on adjoining flowered love seats around a leather-topped coffee table, Smith said, "Okay, tell me about it. Don't mince words, just be direct. I know the death of anyone we know is terribly upsetting, but I'm reading into this something beyond that. Am I right?"

"Yes, you are *very* right."

"What am I right about?"

"I don't know where to begin. I suppose I should just tell you that—"

Ewald and Farmer returned. Ewald pulled a red morocco leather chair on casters up to the table, settled his long, lean body in it, and crossed one leg over the other, the casualness of the pose in stark contrast to the tension-stiffened body of his wife. Farmer stood by a window behind Smith.

"Leslie was just starting to tell me about a particular concern you have with Andrea's death."

Ewald said to his wife, "Go ahead, might as well continue." Smith couldn't decide whether Ewald was angry at Leslie or feeling an anxiety that his outward appearance didn't reflect.

Leslie shook her head and looked down at her drink.

"All right, I'll pick it up from there," Ewald said. "Evidently, Andrea was murdered with a weapon that belongs to me."

The expulsion of air through Smith's lips was involuntary—and necessary. He sat back and listened to Ewald's further explanation.

"I've had a registered handgun in the house for years. Leslie had been expressing concern about the amount of time I'm away, and I thought simply having it on the premises would be comforting to her." He looked at Leslie; she continued to stare down into her port and brandy.

"It was a small stainless-steel Derringer, a three-inch .45 Colt. It's been sitting in a drawer in the bedroom for God knows how long. At any rate, after you called with the news about Andrea, I opened the drawer. Don't ask me why, but I did. The gun is gone."

"Who had access to it besides you and Leslie?" Smith asked.

Ewald looked once again at his wife. "Everyone in the house," she said.

"Family?" Smith asked.

"Yes, family, visitors, household staff, campaign staff. A cast of thousands."

Smith thought for a moment before asking, "Is that what's concerning you so? Or do you think that someone in this household is going to be accused of her murder?"

Ewald didn't reply, but Leslie did, in a low, flat voice. "Yes."

"Someone from your staff, Ken?"

"No," Ewald said, looking at Leslie for the first time as if to receive approval of what he was about to say next. She was without expression. He said, "We feel there is the possibility that Paul will be charged with the murder."

"Why do you say that?" Smith asked.

"Because . . ."

Leslie Ewald finished the sentence. "Because Paul was having an affair with her." Smith started to speak, but Leslie forged on. "Paul was having an affair with Andrea Feldman, and last night he did not return home."

"You're sure?"

"Yes. We talked to Janet."

Smith was processing what she'd said. Both things pointed at Paul Ewald as a suspect, but they were hardly conclusive. Smith added a third element; Paul obviously had access to his father's pistols.

Smith realized Ed Farmer was still standing by the window. He'd forgotten Farmer was in the room. He turned and looked at the campaign manager, then asked Ken and Leslie whether there was any other information.

"Janet knew about Paul's affair with Andrea," Leslie said. "It caused a tremendous rift in the marriage, naturally, and I know Janet had issued an ultimatum to Paul."

Farmer started to leave the room. "Drink, anyone?" he asked.

Smith and Ken Ewald passed, but Leslie asked him to refill her glass. When Farmer was gone, Smith said, "Have you called me here as a family friend, as a lawyer, or for my reaction to this in terms of your campaign?"

"All of that, but especially number two, Mac," Ewald said. "If Paul is charged, we want you to defend him." Leslie sat up straight, closed her eyes tight, and started to cry convulsively.

Ewald moved to her side and put his arm around her. "Take it easy, honey; chances are Paul's not going to be charged with anything. Mac, we just need your advice."

"I think I ought to say something right now," Smith cautioned. They both looked at him. "I've been a quasi–legal adviser to this family on a very informal level, and I *used* to be a practicing attorney. I am now a contented college professor, teaching law at a major university. I'm sorry, but I could not take on Paul's legal defense."

"We know how you feel, Mac, but if we've ever asked a favor of you, this is it. Please, at least consider it."

"Of course I'll consider it. But you have to know where I am. And I just got there in recent years. Look, I want to make a few informal phone calls, maybe pick up some information that will be helpful to you whether or not I have anything more to do with this officially. You know I'll help if I can. I'll get back to you later this morning."

They walked him to the door. As he shook Ken's hand and kissed Leslie on the cheek, he found himself gripped with a sense of pathos and concern. Obviously, the three of them knew that if Paul was charged with the murder, not only would it be a tragic personal experience, it could have a severe impact on Ken Ewald's drive for the White House. And though it seemed unthinkable, a conviction could end that drive. As far as Mac Smith was concerned—despite some reservations about Ewald—that would not be good for the country. He chewed on that thought as he drove back to his home in Foggy Bottom.

SIX

WHILE Mac Smith made phone calls from home the next morning, Colonel Gilbert Morales entered the White House through the Diplomatic Reception Room. He was accompanied by an aide. Two members of the Secret Service had escorted them from the gate, and they were all greeted inside by Richard Morse, an undersecretary from State whose area of expertise was Central America. "The president will be with you shortly, Colonel Morales. Please have a seat. Would you like coffee, tea, a soft drink?"

"No, thank you." Morales surveyed a variety of spindly chairs until settling his large body into the one that appeared to be the most substantial. Even at that, he was uncomfortable. His aide, a young man in an ill-fitting brown suit whose face was deeply pitted, walked to the far side of the room and looked closely at the wallpaper.

"President and Mrs. Kennedy brought that paper to the White House," one of the Secret Service agents said. "It was made in France in 1934 by Jean Zuber and Company." He and his partner were often assigned to conducting public tours of the White House, and were well versed in its decor and history. The agent added to his description, filling the time: "The painter had never visited the United States, but he used engravings he'd seen as a model for his work. That's Niagara Falls," he continued, in the voice he used with tourists. "That's Boston Harbor."

The aide said nothing and took a chair next to Morales.

Undersecretary Morse inquired about Mrs. Morales.

"She is fine, thank you," Morales said. "She is very busy with humanitarian efforts for our people."

"Yes, I'm sure she is," Morse replied. "Gathering medical supplies from private sources, and so on."

Colonel Gilbert Morales had been the military leader of Panama and a staunch ally of the United States. Deposed in a coup staged by the current Panamanian leadership, he'd fled with his family, settled in Washington, and immediately launched an intensive lobbying effort on behalf of forces in Panama still loyal to him. He'd found sympathetic ears in President Walter Manning and his administration.

A door opened, and a young man in a blue suit stepped into the room. He said to Morse in a library whisper, "The president is ready." They all went upstairs to the State Dining Room, where President Manning, Vice-President Raymond Thornton, Secretary of State Marlin Budd, and Senate Minority Leader Jesse Chamberlain were seated at the large dining table. The Panamanian was directed to a chair next to Secretary Budd. His aide stood awkwardly to the side. "Mr. Morse," Budd said, "please see that our young visitor is extended every courtesy downstairs."

"Yes, sir." Morse led the aide from the room.

"Well," President Manning said, "here we are again, Colonel Morales. It's getting to be a habit of sorts, isn't it?"

Morales smiled. "Yes, Mr. President, a habit of which I heartily approve. Your concern for my people, and for justice in my country, is very much appreciated, not only by me and Mrs. Morales, but by every freedom-loving Panamanian."

Morales looked at Chamberlain, a heavyset Texan who'd been elected to the Senate for seven consecutive terms and who anchored the Republican conservative caucus. "You, sir, of course, have always shared President Manning's love of freedom. I bring you fond wishes from my wife."

"Thank you, sir."

"And, when you are elected the next president of the United States, Mr. Vice-President, our fight together for justice and democracy will continue."

"I can pledge you that, Colonel," Thornton said. "Your cause is my cause."

"*Sí*, and I am grateful."

Secretary Budd said flatly, "We wanted to meet today, Colonel, to discuss certain realities that might have to be faced in November."

A wide, radiant smile had been on Morales's face from the moment he entered the room; Budd's words caused it to fade.

"I suggest we have lunch," Manning said, "then get down to business. I don't have much time." He touched a button on the side of the table, and three waiters appeared. "We're ready," the president said wearily. He slumped back in his chair and sighed.

After twenty minutes of aimless chat between the Americans and Morales, the waiters cleared the remains of a grilled swordfish and avocado salad, biscuits, and rice pudding, and served coffee. Secretary Budd then leveled with Morales. "To be blunt, Colonel Morales, we in the administration don't see any hope of further aid to you before President Manning's term ends."

Morales lighted a cigarette and drew deeply on it. He looked at Senator Chamberlain, whose cigar added to the rising blue smoke in the room. "There is no possibility of passage of the new aid bill in Congress?"

"Afraid not," Chamberlain said, coughing. "It's dead, absolutely dead. Damn shame."

"Yes, especially for my people, many of whom will be dead as a result. Of course . . ." He looked at Raymond Thornton, who sat ramrod straight. "You will be the next president, Mr. Thornton." The smile returned to Morales's broad face.

Thornton spoke in measured tones. "Colonel, we fully expect victory in November, but, as you know, nothing is certain on Election Day. Promises to be a tight race. We expect Senator Ewald to be the choice the Democrats will make, and—"

The president interrupted. "Senator Ewald has considerable popularity, Colonel Morales. It is my estimation that the next administration will probably be a Democratic one."

"That might be overstating things a bit, Mr. President," Thornton said, his voice less modulated now. "I wouldn't write us off yet."

"I'm too old, Raymond, to indulge in flights of fancy," Manning replied. "The country's ready for a change. It's the cycle." To Morales, he said, "We vote in cycles in this country, Colonel. We've had a long Republican run, and the odds are against it continuing any longer. As I said, you and your people had better be looking for other ways to regain power."

"I see," Morales said. "There is, of course, the private sector that continues to help us."

"Not as much as it did before," Secretary Budd said. "Any further help from individuals is going to have to be given with much more discretion than in the past. The indictments and the media have seen to that."

"The Reverend Kane has pledged his continued support to me," Morales said. "He has told me as recently as yesterday that he will continue to fund the missions he has established in my country."

Reverend Garrett Kane presided over the most popular and richest television evangelical ministry in America. Blessed with a voice that one writer had described as sounding like "a one-man gang," and with bright blue eyes that promised each television viewer he was speaking only to him or her, Kane had avoided the pits into which other TV evangelists had sunk in recent years. His ministry's financial house was in meticulous order. The Kanes—his wife's name was Martha, although she was popularly known as Bunny—lived a relatively modest personal life, Buicks rather than Jaguars, expensive but conservative clothing, a house in the hills of California's Orange County that would have been appropriate for the president of any medium-sized high-tech company. As Kane explained it, "Jesus meant for us to live decently, but the man who needs to display his wealth is a man for whom Jesus would have wept in sympathetic contempt."

Garrett Kane had not lined his pockets with the millions that poured into his offices every week. Instead, they were directed to other causes precious to him: "Our artistic endeavors will forever mark us as a civilized and a decent people!" or, "The extent to which we devote our God-given energies and resources to eradicate from this earth the evils of Godless Communism shall determine, in the eyes of the Lord, our eventual place in His everlasting kingdom." His favorite cause was the guerrilla resistance movement in Panama, where for years "freedom fighters" had been engaged on behalf of Colonel Gilbert Morales in an attempt to overthrow the regime in power. According to the Manning administration, Morales, and Garrett Kane, the regime was Communist-directed.

President Manning pushed back in his chair and stood. "Colonel Morales, thank you for joining us for lunch. You, and what you stand for, will always have a place at my table."

Secretary Budd stood, too, and said, "Serving you lunch is one thing, Colonel. Money for your cause is another. The reality is that every sign points to Senator Ewald succeeding this president next January. Ewald, as you are well aware, not only vows to cut off any hope of further aid to your cause, he's been pushing for an investigation into Reverend Kane's financial support of you. Those so-called humanitarian missions Reverend Kane has set up in your country are pretty transparent. I wouldn't bank on Kane's support much longer."

Morales was led downstairs by Undersecretary Morse. Thornton left the White House for a campaign meeting across town, while Secretary of State Budd accompanied the president to the Oval Office.

"I think I'll take a nap," Manning said.

"You have two appointments this afternoon, Mr. President. The Canadian trade delegation is due here in fifteen minutes, and—"

"Why are *they* coming?"

Budd frowned. "To discuss extending the free-trade agreement into other areas. We met on that yesterday, remember?"

The president stood in the middle of the room, confusion on his face. "Sir, I can always . . ."

Manning's tone was suddenly angry. "I'll meet with them. I thought you meant some other group that I hadn't agreed to meet with. Let's be a little clearer around here in our communications."

"Yes, sir."

Gilbert Morales and his aide climbed into the backseat of a very long black limousine. Seated on two jump seats were armed bodyguards. Another sat in the front passenger seat, a sawed-off shotgun on the floor beneath his feet. The driver turned and looked at Morales, whose face reflected his frustration. He shook his head and peered through the window at the White House. He realized the driver was waiting for instructions. "Headquarters," he said.

Fifteen minutes later, Morales and his entourage rode the elevator to the eighth floor of an office building across from the Kennedy Center and entered the Panamanian Maritime Mission. Morales ignored the receptionist's greeting and went into a large office on whose door was a sign: DIRECTOR. He picked up a phone and dialed a number. When a male voice answered, Morales said, "Where is Miguel?"

The person on the other end, who seemed confused at the question, said after a false start, "He is on his way to the airport, Colonel. You instructed us to—"

"Bring him back. We may have need of him again."

Morales hung up the phone and looked at the morning's newspaper on his desk. A portrait of Andrea Feldman dominated the space. A headline accompanying the photo read EWALD CAMPAIGN AIDE SLAIN.

He stared at the paper, then picked up the phone and dialed long distance.

"Kane Ministries," a pleasant female voice answered.

"This is Colonel Gilbert Morales. I must speak with him."

SEVEN

SMITH placed a number of calls after meeting with Ken and Leslie Ewald. He was unable to reach MPD detective Joe Riga, but did connect with Rhonda Hamilton, a good friend and one of Washington's best-known investigative journalists. They would get together for a quick lunch at the Foggy Bottom Cafe, a few blocks from his house.

He was about to walk Rufus when the phone rang.

"Mac, it's Leslie."

"I was just on my way out. How are things?"

"Horrible. Could we talk again today? I need very much to see you."

"Yes, of course. Has something else happened?"

"It's all so confusing, Mac, and I desperately need a steady hand like yours to help sort it out. I know I'm imposing but . . ."

"No imposition, Leslie. I'm meeting someone for lunch, have a faculty meeting at three, a wasted hour, but I'll be free after that."

"Could you come by the house at five?"

"I'll be there."

"Thank you, Mac."

"Don't be silly. Is there something I should be thinking about before I get there?"

She sighed. "No, I'll explain when I see you."

The phone rang again. It was Annabel Reed.

"Where are you?" Smith asked. "At the airport?"

"No, I caught an earlier shuttle. I just arrived at the gallery."

Annabel's art gallery, located in Georgetown, specialized in pre-Colombian art. Like Mac Smith, she'd given up a lucrative practice, although their reasons for abandoning law were different. For Smith, it had been fatigue and disillusionment. For Annabel, it represented a more positive career change. Art, particularly pre-Colombian, had begun as an interest, then became her passion. As law had once been for her.

She'd graduated with every conceivable honor from George Washington University Law School, and within four years had built a reputation in Washington as an effective, shrewd, and compassionate attorney. Much of her practice was in divorce cases. Unlike some women specializing in that often-distasteful area of law, she was not known solely as a champion of women's rights. She viewed men going through the pain of divorce with equal sympathy and understanding. At least, she tried to. Whatever her approach and philosophy, they worked, and her income reflected it.

Then she'd bought a half-interest in the gallery from an elderly friend who'd retired as curator of the pre-Colombian collection at Dumbarton Oaks, and who'd opened the gallery to fill his retirement days. It was becoming *too* successful, to the chagrin of his wife, who viewed their retirement as a chance to travel. He needed a partner, and offered Annabel the chance. She didn't hesitate, although she was less than completely honest about why she bought in. She rationalized to friends—more important, to herself—that she'd simply made a wise investment. But she knew deep down that going into the gallery would be a first step toward leaving the law and indulging herself in something with which she had greater psychic affinity. When her partner became terminally ill, she bought his half, continued to practice law and to oversee the gallery's growth for a year, then announced she was closing her offices.

"I heard in the cab what happened last night," she said. "How horrible. You knew her?"

"Yes. Some. I worked with Andrea Feldman on the gala committee. Smart as a whip. She'd been on Ken's staff for about a year. It was a shock to everyone."

"I heard Brian Burns on WRC quoting the police as saying they have a lead in the murder."

"Really? They say who?"

"No. I think they said there'd be a press conference tomorrow morning. The cabbie started talking, and I missed the rest."

"There are some upsetting aspects to this where Ken is concerned," Smith said.

"Yes, the cab driver told me the weapon belonged to Ken. Does that mean . . . ?"

"They've traced it to him already? I didn't know that." He mentioned his scheduled five o'clock meeting at Ewald's house.

"I thought we were having dinner."

"We are, after I see Ken and Leslie. Feel like Italian? I thought we'd go to Primi Piatti."

"Too heavy," she said. "I've been wanting to go back to Nicholas."

"Fine with me. See you there at seven?"

"You aren't picking me up?"

"I'm not sure how long I'll be with them." When she didn't say anything, he said, "Seven. At the bar. We'll have a drink. I'll make a dinner reservation for seven-thirty."

"All right."

Rufus roared his desire for a walk as Smith hung up. "In a minute," he said, dialing a number.

"WRC," a woman answered.

"Rhonda Harrison, please. Mac Smith calling."

"Hello, Mac, canceling lunch on me?"

"Of course not. Look, someone just told me that Brian Burns reported a break in the Feldman case."

"Right," she said. "Brian got it from a source at MPD."

"Specifics?"

"No, except having found the weapon. It was registered to Senator Ewald."

"Is there a press conference tomorrow?"

"Supposedly, although we can't confirm it. Another MPD surprise party."

"A surprise press conference?" Smith laughed. "Should produce a hell of a crowd. Can I talk to Brian?"

"He's in the booth. Want him to call you?"

"If he has any hard news. I'll be out for ten minutes. Thanks, Rhonda. See you at lunch."

As he walked Rufus, Smith felt the surge, the charge, and realized that events last night had opened a small valve in his body, releasing a shot of adrenaline. He was ambivalent about the sensation. Before he'd retreated to the life of a college professor—a decision he made shortly after his wife and son were killed by a drunk driver on the Beltway—those valves used to open all at once, sending a rush of energy and excitement through him. He lived for those moments, was sustained by them.

Not anymore. Those valves had been rusted shut for a time, and he'd become used to doing without the juices.

Until now. This moment.

Rufus pulled on his leash in all directions, large nose to the ground bombarded by the scent of leaves, stilted grass, bricks and concrete, iron railings wet-marked as calling cards by previous visitors out for a walk, and discarded fast-food wrappers, several of which Smith picked up and tossed in a neighbor's garbage can. "Slobs," he muttered.

Rhonda Harrison was seated at the Foggy Bottom Cafe's small bar when Smith arrived. The restaurant, located in the River Inn on Twenty-fifth Street N.W., was packed. Groups of people waited in the hotel's lobby for tables to open.

"Hi, Mac," she said as Smith managed to squeeze in behind her.

"Hello, Rhonda. They must be giving away the onion rings."

"Looks like it." She was an attractive woman in her early thirties. Inky hair cropped close made her small cordovan face seem larger than it was, and the overall effect was pleasing. She'd been with WRC for six years, and in that time had established herself as a tough but fair reporter who had the knack for getting a news source to talk, and who could find in a story an angle others missed. Besides broadcasting, she'd also been doing a considerable amount of writing lately, long, substantial investigative pieces for magazines.

"Mr. Smith," the bartender said over the multiple conversations along the bar. "Your usual?"

"Sure." He turned to Rhonda. "Want some onion rings to get started?" She nodded, and he added them to his drink order. Soon a heaping plate of one of the inn's specialties stood next to Harrison's Bloody Mary, and the glass of Tecate beer with coarse salt and lime that had been served Smith. "Health," he said, raising his glass.

She returned the toast.

"What's new?" he asked.

"Personal, professional, family, or the Andrea Feldman murder?"

"Your choice, but if we opt for Feldman, let's take a walk."

"Sure, okay, let's see," she said in a voice that was familiar to her listeners. "I have fallen madly in love with the man who will be my husband as soon as I get up the guts to ask him out. I got a raise yesterday. My agent sold a piece to *Esquire*. My family, what's left of it, is fine. Okay? That's my capsule update."

Smith placed a large hand lightly on her shoulder. "I'll be invited to the wedding, of course."

"Of course." She looked around; no one was paying particular attention to them. She leaned close to Smith's ear and said, "Your friend the senator is in some mess."

He hadn't expected such a direct statement from her, and his hesitant response testified to his surprise. "Tell me about it," he said.

"I was going to ask you the same thing. Rumor has it that you're smack dab in the middle of it."

"Who's putting that out?"

He felt a shrug of her slender shoulders beneath his hand. "MPD, some press sources. Brian told me."

"Time for that walk," he said. He told the bartender they'd be back, and they went outside. He asked what Brian Burns had told her.

"That you've been called in to handle defense in the event someone in the family is charged with her murder."

"That's news to me, Rhonda. Last I heard, nobody's been charged with anything."

"I know that, Mac, but the scuttlebutt is that the MPD is looking very seriously in that direction. What will you do, take a leave of absence from the university?"

"Washington, D.C.," Smith growled, "a city of tightly guarded, widely circulated secrets. Where did they find the weapon?"

"I have no idea."

"They sure traced it fast."

"Not hard. It was registered. At least they can't arrest him for possessing an unregistered handgun. Maybe that's part of his anti–National Rifle Association shtick—own a gun, if it's registered."

"Small victory."

"Any of what I've said so far true?" she asked.

"Bits and pieces. Are you going with the story?"

She nodded. "We're trying to put together something for tomorrow morning. Care to comment?" She reached into an oversized purse and pulled out a tiny tape recorder.

"Nope."

"Denial?"

"Nope."

"You know what, Mac?"

"What?"

"The shocker to me is that you'd get involved."

He knew that if he *did* get involved, Annabel would have the same reaction.

"Mac."

"What?"

"You suggested we meet for lunch, not me. What are you after from me?"

He grinned. "I was going to see what you knew about the Andrea Feldman murder. I didn't have to probe much, did I?"

"Not with me. I'm a fan, always have been since you treated this new kid in town with respect during the Buffolino case. Ever hear from him?"

"No. Last I knew, he was living in Baltimore."

"Mac."

"What?"

"You didn't have to probe me for what I know about Feldman. Do me the same favor."

"You've got it all. I can't add anything."

"Have you met with the Ewalds?"

"Yes."

"Are they concerned that one of them might be charged with Andrea Feldman's murder?"

Smith hated to lie to her, but he had to. "No, nothing like that was discussed."

"What about the weapon? Did Ewald indicate it was missing?"

"Rhonda, I really can't talk any more about this."

"Will you give me first crack at an interview? If a charge is brought?"

"Of course not. *If* I were to become involved, and *if* what you think is true, I'd be one hell of a lousy defense attorney talking to the press about the case, even to such an outstanding and beautiful member of it. And since I am not officially involved, I certainly don't have any news value."

"Can't blame a reporter for asking."

"Blame? You're good. I *will* promise you that if there's anything I can do for you, I will. Come on, let's finish off the onion rings—why do they remind me today of handcuffs?—and order a couple of salads." He squinted at his watch. "I have a meeting to get to."

"A meeting about the Feldman case?" she asked after they'd returned to their seats at the bar.

"No, a meeting about faculty appointments, tenure, and such— deadly, deadly dull."

Harrison picked up a small clump of the crusty onions in her long, slender, brightly tipped fingers and held them to her lips. Her expression as she looked at Smith was half-amused, half-skeptical. "Do you know what my gut instincts tell me, Mackensie Smith?"

"I would be delighted to know."

"My instincts tell me that we are about to have a bombshell dropped on this city and on Ewald's campaign. And they also tell me that I am sharing onion rings with one of the major players."

Smith winked at her. "All I can tell you, Rhonda, is that you are sharing onion rings with a man who gave up the active practice of law a while back and is blissfully happy in his life as college professor."

"Bull!"

"Even if I were tempted to become involved in a case again, I would have to do it under the threat of dismemberment by my significant other, Annabel Reed. You've never met Annie, have you? I really should introduce you two someday. You'd get along."

"Not if she knew I was mad about you."

They had their salads at the bar. As Smith laid bills next to his empty plate, he said to Rhonda, "This was a more productive lunch than I anticipated. Knowing you're 'mad about' me has made my day. And now that I do know it, I think I'll keep you and Annabel far away from each other. She's . . . bigger than both of us. Thanks for joining me, Rhonda. Looks like I'd better tune in WRC in the morning."

.   .   .

Sᴍɪᴛʜ had no sooner sat down at the conference table with his faculty colleagues when the Feldman murder was brought up. "What's new with that, Mac?" one of them asked.

"How would I know?"

"Come on, Mac, you found the body, and you're an insider with the Ewald family. They're saying on radio and TV that you've been retained in the event anyone from the family is charged. You're a major—"

"Player, yes, so I hear. Okay, I found the body, much to my dismay. To be more accurate, my dog found the body. I have not been retained by anyone. I am very much an outsider and intend to keep it that way, if I can manage it."

"Did you spend time with the deceased at the gala?" another asked.

"Yes. A little." Smith checked his watch. "Good music, a hell of a show. Could we get on with this? I have other appointments."

After Smith left the meeting, one of the professors said, "Sometimes I find it difficult to deal with his arrogance."

The law school dean, Roger Gerry, replied, "The right to be arrogant is earned. Mac Smith has earned that right. But it's confidence and competence you see, not arrogance. He carries it all rather nicely, I think." Gerry adjourned the meeting, a tiny, satisfied smile on his face.

EIGHT

MAC, Joe Riga."

"Hello, Joe, thanks for getting back to me. How's it going?"

"Too damn busy. Here I am with a year to retirement, and you and that beast of yours have to find a body in front of the Kennedy Center. What can I do for you?"

"I was just wondering whether you'd come up with any leads. I heard on the radio—"

"You should know after years of being a defense attorney that anything said on the radio about a murder isn't true."

"Not necessarily. I heard on the radio that you found the weapon."

"That's right."

"Where?"

"A couple hundred feet from the body, in the bushes. It's registered to your friend Senator Ewald."

"Yes, I heard that, too. . . . Prints?"

"Clean."

"I understand you're holding a press conference tomorrow morning. I hate to wait that long like ordinary citizens to get all the sordid details."

"What makes you out of the ordinary in this matter, Mac? Is it true that if anybody from your buddy's house is charged, Mackensie Smith is back in action as the crusading defense attorney?"

There was no sense in making flat denials any longer, so Smith said, "Could be. I don't know yet. What are you announcing tomorrow at the press conference?"

"There is no press conference. We canceled."

"Why?"

"A mistake. We thought we had it nailed down, but something

didn't pan out. We're working on it. What did you know about the deceased?"

"Very little, just that she was smart, hardworking, good-looking— and very bright, in fact. Funny, but I was thinking this morning that I never heard much about Andrea's life, her background, family, that sort of thing. Then again, I really didn't work with her until we helped put together the gala. She was assigned from Ewald's staff to help coordinate things."

"She have any boyfriends?"

"I'm sure she did."

"You were there at Kennedy Center. You talk to her, see her hanging around with anybody?"

"Nothing in particular. Saw her talking, dancing. She danced a lot. She was a good dancer. Caught everybody's attention."

"Not just for her footwork. Who'd she dance with?"

"A couple of young, nice-looking men. They all looked clean and wore conservative suits."

"And maybe one of them got his hands dirty."

"Maybe. Look, Joe, are you working on the assumption that some-body in the Ewald camp killed her?"

"Mac, I'm working on the assumptions, number one, that somebody killed her, and number two, that the gun used traces to the Ewald house. I'm going out to their house in about an hour."

"Really? I'm due out there myself. Mind if I join you?"

Riga laughed, and Smith could see his face, those large, yellowing teeth with the gap in the front. "Sure, why not. I have to get a formal statement from you anyway, something I neglected to do last night. I'll meet you there."

"Fine."

"Hey, Mac, I keep meaning to ask you every time I talk to you whether you ever hear from Tony."

"Buffolino? No."

"Last I heard, he was working private in Baltimore."

"Yes, I heard that, too. Funny, somebody else asked about him recently, too. Good man, Tony."

"Matter of opinion. Maybe we can catch a drink after we leave Ewald. My treat."

"I'm not sure I'll have time, Joe—I'm meeting Annabel for dinner— but let's play it by ear. You're buying? I like that, and if we don't get to do it tonight, I'll remind you of it on a regular basis."

Smith hung up, stretched out on a couch in his living room, and for the moment thought of Anthony Buffolino, one of his last clients as a practicing criminal attorney.

Tony Buffolino had been a Washington MPD detective, a good one, everybody said. He'd had a clean record for fifteen years, a drawerful of citations of merit, letters from appreciative citizens and local politicians, no hint of being on the take, a good cop. Then, after taking three slugs in his right leg—two in the thigh and one in the knee—in a shoot-out during a bank robbery, he was told he was being retired on full pay. That wasn't what he had in mind. He fought being pensioned off despite constant jibes from fellow officers who dreamed of such a situation for themselves, and despite the pleas of his second wife, who hated seeing her husband leave home each morning and never knowing whether he'd return. He went through extensive physical rehabilitation, passed the physical, and continued on the force as a detective assigned to a special unit formed to combat Washington's growing drug trade. That was when all the trouble started, personal and professional.

Smith got up after ten minutes on the couch, shaved, and drove to the Ewald house. He wanted to get there before Riga.

He had trouble reaching the front gate because of the number of vehicles parked outside the house. There were mobile vans from local television stations, automobiles belonging to a variety of reporters, and two MPD squad cars, their uniformed occupants seated glumly inside them. He was passed through the gate by a private security guard. As he drove up in front of the house, he noticed that the video surveillance camera was in place up on the portico.

Marcia Mims, the Ewalds' head housekeeper, escorted him to the study. "I'm early, Marcia," Smith said. "Any problem?"

"They're upstairs, Mr. Smith. We've nothin' but problems. But not you. I'll tell them you're here."

A few minutes later, Leslie Ewald came to the study. Her eyes were puffy; she'd been crying.

"I came early, Leslie, because Detective Riga told me he had an appointment with you and Ken this afternoon."

Her response was to press her lips together, cross the room to a desk, and lean heavily on it with both hands. "I can't believe this is happening," she said in a low voice.

Smith came up behind her. "It's a dreadful thing, Leslie, this suspicion, but it's not yet an accusation, and you and Ken will see it through."

She turned and looked into his eyes. "Mac, things are moving so fast."

They sat in facing chairs. "Obviously, Leslie, the police have to talk to everyone who could possibly have knowledge about what happened to Andrea. Even if the weapon weren't involved, the fact that she was on Ken's staff would be sufficient reason to have detectives talk to him. Have you spoken with Paul?"

"Of course. He's upstairs with Ken. They've been arguing all afternoon."

"About what, or is that none of my business?"

"To me, it's very much your business, Mac, and I'm personally deeply grateful that you're here. Janet has disappeared."

"When did you find that out?" Smith asked.

"This morning. Paul said she packed a bag and left."

"I see," Smith said. "Any idea where she might have gone?"

"None whatsoever. Janet is . . . well, to be kind, Janet is not the most rational of women, especially when the pressure is on."

"You mean . . . ?"

"Yes, I mean Paul's affair with Andrea, and the fact that he never came home last night. Lord knows where Janet would go, or what she would do."

Smith pondered it, then said, "The police will want to talk to her eventually."

"I know that. I suppose we'll have to tell them. When Detective Riga called to arrange to see us, he asked that the four of us be present."

Smith forced a smile and slapped his hands on his knees. "Detective Riga could arrive at any moment, Leslie. I would like to talk to the three of you before he gets here. Could you have Ken and Paul come down?"

"Yes, of course." She called Marcia Mims and asked her to get them. "Not only is this an awful tragedy for that poor girl, and for us as a family, it could be a tragedy for the campaign. Ken had to cancel an appearance this afternoon. He's flying to Philadelphia tonight."

"Are you going with him?"

"Yes. You can imagine the questions the press will have for us at every step."

"Let's not worry about the press now, Leslie. I'm more concerned that everyone here is in sync."

Ken and Paul Ewald came in, and Smith launched into a series of questions that he anticipated would be asked by Riga. He realized he was back in his old role as a defense attorney, preparing witnesses, trying to head off surprises: "Where did you keep the weapon that was used to kill Andrea Feldman?" "Who had access to it?" "When did you last see it?" "Where was it?" "Why wasn't it secured?" "Where were each of you at the time she was killed?" "Can anyone verify your actions during that period of time?" "How well did you know the deceased?" "Was your relationship with her cordial, or had there been a recent strain?"

The list went on. When he was done, he realized some of the answers did nothing to divert suspicion, not just from Ken or Paul but from any of them. No one had an alibi, but Paul had the biggest problem. He claimed he'd had a fight with his wife and had taken a drive into Maryland for quiet time to think. Yes, he'd had an affair with Andrea Feldman, and, yes, Janet knew about it and had reacted vehemently and emotionally. No, he had no idea where she was. A suitcase was gone from her closet; her car was gone, too. He was very concerned about her, he said.

"Has she often just disappeared like this, Paul?" Smith asked.

"I wouldn't say often, Mac, but it has happened before. Frankly, I'm worried about what she might do to herself."

"Is she suicidal?"

"There have been threats, although I think they were just that, attention-getting outbursts. Still, I may as well level with you. Janet has some psychological problems." He looked at his father, who said nothing. "She's been under treatment for quite a while with Dr. Collins."

"Geoffrey Collins?" Smith said. "I know Geof."

Paul stood and walked the length of the room, came back halfway, and said, "Look, I'm so sorry about all of this. I know there's absolutely nothing I can say to either of you to explain it away, or to make it better. I . . . I had an affair, and she's dead now. I know you don't need this kind of complication running for president, Dad, and I would give anything, including my life, if I could go back and make this not happen."

Smith looked at Ken Ewald. Although the senator gave his son a reassuring smile, he obviously did so with some effort.

When Smith asked the senator what he had done following the gala, his answer was terse: "I went to my office across the street and worked until early in the morning. The gala took too much time out of my campaign schedule."

"And you say this Secret Service agent, Jeroldson, was with you the whole time."

"Yes. I mean, I wasn't sitting with him. I was in my office with the door closed, and he was out in the waiting room, the way it always is."

"Riga will want to confirm that with Jeroldson," Smith said.

"Good. Let him. This whole thing is ridiculous. Obviously, no one in this family, or in this household, killed Andrea Feldman. Someone must have broken in, or entered the house under false pretenses and walked out with the pistol."

Smith sighed and recrossed his legs. "Ken, that is always a possibility, but it is, I'm sure you'll admit, a farfetched one. The fact is that Riga's spotlight may sooner or later shine directly on Paul here. As a family friend and unofficial legal adviser who's had some experience in criminal law, I can tell you the evidence is all circumstantial, but still Paul's defense, if he has to make one, is pretty shaky. He had access to the weapon, was sleeping with the deceased, had a wife who was furious about it, and can't account for his—or her—whereabouts."

"Then let them charge me," said Paul, stalking to the door. "I can't do anything about that."

"Don't leave," Smith said, pointing his finger at him. "Riga expects the three of you to be here. It's bad enough that Janet won't be present. That's going to take some explaining in itself."

"I'll be upstairs," Paul said. He closed the door with considerable force.

Joe Riga was accompanied by two younger detectives. Riga was a tall man with a paunch, who wore his black hair slicked back. He handed his raincoat to Marcia Mims and accepted Leslie Ewald's offer to make himself comfortable. His assistants, still wearing their coats, took chairs outside the circle that had been formed by Riga, the Ewalds, and Smith.

"Sorry to take your time, Senator," Riga said. "I guess running for president must have you on the go."

"Yes," Ewald replied dryly.

"I'll try to make this as quick as possible, Senator," Riga said. He nodded at Leslie and Paul to assure them he had them in mind, too.

He went through a list of questions, all asked by Smith during his briefing. Riga was a good interviewer, knowing when to respond to keep an answer going, but most of the time showing no reaction to what was being said, just a few grunts and "ah-hahs," like a Freudian listening to a five-times-a-week patient on the couch.

He asked Leslie to account for her whereabouts at the time of the murder. She said she'd gone to bed following the gala, and assumed none of the household staff would refute that. Riga asked whether any of them could confirm it, rather than just not refute it, and she had to admit they couldn't. "They don't tuck me in," she said rather curtly.

Riga's next series of questions was directed at Ken Ewald. When Smith had asked him about his actions following the gala, Ewald had summed them up quickly. Now, in response to the same question asked by Joe Riga, Ewald went into great detail about what he'd done in his office that night, right down to the memos he'd dictated, notes he'd made, and telephone calls he'd placed.

"We'll want to see a log of those calls, Senator," Riga said in a tone that was neither threatening nor suspicious.

"Of course," Ewald said. "I'll see that you get it, although some of them are highly sensitive in regard to my campaign. I'm sure you can understand the need for discretion in how they're used."

"Sure," Riga said. "You say this agent's name is Jeroldson?"

"Yes, Bob Jeroldson. He isn't assigned to me exclusively, but I seem to end up with him a great deal." Ewald laughed, and Smith sensed the falseness of it, wondered whether Riga had, too. "Jeroldson is a strange type," Ewald said, "although I suppose all Secret Service agents are a different breed."

"How so?" Riga asked. Smith half smiled to himself; never make a statement unless you're prepared for a follow-up question.

Ewald slid over the question like the good politician he was, saying only that Jeroldson seemed to be a brooding, private person.

"Goes with the job, I think," Riga said, offering his own less-than-spontaneous smile.

"I suppose so."

A half hour later, after Paul Ewald had responded to all the detective's questions, Riga seemed to have had enough. He said he wanted to come back the next day to interview household staff, and would also want to spend time with those members of Senator Ewald's campaign staff who had easy access to the house and, by extension, to the Derringer used to kill Ms. Feldman.

After Marcia Mims had been summoned with Riga's raincoat, he looked at Paul Ewald, who sat with what could only be described as a challenging expression on his handsome face, and said, "You know, Mr. Ewald, I'm going to have to talk to you more."

Paul told him he'd be happy to cooperate in any way.

Smith had suggested before Riga arrived that Janet's absence be handled casually, without resorting to an outright lie. "Just say she isn't here, and you don't know where she is," he said. "No sense giving the press or the police something else to chew on." That's the way Leslie handled it when Riga asked about Janet, and he seemed to accept it for the moment. At least he hadn't pressed it.

But now, as he prepared to leave, Riga said, "Please have your daughter-in-law call me the minute you hear from her." He handed a card to Leslie Ewald. "I figured this was a tight family, that you'd know where everybody is all the time, especially when somebody you know's been murdered."

Ewald laughed. "This is a typical American family, running in different directions and trying to find time to sneak one meal a week together."

"Yeah, I know how it is," Riga said. "Thanks for your time and cooperation. By the way, Senator, how's the campaign going?"

"Fine, until this happened," Ewald said.

"I suppose the best thing for you is to get it cleared up as fast as possible."

"It certainly is, and I appreciate the fact that you recognize it," Ewald said.

After Riga and the others were gone, and Leslie and Paul had left the study, Smith sat alone with the senator.

"I have to tell you, Ken, Riga's got a suspicion; maybe a rumor. There's going to be a lot more focusing on Paul."

"I gather that."

"And I suggest we find Janet as quickly as possible."

"My sentiments exactly, Mac. I've never been particularly fond of her. She's so damn flighty, a very difficult person."

Smith didn't respond to Ewald's characterization of his daughter-in-law.

"Mac, if there is a charge brought against Paul, you will represent him?"

"No, I won't," Smith said, not sure whether he meant it.

"You've been a very close and dear friend, Mac, and the last thing I ever want to do with a friend is to put pressure on him. But if this thing gets messy, or messier, there is no one else I feel we can turn to. Please."

Smith averted his eyes and looked at the gun collection on the wall. He thought of Rhonda Harrison's surprise that he would even consider becoming involved, and knew that if he brought the subject up at dinner that night with Annabel, her response would not only be similar, there would be heat and vehemence behind it. Annie liked the fact that he was a professor, was more comfortable with the genteel and quiet pace of the life it afforded them. She had mentioned his health. He also knew there was a certain panache and synergy and symmetry involved—college professor and gallery owner, very intellectual, very noncommercial. He thought of her symmetry.

"Why me? There are plenty of good defense lawyers in Washington. Or elsewhere. You could have almost anyone you might want."

"Because you and I have worked together. You know me, know my family. That's time-saving—and there isn't much time. It will also seem natural. If I call in some high-powered defense lawyer who's handled all sorts of bad characters with money, Paul may get off, but first I get tarred with his attorney's brush. Also, I can trust you. You're bound to learn even more about this one American family, and I need to have whatever comes out known by a man in whom my confidence is absolute, a man I could trust in my . . . Cabinet."

"That isn't a big temptation, if you're trying to bribe me."

"I'm trying to tell you the truth. And there is one other thing."

"What's that?"

"I think you want to see me elected. If Paul gets charged and if this thing drags on, even if we win, we lose. In the next few days or weeks, I either win the nomination and thus the presidency or I'm the next dead body. I don't mean to sound inhumane. I think you want me to be elected—for all the right reasons."

"I'll think about it, Ken. I promise that."

"I suppose that's all I can ask."

Smith got up to leave.

"Mac, can I tell you something in strict confidence?"

"Yes, of course."

Ewald went through a little stutter-step as people always do when they're about to reveal something embarrassing. He shoved his hands in his pockets, cocked his head to one side, and did a toe-in-sand with his foot. "Mac, the fact is, I didn't stay in the office the entire time after the gala."

The comment brought back memories to Smith. He sat down. How many times had defendants held to a story until, suddenly, they felt a need to confide in their attorney? Too many.

"I left the office for about an hour," Ewald said.

"Where did you go?"

"I went to the Watergate Hotel."

"What time?"

"I don't know, maybe two in the morning, maybe a little later."

"Why?"

"I had to see someone."

"That might be helpful," Smith said. "It would be nice to have someone in this family who can verify where they were for a portion of the evening."

"That might be true in a normal situation, Mac, but not in this one. You see . . ."

"Ken, just tell me what it is you want to say."

"I saw someone who would make Leslie very upset."

He waited for Ewald. The story's ending was short. "I've been seeing this woman casually for a while, Mac. I'm not very proud of it, but I suppose that really doesn't matter. If I were a womanizer, somebody who was always on the make, it might be different, but this was one of those things that happens in a man's life now and then. You understand."

Whether Smith understood or not was irrelevant. He said, "Why are you bringing this up to me? Maybe you can ask Riga not to share it with Leslie."

"Well, Jeroldson, the agent, went with me. I tried to talk him out of it, told him I was on a private matter and that I didn't want him with me, but there was no way to shake him. He was doing his job, and if he didn't stay with me, he'd be a former Secret Service agent."

Smith's smile was small. "Must have been a very powerful attraction to agree to take Jeroldson along."

"He didn't know who I met. He never saw her, but when the detective questions him, he'll obviously mention that I went to the Watergate."

"I assume he will. If he doesn't, he's lying in a murder investigation."

"The point is, Mac, that I *can't* allow Leslie to find out about this. There was a similar incident years ago, and although it was all very brief, I'm sure the memory still lingers with her. Obviously, I never dreamed that . . . I mean, how would I know there would be a murder of one of my staff members, and that a weapon I owned would be the murder weapon? Ironic, isn't it?"

Smith looked at him intently. "Ironic doesn't do it. Care to tell me who the woman is?"

Ewald shook his head. "It wouldn't accomplish anything."

"Riga will want to know whom you met with at the Watergate. You can't tell *him* it doesn't matter."

"I know, I know, but for now can't we skip names?" Ewald was angry, chiefly at himself.

Smith shrugged. He had little choice; he couldn't force Ewald to reveal who the woman was. He looked into Ewald's eyes and felt, at once, sympathy and anger. Certainly, adultery was not the greatest sin anyone could commit. He'd come close on more than one occasion during his own marriage, and, he knew, could easily have taken the final step that would have carried him from passing lust to transgression.

What angered him was the possible ramifications to the campaign of the man he believed would make the best president of the United States, the best of the recent lot. Was he looking at another Gary Hart, someone capable of self-destruction at the most crucial time in his life? There were differences, of course. Smith had never viewed Hart as an electable presidential candidate, nor did he see Ken Ewald as a compulsive, promiscuous womanizer. Still, the situation was a lot graver than he would have liked.

What had Henry Adams said years ago? "Morality is a private and costly luxury." Morality, Smith had decided long ago, along with its sister metaphor, religion, had caused the death of too many people to be a dependable criterion for judging others, especially in Washington. The city teemed with ambitious young men and women, many living there only part time, away from home, under tremendous pressure to succeed, and sharing a common love of the excitement of politics and the nation's capital. Whatever their political viewpoint, they came with their dreams and ideals only to learn quickly that politics was a far more pragmatic business, necessity constantly being the mother of compromise. Beliefs usually blew away in the wind like dead leaves when they got in the way of accomplishing goals, political or personal—or, frequently, mixed. Morality? For many, it was every man for himself, and every woman, too.

No, he must not judge this man on the basis of a sexual indiscretion. He would remain angry, however. He was entitled to that.

"Look, Mac, I know this puts you in an awkward position, but try to understand."

"I'm doing my best. Is there much of a possibility that this woman is likely to make your affair with her public?"

Ewald smiled. "Hardly. She's mature and intelligent."

"It may become public no matter how mature and intelligent she is. You realize that. The MPD will end up knowing about it, and that means the press will, too."

Ewald nodded. "Yes, I know you're right. I need a little private time to think, Mac. Maybe you could think about ways to keep this quiet, too."

Smith left the house feeling heavier than when he'd arrived. Don't make judgments, he repeated to himself as he drove to the gate, was allowed to leave, and headed in the direction of the Mayflower Hotel. He didn't notice the sealed pink envelope addressed to *Mac* on the passenger seat until he was halfway there.

He stopped for a traffic light and opened the envelope. Inside was a note on Leslie Ewald's personal stationery:

"Dear Mac, thank you for helping in this time of great need. We shall all be eternally grateful to you. Please accept this as only a token, and rest assured that whatever you need is yours. Fondly, Leslie."

A check made out to him for fifty thousand dollars accompanied the note.

NINE

NICHOLAS'S PALETTE of soft colors on walls and tables, and soft light from a crystal chandelier above, flattered Annabel. She was a beautiful woman in any setting, but, as with all gems—velvet providing a better background than concrete—some settings rendered her invaluable.

She was born with bright red hair, which had burnished over the years into aged copper. She wore it full, creating a glowing frame for her face, which was creamy and unlined. Her eyes were, of course, green, as if ordained, and large, and her nose, ears, and mouth had been created with a stunning sense of proportion.

They'd chosen house specials: salmon with a bouquet of enoki mushrooms for her, lobster in beurre blanc for him, after sharing a cold foie gras with a garnish of beluga caviar. A Muscadet accompanied the meal, inexpensive and unambitious. Mac Smith had had enough of complexity and ambition for one day.

Now, with coffee in front of them, they sat back in their heavy armchairs and looked at each other.

"I am disappointed, you know," she said.

"Obviously. You've played 'the show must go on' all evening, but the actress keeps showing through the character."

"Again, Mac, I ask you why?"

"And, again, Annie, I tell you I'm not sure *why*." He smiled and held up his hand against what she was about to say. "Maybe we should make a pro-and-con list, like when you're deciding whether to buy a house. Let's see. . . ."

"*We?* You've made this decision yourself."

"I can be dissuaded. Go along with me. I shouldn't do it because it will disrupt the quiet lives we've settled into. I shouldn't do it because it's bound to end up a nasty, public affair that will smear everyone involved. I shouldn't do it because . . ." He smiled again, leaned forward, and extended his hand to her. Her smile was smaller, but she placed her hand in his. He held its silken softness and felt its strength. "I shouldn't do it because the beautiful woman with whom I am very much in love promises to scratch my eyes out if I do." He made a point of looking at her beautifully lacquered nails.

"Worse, Mac," she said. "You do this and I will act like a cornered honey badger."

"A direct attack on the genitals?"

She didn't answer.

"That's a powerful entry in the negative column."

"I should hope so." She withdrew her hand, picked up her coffee, and sat back, observing him over her cup. He looked tired. The weight of the decision he was about to make pulled down on the flesh of his cheeks and the corners of his eyes. Although he'd shaved before going to Leslie Ewald's house, a shadow had reappeared. "If I could hold a mirror up to you at this moment, Mac Smith," she said, "you'd see why you shouldn't get involved in this."

He looked at her in turn. There was conviction behind her objections. Nothing frivolous about them. He wished there were a way to bring about a grand compromise, to do the right thing as well as to indulge his instinctive needs at the moment while keeping her happy. At the same time, this urge to compromise was edged with a certain anger at her: He told himself that, ultimately, he would make his choice based on what was good for him, even if it conflicted with what she wanted.

Easier said than done. He did love her.

"Cognac?" he asked. That suggestion wouldn't prompt an argument.

"No. Don't do it, Mac."

"Let's go."

"Let's talk."

"Not here. Come on, a nightcap at my place. Rufus needs a walk."

"Know what I think, Mac?"

"What?" He motioned for a waiter to bring the check.

"I think you're more concerned with what Rufus thinks than what I think."

"He does have a certain wisdom," said Smith, standing and coming around the table to help with her chair. "Most of all, he never argues with me."

T H E Y sat in Smith's den. He sipped a brandy, she an Irish Cream. They said little. Rufus, the Dane, obscured most of a shag rug on which he'd sprawled.

"Okay, I won't," Smith said into his snifter. He'd removed his jacket, tie, and shoes, and sat in his reclining chair. Annabel had staked out a corner of the couch where she'd tucked her stockinged feet beneath her.

"I'm sorry, Mac. I'm acting like an irrational woman."

Smith smiled as he said, "And damned attractive in the process."

"It's just that . . ."

"I think you're right. I don't need the aggravation."

"Maybe you do. Maybe we both do."

"I don't follow."

"Oh, I don't know, Mac, it's just that we're falling into a pretty staid and proscribed life."

" 'Boring' is my translation."

"Not for me, but I sense a certain restlessness in you, especially lately. Don't misunderstand. I love being in love with a college professor. It has a certain snobbish ring to it." She giggled. "And maybe even good for business. But I was thinking as we drove here that maybe getting back into the thick of things is exactly what you need. To make you realize what a nice life a college professor leads, that is."

He narrowed his eyes as he tried to figure out what she was up to. Did she mean what she'd just said? Or was it the old reverse psychology?

He decided to take her at face value. "What about your threat to turn into Annie Honey Badger?"

"Just the animalistic side of Annie. I take it back. No need to buy a metal cup in the morning."

"Whew!" He wiped imagined sweat from his brow.

"Take me home," she said pleasantly, standing and slipping into her shoes. "It was a great dinner." She pressed closer to him, whispered in his ear, "I love you, Mackensie Smith." She kissed him on the mouth, pleasantly, then passionately.

"Sure you don't want to stay awhile?"

"Can't. You have to think. I want your mind focused on me at certain times. Besides, I have a meeting at eight with a dealer from Rio. Tomorrow night. Stay at my place."

"One of these days, we should make it one place," he said.

"One of these days. Maybe."

In her condo in the Watergate's apartment complex, Annabel poured herself a glass of orange juice, lit her one cigarette of the day, and went to her small terrace, where she hunched over the railing and looked out across the Potomac. No sense denying it, she told herself: She was still angry at what would obviously be Mac's decision to become involved with the Andrea Feldman murder.

But she knew it was more than anger she felt; it was something else, and beyond her comprehension at the moment. The fact that it was without definition made it all the more sinister. Yes, that was it. She wrapped her arms about herself as a distinct, sudden chill caused her to shiver. She was afraid of losing Mackensie Smith, not to another woman, but to *something* else.

In that case, the loss would be final.

She quickly went to bed and invited sleep to blot that dark thought from her consciousness.

TEN

MAC SMITH had always been an early riser, although he was capable of sleeping in provided it had been scheduled in advance. Sleeping late had not been planned for this morning, and he awoke precisely at six o'clock to the smell of coffee brewing in the kitchen. To say that Mackensie Smith was obsessive and compulsive about certain ablutions and details was an understatement. No matter what time he returned home at night, he would have trouble falling asleep until he'd prepared the morning coffee and set the timer. Preparing the coffee was a satisfying, relaxing ritual in itself; three scoops of a commercial decaffeinated coffee, two scoops of a water-decaffeinated amaretto blend, and two scoops of amaretto bursting with caffeine. Enough for ten cups; somehow Thursday might turn out to be a long day.

Rufus, the Dane, his nose a finely tuned instrument to most smells, wasn't stimulated by the aroma of coffee. He looked up from where he was sleeping on the floor and observed his master climb out of bed, stretch, yawn, and head for the kitchen. The minute Smith was gone, Rufus climbed up onto the bed and resumed sleeping.

Smith continued his morning ceremonies in the kitchen. He opened windows, turned on WRC, poured his first cup of coffee, then funneled the rest into a carafe so that it would not continue to percolate. WRC's weatherman was in the midst of forecasting a sunny, pleasant day when Smith turned on the station. A minute later, the weatherman turned things over to the anchor, who said, "To repeat our top stories, Paul Ewald, the son of Democratic presidential hopeful Kenneth Ewald, was arrested just hours ago for the murder of Andrea Feldman, a young attorney who worked on Senator Ewald's staff. We'll bring you more details as we receive them. . . .

"The White House has once again avowed its support of rebel forces in Panama loyal to ousted dictator Gilbert Morales. . . .

"A large shipment of cocaine has been intercepted by DEA agents at Dulles Airport. . . ."

Smith called the Ewalds' home. His call was answered by Marcia Mims, whose voice reflected her distress. "No, Mr. Smith, I haven't heard from either Senator or Mrs. Ewald. This is so terrible, so terrible for this family. Oh, my God, Mr. Smith, please do something to help!"

"I'll do everything I can, Marcia," Smith said. "I'll be at my house for an hour. If I don't hear from someone by then, I'll call again."

His next call was to Paul Ewald's place. There was no answer, which didn't surprise him. Janet Ewald was missing, and Paul was in custody. He was hoping—silly game. But you had to try everything, ring every bell, turn over every lead and leaf.

Call number three was to MPD headquarters. He was told Detective Riga wouldn't be back until nine.

"This is Mackensie Smith," he said, and added, "Paul Ewald's attorney. Where is he being held?"

The desk sergeant told him. Smith thanked him and hung up.

He was about to pick up the phone again when it rang. "Hello?"

"Mac, this is Rhonda."

"I just heard on your station about Paul being arrested," Smith said. He sounded gruff, although he had no reason to be annoyed with her. Somehow, getting the news from a radio station rankled, and he couldn't keep it out of his voice.

"Were you called?" she asked.

"No. I'm about to get dressed to go see him."

"You haven't had any conversation with him yet?"

"No. As I said, Rhonda, I heard the news over your station."

"Mac, you say you're going to see him. You are his attorney?"

"Getting dressed and going to see the son of an old friend does not indicate anything, Rhonda. Let's leave it at that."

"Have you talked to Senator Ewald yet?"

"Rhonda, let's drop this. If I am to be Paul Ewald's attorney, that places me under obvious restrictions where you're concerned."

"I understand that, but it doesn't mean I can't stay in touch with you, keep tabs on things through you. We are friends, aren't we?"

"At parties, yes, but our friendship now has some rules."

She laughed. "Sure, it had a few before. But the rules don't preclude me from calling you, or you from answering the phone. Keep in touch, Mac."

"Sure. Do me the same favor."

Showered and dressed, and with Rufus hurriedly walked and fed, Smith was almost out the door when he remembered: He had an early class to teach at the university. He called Dean Gerry at home. "Roger, I can't make my class this morning. I want to call Art Poly to see if he'll cover it for me."

Gerry laughed. "You can cancel it if you want to, Mac."

"No, Roger, they miss enough even when they're there."

"All right, call Art, but I have a feeling I'll be getting more calls like this from you."

"I think you're right," Smith said.

"Look, Mac, I heard the news this morning about Paul Ewald being arrested. I also assume that you're about to handle his defense."

Smith's laugh was rueful.

"Is it true?"

"Probably. I mean, yes, it is. We'd better get together to talk about how to handle this."

"Anytime, Mac. I'm having a few friends over Saturday evening. Perhaps you and Annabel would join us. We can huddle for whatever time you need."

Smith sighed and thought ahead to Saturday. It seemed years away. "I'll ask Annabel as soon as I talk to her. I don't know what my schedule is going to be once I'm in deep in this. If I can't make it Saturday, maybe we can steal some time at the office. I'll let you know."

"Whatever works for you, Mac. Interesting, that you'd get involved in something like this. How well I remember our discussion when you told me you'd decided to close down your practice and join us here in academia."

"I remember that discussion, too. Thanks for understanding about this morning. I'll try to be there Saturday."

Smith opened the front door to leave and was confronted with a half-dozen reporters and photographers who'd congregated on the sidewalk in front of his house. A television remote truck was parked across the street. Smith wasn't sure what to do. His options were to remain inside, give them a statement, or simply walk past without saying anything. The last option seemed the only sensible course, and that's what he did, waving off their questions, saying only to the most persistent, "No comment."

He decided to leave his car in his garage and to walk until he found a cab. The reporters trailed him, but only one continued to match him stride for stride as he put blocks between him and the house. It was a young man carrying a Marantz portable tape recorder and a microphone with the call letters of a station Smith did not know. The young man eventually stopped asking questions and simply continued walking a few paces behind Smith. They reached an intersection where the light was against them. Smith turned and said as pleasantly as possible, "I don't have any comment at this time."

The young man, whose hair was blushing and whose face sported the predictable accompanying freckles, grinned and said, "All I'm asking, Mr. Smith, is whether you're Paul Ewald's attorney. There shouldn't be any mystery about that."

Smith sighed and nodded. "No, there is no mystery about that. Yes, I am representing Paul Ewald in this matter."

The light changed. They looked at each other. Smith narrowed his eyes and said, "You can follow me to Chesapeake Bay, but you won't hear another word."

"Okay," the young red-haired reporter said. "Thanks for answering at least one question."

A few blocks later, Smith found a taxi and had the driver take him to MPD headquarters at Third and C Streets, where, after navigating a maze of members of the press and squinting against flashes from strobe lights, he reached Detective Joe Riga's office. Riga was seated behind his desk, a telephone wedged between ear and shoulder. He was partly obscured by piles of paper and file folders. He saw Smith at the door, waved him in, and resumed his conversation.

Smith went to a window that desperately needed cleaning and looked down to the street. He heard Riga say, "I don't give a goddamn what he wants, the report isn't leaving this office until I get the word from my authorities. Look, I . . . evidently you don't speak English." He slammed the phone down.

Smith leaned against the windowsill and said, "Good morning, Joe.

Still in the State Department? You just flunked diplomacy. You sound angry."

Riga picked up a half-smoked cigar and wedged the soggy end between his teeth. "Yeah, I'm angry at all the wahoos who try to pull rank with me, and I have a feeling you're not here to make me any happier. You're officially Ewald's attorney?"

"Yes."

Riga cackled and put the cigar in the ashtray. "Jesus, Mac, I never figured I'd see you back in the saddle as a criminal attorney." Smith started to say something, but Riga continued. "You know something, you should've stayed at the university. Do you know what you're walking into?"

"Probably not, but that doesn't matter at the moment. You've arrested Paul Ewald. Is he charged with Andrea Feldman's murder?"

"Mac, get your facts straight. We haven't *arrested* Paul Ewald. We brought him in for questioning."

"In the middle of the night."

"Yeah. People tend to be home then."

"You didn't have to detain him to question him, Joe."

"In this case, I figured it might be a good idea." Riga shrugged, grimaced, picked up his cigar again. "His wife cuts out, which makes me a little uneasy, you know? I feel better having him cozied up here."

"I don't give a damn what you feel better with, Joe. You have no right to detain him unless you're ready to charge and indict him."

"Yeah, yeah, I know, but *you* know I've got a little time."

"Damn little. Why wasn't I called immediately?" Smith asked.

"We told him he had a quarter to call his attorney, but he didn't. Maybe he doesn't want you."

"I don't think that's the case, Joe. His rights were read to him, I assume."

Riga laughed. "Yeah, we read him his rights. We read them a couple of times, because of who he is."

"With the video running."

"Yeah. We made sure we shot his best side."

"Did he make any statements?"

"Just that he didn't kill her."

"Anything else?"

"Nothing important. They all sound the same when you pick them up and question them about a murder. They go through their shocked routine, then get angry at the outrage of it all, and then they clam up. He followed the pattern. You wanna see him?"

"Of course. Before I do, though, let me ask you a question."

"Shoot." The phone rang and Riga picked it up, scowled at what he heard, and hung up.

"Joe, doesn't it strike you as a little strange that the son of a prominent senator and presidential candidate sleeps with a member of his father's staff, then chooses to shoot her, of all places, in front of the Kennedy Center and with a weapon that belongs to his father?"

Another shrug from the detective. "Maybe twenty years ago. Nothing surprises me in this looney-tune society."

Smith pushed away from the windowsill and took a chair across the desk. "There still has to be some question in your mind about the probability of all this. Paul Ewald isn't a nut by any stretch of the imagination. He's well educated, has a successful import-export business, and has never been in trouble in his life."

"Come on, Mac, what the hell does that mean? What we've got here is a guy who's been importing and exporting with some chick with a body and brains. He's cheating on his old lady. The broad threatens to bust up his marriage, which, because he happens to be the son of maybe our next president, could screw up his father, too. He tells her to back off. She won't back off. He pulls out the gun and figures that'll get her attention, get her to listen. She doesn't. Boom! Another crime of passion, just like in the good old-fashioned murder mysteries. Nothing new. The strength of a single pubic hair is stronger than ten thousand mules."

Riga laughed at his own joke. "I think Freud said that," he said.

Smith realized he was wasting time trying to get Riga to at least acknowledge some doubt about Paul Ewald's guilt. "Yes," he said, "Willie Freud from Anacostia." The phone rang again, and Riga picked it up. Smith stood and pointedly looked at his watch. Riga put his hand over the mouthpiece and said, "All right, I'll get somebody to take you down." He pushed a button on his intercom: "Send Ormsby in here." Riga went back to his telephone conversation. A sergeant entered the office. Again cupping a hand over the mouthpiece,

Riga told him, "This is Mackensie Smith, Paul Ewald's lawyer. Take him down to see his client."

Twenty minutes later, Smith sat with Paul Ewald in a room reserved for lawyer-client meetings. It was furnished in pure postmodern police station: a long wooden table and four wooden chairs without arms. At least all four legs on the chairs were the same length. In the interrogation rooms, a half inch of the front legs was sawed off to keep suspects constantly leaning forward. A bright bulb covered by a green metal shade hung above the table. Heavy wire mesh covered the windows, as well as a small window in the door. A uniformed officer could be seen through the window.

Smith and Ewald shook hands. "Thanks for coming, Mac," Ewald said.

"Sorry you're going through this, Paul. You won't have to much longer." They sat at the table, Smith at the head of it, Ewald to his left.

"Let me say a few things at the outset, Paul. I don't know what evidence the district attorney thinks he has to make a case against you, but I'll be informed of that in short order, if he does decide to proceed with charges. I know that you didn't come home that night after the show at the Kennedy Center. I know that you had access to the weapon that killed Andrea Feldman. And I know that you'd been having an affair with her. If that's all the DA is going on, he won't dare seek an indictment. I can assure you of that."

Ewald drew a deep breath, sat back, and looked up at the ceiling. His eyes were closed, and he pressed his lips tightly together. Smith took the moment to observe him. Paul Ewald was a presentable young man. Smith thought of the actors Van Johnson and Martin Milner. Paul had the same boyish quality as his father, although there was a subtle ruggedness to his father's face that Paul did not possess. In fact, Smith had often thought that there was a softness in Paul Ewald that was almost androgynous, half-effeminate, with a certain vulnerability— call it weakness—that was, at once, appealing yet off-putting. Ewald was wearing socks; his shoes had been removed as a matter of procedure. He had on a white shirt open at the collar and gray trousers. As he opened his eyes and looked at Smith, his fatigue was apparant.

"Paul, did you kill Andrea Feldman?"

"Of course not."

"You were sleeping with her, and she threatened to break up your marriage and ruin your father's chances."

"No. Andrea was demanding, but not to that extent. I'd come to hate her, though." Ewald laughed. "Maybe I should have killed her. I'm ending up in the same position whether I did or not."

"Not true, Paul. They have to *prove* you killed her, and if you didn't, they'll have a tough time with that."

Ewald shook his head. "Pardon me, Mac, if I don't enthusiastically agree with you. Have you ever had nightmares that you'd be accused of something you didn't do, but you'd end up paying for it for the rest of your life?"

"Only after I've read novels in which that happened. It won't happen here."

"I hope you're right."

Smith broke the ensuing silence. "Do you have any idea who might have killed Andrea?"

"No, I don't, although women like Andrea Feldman can get people pretty upset."

Smith thought of Riga's comment about mules, but kept it to himself. He rolled his fingers on the tabletop and chewed on his cheek. "Paul, had you been with her to the Buccaneer Motel, the place she had a key to?"

"Yes."

"The night she was murdered?"

Ewald shook his head. "No, we didn't have sex that night."

"Didn't Andrea have an apartment here in D.C.?"

"Yes, she did, but we never went there. I thought it was strange, but she said we should be more discreet than that, go out of town every time we got together." He banged his fist on the table. "Damn it, I should have known better. If things weren't so . . . rotten at home, maybe I wouldn't have . . . hell, no sense blaming circumstances. No sense blaming Janet. The fact was, *we* did not have the kind of life recently that, among other things, promotes a healthy sexual existence between man and wife."

Smith made a few notes on a pad. He asked, "When did you meet Andrea, Paul—*after* she'd joined your father's campaign staff?"

"No. I met her several years ago at a party in Georgetown, sort of a business gathering at the home of one of my important customers. She was there with a date, but we had one of those locked-eyes reactions to each other all night. Before she left, she slipped me her phone number. I sat on it for a while. Then, one night, I had a fight with Janet, left the house, and called her. She suggested we meet for a drink. We did. One drink led to several, and we ended up driving to Maryland, where we made love for the first time."

"I see," Smith said. "Then what? Did you suggest she join your father's staff?"

"I guess so. She told me how much she believed in my father's cause, and how all the issues he stood for represented how she felt about things in this country. I probably did suggest that she apply for a job on his staff. Yes, exactly, that's the way it happened. I suggested it, and told her I would put in a good word for her. She was hired about a week later."

"What did you know about her background, Paul?"

"Not much, Mac. She was actually a very private person. Maybe that's why I trusted her. Maybe that's why we never went to her apartment. Maybe she didn't want anybody there. Sometimes I wondered whether she had a live-in boyfriend, but it really didn't matter."

"Did you ask her whether she had a boyfriend living with her?"

"No. I didn't want to do anything to jeopardize the relationship. To be honest with you, Mac, I loved every minute we were together. It was sex the way you read about in cheap novels. She was *good.*" He looked at Smith, who said nothing. Ewald shrugged. "What can I say? I'm weak."

"You do know that Janet is still missing?"

"Yes."

"You have no idea where she might have gone?"

"None whatsoever. I called every place I could think of with no luck. Janet hates confrontation."

"It seems she confronted you pretty directly about your relationship with Andrea."

"Sure, but those were hysterical moments, times when she'd fly off the handle. She did that a lot. Janet's kind of a split personality. She either reacts emotionally to something and throws a fit, or goes into a shell, runs away and hides. I guess she's in her shell period now."

Smith was taken by the fact that Paul seemed to have little concern about his wife's disappearance—even whether she was alive or dead—but he chalked it up to the strange relationship between them, and the emotionally unsettling situation Paul Ewald was in at the moment. He said, "Paul, I want you to say nothing to anyone unless I'm present. Do you understand that?"

"Yes, I do."

"Not only do you understand it, Paul, will you follow that advice?"

"I'll do my best, Mac. Have you talked to Mom and Dad?"

"No, they're out of town. I intend to touch base with them the minute I leave here. I'm sure they've heard the news by now. You haven't heard from them?"

"No." His eyes misted. "God, Mac, it's bad enough sitting here with you under these circumstances. I'm not sure I can face them. They won't even let me wear shoes—it's like I was a convicted murderer."

Smith patted Paul's arm and smiled. "You'll be out in a couple of hours, Paul, I promise you that." He stood. "MPD's got its neck way out on this, pulling you in like this."

Paul looked up at him. "I can't believe you're agreeing to help me, Mac. I thought you'd decided to never practice law again."

"Which just goes to show how weak *I* am. I don't see how I can do otherwise, considering my long friendship with the family and caring for the cause, you might call it. By the way, Paul, I assume you'll accept me as your attorney?"

Paul's lower lip trembled. "Accept you? How can I not? You're the best." He was crying. "Just lucky for me, I suppose, that I was born . . . with advantages."

Smith was tempted to wrap his arms around him and give him a bear hug, kind of a manly shoring up of his spirits, but he restrained himself. This was no time for gestures of sentiment. At best, they would be misunderstood. Still, he put his hand on Paul's.

Smith indicated to the guard that he was leaving. The door opened. Smith looked back at Ewald, who stood with his back to the door, his body moving in rhythm to his sobs.

"I'll be back, Paul. In the meantime, remember what you've promised me."

. . .

SMITH placed a call from MPD to the office of Leonard Kramer, the District of Columbia's district attorney. He was told that Kramer was out of the office and would not return for an hour. "Please have him call me the minute he comes in," Smith said, not trying to soften the anger in his voice. He identified himself to the secretary, indicated that he was representing Paul Ewald, and reiterated the urgency of his call.

A few reporters from early that morning had continued to wait outside Smith's home. He took the same tack—"No comment, sorry"—and entered the house, where Rufus greated him in his usual exuberant fashion. "No comment for you, either," Smith said, rubbing the huge animal behind the ears. He poured himself coffee from the carafe and sat at the desk in his study. Twenty minutes later, Leslie Ewald called. They'd just returned to Washington. "This is outrageous, Mac," she said. "How dare they arrest Paul!"

Smith thought of Riga's word games and decided not to play them with Leslie. "My sentiments exactly, Leslie. I just came from visiting Paul. He's all right, shaken naturally by the events, but holding up very nicely. I assured him he'd be out before the day is over. I have a call in now to the district attorney."

"Can they do this legally, abduct him out of his own house in the middle of the night?"

"No . . . well, they shouldn't, but they did, and they'll get away with it unless Paul wants to bring civil charges."

"I'm sure that's the last thing on anyone's mind," Leslie said. "Can we see him? I mean now?"

"I could arrange it, but I recommend against it. Give me until early afternoon. I'll be in touch. For now, let me clear the line for the DA's call. I'll be back to you as soon as I know something."

Kramer called and said in a low, rich voice that always seemed to contain an imminent laugh, "The last thing I thought I'd be doing was calling Mac Smith as defense counsel. How are you, Mac?"

"I'd be a lot better if Paul Ewald were sitting at home right now eating a tuna-fish sandwich. What the hell could have prompted you to haul him in this way?"

"Hold on, Mac. There's a division of labor here. We prosecute, MPD investigates."

"You aren't suggesting that Joe Riga did this of his own volition without an okay from you? I know Joe. Doesn't wash."

"You do realize, Mac, that we aren't dealing here with your run-of-the-mill murder case."

"True, but we are dealing with a run-of-the-mill Constitution under which we function. That make sense to you?"

Kramer was silent a moment, then he said, "It was MPD's opinion that Paul Ewald was a threat to disappear. They acted on that instinct, and I can't say I blame them."

"Are you charging Ewald?"

"Not at the moment. He's considered a prime suspect, and sure as hell is an important material witness. We're operating under the theory that Mr. Ewald, the younger of the two, is damned important to the case."

"Who concocted that theory, Len? I get the feeling you're talking about someone other than yourself."

There was silence. Then Kramer said, "There's been a little pressure."

"Pressure? Who'd put pressure on you, Len? Ken Ewald is a Democrat. You wouldn't be sitting in your chair if you weren't, and your boss, too."

"Look, Mac, let's drop this."

"Happy to, Len, provided Paul Ewald is back at home eating a tuna-fish sandwitch by two o'clock."

"We can arrange that."

"I know you can. The question is will you?"

"You have my word."

"Good. You are, of course, aware of the embarrassment to Paul's father, Senator Ewald."

"I'm not in the business of embarrassing presidential candidates." He was angry.

"That may be true of you, Len, but somebody sure as hell knows what the embarrassment factor is here. Thanks."

"Welcome back to the nasty side of life, Professor."

Smith worked through the lunch hour making notes on a yellow legal pad. The ringing of the phone stopped him. It was Annabel Reed calling from her Georgetown gallery. Smith filled her in on what had happened that morning and asked what was new with her.

"I think I'm going to be able to buy Tlazolteotl."

"Tlazolteotl?"

"You mispronounce it."

"So what? What is it?"

"The ancient Aztec goddess of childbirth. I've been negotiating for it with a dealer in New York for a long time. Dumbarton Oaks wanted it, too, but they already have a superb example. That was the point I kept making. I guess I was effective in making it. It's mine!"

Smith smiled at her enthusiasm. He loved her in all weather and temperaments, but responded with special verve when she was high on having captured a prize for her gallery.

"When do you take possession of Tlazolteotl?"

She laughed. "You mispronounced it again."

"Sorry. I've seen pictures of it. That's the stone rendering of a woman squatting in childbirth, right?"

"Yes, but you don't have to be so crude about it. A celebration is definitely in order. My treat, your choice. I'll even go to one of those macho steak houses you like."

"I have a better idea. Let's celebrate at your place. I'd like to stay away from the public for a while."

"Fine, but if we're celebrating at home, the meal is on you. Cook it, or bring it in."

"I'd love to cook it, but I won't have the time to do justice to the sort of meal the goddess of childbirth deserves. Trust me, as they say in Hollywood. Six o'clock?"

"I'll be waiting."

Smith's phone rang all afternoon, causing him to put the answering machine on so he could screen calls and decide whether or not to take them. He debated returning to MPD headquarters to be present when Paul was released but decided against it. Len Kramer was a man of his word. That was confirmed when the phone rang at 2:15. It was Kramer. "Paul Ewald is on his way home to make a sandwich, Mac."

"Thank you," Smith said, "for letting me know."

He called Leslie Ewald and told her that Paul had been released and should be home shortly. He made a couple of other calls before a wave of fatigue came over him. He took a shower and a short nap. Then, before leaving for Annabel's house, he called the Information operator in Baltimore and said, "Last name is Buffolino, Anthony Buffolino. It might be listed as a residence or as a private detective agency." The operator gave him both.

He hung up and stared at the phone, then lifted the receiver and dialed Tony Buffolino's home number.

"... AND so I called his home and got an answering machine. He sounded angry on his message. He said something like, 'I'm not here, so come on over and rip me off if you want. Otherwise, say what it is you have to say and I'll get back to you sometime."

Annabel raised her eyebrows and shook her head. "Lovely dinner you brought in. For you, it's takeout; for me, bringing in. Are you sure you want to get involved with him again, Mac?"

"Yes, I think I do. He's exactly the person I need."

"Why do you need anyone?" she asked. "Paul has been released. Do you think there's a likelihood he'll be charged with the murder?"

"I don't know, but it remains a distinct possibility. Besides, if it isn't Paul, it could be someone else very close to Ken and Leslie. Paul's release doesn't end anything, Annabel. To the contrary, I think it represents the beginning of something long and difficult. Tony was a superb investigator, probably the best MPD had. Yes, I think I could use him . . . *if* he calls back, and *if* he's interested. We didn't part company on the best of terms."

"I could never understand that. You saved him from criminal prosecution. He should have been grateful."

"He didn't see it that way. He was bounced off the force, which, for him, was the ultimate penalty. He loved being a cop, loved it like no one I've ever known. At any rate, I asked him to call me at home. If he does, he'll get my answering machine, which, as you know, takes a more civil tone than his."

Annabel laughed. "Of course I know it. It's my voice. I even tried to come up with a British accent for you."

"And you were good. A Brit wouldn't buy it, but Tony will." He moved to where she was sitting on her living room couch and put his arm around her. "When do you take possession of the woman hunched over in childbirth?"

"So crude."

"Just practicing for Tony Buffolino."

"Two weeks. I pick it up in New York."

"I'll go with you, to guard you and the stone brood mare."

"That would be nice. We can make a weekend of it."

He pressed his face to her long white neck. "You know I love you, Annabel."

"Sometimes." The feel of his hands on the front of her robe was too pleasurable to protest. He continued to stroke her, his fingertips tracing the lines of her body beneath the silk, soon teasing, provoking, causing her to make sounds that to Smith sounded like the "meow" of a contented Siamese. She began to touch him, too, and brushed her lips across his, then stabbed fiercely at his lips, laughing until he parted the sash of her robe and moved his fingers over her skin.

"I am at a large disadvantage . . . ," she said playfully, her voice trailing off like his fingers. "Get naked, Smith."

He hated to break the bond between them, but he did. Moments later, they were both nude and heading for the bedroom.

Her housekeeper had changed the linen that morning. Between the clean, smooth sheets, they easily slid into first a gentle, then a more aggressive, display of their hunger for each other.

After they were spent, she whispered only, "Whew!"

"I hate to bring up a rival," Smith said, getting up from the bed, "but I want to call my machine." He picked up the phone, punched in his code, and listened to messages.

"Did Buffolino call?" she asked when he was finished.

"Yes. He said, 'A blast from the past.' Then he added, 'Smith, I want to tell you to drop dead. But I learned a couple of lives ago never to shut the door to anything. Call me. Any hour. I'm up late. I got this thing for old movies.' "

"A character."

"That and other things. Do you mind if I call him now?"

"Why should I mind? You've already seen to it that I've suffered my delightful 'little death.'. . ." She smiled. " 'Deaths' is more accurate."

"I'll use the phone in the living room."

"No, stay here. I can touch you while you talk."

He dialed. "Tony?"

"Yeah. Smith?"

"Yes. I got your message."

"I got yours, too. Hey, I heard about you finding the body of that chick who got it."

"Yes, I was walking my dog, and . . ." Nobody cared that he was walking his dog. "Tony, I have a case that I thought you might be interested in working on."

"A case?" He snickered. "What'd they do, fire you at the U? What'd you do, put the make on a Betty Co-ed?" A louder laugh this time. "Nice young stuff at the U, huh?"

"Nothing like that, Tony. I'd like to talk to you tomorrow."

"That'll be tough. I'm in the middle of . . . renovations . . . on my office . . . suite. I got a big case going. I may win it. It's called prosperity. You want breakfast? You want to *buy* breakfast? I'll come to D.C., any place you say as long as it's good. No greasy spoons, okay?"

Smith couldn't help but smile as he listened to that voice he'd heard so often when he was defending Buffolino. "Sure," he said, "breakfast, my treat, my pleasure. Seven o'clock at the . . . ?"

"Seven o'clock? What, are you crazy? I work nights, man. Make it nine."

Smith sighed. "All right, nine, Tony. Be on time."

"I'm always on time. You know that. I just like to be realistic. You know the airlines build in their schedules all kinds of time so that they look like they arrive on time? All a fraud. All a fraud. I pick a realistic ETA and I make it. I'll see you at nine."

"One question, Tony."

"What?"

"Are you available to take on a case that could run a while?"

"I'm up to my duff in cases, Mac, but I'll check my calendar. Maybe I can juggle things, *if* I decide to work for you. Know what?"

"What, Tony?"

"It'll be good to see you again."

"I'll enjoy it, too. Nine o'clock at . . . where are we meeting?"

Buffolino said, "The Jockey Club in the Ritz-Carlton. We'll have a . . . whatta they call it . . . a power breakfast."

"Fine. Nine at the Jockey Club."

"You got it, Mac Smith." He paused. "Hey, you okay?"

"Yes."

"You sound different."

"You don't. Good night, Tony."

Smith hung up, and was at once amused and annoyed. Buffolino's bravado and bluff was the stuff of all losers. On the other hand, Tony had attributes, strengths that Smith needed, including candor, know-how, street smarts. Smith had once had a good staff, good people, who'd drifted away into other lives when he closed his practice. The little speech he'd made that day informing them of his decision had been difficult. A few cried, a few swore, one or two shrugged it off and promised to go on to bigger and better things. Each handled it in his or her own way. Of course. Just another instance of life happening while other plans are being made.

"Mac," Annabel said, touching him.

"What?" He drew a sharp breath.

"Spend the night."

Even though he was an experienced lawyer, there was no argument from him.

ELEVEN

TONY BUFFOLINO sat at a folding metal kitchen table and applied polish to black wing-tip shoes. He seldom wore them. They were tight and pinched his toes, but they went with the blue suit he intended to wear to his breakfast meeting that morning with Smith.

Abercrombie, the smaller and younger of two black-and-white cats (the other was Fitch, of course), walked across the table and pushed his head against Buffolino's hand. "Not now, baby, Daddy's got to get out a' here and earn some cat food." Abercrombie looked at him as though understanding and approving, arched his back, and sashayed away.

A squeal of brakes caused Buffolino to turn and look out through a dirt-crusted, smeared window at the street one flight below. It was an industrial area of Baltimore. A ready-mix cement company was across the street, flanked by two automobile body shops, both of which, Buffolino knew, were part straight, part chop shops. The car with the loud brakes had almost hit a homeless drunk named John who slept in wrecks behind the shops. The driver leaned out his window and cursed at John, who answered with a series of jerky arm and finger gestures.

Buffolino shook his head as he stood and stretched, causing his sleeveless undershirt to pull out of his striped boxer shorts. He pushed dirty dishes aside in the kitchen sink and used a Brillo pad to scrub the black polish from his fingers. Taking a bowl from the pile, he filled it with milk and placed it on the floor next to three other bowls that had been licked clean.

The bedroom was in the rear of the railroad flat he'd called home for the past two years. It was large enough for an earthquake of a double bed, a dresser rejected by the Salvation Army, and a yellow plastic table that served as a nightstand. A telephone, answering machine, windup alarm clock, and dog-eared copies of *Penthouse* and *Playboy* covered the surface. Because there was no closet in the room, he'd suspended a piece of iron pipe with wire attached to hooks screwed into the ceiling. His blue suit was covered with a dry cleaner's plastic. He slipped on the trousers, which were tight around his waist, and swore softly as he sucked in his stomach and hooked them closed. He rummaged through dresser drawers for the blue silk shirt, unhooked his pants, breathed deeply, tucked in the shirt, and tied a white tie around his neck, the skinny end dangling below the fat end.

In the tiny bathroom, he carefully peeled away a piece of toilet tissue he'd used to stem the flow of blood from a shaving cut, ran a comb through thick, wavy black hair with gray at the temples, and turned his head back and forth as he scrutinized his mirror image. Some people said he looked like Dave Toma, the former cop turned actor and antidrug crusader, although Buffolino thought there was more Paul Newman in his face than that. Victor Mature, his first wife had decided. Peter Falk, said wife number two. But neither of them spoke that way after the first few years. Mussolini, said one; baboon said the other.

He strapped on a shoulder holster, poured himself a cup of coffee, and turned on the radio. The weather would be sunny and warm. Yeah, and maybe Buffolino would earn a few dimes to buy his Billy a thing or two.

He let the phone in the bedroom ring until the machine picked up, and he heard the voice of his second wife, Barbara, through the speaker. He picked up. "Hello, Babs. I was on my way out. I got an important meeting in D.C. at the Jockey Club. That's at the Ritz. I got to step on it."

"Tony, is there any chance of getting some extra money this month? The doctor wants Billy to see a bone specialist, and I don't have it."

"Bone specialist? What for? It's in his bones now?"

"No, Tony, no, but the radiation does things, I guess. I'm not sure, but the doctor says I should take him."

"Goddamn doctors. Bloodsuckers. What do they think, we live in Bethesda? Jesus. How much?"

"I don't know. I just need to know you can help out if it's a big bill."

"Yeah, yeah, I'll help out. I got this meeting this morning about a case. You remember Mac Smith? Yeah, he called me and needs me. How's that, huh? It's a big one. Yeah, sure, you got it, Babs. Is he there?"

"No. My mother has him for a few days."

"How's your mother?"

"Fine. She's a big help."

"Yeah, I know. Well, Babs, I got to go. I don't want to be late, huh? Let me know."

"I will. Thanks, Tony."

"Yeah. Say hello to Billy. Maybe I can get out to see him this weekend."

"Try. He asks about you all the time."

"Yeah. This weekend. I'll be there unless this case sends me out a' town. I'll call ahead. So long."

His car, a faded red 1978 Cadillac with a cracked white landau roof and white leather interior gone grimy with age, was parked in front of a body shop. It wouldn't start. "You should junk this, Tony," the body-shop owner grumbled as he always did when Buffolino persuaded him to give him a jump-start. "I can get you a nice '85, '86 cheap. Maybe even the color you want."

"Yeah, that'd be nice," Buffolino said, looking at his watch.

"You tell me what you want, Tony—year, color, accessories, and I get it for you, a couple days." The car started.

"Thanks, man," Buffolino said. "We'll talk about it."

"Foreign, too—BMW, Mercedes, Jag. Whatever."

"Good, great, thanks, Mickey. I owe you." No thanks, he thought. As much as I need new wheels, no custom-stealing for me.

It was stop-and-go traffic once he reached the D.C. city limits. His engine stopped and went, too, dying multiple deaths but recovering each time with distinct moans of protest. Shame innocent murder victims can't do the same, he thought.

By the time he parked around the corner from the Ritz-Carlton, he was fifteen minutes late. "Damn, man," he muttered as he ran around the corner and sped past the doorman.

Smith was waiting at a table. Buffolino paused in the doorway, drew a deep breath, ran his hand over his hair, and sauntered up to the table. Smith stood, extended his hand. "Hello, Tony, good to see you again."

"Yeah." He sat and looked around. "Nice place."

"I assumed you'd been here before."

"Nah. Always wanted to. My girlfriend comes here."

"Girlfriend? Getting married again?"

"Nah. Three times you're out, huh?" He smiled. "You look good, Mr. Smith. A couple a' pounds more maybe, but good. The U treats you good?"

"Yes." Smith motioned to a waiter for menus. "I suggest we order," he said. "I'm sure we both have commitments to get to."

"Yeah. Up to my neck." Tony's schedule called for him to sit in a small spare office he rented from a real estate broker and wait for the phone to ring, hoping it was not someone selling subscriptions or a recorded voice offering choice bargains in travel, real estate, or jewelry.

After they'd ordered, Buffolino asked, "What's this case you called me about?"

What Smith wanted to accomplish from this initial meeting was a sense that Buffolino was still the person he needed, to become reacquainted with the man he'd defended years ago. He answered the question with, "Tell me about yourself these days, Tony. Fill me in on your business. How are your children?"

"They're good. One's got a medical problem . . . Billy . . . I guess you remember. . . . Yeah, well, sure you do. . . . anyhow, nothing I can't handle." He almost asked about Smith's son, but caught himself.

"You have your own agency now?"

"Yeah. Natural move to make, huh? What's an ex-cop know except being a cop? Working private's good. I can pick and choose the slobs I'll work with. Lot a' slobs out there, Mac. This whole country's la-la land. You find that?"

Smith smiled and sighed. "We do have more than our share of strange ones. Another orange juice?"

"I guess so. Fresh-squeezed. It's better than canned."

They filled the next few minutes with small talk. When their breakfasts were served, Smith said, "This case, if it develops, will be a tricky one, Tony. It involves the son of . . . a prominent politician."

"Somebody ice him?"

"No. *He's* suspected of 'icing' someone."

"Yeah? You say *if* the case develops. You're not . . . we're not a sure thing?"

Buffolino tried to hide his disappointment, but Smith picked up on it. "I'm here this morning, Tony, assuming we're going ahead. Naturally, I have a retainer for you." He pulled an envelope from his jacket. In it was two hundred dollars. "If we go forward, there'll be whatever we agree on."

"The family's rich?"

"Yes."

"A big shot. Who they say he kill, somebody in the family?"

"No, it was his lover."

"Happens," Buffolino said.

"Too often. Tony, can you start now?"

"Start?"

"Yes. I've typed out the details." Smith pulled papers from his breast pocket and handed them across the table. "My client is Paul Ewald."

"The senator's son."

"He's a prime suspect in the murder of a young woman with whom he had an affair. Named Andrea Feldman."

"The broad you found outside the Kennedy Center."

"Yes."

Buffolino whistled. "What every candidate for president needs, a son who bumps off a bimbo."

"Andrea Feldman was no bimbo, Tony. She was an attorney working on Senator Ewald's staff. Look, I have to move on. You stay here and read what I've given you. What I want you to do first is to go out to a motel in Rosslyn called the Buccaneer."

"I know that joint. They change the sheets every hour."

"Yes, I'm sure they do. Feldman had a key in her purse to room six at that motel, and my client indicates he'd been there with her, although not on the night she was murdered. I just have a feeling it ought to be checked out. Paul Ewald's picture's in the papers. Show it to the owner if you can, see if he remembers ever seeing him there. All the details are on the notes I gave you. Also, Paul Ewald's wife, Janet, has disappeared. I want you to see what you can do about finding her. And I want you to do some digging into Andrea's background. I've given you what I have, but it's pretty sketchy."

Buffolino sat back and quickly scanned what Smith had written out. When he was finished, he looked up and said, "You want me to check out a murder scene, find the missing wife of the accused, and dig into the background of the deceased, all for two hundred bucks?"

"I told you that was a retainer, Tony."

"And I told you, Mac, that I got some big cases I'm working on back in Baltimore. If I do this for you, I got to drop some of them, and that takes mucho money out of my pocket."

Smith scrutinized him across the table, and although he knew Buffolino was putting up a front, he also knew that the assignments he'd given him were going to take a lot of his time. He said, "Okay, Tony, I'll write you a check for a thousand. Get moving on this and we'll discuss what the real fee will be. Fair enough?"

"Yeah, I trust you, although I don't know why I should."

Smith ignored the comment and said, "Some rules, Tony. You discuss this with no one unless I tell you you can. Everything is reported directly back to me. Agreed?"

"Sure. The usual routine."

"Fine. Enjoy your breakfast," Smith said. "You have my address there." He pointed to the papers in Buffolino's hand. "Meet me at my house tonight at eight."

"Okay. You'll have a check for me? My kid needs some more medical help."

"Yes, I'll have a check for you. You look good, Tony. It's good to see you again, and I appreciate your taking time out of a busy schedule to help me with this."

Buffolino looked into Smith's eyes and remembered the last time they'd been together. When they'd parted company on that previous occasion, he'd felt betrayed. Would he feel the same way again when this was over? It really didn't matter at the moment. He needed the money. He *desperately* needed the money.

"See you tonight at eight," Smith said.

"Yeah, I'll be there. *Ciao.*"

TWELVE

BUFFOLINO took his time finishing breakfast. When he was through, he went to a pay telephone, consulted a pocket address book, and dialed the number of police headquarters in Rosslyn, Virginia, across the Key Bridge from D.C. "Detective Glass, please," he said to the desk sergeant.

"Not here. Who's calling?"

"Buffolino, Tony Buffolino. I'm working private on the Feldman case." The sergeant hesitated, obviously not sure whether to believe him or not. Then the sergeant said, "Aren't you the former D.C. cop who . . . ?"

"One and the same, pal. Look, I got information Glass needs on the case. Where is he?"

"Out on an investigation."

"The Buccaneer Motel?"

"Yes."

"Thanks."

He stopped at a newsstand on the way to his car and bought the latest edition of the newspaper. On the front page was a photograph of Paul Ewald that looked as though it might have been taken from his college yearbook. Buffolino retrieved his car and headed for Rosslyn. The radio in the Caddy was as unreliable as the rest of the vehicle. This morning, however, it was working, and he listened to all-news WRC.

"Here's an update on the arrest and release of Paul Ewald, son of the Democratic candidate for president, Senator Kenneth Ewald. According to sources who have asked to remain anonymous, Paul Ewald and the deceased, Andrea Feldman, left the party at the Kennedy Center in honor of his father and went to a motel in Rosslyn called the Buccaneer. The same source has told us that a positive identification was made of Paul Ewald from a photograph shown the motel's owner by police officials. We've also learned that Paul Ewald's wife, Janet, has been missing since the murder, and her whereabouts are still unknown. Finally, Mackensie Smith, formerly one of Washington's leading criminal attorneys and more recently professor of law at George Washington University, has been retained to represent Paul Ewald in the event he's charged with the Andrea Feldman murder. Stay tuned for further developments in this and other stories we're following closely. A Defense Department spokesman said today that . . ."

Buffolino, who was on M Street, thought, Yeah, and Mac Smith and me are a defense department. He cut a hard right onto Wisconsin Avenue, drove four blocks, pulled into a parking space, and ran into a store whose sign said it sold movie and theatrical memorabilia. He came out ten minutes later, made a U-turn, went right on M again, and crossed the bridge into Rosslyn.

It took him a few wrong turns before he came upon the motel, a one-story cement-block building that was located in an area awaiting gentrification or demolition. Most of its yellow paint was a memory, flaked off years ago. It was flanked by a gas station and a rubble-filled empty lot. A large sign heralded its features—waterbeds, adult movies, and special short-stay rates. The doors had once been red. Red draperies hung precariously over each room's single window.

Neighborhood residents, mostly black and Hispanic, dawdled in small groups in front of it. There were a couple of news vehicles parked across the street, and a Rosslyn MPD patrol car blocked the entrance to the parking lot. A uniformed officer leaned against it.

Buffolino went up to the officer. "Hi, Tony Buffolino, working private on the Feldman murder. I'm looking for Detective Glass."

The officer, whose bored expression testified that he'd been on the force more than six months, nodded toward the only open door in the motel—number 6. "He's in there."

Good timing, Buffolino told himself. He said to the officer, "Could you tell him I'm here? He'll want to see me. Tell him Tony Buffolino is here."

The officer slowly walked to the open door and poked his head inside. A few minutes later, Detective Robert Glass emerged, and squinted against a hazy sun. "Hello, Tony," he said, extending his hand.

"Bobby, good to see you. They threw this one at you, huh? What've you got, a couple years to the pension?"

Glass, who looked more like a man who belonged in a corporate office than a police precinct, laughed. "Afraid so. What brings you here? He said you were working private on this case."

Buffolino had rehearsed the answer to that question on his way to Rosslyn. "I've been doing a lot of work the past couple a' years for Mac Smith, the big-shot attorney in D.C. He's the one who defended me, and he's wired tight into the Ewald family. In fact, he's Paul Ewald's attorney. He asked me to stop down here and see what's happening."

"You probably know as much from TV as I do, Tony. Riga from D.C. found a key to this place in her purse, and asked me to check it out." He looked over his shoulder toward the empty door. "That's the room they had."

"You find anything in there?"

Glass shook his head. "We've already dusted the place. There were prints, but not good ones. Prints don't read on sheets." He laughed.

Buffolino laughed, too. He said, "I heard on the radio that the owner of this dump identified Paul Ewald from a photograph. You show him the photograph?"

"Yes."

"No question about it with him? He ID'd him right away?"

"Well, he's an older man, but he didn't seem to have any doubts."

"What about the girl? You show him a picture of her?"

"No. You want to see the room?"

"Nah. I think I'll just hang out a while, maybe talk to the owner."

"Well, we're out of here. I'm leaving a uniform until Riga clears the joint. You look good, Tony. Things are good for you?"

"Yeah, great. You?"

"Good. You ought to come over sometime just for fun. My wife asks for you. Come for dinner. Bring somebody. You married again?"

"Nah. Two was enough. Three you're out. Hey, Bobby, does this thing play for you?"

"What do you mean?"

"I don't know, it's just that I have trouble with the idea that Ewald's son is having a fling with this chick, leaves a big party in honor of his father at the Kennedy Center and brings the broad to this fleatrap, makes it with her, then drives back to D.C., ends up in the bushes across from the Kennedy Center with her, and does her."

Glass smiled. "People do funny things when they're in love. Have to go, Tony. Good to see you again." He shook his hand.

"Who owns this dump?" Buffolino asked. Glass looked toward the motel office where a wizened little old black man stood with a couple of friends. "Him," Glass said. "Nice old guy. Never have much trouble with him. Runs a decent bang-and-run operation." He laughed. "Take it easy, Tony, and remember the invitation to come to the house."

Buffolino got back into the Caddy, found a diner, had coffee and read the newspaper, tearing out the front page and the inside page on which the story about the murder was continued. He shoved them in his pocket and returned to the motel. The red door to number 6 was closed. A uniformed officer sat in front of it.

The motel owner stood outside his office with friends. "Buffolino, United Press," Tony told him. "Can I ask you a few questions?"

"You-nited Press?" the owner said.

"That goes all over the world," one of his friends said, her voice indicating how impressed she was.

The owner, whose name, he said, was Wilton Morse, shook his head. "I'm not talking to nobody. Leave me alone."

"Hey, man, you already talked to the police. I'm just interested in finding out a little about you and your establishment here, maybe give you some good publicity."

Morse seemed unsure whether to continue the conversation or to bolt to the safety of his office.

"That's right, Wilton," a woman said, laughing. "Might turn this place into some kind of Holiday Inn, maybe even a fancy Hilton Hotel where people stay the night." Others laughed with her.

Buffolino grinned. "Mr. Morse, what kind of car did they arrive in?" Morse shook his head.

"No plate number? You didn't get the plate number when they registered?"

Someone else answered. "People don't register here. Just cash up front."

"I done all my talking to the police," Morse said.

Buffolino knew he was about to lose the motel owner. He said quickly, "You know something, Mr. Morse, you're quite a hero. I mean, hell, you're the one who identified the picture." Before Morse could say anything, Buffolino opened the flap on the envelope he carried and pulled out an 8 × 10 black-and-white glossy print. He shoved it in Morse's face. "I mean, Mr. Morse, when you looked at this picture and said, 'Yeah, that's the man who brought that poor lady here the other night,' you did everybody one hell of a service."

Morse squinted at the photograph, and pulled back to focus better. Others moved in and looked, too.

"You've got good eyes, Mr. Morse, recognizing him from a picture like this."

Morse said, "I always remember a face."

"And a good thing for the citizens of Rosslyn and D.C.," Buffolino said, replacing the photograph in the envelope. "Well, thanks for your time, Mr. Morse." He looked past him at the motel. "You got a real nice place here."

BUFFOLINO didn't arrive at Mac Smith's house in Foggy Bottom until almost nine that night. "You're late," Smith said.

"I got hung up. You got any coffee?"

"Yes." Smith poured them each a cup, and they sat at the kitchen table.

"Well?" Smith asked.

"Well, I spent some time at the motel, and then I headed over to where Andrea Feldman lived, near Dupont Circle."

"Find anything interesting?"

"Yeah, I think so," Buffolino said. "You heard the owner of the Buccaneer identified Ewald from a photograph, right?"

"Yes, I heard that."

"I had a few words with the gentleman who owns that dump. Name is Wilton Morse. Nice-enough old guy. I showed him a picture of the man who checked in with Andrea." Buffolino reached into the envelope, pulled out the photograph he'd shown Morse, and slid it across the table to Smith.

Smith stared at it. "That's Van Johnson."

"It sure is," Tony said after his second cup of coffee and third doughnut. "And it cost me ten bucks. I'm keeping track of expenses."

"Of course."

"I showed this to Morse, the owner, like it was the picture the cops showed him, and he didn't tell me it wasn't Paul Ewald."

"Did he confirm that this was the person he saw come into the motel with Andrea Feldman?"

"Nope. But he didn't deny it either."

Smith sat back and shook his head. "What made you take this photograph there, Tony?"

"I done it before. I saw Ewald's picture in the paper and he looked a little like Van Johnson to me, so I figured I'd try it. Sometimes it works, sometimes it don't."

"Anything else at the motel?" Smith asked.

"No, except Morse, the owner, needs glasses but don't wear them. I could tell the way he was squinting at the picture."

"Very observant. What about Andrea Feldman's apartment. You got into it?"

"No, but I knew the cop guarding the scene. I asked him about where she lived, and he told me it was kind of strange."

"In what way?"

"Well, he said it looked like nobody lived there, real sparse, no pictures, just a couple a' books, clothes in the closet. You know, you figure a career dame like this wants to live good, have comfortable surroundings, but my friend told me that ain't the way it was."

"You've had a busy day, Tony."

"Yeah, and I'm beat. You got anything to lace this coffee with?"

"Sure." Smith placed a bottle of Nocello on the kitchen table and refilled their cups. "Tony, I'm going to need you for a while. Can you shake your other commitments and work with me?"

"I been thinking about that. You know something, Mac, it's good to be back with you. I know we parted on lousy terms the last time, but you can understand that. Hell, it was my career that went up in smoke." Smith started to say something, but Buffolino continued. "Besides, this Ewald thing fascinates me. Yeah, count me in, but it's going to cost you."

"Meaning?"

"A grand a week, plus a place to stay in D.C. I can't be drivin' back and forth to Baltimore."

"Lots of people do."

"Yeah, nine-to-fivers. I'm on a case twenty-four hours."

Smith frowned. "All right," he said, "that can be arranged. A thousand dollars a week and a place to stay."

"I figure I ought to be close to you here, and close to the Kennedy Center."

"Why?"

"Why what?"

"Why do you want to be close to the Kennedy Center?"

"I don't know, Mac, just a hunch. I mean, that's where she bought it, and our client was at that party there. How about springing for a suite at the Watergate?"

Smith sat up straight. "At the Watergate? A suite? I wouldn't have supposed you'd want that after what happened."

"Well, time goes by, huh?" Buffolino grinned. "Whattaya say? Think of it this way, Mac. We're going to need someplace to work out of, right?"

Smith nodded. He'd been thinking the same thing.

"So, we get a suite at the Watergate, you get an office, I got a place to live that's decent and close to everything, and we all get somethin' out of it."

Smith couldn't help but smile. "Okay, Tony, a suite at the Watergate it is."

"Great. Call 'em in the morning, and I'll get over and pick the room. I got to go back to Baltimore and pack some things, get somebody to take care of my cats."

"Pick the room?"

"Yeah. Anything wrong with that?"

"I suppose not. I'll call and tell them you're coming."

"Good enough, Mac." Buffolino stood and slapped Smith on the arm. "Hey, I think we're gonna make a hell of a team."

Long after Buffolino had left, Smith sat in his study, Rufus at his side. He didn't read, didn't make notes, just sat and thought. He realized his head was beginning to droop, looked at his dog, and said,

"There is something very strange going on here, Rufus, very strange indeed."

Rufus raised his head from the floor and looked at Smith as though he understood every word. Smith got up. "Come on," he said. "Time for you to go into the great outer world—or outer john. We'll discuss this further in the morning."

THIRTEEN

"**MAY I HELP YOU, SIR?**" a pretty desk clerk at the Watergate Hotel asked Buffolino.

"Yeah, probably. Mr. Mackensie Smith made arrangements for me to choose a suite, and to stay in it for a while. The name's Buffolino, Anthony Buffolino."

The clerk smiled at him and pulled a computer printout from a file folder. "Yes, sir, I have the reservation here. You'll have suite—"

"As a matter of fact, I have a preference. I'd like suite 1117."

"Suite 1117? Let me see. Yes, it's available for the next four days. We have someone coming in after that."

"You can give them another room."

"I don't think so, Mr. Buffolino."

"Let's not worry about it now, I'm sure Mr. Smith can work it out. In the meantime, I'll just go up."

"Of course." He filled out the registration card. "Luggage?" she asked.

He pointed to a battered steamer trunk and two canvas duffel bags.

"I'll have . . . them . . . sent up right away," she said. An incinerator would be more appropriate, she thought.

He was handed the key and rode the elevator to the eleventh floor, opened the door to suite 1117, and stood in the archway, his eyes embracing the suite, his tongue almost tasting it—every wall, corner, every brass-framed picture, lush and large plant, piece of furniture.

He stepped inside and rocked back and forth, his toes and heels sinking into the foyer's thick gold carpeting. Closets were to his right. He looked at himself in a mirror that hung over a marble table. A few steps and he was on the fringe of a huge living room. A seven-foot leather couch, three leather chairs, and a large black lacquered coffee table occupied the right side of the room. In front of him, twenty feet away, was a twenty-five-inch color TV. He took a few more steps and turned left. A heavy white table surrounded by four chairs with cane backs and floral print fabric provided a dining area for a full kitchen hidden behind fanfold doors.

He passed the smaller of two baths as he went to the bedroom, a large and airy space with two queen-sized beds, a TV, desk, and a sitting area formed by white leather chairs and a brass table. A brisk breeze through slightly opened sliding glass doors sent gossamer white curtains fluttering into the room.

Outside, on the Astroturf-carpeted balcony, he looked down over the sprawling Watergate complex, then slowly walked the length of the balcony on the bedroom side until reaching the point where it wrapped to the left, around the corner of the suite. From there, he looked down onto the Potomac. Small boats of all descriptions, including an eight-man racing scull, moved with varying speeds through the brown water. Across the river, spires on old Georgetown University buildings spiked up into heavy gray air that had descended on the city.

For a moment, there had been a small satisfied grin on Buffolino's face during his tour of the suite. Now—and suddenly—he closed his eyes and grimaced against an unseen invasion of sound and image. Day turned to night, and time fell away, taking him with it to a night six years ago outside suite 1117. . . .

He was in the hallway, looking right and left. He knocked. The security chain was slipped from its notch, and the door opened. The man was young, black, and dressed nicely. He scrutinized Tony before allowing him to step into the foyer. The door closed. Tony looked in the direction of the bedroom. A tall roses-and-cream blonde wearing a silk robe loosely secured at the waist smiled at him.

"My man," a male voice said from the living room.

He was on the leather couch, his feet up on the black lacquered coffee table. "Tony, right on time. Come in and sit down." Another woman, brunette and still more luxurious than the blonde, sat in one of the leather chairs. She, too, wore a revealing robe. "This is Joanna, Tony, a friend of mine." He laughed and patted her bare knee.

Buffolino sat in a chair facing her. The man on the couch, who was in his early thirties, was Panamanian, although there was little trace of it in his speech. He wore a red silk shirt open to his stomach. Three thin gold chains nestled in a heavy mat of black chest hair. Thick fingers supported multiple rings. Light from a table lamp revealed skin that was pockmarked and sebaceous. "Why don't you and your friend spend a little time together in the bedroom," he said to Joanna. "Freshen up, get pretty for us. We'll see you later." She touched Buffolino's neck as she passed him. Moments later, he heard the bedroom door close.

"So, Tony, my man, we finally get together. That's nice. That's the way it should be, doing business together instead of being competitors. It's like a merger."

Buffolino didn't respond.

"Hungry, Tony? Help yourself." He nodded at the white table near the kitchen. On it was a cut-glass bowl of caviar, surrounded by thinly sliced and crustless toast, lemon wedges, chopped onions, and cooked egg yolks. "The best, man. I ordered up the best for my new partner. What do you drink?"

"Ah, anything. Scotch, vodka, a beer."

"Take whatever you want, baby. It's all there."

Tony poured himself half a glass of Absolut over ice and returned to the chair. The man on the couch raised a partly consumed glass of orange juice in a toast. "To our merger, Tony. To good times for everybody." Buffolino lifted his glass, but only to his mouth.

"Like this suite, Tony? I do. Somebody said once that living well is the best revenge. I like that. It's true. People like you and me should always live well, high style like. Now that we're partners, you'll be living like this, too, as long as you keep doing what I'm paying you to do."

Buffolino stared at him over his glass.

"You're not a big talker, are you, Tony? That's good. Talkers get in trouble. You're a *silent* partner. I like that."

"I got one question for you, Garcia."

"Hey, you got a right to ask questions."

"What happens if this thing goes sour? I mean, you realize my neck is way out, huh?"

Garcia opened his eyes wide and smiled. "And, Tony, my man, you are being paid plenty of green for stretching your neck a little. Besides, anything goes bad on the deal, you come visit me in Panama. I got plenty of room, and plenty of friends who'll take real good care of you."

Buffolino knew Garcia was referring to the strongman Colonel

Morales, who not only ran Panama with an iron fist, but who was alleged to run that country's multibillion-dollar drug industry, too.

"Look, I got to go, Garcia. Just give me the money and let me get out of here."

"Sure, sure, only I thought we could celebrate a little. You order up anything you want, drink, eat, spend a little time with my friends in there."

"Nah, I got other things to do."

"As you wish. You like to keep things all business, that's fine with me. I like that. All business. So, you do understand what our deal is?"

"Yeah."

"Instead of busting my chops like you've been doing, you leave me alone here in D.C., like happens in other cities where I have partners. You keep me out of trouble, let me know when trouble's brewing, make sure your cop buddies don't bust my chops. Right?"

"Right. I don't need a lesson in how this goes down. Come on, Garcia, give me the money before I change my mind."

Garcia crossed the expansive room and returned with a black leather Gucci briefcase, placing it on the table in front of Buffolino. "There it is, Tony. You even get the briefcase as a bonus." He laughed. "I don't mess around. I go first class all the way, like you'll be doing from now on. Every month, you get the same. Oh, but not a new briefcase." Another laugh. "The same bread, twenty-five grand, and all you have to do to earn it is do n-o-o-o-th-i-i-i-n-g." He dragged out the word.

Buffolino took the briefcase and started to get up.

"Come on," Garcia said, "relax. You got the money, right? One more drink between partners." He didn't allow Tony to respond, simply went to the table near the kitchen and refilled his glass. "How's it feel to have twenty-five grand in your hands?"

Buffolino looked at the briefcase, and a wave of disgust came over him, so strong that he wondered if he might become ill. "Listen, I . . ." Garcia rejoined him. "What's the matter?" he asked. "Feel like dirty money because it's drug money? You'll forget about that once you start spending it. It spends the same as clean money, only it's easier to come by. You see that. All you have to do is leave my operation alone, give me a word or two now and then, and get rich, with nobody knowing the difference."

Buffolino took a long swig of his drink. As he was placing it on the table to leave, the first sounds and sights erupted. The whirling blades of a helicopter suddenly loomed up outside, a brilliant light from it pouring through the glass doors and painting everything in the room in harsh whiteness.

"What the . . . ?" Buffolino bolted from the chair and headed for the door. It opened before his hand could reach the knob. Standing in the hall were four men, their guns drawn.

"Cool out, Tony," one of them said. Officers from Internal Affairs. "Nothing stupid."

Buffolino turned and looked at Garcia, who was leaning casually on the television, a smug grin on his face.

"Cuff him," a cop said as another removed Tony's service revolver from where it sat beneath his jacket.

There were so many things Buffolino wanted to tell them instantly, how he never took from anybody before, how his youngest child was sick with cancer and needed expensive medical treatment beyond what his benefits as a cop would cover, how backwards it was to use a notorious drug kingpin like Garcia to trap a cop who'd always been honest, to make a deal with that scum. He said nothing, and was led to a waiting car downstairs.

TONY Buffolino opened his eyes and blinked. That scene had played in his mind thousands of times since it happened. Early—during the hearings, and shortly after his dismissal from the force—he wished he'd run from the suite to the balcony and gone over. Then, as the banal realities of every day prevailed, that thought dimmed. Not the scene itself, not the disgrace, the second divorce, being shunned by friends in MPD, the hatred he felt for those who'd set him up, wired Garcia, caused him to lose what had always meant most to him. That Mackensie Smith had successfully prevented a criminal action being brought against him meant nothing. Anthony Buffolino died that night in suite 1117.

But as he went inside from the balcony and again surveyed the living room, he felt an unmistakable twinge of life. He'd felt it the morning he'd met Smith for breakfast, a sense of having something important to do that day, a meeting, a case, a reason for shining shoes that went unpolished month after month. Something positive to report to Barbara and Julie. Although they were no longer his wives, they meant a great deal to him. Money. Clean money. A sense he was doing something worthwhile for Billy without the accompanying sense of constant deprivation.

"Damn," he said aloud, smacking a fist into a hand. He rode the elevator down and walked into the elegant Jean Louis restaurant.

"We're open at lunch only to club members and hotel guests. Are you a guest of the hotel, sir?"

"I certainly am. Suite 1117."

"Will you be dining alone?"

"Today, yes. I'll have guests other days. I'll be here a while."

"Good, sir. This way, please."

After a quick study of the menu, he said to the waiter, "I'll start with this terrine of fresh and smoked salmon with caviar. Let's see, how about some Maryland crab cakes for a second course, this here—how do you pronounce it?—mousseline of lobster filled with lobster sauce for the third, and the venison stuffed with mushrooms. No, no dessert. I got to stay in shape."

To the wine steward, he said, "Latour? Whatever you say. I'm in suite 1117. I'll be here a while. Remember me, okay?" He handed him a twenty-dollar bill.

FOURTEEN

AS BUFFOLINO finished up his several lunches that day at Jean
Louis, Leslie Ewald was finishing up a speech to the Democratic Woman's Association at their luncheon in the Mayflower Hotel's
main ballroom.

"I suppose the best way to describe Ken's vision of America is to say
that he believes with all his heart that every American must have the
right to be treated as he wishes to be treated, and would want his own
children to be treated. This is not the case in today's America. My
husband, when he is president, will work hard to bring this about, and
to return us to a nation with a keen sense of justice, equality, and
fairness for every man, woman, and child."

Two hundred women stood and applauded. Once the applause had
subsided, the press representatives, who sat in a cordoned-off area in
the front of the room, tossed a barrage of questions at Leslie. She held
up her hands and smiled. "Please, I do have another commitment I
must get to, but I will be happy to take a few questions. Before I do,
let me say that Ken and I are naturally delighted that our son has been
released, and we stand firm in our love and support of him. We feel
totally vindicated, as I know he does, but please, it would be inappropriate for us to discuss any aspect of that."

She recognized a reporter, who asked, "Mrs. Ewald, a poll released
earlier this morning indicates that your husband's standing has slipped.
Do you think this unfortunate affair, even if it's resolved to your
satisfaction, has seriously damaged his chances for the Democratic
nomination in July?"

Leslie shook her head and said with strength, "Absolutely not. The
American people . . . every family in this wonderful country . . . has
had to face problems, and they understand the problems we're facing
as a family. It is distinct and apart from the leadership qualities that

Ken will bring to the White House, and I am confident that the American people will sympathize with our pain, and will focus on the issues that are really important to them."

Another questioner asked, "Not only is your son a prime suspect in Andrea Feldman's murder, Mrs. Ewald, but his wife . . . your daughter-in-law . . . has been missing for a few days now. Would you comment on that?"

"No, I won't. Janet, whom we love very much, has undoubtedly gone off to find some solitude, which, I must add, sounds like a very good idea." Some of the audience laughed quietly, and Leslie joined them. "All of this will be resolved shortly. In the meantime, we're pressing ahead and know that we will be successful in July at the convention."

Other questions came from the press section, but one of Leslie's press aides quickly came to the microphone, waved his hand, and said, "Sorry, Mrs. Ewald has another appointment. Thank you very much."

A loud voice from a reporter asked, "What will your priority as First Lady be?"

Leslie, who'd started to leave the podium, leaned back to the microphone and said, "Day care. The right of every mother to know that her children are in a safe and enriching environment when it's necessary for her to work outside the home . . . or simply because she wants to work."

Leslie's aides and Secret Service agents led her from the podium and out of the ballroom. Outside, in the lobby, another small knot of reporters waited. As Leslie passed them, a young woman in jeans with long, matted blond hair pushed close to her, shoved a microphone in her face, and asked, "Will you be the first First Lady to be divorced while in the White House?"

Leslie stopped and looked at the reporter as though she'd spoken a foreign tongue.

The reporter added, "Everyone knows that you and Senator Ewald have been estranged for years."

The aides tried to move her on, but Leslie stood firm. She looked the reporter in the eye and said, "First of all, I find you personally offensive. Second, I respect your right as a journalist to ask anything you wish. Third, my private life is exactly that, private. And fourth, you are talking to a happily married woman, whose husband is a fine and decent man and who will be the next president of the United States, your country. Knowing my husband, I know he will defend to the death your right to be offensive and boring. Have I answered your question?"

The reporter's expression was defiant, but her voice was weak. "Yes," she said, backing into the crowd.

After the Ewald entourage had left the hotel, a veteran campaign reporter from the *Washington Post* joined a colleague for a drink in the Mayflower's refurbished Town-and-Country bar. "She talks like Ewald does," he said as the bartender served him a shot of rye and a glass of seltzer. "They don't even try to change the quotes. Jack Kennedy gave that speech about America treating everybody and their kids the way they want to be treated during the civil-rights movement. Almost word for word. Doesn't anyone remember Joe Biden's campaign?"

His friend, who'd ordered a beer, laughed. "Hey, it could be worse. They could be quoting James Watt or Jimmy the Greek."

"True." He downed the rye and waved for another. "I just wish there were some goddamn basic honesty. The kid who asked about their relationship was on the money. 'Happily married woman,' my ass."

Mac Smith watched Leslie's confrontation with the young reporter on a newscast an hour later. He was in a TV room in the Ewald house in Georgetown. "Nice work," he said to Leslie on the TV screen as she told off the reporter. He did admire the way they'd forged ahead despite the brewing scandal about Paul. They conducted themselves with dignity, and without apology. He liked that. At the same time, he knew that their statements that what had happened to them personally would have little effect on Ken's bid for the White House were at best naive, or, more likely, planned bravado. The campaign had to have suffered, and he wondered what kind of strategy was being planned at the moment.

The door to the TV room opened, and Marcia Mims asked Smith if he would like something to eat or drink.

"No, thank you, Marcia."

She lingered in the doorway, as though she wanted to say something else but wasn't sure she should. Before Smith could encourage her to speak, she backed out and closed the door.

. . .

MARCIA Mims had been with the Ewald family for twenty-two years. She'd come to Los Angeles from Martinique as a young woman, after a charlatan beauty-contest promoter there convinced the beautiful and shy Marcia—as well as her mother—that he had arranged a screen test at a major Hollywood studio for the newly crowned "Miss Fort-de-France." Marcia's mother forked over every cent they had in savings, and Marcia headed for Hollywood, the family's future riding on her certain rise to screen stardom. Of course, there was no screen test, nor was there money to return to Martinique. Prostitution? Domestic work? Marriage? She had tried them all, and after two divorces, instead of becoming a star and rich, settled for running a household of a possible political star who was rich—an aspiring California politician named Kenneth Ewald.

Aspirations then turned to reality for Ewald, and Marcia Mims was promoted to the Ewald Washington house in Georgetown when he became a United States senator. "La-dee-da," her friends said when she announced she was leaving for the nation's capital. "Just don't let massa get his hands on your butt. He looks like he likes 'em all shades," they joked. A lot of giggling. And envy. In fact, Marcia had hit it off pretty well from the start with the Ewalds. They liked her and showed it in many generous ways, gradually promoting her. She was reluctant to express too much appreciation lest she seem to be playing the house-slave role, but she knew that considering who she was and where she'd come from, there were worse things than being surrogate mother, wife, and chairman-of-the-board in a wealthy and exciting household, with gardeners, two chauffeurs, kitchen workers, and serving staff under her managerial thumb. "I don't know what I'd do without you," Leslie Ewald often said—said too often—and Marcia never failed to return the compliment, probably with as much sincerity as she perceived the lady of the house possessed.

Now, it seemed possible that she would be promoted again, this time to the White House, and the thought of it frightened her. She had begun to read books on what the White House was like, and wondered what extra demands would be placed on her, what additional duties she would be called on to perform once she was there. The White House!

Serving the president of the United States! Someday, *she* would write a book and be famous. What stories she'd have to tell! Her diary was already a treasure.

E D Farmer, Ken's campaign manager, poked his head in. "Sorry, Mac, didn't realize you were here," he said.

"No problem, Ed. I was just watching Leslie on television. She handled herself beautifully."

Farmer, whose expression was consistently dour, raised his eyebrows and leaned against the door frame. He fiddled with his bow tie as he said, "Between you and me, Mac, they're performing a lot better than the situation really is. We're in trouble. Some of the faithful are losing faith, even whispering defection."

Smith nodded. "I suppose we couldn't expect anything else, considering the serious nature of what's happened. What's the term—'damage control'?—how is that coming?"

The question brought forth a rare smile from Farmer. "The water has started pouring in, and we're trying to bucket it out as fast as possible. Sorry, I have to run." And he was gone.

Smith spent the next few minutes consulting notes he'd made on a legal pad, and added more. There was a knock on the door. "Come in." Marcia Mims reappeared. "Mr. Smith, you have a telephone call."

"Who is it?"

"The gentleman says his name is Mr. Greist, Herbert Greist, and he's calling from New York."

Smith glanced around the TV room in search of a phone. Marcia said, "Why not take it in the second-floor office?"

Smith went to the office on the second floor, which was fully equipped with fax and copying machines, an IBM computer and printer, two multiline phones, dictating equipment, and a broadcast-quality cassette tape recorder on a shelf high above the desk. He picked up the lighted extension and said, "This is Mackensie Smith."

Greist, whoever he was, seemed surprised to hear a voice on the other end of the phone. He coughed, excused himself for a moment, and Smith could hear papers being shuffled in the background. "Ah, thank you, Mr. Smith. I had to find Mrs. Feldman's file."

"Mrs. Feldman? What is this about?"

"I've been retained by Mae Feldman, regarding the murder of her daughter, Andrea." He had the tired voice of a person whose successes were few and far between, or never.

There had been some mentions in the press coverage of Andrea Feldman's murder that attempts to reach her only known family member, her mother, had been unsuccessful. Frankly, Smith hadn't given much thought to that. Damn. Dumb. Now, he would. "Go on," he said.

"We intend to file suit over the loss of Andrea Feldman's civil rights, and to ask for substantial damages from your client for my client's pain and suffering in losing her only daughter."

Smith said nothing. Greist asked if he were still on the line.

"Yes."

"And so, Mr. Smith, I think it would be in the best interest of both parties for you and me to meet to see whether there is some accommodation we could reach that would avoid further embarrassment and pain to Senator Ewald and his family."

The words "cheap hustler" ran through Smith's mind. What would it cost to not further embarrass a man running for president? Lots. Smith's inclination was to politely tell Mr. Greist to get lost. But he was no longer a free man. He couldn't. Andrea Feldman's mother certainly had the right to sue over her daughter's death. No matter what might happen in any criminal proceeding, there was lately the chance to sue for the loss of an individual's "civil rights," i.e., life. If Greist were any good—which Smith doubted—they might mount a compelling case. But Greist obviously wasn't interested in filing cases or going to court. His message was clear. Come up with enough money and they'd go away.

"When will you be in Washington, Mr. Greist?"

"My, ah, plans will keep me here in New York for some time, Mr. Smith. Perhaps you could come here for a conference."

"I'll consider it."

"I would suggest that you not wait too long. Mrs. Feldman is . . . well, she's most anxious to put this behind her, as you can well imagine."

Translation: Get money now.

"I'll be in touch, Mr. Greist. By the way, it was my understanding that Mrs. Feldman hadn't been located."

"She travels."

"She lives in San Francisco?" Smith asked.

He cleared his throat. "Well, yes, but New York is a second home for her."

"Because of her profession? Which is?"

"We can discuss that when we meet. I repeat, Mr. Smith, time is of the essence."

"Yes, I'm sure it is, Mr. Greist. By the way, I assume you're the attorney handling the disposition of whatever estate Andrea Feldman left."

"That is correct."

"She had a will?"

"Well, she . . . her affairs are in good order, Mr. Smith."

"I'm sure they are. You'll hear from me . . . or from someone on my staff. Good-bye."

Smith hung up and left the room, never noticing that the tape recorder on the shelf above him had begun recording the moment he lifted the receiver.

Downstairs, Smith checked his watch; he wanted to run home before going to the gathering at Roger Gerry's house. He'd asked Annabel to go with him, but she was busy, which was okay with him. He didn't intend to stay long, wasn't in the mood for polite parties.

He strolled to the rear of the house and found Marcia Mims in the kitchen. "I'm leaving now, Marcia. Thank you for everything."

She looked up from salmon filets she was garnishing for dinner that night and said, "Anytime, Mr. Smith."

"How are you holding up under all of this, Marcia?"

She looked down at the glistening pink flesh beneath her hands and slowly shook her head. "I don't know, Mr. Smith, how all this will end up, but I know this household is full of mess. There's serious trouble here."

Initially, Smith thought she was referring to the trouble caused by Paul's arrest, complicated by Janet's disappearance. But then he realized she was referring to something beyond that. He asked what she meant.

"It just makes me so sad to see this mess—and a wonderful family destroyed."

"Because of what happened with Paul?"

"Yes, and . . ."

"And what, Marcia?"

"And lots of other things that most folks just don't know about." She didn't give Smith a chance to press the question. "Excuse me, Mr. Smith, I have a lot of work to do."

Smith stared at her until she looked at him again. "I'll be back, Marcia. Maybe we could find some quiet time to talk."

She went back to working the fish.

SMITH sat with his dean, Roger Gerry, in a comfortable study in Gerry's home. The sound of the guests mingling in the other rooms was agreeably muffled.

"I need time off," Smith told him.

Gerry, whose round, pink, and pleasant face belied a leg-trap intellect and rock-hard convictions, raised his white eyebrows. "A leave of absence?"

"Maybe not that formal, Roger. Without going into too many details at this stage, let's just say that my involvement with the Ewald family is going to keep me occupied for a period of time."

"How long do you anticipate this will go on?" Gerry asked.

Smith shrugged. "Could be a couple of months. I possibly can handle an occasional class, but I can't be bound to it. How about Tony Peet covering for me when I can't make it?" Peet was the youngest member of the law school faculty, a brilliant Harvard scholar who made no attempt to hide his aspirations to one day become a justice of the Supreme Court. Few doubted he'd achieve his goal, except those who knew what a roulette wheel court appointments were.

"All right, Mac, but you discuss it with him. If it's okay with him, it's okay with me. I need you both. Tell me, is the Feldman murder something you really want to be involved in?"

Smith laughed. "I've been asking myself that question ever since she was killed, and Ken and Leslie Ewald asked me to advise them. Annabel has been asking that question, too, and I'm not sure we've come to the same conclusion. She says she understands why I feel compelled to do this, but I don't think she really does. We both left the active, hectic practice of law to pursue things that were gentler and longer term. I suppose I can view this as a momentary digression, sort of keeping my hand in something. Besides, I've known Ken and Leslie for years. And . . ."

Gerry's white eyebrows peaked again like mountaintops, and a smile crossed his face. "And Mackensie Smith was getting bored, needs a little action in his life, sort of like an older man taking up with a young woman. Just remember one thing, Mac—old men who have flings with young women enjoy it for a brief period of time, but find that if it lasts for any duration, against all odds, it loses its appeal. And I'm not speaking legally."

"I'll keep that in mind, and please refrain from using that analogy with Annie next time you see her." Smith checked his watch. "I really can't stay long, Roger. It was kind of you to take time from your guests for this discussion."

"You will have something to eat with us?"

"Would you be offended if I didn't?"

"Of course not. I know you have many things to do, all of them undoubtedly due yesterday. Go on. Just say good-bye to Charlotte, and promise me one thing."

"What's that?"

"To keep me informed on all the sordid, inside details as they develop. I may be a law school dean, but I haven't lost my interest in the hectic, active practice—or in gossip."

"I'll give you a regular report, Roger. And thanks again. I appreciate your understanding."

Mac took Rufus for a long walk. Such a pleasant and easy conversation with Gerry seemed out of place, almost perverse. The son of the man likely to become the Democratic presidential nominee was a prime murder suspect, and he, Mac Smith, had accepted the responsibility of trying to keep *suspect* from becoming *accused.*

As he headed back toward the house, he said to himself, Pull out, pull out before it's too late.

That was as long as the thought lasted. He wouldn't pull out. The surge of purpose—and, yes, he admitted to himself, importance—

would override any cautious evaluation of the situation in which he'd placed himself. He was in, all the way in, and there was a lot of work to do, the contemplation of which was full of mess, as Marcia put it, but also of an odd, fulfilling pleasure.

FIFTEEN

"ARE YOU AWAKE?" Smith asked Annabel, looking over at her. The sight of her copper hair strewn over a pillow never failed to delight him.

She mumbled and buried her head a little deeper in the pillow.

"It's important."

"What's important?"

"We should have made coffee last night," Smith said.

"Uh-huh."

They'd decided to stay at her place Saturday night to avoid the constant ringing of the telephone in Smith's house.

"I'll get up and make some," he said.

"Good," she said, and sank into sleep again.

He kissed a small exposed portion of her cheek, rolled out of bed, and went to the kitchen, where he prepared the coffee using the various blends that he had made certain were always stocked there. He found fresh eggs, scrambled them expertly, popped oatmeal bread into the toaster, poured orange juice, and when everything was ready, shouted, "Get up! Eat. Breakfast is ready. The world is waiting."

They finished breakfast by eight, and sat at the dining room table drinking second cups of coffee and reading the Sunday paper, enjoying an interlude both sensed must be brief. There was a long feature on the Feldman murder, including pictures of Paul, his mother and father, and the deceased. There was also a shot of Mac Smith taken outside the Ewald home.

Annabel giggled. "I never knew you had a double chin, Mac."

"Shadows from the lighting," he said.

She laughed again. "Since you're going to be the subject of media attention, maybe you should hire a media adviser, like politicians do."

"Or a surgeon, for a tuck or tug." Smith went to the funnies. He was reading *Doonesbury* when Annabel said, "Mac, time to fill me in on everything."

Which he did, in as much detail as he could summon. He told her about the call from the New York shyster Herbert Greist, replayed his interview with Paul Ewald, his conversations with Ken and Leslie Ewald, what had transpired during his meeting with Joe Riga at Riga's office, and his brief talk with Ken Ewald in which Ewald had said he hadn't stayed in his office the night of the murder but had instead gone to the Watergate Hotel for a tryst with an unnamed woman.

"Interesting, that he would tell you about that but not tell you who she is," Annabel said.

"Dumb but not unusual," Smith commented. "It's known that Ken has had a proclivity for pretty faces other than Leslie's, but he's always been mostly a model of discretion, thank God for her sake."

"Aren't you curious about who she is?"

"Yes, I'd like very much to know who she is. I need to know everything so we are not surprised, caught off base. I've learned too much from the radio so far. I'll have to know eventually. Unfortunately, so will too many other people."

"Think he would tell you if you asked him again?"

"Yes. I will—ask him, I mean. I also want to ask you a favor."

She cocked her head and raised her eyebrows. "My dear . . . asking for my favors on this Sunday morning?" Sunday mornings were a favorite time with them for making love, like the rest of the world, with the alarm clock turned off.

"That's favor number two," he said. "First, I want to set up a meeting in New York with this Greist character as quickly as possible. I thought I'd try to call him today and see if he's available sometime tomorrow. His type can be in the office Sundays—not always working. My problem is that I *have* to spend time here getting organized, hiring a temporary secretary to work out of the suite, lease some word-processing equipment, get a couple of extra phones in there, a copying machine, all the things I used to take for granted when I had the office. Would you go to a meeting with Greist in New York?"

"Mac, I own an art gallery, remember? I *used* to be a lawyer."

"Once a lawyer, always a lawyer, and you know it. Look, if you're really jammed up at the gallery, I'll try to figure out something else, but if you could go to New York as a representative of my . . ." His voice took on a certain pomposity. "As an associate in my law firm"—his voice returned to normal—"I would be forever grateful."

She poured them more coffee, and the sight of her voluptuous body beneath her robe, hair hanging loose and natural, pretty bare feet with red-tipped toes on white terra-cotta tiles, took his mind off murder for the moment. When she sat down, he repeated his request, adding, "I'll make it up to you."

"How?"

A shrug. "I don't know, a long trip somewhere exotic once this is over."

She sat back and looked at him. What she saw was a different man. Always intelligence itself, he now had the look of someone with a large commitment, almost religious in intensity. He was very much alive. She liked what she saw, even if she didn't like the reason for it. "How are things going with Tony Buffolino?" she asked.

He laughed. "He's as big a character as ever, but no matter what Tony is or isn't, he's a damned good investigator, very creative." He told her of how Tony had used the movie-star photo.

She shook her head. "You're an amazing man, Mac Smith. You have Ken Ewald, who, if he were to become president, would want you as his attorney general. You've counseled the rich and famous, and you've become a distinguished professor of law at a leading university. At the same time, you hire a foul-ball ex-cop, put him up in a suite at Watergate, and pay him probably a lot more than he, or any other private investigator, is worth, I'm sure. What's next, a limo and dancing girls?"

"I hadn't thought of that, Annabel. I will . . . think about it . . . the dancing girls part. For Tony. In the meantime, will you go to New York and talk to Greist for me? I'm going to get Tony moving tomorrow on checking into Andrea Feldman's past. I think I'll send him to San Francisco."

She assumed a pout. "He gets to go to San Francisco, and I end up in New York talking to some sleaze?"

"Do it for me and do a good job, and we'll go to San Francisco together. Soon."

"When?"

"As soon as . . ."

"All right," she said. "James can handle things at the gallery while I'm gone. He's working out very nicely."

"Good."

"I'll stay an extra day or two in New York. There are some pieces I'd like to track down, and I may as well do it on your generosity."

"Of course." She was having fun at his expense, and he found it amusing.

"You will put *me* up in fancy digs, of course."

"Of course. The Y on Forty-seventh Street. No, seriously, Annabel, you name it. Then you'll go as my associate?"

She flashed a wide and warm smile. "I'll go as your *partner.* I'll name the hotel—and my fee. Count on it."

With favor number one out of the way, they proceeded to favor number two, fell asleep in each other's arms for a half hour, then showered and went about their individual projects for the day. For Annabel, it was to sort out clothing to get ready for Washington's infamous heat and humidity, a season that would surely arrive soon. Smith settled by a phone in the living room and called the number he had for Herbert Greist. He thought he might get an answering machine, but Greist answered.

"I'm impressed, Mr. Greist," Smith said. "This is Mac Smith. You must have a heavy caseload to be working on a Sunday."

Smith's attempt at conciliatory chitchat fell on deaf ears. Greist said only, "Yes, I do."

"Mr. Greist, one of my associates"—he glanced at the bedroom— "my partner, Annabel Reed, will be in New York tomorrow on other business. I thought it might be a good time to make contact with you and to see whether there is some field of understanding that could be established."

"I'd rather see you, Mr. Smith."

"Well, as you can imagine, being the Ewalds' attorney in this matter is going to keep me anchored to Washington for quite a while. You seemed anxious to move on this. Ms. Reed has my total confidence and can speak for me." He wanted to add, "Take it or leave it."

"Yeah, I suppose so. Will four o'clock be convenient?"

"Yes, I'm sure it will be. Her other appointments are in the morning." They made the date, and Greist gave Smith his address on Manhattan's West Side.

Smith picked up the phone and called an old friend in Connecticut, Morgan Tubbs, a partner in a Wall Street law firm. He reached Tubbs at his home, and after the smallest of small talk, got to the point. "Morgan, could you have someone up there run a background check for me tomorrow morning on a New York attorney named Herbert Greist?"

"Happy to, Mac. What's his connection with Ewald?"

"No connection."

"I was really shocked, I have to tell you, when I heard you had agreed to represent the Ewald son. I thought you were out of litigation for good."

"Nothing is forever, as they say."

Tubbs laughed. "I heard a rumor that you were doing this for Senator Ewald to try and keep his campaign on track. I'd like to think that was an altruistic act on your part, but rumor also goes on to say that if Ewald becomes president, I'm talking to our next attorney general."

"No, you're speaking with an old friend who's taken some time off to help another friend, and who will be scurrying back to academia as soon as possible."

"As you wish, Mac. I'll be happy to see what I can come up with on Greist. Where can I reach you tomorrow morning, at home?"

Smith started to affirm that, then said, "No, Morgan, I've established an office in the Watergate Hotel. It's suite 1117. I should be there by late morning."

"Talk to you then."

Smith told Annabel that he would call her in New York before her meeting and fill her in on what he'd learned about Greist from Tubbs. Then he called Tony Buffolino at the Watergate, but there was no answer.

That afternoon, they went to Smith's Foggy Bottom house, where he prepared a list of things he wanted to accomplish the next day and fed Rufus. Later he suggested, "Let's take a nice, long, leisurely walk. It might be the last time for a while we can just do nothing together."

"Were we doing nothing together this morning?"

"No," he said, smiling, "we were doing everything."

They ended up at the Mall, where they strolled through the Museum of American History, had an early dinner at Clyde's in Georgetown, and spent the rest of the evening at Annabel's. She finished reading the newspapers, and he skimmed through a copy of *The A.B.C. Murders*, an old Agatha Christie novel that he found on Annabel's bookshelves, and that set his mind toward detection, discovery, and looking twice at the obvious.

He returned to his house at eleven, walked Rufus, and immediately went to bed.

SIXTEEN

AFTER dropping Annabel off at National Airport to catch the crowded 8 A.M. shuttle, he went to a business machine store and arranged to have necessary office equipment delivered to the Watergate. He made another stop at an office supply store and ordered basic supplies.

Buffolino was at the suite when Smith arrived shortly before eleven.

"Nice suit," Smith said.

"Thanks. I needed some new threads if I'm going to be hanging around a place like this."

"Where did you get it?"

"Downstairs. They got a men's shop."

Smith raised one eyebrow.

"It was on sale."

"I see. Are you comfortable enough here, Tony?"

"Jesus, sure I am. I really appreciate you going for this, Mac." Buffolino looked around the living room. "Brings back old memories."

"Unpleasant ones, I assume," said Smith. "Frankly, I was surprised . . . no, shocked is more like it, that you actually chose this suite to stay in."

Buffolino shrugged. "Yeah, well, I figured I'd relive the crime, like. Know what I mean? You see, I was afraid of this place. My life went south here. Actually, it's not as unpleasant as I figured it might be. Funny, when I walked in here, I could almost see that dirtbag Garcia sitting in the chair. That's one thing I'd like to do before I pack it in, Mac."

"What's that, Tony?"

"Find him and settle the score."

"Tony, that case is closed. Still, when this one is over, you'll have enough money to buy a plane ticket to Panama, if you want. He went back, didn't he?"

"That's what I heard."

"You'd be on his turf."

"That's okay," Tony said grimly. "He was on mine."

Smith told Tony about the things to be delivered that day, and also said that there was the possibility he'd have to go to San Francisco, not only to dig a little further into Andrea Feldman's background, but to find her mother, too.

"Hey, great," Buffolino said. "Always wanted to see Frisco. Good thing I bought this suit. Maybe I should get another."

"That one looks like it will travel well, Tony."

The message sank in, and Buffolino made a mental note not to bring up any further mentions of personal expenditures. He said, "You know, Mac, you're okay, putting me up in a place like this. I never figured you'd pop for it, but . . . well, I just want you to know I appreciate everything you've done for me. Including what you done for me when IA set me up in here. I didn't much go for it then, but I know you did right by me."

Smith was becoming slightly embarrassed, and was relieved when the phone rang. He picked it up.

"Mac, Morgan Tubbs."

"Good morning, Morgan. Come up with anything on Greist?"

"An interesting, albeit unsavory, character," said Tubbs. "Let's see, Herbert Greist is fifty-eight years old, a graduate of City College Law at the age of thirty. After passing the Bar, he worked for the public defender for four years after which he became deeply involved with the ACLU, but only for a year. He's been in private practice ever since. There seems to have been a series of offices, the latest of which is on West Seventy-eighth."

"Yes, I have that address," Smith said. "So far, I fail to see why you consider him to be unsavory—or even interesting."

"Well, Mac, here's what led me to say that. Herbert Greist seems to have a penchant for affiliating with what some would see as our less patriotic element."

" 'Less patriotic'?"

"Yes. Of course, none of this comes from official sources, but as it happens, we have a young attorney here whose uncle was once involved with Greist through—well, none of that matters. What our young associate tells me is that he called his uncle, and his uncle informed him that Greist's practice is rather restricted to lower-echelon socialist and Communist sympathizers who run afoul of authorities. According to the uncle, the FBI and CIA have dossiers on Greist several yards in length and continue to add to them."

Buffolino motioned to Smith across the room that there was a carafe of fresh coffee. Smith nodded—yes, he wanted a cup—and said, "The FBI and CIA run files on anyone who subscribes to *The Nation* and who drinks pink lemonade. That doesn't mean Greist is a fellow traveler." His use of that old-fashioned, McCarthy-era term made him smile.

"True, but there is more juice here than pink lemonade, Mac."

"Being facetious," Smith said.

Tubbs's voice suddenly turned jarringly proper. "I certainly hope so."

Smith asked, "Any indication that Greist ever practiced law in San Francisco?"

"As a matter of fact, there is. He evidently was general counsel for a little more than a year to the Embarcadero Opera Company." Tubbs laughed. "Pornographic opera, no doubt, being in San Francisco."

"Wrong," Smith said. "It's a small, ambitious, and pretty damn good opera company. General counsel? Doesn't make sense. Performing companies like that are lucky to get a young opera-buff attorney to look over their lease. They don't have general counsels."

"Well, that's what I was told. That's right, I forgot you were an inveterate opera lover. You must miss New York."

"Not at all," Smith said. "The Washington Opera Company is first-rate. You say he was general counsel to the Embarcadero group. When was he out there?"

"Three years ago, I believe."

"Hmmm," Smith said, thinking back to a benefit performance for the Embarcadero Company he had attended in that same year at which an impressive array of singers had appeared. He'd had that same thought during Roseanna Gateaux's performance at the Ewald gala the night Andrea Feldman was murdered: She'd been one of the stars who'd lent her name and talent to the fund-raising event for the struggling San Francisco company.

"Anything else interesting?" Smith asked.

"No, Mac, that's about it. There were some Bar Association complaints against him, but action was never taken other than a few talks. Just your average, run-of-the-mill lowlife barrister." He gave forth with a hearty laugh.

Smith winced at the characterization. It was undoubtedly true, but Morgan Tubbs made such characterizations of anyone who hadn't graduated from an Ivy League school, and who dealt in any aspect of the law other than corporate high finance. "Thanks, Morgan, I appreciate your help."

"My pleasure, Mac, but you have to promise to fill me in on all the intrigue the next time you get to New York."

Smith managed not to commit to that before hanging up.

He sipped from the cup of coffee Buffolino had handed him, found a phone number on a scrap of paper in his pocket, and called it. Moments later, he was connected to Annabel's suite at the Plaza. "How was the flight?" he asked.

"Fine. The suite is lovely."

"Glad to hear it." He filled her in on what he'd learned about Herbert Greist.

"Mac."

"What?"

"I just had a chill."

"Turn up the heat," he said.

"Not that kind of chill, Mac, one that comes from inside. I can't explain it, but something tells me this is about to become a lot more complicated than you anticipated."

Smith laughed. "I think it will all be considerably simpler when you've had a chance to hear what Greist is really after. By the way, Annabel, see if you can get a handle on where Mrs. Feldman is."

"I have that on my list of questions. Where will you be when I'm done with him?"

"Hard to say. I might be here at the Watergate." He told her of steps he'd taken that morning to equip the place. "I want to get over to Ken and Leslie's house sometime today. I know they're about to hit the campaign trail again, and there are questions I need to have answered. I also want to stop in and see Paul, and to keep looking for Janet. In the rush of things, I've almost forgotten I have a client. Try me at home if you can't get me at either of those two places. I'll be anxious to hear how it goes."

Smith had no sooner hung up when there was a knock on the door. Buffolino, who was reclining on the couch, jumped up and said, "Hey, must be lunch. I forgot I ordered it." He opened the door and a young man in a starched white jacket, white shirt, and black bow tie wheeled in a serving cart covered with pristine linen. He removed metal covers from dishes, and took pains to make sure all the elements were in perfect order.

"Yeah, thanks, looks great," Buffolino said, handing him some bills.

Smith came over to see what was on the table. There was a large shrimp cocktail, filet mignon, shoestring potatoes, an arugola-and-endive salad, hot rolls, and a shimmering, undulating crème caramel.

Buffolino gave Smith a sheepish grin. "Want some?" he asked. "I can't eat all of this."

"No, but thanks anyway, Tony. Go ahead and eat before it gets cold."

Buffolino wedged the linen napkin between his shirt collar and neck and started in.

"What are your plans for the rest of the day?" Smith asked.

"I got some calls in around town, and out on the Coast. I figure I'll concentrate on trying to find Ewald's wife, Janet, unless you got something else for me to do."

"Nothing specific. Be here when they deliver the equipment and supplies, if that won't inconvenience you."

Smith's sarcasm was sharper than the knife Buffolino was using to cut his steak. He shook his head. "Hell, Mac, I'm yours. You can count on me."

Smith left for the Ewald house. Tony Buffolino wiped his mouth, got up, and called the house where his second wife and two daughters lived. One of them, Irene, answered. "Hey, babe, it's Daddy," Buffolino said.

"Hello, Daddy." Her response was pointedly cold, but Tony knew better than to mention it. He was a lousy father, and he'd never denied it. He hadn't seen Irene or her younger sister, Marie, in over six months. "Hey, look, Irene," he said, keeping his tone upbeat, "your old man's made a score, a big one, big names, the biggest. You know them all, you read about them in the paper. They're paying some good dough, and I'm set up here at a suite in the Watergate Hotel like some rich Arab in with the oil money." He waited for a response, received none. "I want you and your sister to come up for a little party. Mom, too. It'll be nice to spend a little time together. They got swimming pools inside and out, the best food you ever ate, the works. It's a suite, a real big suite with more than one room. The furniture is all leather. What do you say?"

"I'll have to ask Mommy."

"Her, too, remember. Dinner's on me, for her, too."

His daughter put down the phone, and Buffolino heard soft female voices in the background. When she came back on the line, Irene asked, "When?"

"I was thinking about tonight, if you guys can make it. I think I'll be heading for Frisco—San Francisco—in a day or two, maybe be gone a week, who knows? Yeah, how about tonight?"

His ex-wife took the phone from her daughter. "Tony, what is this crap?"

"No crap, babe. Come see for yourself. Please, you and the girls."

"You're sure?"

"Yup, I'm sure. Seven o'clock, suite 1117. Make it seven-thirty. I got to run some errands."

"Tony, if this ends up some . . ."

"Trust me, babe, and everybody dress up. Remember how you always wanted to try caviar?"

"Yes." She couldn't help but laugh.

"You tasted it since we split?"

"No, but everything else has tasted better ever since."

He let the comment slide. "Tonight's the night, babe, all the caviar you want, and buckets a' champagne. *Ciao!*"

As Buffolino finished his lunch at the Watergate, a limousine carrying Senator Jody Backus and Ken Ewald's campaign manager, Ed Farmer, pulled up in front of Anton's Loyal Opposition Bar and Restaurant. Since opening a few years earlier, on First Street NE, on

Capitol Hill, it had become a favorite hangout for members of Congress. Backus hadn't been there since deciding to run against Ewald, but he'd been announcing to his staff lately that he missed it, needed "someplace normal where this ol' boy is comfortable." His staff knew that his real need was Anton's blackened redfish. He'd been expressing a yen for it for the past three days.

"What a pleasure to see you again, Senator," a tuxedoed host said at the door.

"Same here, Frank," Backus said. "Trouble with runnin' for office is that everybody wants you in places you damn well don't want to be. You've got the black redfish ready?"

Frank laughed. "Of course. The minute your office called, I made sure we did. Your usual table?"

"That'll be fine."

They were led through the restaurant, where Backus, to the trailing agent's chagrin, stopped to shake hands. Farmer watched the senator from Georgia with intense interest. Despite being overweight and crass, and with a tendency to sweat even in the blast of an air conditioner, there was an unmistakable dignity to the man. He almost looked elegant, which, Farmer rationalized, was the result of the power he wielded. Power seemed to iron out wrinkles in suits, and to assign a certain charm to crude behavior.

They moved past two large glass panels on which a donkey and elephant were etched, and to a banquette in the rear. Etched-glass panels along the back of each bench created a relatively private setting. Backus struggled to maneuver his bulk into the banquette. Across from him, the lithe Farmer slid easily into place.

Backus was sweating as he said to the host, "Bring me my usual Blanton's on the rocks and a side a' soda water. What are you drinkin', Mr. Farmer?"

"Perrier, please."

Backus's laugh was a low rumble. "Someday, Mr. Farmer, somebody will give a satisfactory explanation to this simple ol' farm boy why people pay for water in a fancy bottle when it's free out a' any ol' tap."

"Marketing, Senator," Farmer said.

"Like sellin' a politician, huh?"

"I suppose you could draw the analogy." Farmer's small face was particularly tight above his yellow-and-brown polka-dot bow tie. His glasses were oversized on the bridge of an aquiline nose. He glanced quickly across the room to where the Secret Service agents sat in their own banquette. He said to Backus, "I would have preferred to meet in an office."

"I know you would prefer that, Mr. Farmer, but I had to get out of offices, settle in a public place where real people congregate. I need that like a drug addict needs his daily fix." Farmer started to say something, but Backus continued. "Your boss could use a little of that, too, you know. He's an insular fella, I'll say that for him. Likes to be alone too much. Sometimes, I see a little Richard Nixon in him." Backus's fleshy face sagged. His smile was gone. He leaned as far forward as his girth would allow and said, "I worry about Kenneth Ewald. He's like a son to me. I think the rigors of this campaign"—a slight smile returned—"and the rigors of an active social life, to say nothin' of fulfilling his role as a family man and havin' to stand tall where his son is involved, are takin' their toll. You agree?"

"No, sir, I don't. Senator Ewald is holding up quite nicely."

"Damn shame what happened to that Feldman girl the other night."

"A tragedy."

"Certainly for her. Have you seen Paul?"

"Since his arrest? No."

"Awful thing for a mother and father to have to face, havin' your only son a murder suspect."

"That's all he is at this point, Senator, a suspect."

"Don't think he did the evil deed, huh?"

"I don't know."

Backus sat back and slapped beefy hands on the dusty rose tablecloth. "Take a look at the menu, Mr. Farmer. I recommend the blackened redfish, but everything's pretty good here."

A waiter brought their drinks. Backus raised his glass filled with rich, amber bourbon, and said, "To the next four years of a Democratic administration. A-men!"

Farmer sipped his water and stared at Backus. Personally, Farmer found Backus to be everything he despised in politics. But one thing Ed Farmer never wanted to be accused of was naiveté. Personal responses meant little in Washington and politics. More important was the aura of power that Backus exuded, his crass style be damned. The big southern senator's body count topped that of everyone else in Congress, and he knew the location, width, and depth of every grave.

Backus locked eyes with Farmer as he downed his drink and waved for a waiter to bring him another.

"Sir?" the waiter asked Farmer.

"A small bottle of Château Giscours Margeaux, '83, please."

"That's what I like to see," said Backus. "I don't much care for wine, but—"

"Senator, could we get to the point of why we're here?"

Backus swallowed his annoyance at being interrupted. "That would be sincerely appreciated, Mr. Farmer. Proceed. This is your meeting."

"And your check?"

"If you insist. I suppose Ken Ewald doesn't pay you a hell of a lot."

"Money didn't motivate me into politics. Public service did."

"Just like me," Backus said. "What'll Ken Ewald toss you if he makes it, Mr. Farmer, chief a' staff? Press secretary? Health, Education and Welfare? I'd heartily endorse the latter. You'd be damn good givin' out welfare to the shiftless nonproducers of this society."

Farmer sniffed the wine, tasted it, nodded to the waiter, and returned his attention to the large man across from him. "Some people are suggesting it might be time to talk about a coalition."

"Coalition? With who?"

"You and him."

Backus laughed. "I figured that'd be comin' up. Senator Ewald must be a mite nervous these days about the way things are goin'."

"There's some truth to that," Farmer said flatly.

"No wonder. I heard him say in that speech he gave last week that the Republicans have had a lock on the White House all these years, and that he is the one who has what it takes to pick that lock. Nice phrase your speechwriters came up with, but the fact is, I don't think your master, Ken Ewald, is in a position to pick anybody's lock these days, not with havin' one of his staff members murdered with his own weapon, and havin' most fingers pointin' at his own son. Tell me, Ed, what's your honest evaluation of the possibility that Paul Ewald killed that poor young thing?"

Farmer hesitated before saying, "I don't think Paul Ewald killed Andrea Feldman."

"You don't sound like you're brimmin' over with conviction, Ed."

"No one knows what happened," Farmer said.

"And from Ken Ewald's perspective, just as well nobody does know, least not till after November." Backus cocked his head and smiled smugly. "Know what, Ed? I don't think your boss is goin' to make it at the convention. What do you think?"

Farmer sipped his wine.

"Just how nervous is your man?" Backus asked.

"Probably not as nervous as you hope," Farmer replied. "He's ignoring any pressure to offer you the vice-presidency up front."

"That's about the only thing I agree with him about. I don't intend to be anybody's vice-president. You hear me? You make sure Senator Ewald hears me."

"Yes, I heard you," Farmer said, touching the end of his bow tie, then examining a class ring on his finger.

"I suggest we eat," Backus said, "unless you've got more to say."

"No, I have nothing more to say, Senator Backus, except that your toast to a Democratic administration won't mean much if Ken Ewald doesn't make it at the convention."

"I don't read it that way. Seems to me that all he has to do is keep on the course he's takin', and this country might be proposin' a toast to this ol' southern boy on November nine. That wouldn't upset you too much, would it, Ed?" Backus's moonlike face was quiescent; the liquor had added a touch of color.

"I suppose not," Farmer said, "although having you as president, Senator Backus, wouldn't represent much of a change from the past eight years, a donkey instead of an elephant, but not much else different."

Backus looked above Farmer's head to the etched donkey and elephant on the glass behind him. He smiled, said, "At least we'd have a president who's in the mainstream of American thought."

"Like President Manning," Farmer said.

"Manning's not a bad fella, just handin' out favors to the wrong people."

"Like Colonel Morales and the Reverend Kane?"

"Hell, no. Morales is fightin' for freedom in Panama, and the last I heard, the American people stand up for freedom. As for the Reverend Kane, he tends to people's souls."

"Unless they're Panamanian. Then he tends to their stockpile of weapons."

"You sound like your boss, Ed," Backus said.

"I'm supposed to sound like him. I'm his campaign manager."

Backus nodded and narrowed his eyes. "I like you, Ed. I like a man who says what he's supposed to say even though it don't necessarily represent what he thinks."

"I believe in what Ken Ewald stands for," Farmer said.

"Unless he's not sittin' in a chair where he can put his ideas into action."

Farmer's smile was thin. "Like you, Senator Backus, proclaiming your wholehearted support of Ken if he gets the nomination."

"I'm a Democrat. I owe my allegiance to whoever comes out of the convention as the candidate. I just hope it isn't Ken Ewald. I got grave doubts about where he might lead this country."

"And you would prefer someone, Democrat or Republican, who espouses the Manning doctrine."

Backus leaned forward and his voice became slightly fatherly. "Ed, we've still got us a two-party system, Democrats and Republicans, but that doesn't mean a hell of a lot anymore. What matters today is political vision, not party labels."

Farmer listened silently to the quiet speech he was given by Backus. The southern senator was right, of course. There had been a shift from a two-party system in which Democrats and Republicans competed for elected office, to one in which conservatives and liberals did the vying, Democrats and Republicans sometimes joining forces on the Right, against Democrats and Republicans hooking up together in an equally uneasy alliance on the Left. Philosophy or ideology had supplanted party politics. "The cause," no matter what it was, had been elevated above allegiance to party which, some claimed, represented a positive step in that it caused the men and women of Congress and the executive to act according to their consciences, rather than along strict party lines. Under the old system, it would have made sense to pair people like Ewald and Backus together to combine the liberal and conservative voters. North and South. Big-city guy and rural American representative. But such coalitions were no longer viable. Ewald and Backus were polar opposites. The fact was—and Farmer knew it—Ken Ewald, despite his seemingly immense popularity, and his victory in a majority of the primaries, did not represent the mainstream of American thought. He was too liberal, too linked to big-budget social programs, perceived as being too soft on crime and national defense. Ewald's nomination could end up yet another example of the Democrats' penchant for self-destruction, a candidate who stood for the principles of the party but not the principles of the majority of the American voters. McCarthy. McGovern. Carter. Dukakis. Ewald.

After they ordered, Backus said, "You're obviously an ambitious fella, Ed."

"Yes, I have ambition."

"Seems like everybody in Washington has ambition."

"You aren't critical of that, are you, Senator? I'd say Senator Jody Backus has demonstrated a fair amount of ambition in his career."

"A different thing, Ed. A politician's ambitions are based upon his desire to serve the public. Then there are all those ambitious men and women lookin' to grab onto his coattails. That's how some politicians get in trouble, havin' the wrong young men and women hangin' on their coattails."

Farmer's thin nostrils flared. "Are you including me in that category, Senator Backus? It seems to me you ought to be more respectful of my ambition."

Backus gave him a conciliatory smile. "Don't take personal offense, Ed. I just call it like I see it. Your level of ambition certainly hasn't been lost on me."

Farmer said nothing.

"You see, Mr. Farmer, I *like* ambition in young men, big dreams, feet gettin' bigger along with the head, climbin' and stretchin' and sniffin' around the ones who can do them the most good. Of course, I'm not talking about loyalty here. Lots a' times, loyalty and ambition don't go hand in hand."

"I'm not sure I appreciate the tone this conversation is taking," Farmer said.

"Now ain't that too bad."

"I happen to be a very loyal person, Senator."

"Depends on how you define it, Ed. What do you figure got that nice young woman killed—too much ambition, too much loyalty, or not enough common sense when it came to the people she chose to run with?"

"I wouldn't know," Farmer said in a low voice.

The waiter arrived with their appetizers. Farmer touched his mouth with his napkin, slid out of the booth, and said to the restaurant host, "I just remembered an important appointment." He turned to Backus and said as pleasantly as possible, "I really hate to leave, Senator. Enjoy your blackened redfish, and thank you for the wine. It was palatable."

M A C Smith waited a long time in the study before Ken Ewald came through the door. "Sorry, Mac, but things get crazier every day."

When they were seated, Smith asked Ewald a number of questions that had been on his mind. Then he said, "Ken, we are alone in this room. You mentioned to me that the night Andrea Feldman was murdered, you'd left your office to meet with a woman at the Watergate Hotel."

Ewald glanced nervously at the door.

"I'm not in the habit of informing wives about husband's indiscretions, Ken, but I have to know everything that occurred that night, with every*one*."

"I don't see why."

"Because you've brought me into this situation. You've asked me to be Paul's attorney if he's charged, and although he hasn't been yet, there is every possibility that he will be, depending on what MPD manages to come up with. You can't bring me in and then stonewall me."

"Yes, of course, you're right, Mac, but what contribution could revealing this woman's identity possibly make to your defense of Paul, if it comes to that?"

"I don't know, Ken, but I learned long ago not to censor myself until I had the facts. When I have the facts, I can make a determination whether it contributes or not. I do not intend to be surprised at answers the DA may come up with."

Ewald sighed and said, "Okay." He cast another quick look at the door, lowered his voice, and asked, "What is it you want to know?"

"Simple. Who was the woman at the Watergate?"

Ewald frowned. "Mac, I really don't think . . ."

Smith stared at Ewald across the small space separating them. "Who was it?" he asked again.

"All right. But I'm putting tremendous trust in you."

"You have to. Do it with confidence."

"I worked in my office until about two in the morning," Ewald said. "And then . . ."

HE'D called his home before leaving the office, got Marcia Mims, and said to her, "Tell Mrs. Ewald I'll be here quite late. A last-minute meeting has come up."

"Yes, sir," Marcia said.

His unmarked blue Cadillac was at the curb in front of the office building. The driver opened a rear door for the presidential candidate and his bodyguard, Agent Jeroldson. "To the Watergate," Ewald told the driver. "Go in the garage."

The driver made a U-turn, and a few minutes later came to a stop in front of a small service elevator beneath the Watergate. "I'll be back here soon," Ewald said as he and Jeroldson got out of the car and pushed a button next to the elevator. They stepped in and rode to the twelfth floor, where Jeroldson fell behind Ewald as they walked down the hushed, carpeted corridor until reaching the door to a suite at the far end. Ewald poised to knock, then looked back at Jeroldson, who momentarily locked eyes with him, then looked away at an elaborate flower arrangement on a table. "Meet me downstairs at four," Ewald said. "You're free until then."

Jeroldson nodded, which angered Ewald. Every other Secret Service agent who'd been assigned to him was courteous, would have said, "Yes, sir." Ewald almost said so, but stopped himself. Another time. "You're relieved," he said. "Please go." He watched the square-shouldered, thick-necked agent slowly turn and walk toward a bank of public elevators. He waited until Jeroldson had punched the button before knocking.

"Ken?" a voice asked from behind the door.

Ewald looked to where Jeroldson stood. The elevator had arrived, but Jeroldson hadn't entered it. He was looking at Ewald, motionless, his eyes conveying one final, mute message. He stepped into the elevator.

An eye confirmed the identity of the visitor through the peephole. The door was unlocked and opened. Ewald stared at the thick, loose black hair flowing over the shoulders of the white silk robe she wore. A large diamond suspended on a gold chain rested on the upper ivory reaches of her stunning breasts. Her fingers, bright crimson nail polish at their tips, were laden with rings. Her bare toes were tipped in the same red. A heavy scent of Joy filled the doorway, the perfume causing an instant and involuntary physical reaction in him. Leslie used only an occasional dab of Mitsouko, or L'Air du Temps, preferring the smell of soap. Ewald liked that smell, too . . . on her. But this—this you could swim into. . . .

Roseanna Gateaux stepped back, a smile on her lips. Ewald gave one final glance at the hallway, stepped over the threshold, embraced the voluptuous, warm, and welcoming body of the famous diva, and gently kicked the door shut.

"SATISFIED?" Ewald asked.

"Nothing to be satisfied about, Ken, but at least the question has been answered."

"I assume you know the great faith I have in you to have told you."

"Yes, okay." Smith stood. "I really have to go. We'll keep in touch."

As they stood at the front door, Ewald said, "I just want you to know, Mackensie Smith, how much Leslie and I appreciate what you're doing for us. I don't think there is another person in this country we could turn to with such confidence."

Smith grunted. "I'm doing it for you and for Paul. I'll be in touch."

SEVENTEEN

ANNABEL REED sat in a closet-sized, sparsely furnished office on West Seventy-eighth Street in Manhattan. A small sign on the door read HERBERT GREIST ATTORNEY-AT-LAW. He had no receptionist or secretary. If there had been one, she wouldn't have had a place to sit.

Greist was a big but stooped man with flowing gray hair. He wore a rumpled black sharkskin suit; a tailor's nightmare, Annabel thought. His right shoulder was considerably lower than his left, and his right arm noticeably longer than his left. It gave the overall effect of a man about to fall to one side. His face was sallow and loose. Sunken eyes were surrounded by circles the color of forest mushrooms.

"Sit down, Ms. Reed, please sit down." He held out his hand and she took it, glad she was wearing gloves. "You'll have to forgive this office. I'm in the process of moving to quarters in midtown and am using this temporarily."

Sure you are, Annabel thought.

She sat in a rickety cane chair while Greist went back behind a cheap wooden desk, the veneer chipped off in places, the edges scarred from too many unattended cigars. "Mind if I smoke?" he asked as he drew one from his inside jacket pocket.

"No, not at all," she said, knowing that to protest would have been futile. She watched him light up and drop the dead match in a large once-amber ashtray overflowing with ashes.

"Frankly, Ms. Reed, I would have preferred to speak directly with Mr. Smith," Greist said, exhaling smoke.

"That may be," Annabel said, "but Mr. Smith is terribly busy in Washington. I'm completely familiar with the content of your telephone conversation with him, and have full authority to act on behalf of Mr. Smith, and our clients."

"Clients. The Ewald family. It's a fortunate law firm that has as a client the man who could be the next president of the United States."

"We were involved with the Ewald family long before Senator Ewald chose to run for the presidency. Now, Mr. Greist, could we get to the point? You indicate that Mrs. Feldman intends to file a federal suit for the loss of her daughter's civil rights."

Another cloud of blue smoke left his mouth as he leaned back and thought for a moment. "Yes. She is thinking of doing so. And certainly with justification."

"We would debate that. Still, you indicated that your client, Mrs. Feldman, was open to the idea of a settlement. Settlement is probably out of the question. But if it were a question, what kind of numbers are you talking about?"

Greist placed the cigar on the heap already in the ashtray, leaned forward on his elbows so that his chin rested in the palms of his hands, and managed a weak smile. "Directly to the point, I see," he said, with little energy behind his words.

"Yes, I don't see anything to be gained by sitting here stringing out this discussion. How much money does your client feel will adequately compensate her for the loss of her daughter?"

"That is hard to say, Ms. Reed."

Annabel smiled. "I would suggest it become easier soon, or we have nothing to talk about, Mr. Greist."

He retrieved his cigar and leaned back again. "Let me see," he said. "Would a half-million dollars shock you?"

"I don't shock easily," she said. "The fact that it is a ludicrous number probably has more effect on you. You are, of course, joking."

"Not at all." Smoke clouded his face. He coughed and rubbed his eyes.

She stood and waited until he could again speak. Looking down at him, she said, "Mr. Greist, you have wasted my time and my law firm's money in arranging this meeting. I would like to speak with your client. Perhaps we could arrange it while I'm in New York."

"My client is not in New York."

"Then why are you representing her?"

"I, too, go back a long way with my client's family. Of course, I don't have the luxury of representing rich and powerful political figures as you and Mr. Smith do, but I assure you our resolve is no less adamant." He stood, taller than she'd remembered when he first greeted her. He said, "I suggest that there are other, mitigating circumstances that might cause you and Mr. Smith to reconsider the amount of compensation with which we can be comfortable. There are aspects of Senator Ewald's life that came to be known to my client, and to her daughter. Those 'things' have a certain intrinsic value—once you are aware of the nature of them, I'm sure you will agree."

Reed wasn't sure how to react. "You are suggesting blackmail of Senator Ewald and his family."

It was the first wide smile Greist had exhibited, and it revealed teeth that had been tortured or neglected. "Blackmail? That is a terrible word. I prefer to view the sale of information as being simply that, a commercial transaction. My client has information that your client would benefit from, and I am suggesting it has a certain worth."

"More than the loss of your client's civil rights, I assume."

"As you wish."

"What is this information that Senator Ewald would want to pay a great deal of money to retrieve?"

"That, Ms. Reed, is for another day, another meeting. You'll be here a few days?"

"Yes. I'm staying at the—I'm at a hotel."

"Are you free tomorrow evening?"

"No, I am not, and I must say that I resent the entire tone of this meeting."

"Might I suggest, then, that you call Mr. Smith and tell him what has transpired at this *distasteful* meeting. As counsel to the next president of the United States, he might put a more liberal interpretation on it than you exhibit. I can be reached here tomorrow between one and three in the afternoon. Thank you for coming."

She walked back to the Plaza, her mind racing, her anger barely under control. There was a nip in the air; she pulled her gloves from the pocket of her raincoat, and in her annoyance, one of them fell to the pavement. She stopped quickly and turned to pick it up. The man behind her seemed startled at her abrupt halt and change of direction. He looked away, then pretended to peer at items in a store window.

Lingerie. Reed picked up her glove, glanced back at him one more time, and walked quickly to the hotel, where she took a shower—which seemed symbolic—ordered a bottle of white wine to be sent to the room, and called Smith at the Watergate. She got the new answering machine. She had the same luck with his home number. Finally, with some hesitation, she dialed the Ewald house. The phone was answered by the head housekeeper. "Yes, ma'am," Marcia Mims said, "he was here, but he's left."

Annabel gave the housekeeper the same message she'd left on both of Smith's answering machines; that he was to call her in New York as soon as possible. She gave Marcia Mims her number at the hotel, and hung up as room service arrived.

Glass in hand, she stood at the window and looked down over the street where people were heading home from their jobs. How routine our lives are so much of the time, she told herself. Then she was forced to smile. She could understand a bit better why Mac Smith had accepted the offer to defend Paul Ewald. It broke the sought-after routine of the college professor, just as coming to New York to meet with Greist had broken her routine at the gallery. Maybe she should ease up on Mac a little. Maybe not.

She sat on the housing that covered the suite's heating system and shook her head. Herbert Greist trying to blackmail the next president. Tony Buffolino going to San Francisco to find the mother of a slain girl. Politics. Adultery. Blackmail. Murder.

"Hey, kids," she said softly to the passersby below, "you don't know what you're missing."

B Y the time Mac Smith returned to the suite at the Watergate, all deliveries had been made and the living room had begun to look like a working office. There was a note on the table: "Be back around six—I got something to talk to you about. Tony."

Smith called Annabel in New York, and she recounted for him her conversation with Herbert Greist. Smith took notes while she talked. When she was finished, he said, "He told you that there was damaging information about Ken that both Andrea Feldman *and* her mother had?"

"Yes, that's what he said, Mac. I made notes after I got back to the hotel."

"No idea what information that might be, or how the Feldman ladies got it?"

"No. I should have asked more questions, but frankly, I was anxious to get out of there. He's a communicable disease."

Smith considered telling her what he'd learned about Ewald's liaison with Roseanna Gateaux at the Watergate the night of the murder, but decided not to do it over the telephone.

"Greist wants to get together with me again tomorrow night," Annabel said.

"Are you?"

"I told him I couldn't, but I'm thinking now it might be a good idea. He gives me the creeps, but maybe I can find out more."

"Do whatever you think is right, Annabel, but be careful. Somebody murdered Andrea Feldman, and I don't think it was Paul Ewald."

"I'll watch myself," she said. The man who'd been behind her when she dropped her glove suddenly flashed across her mind. She didn't mention him. Overactive imagination.

"Good luck with whatever it is you're going after for the gallery," he said.

"I almost forgot about that," she said, laughing with relief. "I'll fill you in when I get back. Or sell it to you."

Smith had just poured himself a well-watered drink when Buffolino returned.

"Where've you been?" Smith asked.

"Having a pop with an old friend of mine from the IRS."

Smith smiled. "Not a bad friend to have."

"Yeah, he's come in handy over the years. I got him out of a jam when I was still on the force, one of those personal sex things that would have blown him out of the water. Anyway, he owes me, and every once in a while I remind him."

"Having tax problems, Tony?"

"Me? Nah. I don't make enough to have tax problems."

Smith raised his eyebrows.

"Well, until now. I mean, I wasn't doin' as good as I told you I was."

Smith said nothing.

Buffolino sat in a leather chair and put his feet on the coffee table. "I had my friend check out tax returns for Feldman and her mother."

Smith cocked his head. "And?"

"And they file every year, only there isn't a lot of money to account for. Andrea Feldman never got paid much working for causes. Her mother lists some income from work, but she basically is on Social Security and some interest from small investments. Nothing major league."

"What kind of work does the mother do?"

"My friend says she lists herself as a consultant."

"What kind of consultant?"

"Like all consultants, unemployed."

"Any leads on where the mother might be?"

"Disappeared, like Janet Ewald. I checked a friend at the PD. He tells me no one was ever able to make contact with the old lady to tell her her daughter was dead."

"She knows, Tony."

"How could she miss it, with all the stories on the tube and in the papers?"

Smith had been debating with himself about how much to tell Buffolino. As a good lawyer, he knew he could only be as effective as information given him by a client, and the same tended to be true for an investigator. Yet he was reluctant to reveal too much of the Ewald family's private affairs. He decided to tell Buffolino about the blackmail attempt by Herbert Greist, but keep Ken Ewald's liaison with Roseanna Gateaux to himself.

When he was finished recounting what had transpired with Greist and Annabel in New York, Buffolino said, "Weird family."

"Certainly not conventional."

"Maybe the old lady doesn't want to be found because her daughter was murdered."

"I don't follow," Smith said.

"Why else would she lie low? People who get murdered make their families feel guilty somehow. Like they were all victims—or all at fault, know what I mean? You got any better answers?"

"No, I don't. Except that I think you'd better get out to San Francisco as quickly as possible and see if you can track her down. You might also try to find out where she did her banking, whether there were any accounts for her or for her daughter. Since you seem to have friends everywhere, I assume that extends to California."

Buffolino smiled. "Mac, I got friends in every state, including a good one with Wells Fargo in Frisco. When do you want me to go?"

"How about tomorrow?"

"On my way."

"Nothin' new on our other missing person? I came up dry so far," Buffolino admitted as he went to the kitchen to make himself a drink."

"No, nothing. That's really the most pressing matter to be resolved. If it weren't for this Greist character in New York, I wouldn't be so concerned with finding Mae Feldman. Any ideas on how we can push the police to find Janet?"

"They don't take any push from me," Buffolino said. The phone rang. "I'll get it," he offered. "It's for you, Mac."

"Mr. Smith, this is Marcia Mims."

"Yes, Marcia, how are you?"

There was a long pause. ". . . Mr. Smith, I really think we should talk."

Smith heard music and voices in the background. He also heard both the urgency and the hesitation in her voice. "I'll be happy to talk to you any time, Marcia," he said.

"There are things you have to know, Mr. Smith, and I really have to talk to somebody I can trust."

"Fine. When would you like to get together?"

"I was hoping . . ."

"You were hoping we could do it right away. I don't see any reason why not. I have a suite here at the Watergate. Maybe you could—"

"Mr. Smith, I know you're very busy and I don't want to inconvenience you, but I'm not in the city. Tomorrow is my day off, and I came to Annapolis to stay with my cousin Tommy tonight. He owns a crab-cake restaurant in the Market House."

"What's the name of his place?"

"Tommy's."

"Of course. I can head over there in a little while."

"I'll be here waiting for you, and thank you, thank you very much."

"Just sit tight, Marcia. See you in about an hour."

"What was that all about?" Buffolino asked after Smith hung up.

"The Ewalds' housekeeper, Marcia Mims. Wants to meet with me about something. I'm driving over to Annapolis."

"I'll go with you."

"No, that might put her off. She's very delicate right now. You get ready for your trip, make a reservation, get set to go tomorrow. Here, copy this down and use it." He handed Buffolino his gold American Express card. Tony noted the account number.

"Where are you going to be in Annapolis, in case I need you?" Buffolino asked.

"A crab-cake restaurant called Tommy's, in the Market House."

"Sure you don't want me to come with you? I love crab cakes."

"I'll bring you a doggie bag."

Buffolino smiled, looked at his watch, then slapped the side of his head. "Jesus, I forgot."

"Forgot what?"

"I forgot I'm havin' a party up here tonight."

"A *party?*"

"Well, not really a party. I invited my wife and daughters up here for a little dinner, a quiet thing, you know?"

"Tony, I—"

"Hey, Mac, I owe 'em. This is on me. I'll pick up the tab."

"That's generous of you, Tony. And I won't bother with that doggie bag. I'm sure you'll make do."

EIGHTEEN

HE FOUND a parking spot near the distinctive harbor that forms the center of Annapolis, and a few minutes later walked into Tommy's Crab Cake House. Business was good; there was a wait for tables, and a lively group was congregated in the small barroom.

A handsome black man wearing a perfectly fitted double-breasted gray suit came from the dining room and nimbly made his way to a podium near the front door. Smith asked, "Are you Tommy?"

The man nodded.

"My name is Mackensie Smith. I was supposed to meet your cousin, Marcia Mims, here."

"Oh, yes, Mr. Smith, Marcia told me you were coming." He looked around before leaning close and saying, "I'm glad you're here. She's very upset. If you'll give me a minute, I'll take you to her."

Tommy seated a party of six, told one of the waiters to cover the front, and motioned for Smith to follow him. They walked through the dining room, entered the kitchen, went through a door leading to a short, narrow hallway, and stepped into Tommy's cramped and cluttered office, where Marcia Mims sat on a couch, obviously having made room by pushing piles of paper and magazines aside. She stood up when she saw Smith.

"Hello, Marcia," he said.

Marcia looked at Tommy, who gave her a reassuring smile. "Relax, honey, everything's going to be all right." He said to Smith, "I have to get back. Just yell if you need anything."

"Please, Marcia, sit down," Smith said. He pulled a folding metal chair close to the couch. They said nothing for a few moments, just sat and looked at each other. Smith broke the silence. "I haven't been to Annapolis in a long time. I guess the last time was a football game at the Naval Academy. Must be three years ago."

"I come here whenever I can," Marcia said. "Tommy and his wife are very good to me."

"Seems like a nice fellow, and it looks like he's made a smiling success out of crabs."

Marcia laughed, and Smith was glad to see it. She'd been as taut as a violin string when he first came through the door. Now, she relaxed slightly, the tightness in her body visibly falling away into the soft cushions.

"Mr. Smith, I . . ."

"Yes?"

"I called you because . . . I called you because I don't know what to do. It's about Janet."

Smith sat up straight. "Janet?"

"Yes."

"Do you know where she is?"

"Yes."

"How do you . . . I mean, did Janet call you, or have you known all along?"

"She called me two days ago. She's very frightened."

"Frightened of what?"

"Of what will happen to her if she comes back."

"I don't understand, Marcia. What would she have to be frightened about? Does she think someone would hurt her?"

"She doesn't know what will happen to her, that's all. Mr. Smith, Janet has never been comfortable in the Ewald family. She's always considered herself an outsider."

Smith shrugged. "That's not uncommon for daughters-in-law. It's not a reason to be really frightened. Why did she call you, Marcia?"

"Janet has always turned to me, Mr. Smith. She says I'm the only one she feels she can trust and confide in."

"That's flattering to you, and deserved, I imagine. Where is she?"

The tension returned, and she looked away.

"I want to help, and I assume you called me because you thought I could help Janet. She certainly shouldn't be frightened of me."

The housekeeper looked at him again. "I know that, Mr. Smith. I think she knows that. It's just that I'm not sure what to do. I told her she should come back and face whatever is going to happen with Paul, but she's too confused at this point."

Smith decided that to press for Janet's whereabouts would be counterproductive. But he had to get more out of Marcia. He said, "Well, Marcia, at least she's safe. I was beginning to wonder whether something terrible had happened to her." He stood. "I suppose you'll have to make your own decision about what to do with Janet. I agree with you that she should come back, but she can't be forced to. Is there anything else you want from me at this point?"

"Please, sit down, Mr. Smith."

Smith resumed his seat and waited for her to say what was on her mind.

"I told Janet I would talk to you, and if I thought things were right, I would take you to her."

"Is she here in Annapolis?"

Marcia nodded.

"Well, here I am," he said. "Frankly, I'm going to leave one way or the other, either by myself or with you to see Janet. The smell of crab cakes is getting to me. I haven't had dinner yet."

She smiled. "I'm sorry, Mr. Smith, but I just want to do the right thing by her."

"Of course. That's why she trusts you."

"Tommy has a little apartment here in town that he only uses occasionally. Janet is there."

"Has she been there the whole time?"

"No, she stayed in a motel in Virginia before she called me."

"Let's go," Smith said. He could see that she was grappling with the decision she'd made, and he reached out and touched her hand. "Everything will work out, Marcia, for Janet and for everyone."

They stopped at the front of the restaurant to tell Tommy they'd be back, then walked slowly along the edge of the harbor, in which small boats of every description were anchored. The night was humid; a fog had begun to roll in off Chesapeake Bay. They went up a narrow street lined with shops until they reached a two-story building at the end of it. The ground level was a men's clothing store. A separate door provided access to the second floor. Marcia pulled a key from her purse and opened the door, and they proceeded up a narrow flight of stairs.

There was a single door off the landing. Marcia knocked.

"Who is it?"

"It's Marcia, honey, and Mr. Smith." They waited, long enough for Smith to wonder whether Janet had decided to not let them in. Then there was the turn of a lock, and the door opened.

Tommy's apartment consisted of a living room–bedroom combination, a pullman kitchen, and a bathroom. If it weren't for the kitchen, it would have looked like any moderately priced hotel room. Tommy must put his money into clothing.

Marcia immediately went to Janet and hugged her, then stood at her side. Janet had always been frail, her features thin and birdlike, but at this moment she looked absolutely fragile. There was virtually no color in her face. The yellow sweater and black skirt she wore had undoubtedly fit her a week ago, but now hung loosely on her. She was considerably shorter than Marcia; oddly, had it not been for their color difference, they could have been mother and child.

"How have you been, Janet?" Smith asked.

Janet played with her bony white fingers. "All right, Mac. No, not all right. Not good at all."

He wondered if she might collapse, and he suggested they sit down. "Would anyone like something to drink?" Marcia asked.

"Anything cold, a soft drink," Smith said, not taking his eyes off Janet, who sat on the edge of a chair and continued to pull at her fingers.

As Marcia went into the tiny kitchen and opened the refrigerator, he said to Janet, "Marcia says you're afraid to come back, Janet. Do you know that I'm handling Paul's defense in the event he's charged with Andrea Feldman's murder?"

She looked at him with wide eyes. "Yes, I heard that. I mean, I read that." Smith started to say something, but Janet added, "Marcia told me, too. She said you've been helping everyone."

"I'm trying."

"How is Paul?"

"Doing quite well, considering the circumstances." He thought of Paul's indifference to her disappearance, said instead, "He's been frantic about you. It would be very helpful to him if he knew you were safe and if you were there at his side."

She quickly shook her head. "I can't."

"Why? What made you run the way you did?"

Marcia returned with three glasses of diet soda. Smith repeated his question to Janet.

"I had no choice. I knew they would think it was me."

"Think it was you what?"

"Who killed Andrea Feldman."

"Kill Andrea—you?"

"Yes, or they'd make it seem as though I did."

"Who would do that, Janet?"

"Ken and Leslie."

Smith looked at the floor, then back at her. "Janet, I don't know the kind of relationship you've had with your in-laws, but I don't think they're the kind of people who would falsely accuse someone of murder."

Marcia said, "Mr. Smith, there is a great deal that goes on in that house that most people wouldn't dream of."

"Like what?" he asked.

"Like . . ." She and Janet looked at each other before Janet said, "Paul wasn't the only one who had an affair with Andrea."

Smith measured his words. "Ken did, too." So Ken might have had a motive to murder Andrea himself. He looked at Marcia Mims and asked, "Is that true, Marcia? Do you know that Senator Ewald had an affair with Andrea Feldman?"

"I don't think it's my place to—"

Smith said loudly, for the first time, "Marcia, let's not play games. Can you confirm that he had an affair with her?"

"Yes."

"Quite a young woman," Smith said, more to himself than to them.

Smith pondered the situation. According to Ken's claims about what he'd done the night of the murder, he'd spent time with Roseanna Gateaux in the Watergate; she could certainly confirm that, assuming she was forced to be honest about it. Secret Service agent Jeroldson was with Ewald the rest of the night. Smith had to ask Joe Riga what had come out of his interview with Jeroldson.

As Smith looked at the two women across from him, he thought of other possibilities: Either of *them* could have killed Andrea. If Paul

Ewald had gone to the Buccaneer Motel after the party and before Andrea was killed, he could have dropped her back at the Kennedy Center, left . . . and someone else could have killed her. Paul had denied having gone to that motel with her after the party. Had he or hadn't he? If he had, why lie about it? If he hadn't, and she'd gone there with someone else, that would make the motel owner, Wilton Morse, either a liar or severely mistaken because of poor eyesight. No, according to what Tony said, Morse's eyesight wasn't *that* bad. That left lying. Why would Morse lie? Had he been paid to? And, if so, who would have that much to gain by pinning Murder One on Paul Ewald?

"Janet," Smith said, "do you think your father-in-law had a motive for killing Andrea Feldman? Was Andrea blackmailing Senator Ewald?"

Another look between the two women. Marcia Mims said, "*I* don't know anything about motives, Mr. Smith, and I really don't want to be involved. All I know is that Janet means a lot to me and I want to help *her*, nobody else. That's why I called you."

"Yes, of course, and I think Janet is fortunate to have a caring friend like you. But she's opened this whole line of conversation, to which I have to respond. After all, I am her husband's attorney, and he's a prime suspect in the murder. I don't believe he did it, and if his father is the murderer, the ramifications of that are clear enough."

Smith turned to Janet. "I was brought here by Marcia to help you, Janet, and I thought perhaps to offer some advice. Well, my advice is for you to come back to Washington with me and face this thing head-on."

Janet's nervousness returned, and she shook her head. "I can't do that. I'm too afraid."

"That they'll say *you* killed Andrea Feldman? It won't happen, believe me."

"No, Mac—I'm afraid that they might kill me, too."

Smith's laugh was involuntary.

Janet's face hardened.

"I'm not laughing at *what* you're saying, Janet, but the idea is simply too farfetched for me to give much credence to it. Will you come back with me? If your physical safety is a legitimate concern, I can arrange to have you protected."

"How?"

"Leave that to me. Will you come?"

She shook her head.

Smith stood. "Well, you put me in a difficult situation. The police are looking for you, because they must talk with you as they have with everyone else. I know where you are now, and if I fail to make that known to them, I'm obstructing justice, something no one, especially an attorney, is supposed to do."

Janet turned to Marcia and said, "See, I told you this was a mistake." Marcia put her arm around her and said, "It wasn't a mistake. I trust Mr. Smith. He won't tell anyone."

"Don't place that burden on me, Marcia," Smith said sternly.

"Please, Mac, don't tell them where I am. Oh, go ahead, I won't be here anyway." She jumped up from her chair and paced the room, her thin arms wrapped around herself as though an arctic blast had hit.

"Look, Janet," Smith said, "let's leave it this way: Think about it. I won't tell anyone that I've seen you and had this conversation, no one. I promise you that. Think about it for twenty-four hours, and then let's talk again. I'll come back here tomorrow night. Promise you'll be here."

She turned and said angrily, "I don't trust anyone connected with that family."

"Suit yourself, but I'll keep my part of the bargain. I'll be here tomorrow night at the same time. I hope you'll be here, too." He looked at Marcia. "Are you coming with me?"

She shook her head. "No, I'll stay with her a while."

"Fine. You know where to reach me. Good night."

Smith was angry, and the speed at which he drove back to Washington reflected it. He went to the Watergate suite, where Tony Buffolino sat alone watching television.

"Where're your wife and kids?" Smith asked.

"Ah, they came up here, but I got into a hassle right away with my wife and they took off. Typical, man—I want to do good, but I shoot off my mouth and we end up in a brawl. I'll make it up to them. What was your trip all about?"

"Nothing, wasted time. Anything new here aside from a near-homicide fight with your wife?"

"I made my reservation to go to Frisco tomorrow."

"Good." Smith picked up the phone and dialed Joe Riga's number. To his surprise, he reached him immediately. "Joe, Mac Smith, I need to talk to you."

"Now?" Riga said.

"Now, or in the morning."

"Let's make it tomorrow, Mac."

"As early as possible. Will you be in at eight?"

"Yeah, I'll be here."

"Sorry your party didn't work out, Tony," Smith said as he prepared to leave for home.

"Story of my life, Mac. Have a good night. I'll keep in touch from Frisco."

NINETEEN

"YOU WANT SOME tonsil varnish, Mac?" Joe Riga asked. Smith laughed and shook his head. It was apt slang for stationhouse coffee and, for a coffee snob like Mac Smith, it was even worse than that.

Riga fussed with paperwork on his desk before asking, "What can I do for you?"

"Tell me what's going on with the Andrea Feldman investigation."

Riga crumpled a piece of paper into a ball and tossed it over his shoulder. It missed the wastebasket. "Just plodding ahead, Mac. Lots of players, but no scorecard yet. Why do you ask? Your boy Ewald hasn't been charged with anything."

"True," said Smith, "but he's spending his days waiting for the proverbial second shoe to drop. Is he still your prime suspect?"

Riga smiled, exposing yellowed teeth. "Let's just say that we haven't crossed his name off the list."

"When can we expect the autopsy report?"

Riga took a sip of his coffee, made a face, and said, "*We?* You don't have any official connection. You don't even have a client."

"Not necessarily true, Joe. Yes, Paul Ewald has not been charged with the murder, but I'm on tap with the Ewald family. I just want to be ready in case you decide to send a couple of wee-hours visitors to his house again. Only for questioning, of course."

Riga threw a couple more spitballs at the wastebasket. "If I didn't know you better, Mac, I'd think you were ambulance chasing."

"Careful, Joe."

Riga's smile was big enough to assure Smith he was half kidding.

"What about the autopsy?" Smith repeated.

"Nothing's come down on it yet."

"Any preliminary findings?"

"Just scuttlebutt."

"Any determination whether she'd had sex that night?"

"Check Forensics."

"I will."

Riga leaned forward and said, "Look, Mac, let me level with you. All of us . . . me, the DA, a couple of others . . . wanted to break this case fast. We figured Paul Ewald did it, and we brought him in hoping he'd decide to make it easy for us, 'fess up. We figured with the circumstantial we had, plus the ID by the motel owner in Rosslyn, we could shake Mr. Ewald up enough to get a confession out of him."

"You could go to jail for that kind of police procedure," Smith said sternly.

"Why, because you claim I told you this? Come on, Mac, I'm being up front with you because we go back a ways, huh? We got a little pressure on us to solve this thing."

"I can imagine. You must have been disappointed when Paul Ewald didn't hand you a written, notarized confession when you knocked at his door in the middle of the night."

A grin from Riga. "Yeah, that would have been nice. Look, we took a shot and it didn't work, so we let him go. You came on strong with Kramer, and your client took a walk. Wanna know something, though, Mac?" Riga asked, leaning even more forward and staring at Smith.

"Life is a continuing education, Joe. Go ahead."

"I still think he did it. We've interviewed more than a hundred people so far, and when I line everybody up in my mind, I keep seeing Paul Ewald stepping forward, raising his hand, and saying, 'I did it!' "

"Not a very open-minded way to conduct a murder investigation," Smith said.

"That's for juries, Mac, not for cops. I go into an investigation with my mind closed against all the distractions, you know? My gut tells me who the major players are, and I keep the spotlight on them."

Smith went to the window and leaned against the sill. He'd come to Riga's office hoping to learn whether MPD's questioning of Secret Service agent Robert Jeroldson had revealed Ken Ewald's rendezvous with Roseanna Gateaux the night of the murder. He was reluctant to ask, but decided that if he didn't, he wouldn't learn anything. "A hundred people, you say. Everybody had an alibi except Paul Ewald?"

Riga shook his head.

"Any of the others people I might know?"

Riga nodded. "Yeah, Senator Ewald for one."

Smith raised his eyebrows and looked surprised. "Why do you say that?" he asked.

"Your senator buddy cut out of his office that night for a couple of hours."

"Oh?"

"Yeah, he and the Secret Service agent, Jeroldson, went to the Watergate Hotel."

"What did they do there?"

"Beats me, but it's on my list of questions the next time I talk to Ewald. Jeroldson says Ewald insisted they split up, and Ewald went into a room at the hotel."

"Whom did he see?" Smith asked.

"Damned if I know, but I will." Riga leaned back in his wooden swivel chair, bringing forth a loud groan from its metal tilting mechanism. "I got a feeling you're not leveling with me, Mac, and that means we're playing with two sets of rules here this morning. I showed you mine, now you show me yours."

Smith laughed and came to the desk, perched on the edge of it. "What is this, a game of doctor-nursey? Why do you want to know whom he saw that night? Maybe it was personal."

"I assume it was. Last I heard, Senator Ewald wasn't up for any Husband of the Year awards."

"Looking for gossip, Joe?"

"I got no use for gossip. What I got is a murder to solve."

"Is Senator Ewald high on your list of suspects?"

"He's part of the crowd. Anything else you want to discuss, Mac— the baseball season, Star Wars, spring fashions?"

"No, Joe, I just wanted to touch base with you. As I said, I'm on retainer to the Ewald family, and would like to avoid being blindsided. By the way, the motel owner in Rosslyn. He's a liar. Paul Ewald wasn't at that motel that night."

"I know that. Well, maybe he's not a liar, just a guy who likes to cooperate with the law to keep the law off his back. Besides, he's not what you'd call a prize witness for the prosecution. I don't think he could pass a driver's test eye exam."

As Smith went to the door, Riga asked, "How's the senator's campaign going?"

"All right, I guess. I'm not involved much in his political life."

"This kind of thing could hurt him, huh?"

"Depends on what you decide to do, Joe."

"What *I* decide to do?"

"Yes. Think of the awesome responsibility you have. Accuse anyone in the Ewald family of murder, and you potentially blow Ken Ewald's campaign for president away in smoke. You're a regular king-maker. Thanks for the time, Joe. I'm still looking forward to having that drink with you."

A long black limousine carrying Colonel Gilbert Morales, his aides, and bodyguards, passed through the Lincoln Tunnel and moved slowly in clogged Manhattan noontime traffic until it went past the front of the Waldorf, turned right at the corner, and stopped at the smaller entrance to the Waldorf Towers. The sidewalks had been barricaded by New York City police, and a cadre of uniformed officers lined the length of them. A group of onlookers strained to see who was arriving by limo.

"Who's that?" a man from Cleveland with a large video camera around his neck asked his wife.

"It's that Morales from Panama, the one fighting Communism there."

"Good thing we have Manning in the White House," the husband said gravely. "If that jerk Ewald becomes president, all Central America will go Commie."

Morales and his entourage were greeted in the small lobby of the Waldorf by a representative from a public-relations agency that had been retained to promote Morales's cause in the United States.

They all went up to a large and ornately furnished two-bedroom suite, where, after food and drinks had been delivered, they discussed Morales's scheduled appearance that night on Ted Koppel's *Nightline*.

When that discussion was concluded, one of Morales's aides and a bodyguard were assigned to escort the securely girdled, long-lashed Mrs. Morales for two hours of shopping. Everyone departed, leaving

Morales alone to go over answers he'd prepared to questions that Koppel was likely to ask.

A half hour later, the phone rang.

"*¿Sí?*"

"It is Miguel," the voice on the other end said. "I am downstairs."

"*Bueno.* Come up."

A few minutes later, Morales opened the door to admit a rapier-thin young Panamanian wearing an expensive, tightly tailored blue pinstripe suit. His silk tie was the exact color of the suit. His shirt was medium blue; the collar stood high above his jacket neck, and his cuffs were below its sleeves. He wore a plain gold wedding band; a thin gold chain dangled from his left wrist.

"Come in, come in, sit down," Morales said, continuing in Spanish.

Miguel went to a sideboard, where he poured himself a glass of tomato juice. He turned and looked at Morales, who had resumed his seat.

"Sit down," Morales repeated, gesturing to a chair next to him.

Miguel sat. Morales looked into his youthful face and smiled. "So young," he said.

There was no response from Miguel, who simply took a tiny sip of the juice and placed the glass on a table in front of them.

"So young to be so good at your craft," Morales said.

"Good *because* I am young," Miguel said in an evenly modulated voice.

"*Sí, sí,*" Morales said. "You are ready?"

Miguel narrowed his eyes and said, "I am always ready."

"*Bueno.* Then let us go over this again."

TWENTY

TONY BUFFOLINO retrieved his .22 revolver from Security at San Francisco International Airport. He was licensed to carry the weapon, and had checked it with airline security in New York before boarding the flight. Revolver securely nestled beneath his arm, he pulled the new suitcase he'd bought at a Watergate luggage shop from the baggage carousel and went out front to take the shuttle bus and pick up the Hertz Continental he'd reserved.

"Nice, nice," he said aloud as he settled behind the Lincoln's steering wheel and adjusted the seat and mirrors. He read over the printout he'd gotten from the Hertz direction-giving computer, and carefully studied a map of San Francisco, placing an "X" on Santiago Street, in the Sunset district. He'd intended to go to the hotel first, but changed his mind. He started the engine and headed for the "X" on the map, reaching it almost an hour later after a series of frustrating, obscenity-producing wrong turns.

The house he was looking for was nondescript, on a nondescript street, in a nondescript neighborhood. Still, there was a refreshing neatness and cleanliness to the area. The houses were all painted in pastels, as was most of the city; a shower of sun gave them a recently washed look. He parked across the street from number 21, got out of the Lincoln, spent a moment taking in more of his surroundings, then crossed to a two-family house; the numbers were 21A and 21B. The only number he'd been given by Mac Smith was 21—no letters. He took a chance on 21A and rang the bell. When there was no immediate response, he rang again, longer this time. Eventually, he heard an interior door open and close, and a female hand with chipped red nail polish pulled a flowered green curtain aside. Half her face was visible.

Buffolino flashed his biggest nonthreatening smile. The half-face continued to stare at him. "I need some help!" he yelled through the glass. The curtain returned to its original position, a key was turned, and the door opened as far as its chain would allow.

"Mrs. Feldman?"

"Next door." She had a deep booze-and-cigarette voice.

"Thank you," Buffolino said.

"She's not here."

"Do you expect her back soon?"

"No. She's gone away."

"Is that so? Has she gone away for good?"

"She still pays the rent."

"Then I suppose she'll be coming back," Buffolino said, annoyed at the crabbed conversation and the narrow opening through which it was being conducted.

"Are you a friend of Mrs. Feldman?" the low voice asked.

"Yeah, I am, from New York."

"I used to live in New York."

"Yeah?"

"Yes. Are you with a company?"

"Huh? No, I work by myself."

"An opera company."

"Opera company? No, ah . . . I dabble, if you know what I mean. Opera! Hey, are you an opera singer?" Before the low voice behind the door could answer, Buffolino said, "Opera is my chief love in life. What a coincidence. How about a cup a' coffee and some opera talk?"

She looked him up and down.

"I mean, just open the door and let's talk for a minute." The chain was released and the door opened, revealing a tall, full-bodied woman with dyed red hair and an imposing bosom that threatened the thin fabric of a pink housecoat.

"Anthony Buffolino," he said, extending his hand.

"A pleasure to meet you, Mr. Buffolino. I am Carla Zaretski."

"Pleased, I'm sure. Gee, I'm sorry I missed Mae. Any idea when she'll be back?"

Carla slowly shook her head. "She had family business to attend to."

"That so?"

"Yes. There has been a tragedy in her life."

Buffolino looked serious and said, "Andrea being murdered. I guess Mae had to make a lot of arrangements."

Carla placed her hands over her bosom and sighed. "A terrible thing to lose your only daughter. It devastated Mae, absolutely devastated her. Poor thing. Andrea was her only child . . . and such a good daughter. She visited often, always bringing things. And then *that* news. So tragic."

"Like opera," said Buffolino.

Carla glared at him.

"I mean, it's just that opera is always . . . tragic . . . the plot, I mean."

Carla's sudden flash of anger subsided as quickly as it had flared. "Great tragedy is what opera is made of."

"That's what I was saying. Where do you figure Mae went?"

"To New York."

"How come New York?"

"To find solace with her many friends. You say you are a friend?"

Buffolino shrugged and shifted from one foot to the other. "Actually, I was more a friend of Andrea's. We were . . . well, we were pretty close once."

The expression on Carla Zaretski's face was sheer horror. "Then you, too, have suffered a great loss. Were you there when . . . when it happened?"

Buffolino looked at the ground and slowly shook his head. "No, and that makes it even harder. If I had been, maybe I could have done something. I can't get that out of my mind, you know, always wondering if I could have done something to prevent it."

Carla, who was a few inches taller than Buffolino, looked down into his eyes and asked, "Would you like a drink?"

Buffolino gave her his best aren't-you-a-wonderful-person-for-thinking-of-it look, and broke into a smile. "That's very kind of you. Yes, I would enjoy a drink, but only if you'll join me." He had no doubt that she would.

A few minutes later, he stood in the middle of her modest living room, a glass of warm whiskey in his hand. The walls were filled with photographs, all of them featuring Carla Zaretski. A badly scratched recording of Mozart's *Marriage of Figaro* came from small, cheap speakers.

"Memories," Carla said from where she'd arranged herself on a chaise longue that bore the scratch marks of four cats that roamed the room.

"You were a star, huh?" Buffolino said.

"No, never a star, but I sat on the threshold of stardom. The voice is such a fickle slave. I lost my portamento prematurely."

Buffolino stared at her. "Jesus, I'm sorry to hear that. What'd you have, an accident?"

"Accident?" She started to laugh. "You are absolutely charming. Portamento, you know, is when the singer is no longer able to smoothly transverse the octaves."

Buffolino joined her laughter. "Yeah, right, *that* portamento." He quickly turned his attention to the photographs on the wall. "Who's this with you?"

"My dear friend and one of the world's great divas, Roseanna Gateaux. Surely you recognize her."

Buffolino had certainly heard of Gateaux, and remembered Mac Smith mentioning her as part of his blow-by-blow description of the events at the Kennedy Center the night Andrea Feldman was murdered. "Sure," he said, "but that picture must have been taken years ago."

"She is here now, singing Leonora in *Il Trovatore*. How sad Mae can't be present."

"Yeah, I know. Let's talk about that. Talking eases the pain sometimes."

An hour later, Buffolino decided it was time to leave. His hostess had lapsed into a nonstop recounting of her failed operatic career, which, the more she talked, Buffolino realized had never amounted to much except unrealistic dreams and empty, childish artistic pretensions. Still, he knew that Miss or Mrs. Zaretski represented the sort of direct link to Mae Feldman that he needed. Mac Smith had told him to find out everything he could about Andrea Feldman's mother. This was paydirt.

He told her he had to leave, but added, "I'll be staying in town a few days. How would you like to have dinner with me?"

"Dinner? On such short notice?" She fluffed her hair. "You mean tonight?"

"Let's make it tomorrow night," Buffolino said lightly. "Hey, you were some knockout. I can see from the pictures. You haven't lost much as far as I'm concerned."

She giggled like a schoolgirl.

"Come on, I don't know anything about San Francisco. Dinner's on me, and you show me the sights. Whattaya say?"

When she didn't immediately accept, he asked, "Are you going to see your friend Roseanna while she's here?" He knew the answer; Roseanna Gateaux was not her friend, and she probably didn't have enough money to buy a ticket. "I'd sure like to hear her sing," Buffolino said. "*Traviata.* That's one of my favorites. What do you say we go together?"

"*Trovatore,*" she said, but there was no hesitation now. They made a date for dinner the next night. She suggested he buy tickets to the opera, but he reached into his pocket and tossed a hundred dollars on the table. "You do it, pick some good seats. Is that enough?" She frowned. He tossed down another hundred. "Get the best."

"I will."

"Great, I'll be staying at a hotel called the Mandarin Oriental, down in the financial district. Maybe you could call me there tomorrow and we'll set it up."

She walked him to the door. "You are a very sensitive and kind man," she said.

"Well, I . . . hey, I'll level with you, I just happen to have taken a shine to you, you know? And opera, a chance to see Roseanna Gateaux. My lucky day."

TWENTY-ONE

THE LUNCH at the Four Seasons was pleasant, but turned out to be mission impossible. Annabel spent the lunch negotiating with a collector of pre-Colombian art for a sculpture of were-jaguar. The collector was a prissy little man who wouldn't budge on the price, which, Annabel knew, was far in excess of the piece's worth. They parted and agreed to keep in touch, although she decided the only way that would happen was if he called to announce he'd cut his price in half.

She had time to kill; the appointment she'd made with Herbert Greist wasn't until six. It was a lovely day in New York, sunny and mild but with enough nip in the air to remind you that summer wasn't here yet.

She decided to take a leisurely walk, and chose upper Fifth Avenue. Although she'd dismissed the notion that she'd been followed yesterday, the thought had come back to her a few times that morning, causing her to look behind in search of the same man. He was never there, and by the time she'd reached the Four Seasons, she'd put him out of her mind again.

Now, as she took her post-lunch stroll up Fifth and over to Madison to browse shop windows, she stopped to admire a good collection of antique jewelry in a small store. The light was such that Annabel could clearly see her reflection in the window, and she moved to avoid it to see the jewelry more clearly, and saw instead the reflection of a man across the street. It wasn't the same man as the day before, but he was dressed similarly in a tan raincoat, and seemed to be reading the pick-up times on a corner mailbox. She wouldn't have thought much of it except that she wondered how much information could be on the box to keep him engaged so long. Either the entire Constitution was pasted there, or he was illiterate.

She went to the corner and waited for the light to change, looking straight ahead but seeing in her peripheral vision that he'd crossed the street against the light and now lingered on the far corner. This time, he looked down at what appeared to be a map in his hands.

The light changed in her favor. She started to cross, quickly reversed herself, and walked east on the cross street, stopping halfway down the block in front of a restaurant. She looked inside. There was a bar by the window with one man sitting there. She entered and went to a bar stool that placed her in front of the window.

"Yes, ma'am?" the bartender asked.

Annabel, who had swiveled on the stool to look out the window, said without turning, "Club soda with lime, please."

She saw the tan raincoat pass on the opposite side of the street. He didn't seem to be looking for her; he'd probably seen her enter the restaurant. He never looked in her direction as he passed from her view. She paid for her drink, stood at the window, and looked up the street. He was gone.

She left the restaurant and scanned the block. No sign of him. He'd either decided to keep going, or had found a spot from which he could observe without being seen.

"Damn," she said as she retraced her steps to Fifth and continued uptown. She stopped occasionally to see if he'd fallen in behind her, but saw no more of him.

Greist had wanted to meet at his office again, but Reed insisted they meet in a public place. His office was just too stifling and tawdry. They agreed on the Oak Bar in her hotel.

When Greist arrived, Annabel sensed he'd already been drinking—nothing overt, just that tendency to reach for the floor with his feet rather than finding it naturally. He was also outwardly more pleasant, which, she assumed, went hand in hand with whatever he'd consumed. He joined her at the small corner table she occupied.

"Did you talk to Mr. Smith?" Greist asked after he'd been served a scotch and soda.

"Yes, I did. His attitude matches mine, Mr. Greist. Unless there is some specific indication of the nature of the information you wish to sell, and proof, we couldn't even begin to consider it."

He sat back and held his drink in both hands, staring into it as though seeking his next line from the quietly bubbling liquid. He said to the glass, "That's a shame."

Annabel's laugh was sardonic. "You wouldn't expect us to recommend to our client that he pay half a million dollars for something we haven't seen, would you?"

"Faith, Ms. Reed. There is no such thing anymore as faith and trust."

"There certainly isn't in this situation, and I think you're absurd to expect it."

A tired smile formed on his lips. "Ms. Reed, this is a treacherous world. Information can be its salvation, or its ultimate destruction."

The word "crackpot" crossed her mind. She had the feeling he was about to give a speech, something vaguely political and filled with clichés about the state of the world as he perceived it. She could do without that, did not want to waste time being on the receiving end of it. He slowly turned to her and said, "The information I offer your client, the honorable senator from California Kenneth Ewald, could change the course of events in this country, perhaps in the world, if it were to get into the wrong hands."

Annabel couldn't help but laugh. "Mr. Greist, you're not making any sense at all. I think we'd get a lot further if you would be specific instead of talking in grandiose terms about world change."

"You get what you pay for, Ms. Reed."

She asked, "How did your client come into possession of this so-called world-shaking information?"

"Irrelevant."

Should I say "overruled"? she wondered. "Maybe to you, but not to me or to Mackensie Smith. Is your client here in New York now?"

"Ms. Reed, I did not agree to meet you again to answer *your* questions."

"Fine," she said. "Then you'll just have to go ahead and file your suit on behalf of Mrs. Feldman for the loss of her daughter's civil liberties, and for her pain and suffering." She motioned for the check.

Although Greist had had a drink on top of what he'd earlier consumed, he seemed more sober than when he'd walked in. He stood and said through slack lips, "You and Mr. Smith are making a grave mistake, and obviously do not have your client's best interests at heart."

"I take it the drink is on me," Annabel said.

"I'm sure your wealthy client provides you with a large expense account. Good evening, Ms. Reed."

She watched him disappear into the lobby. Was this all one grand bluff on his part, a transparent shakedown, or was there even a modicum of truth behind his threat? The waitress brought the check; Annabel quickly laid more than enough money on top of it and went to the lobby. Greist was gone. She moved to the street and saw, far in the distance, a man across Fifth Avenue, beyond the fountain. It might have been Greist. She ran to the corner, crossed, slowing to a walk as she reached the figure. It was Greist. He was walking east, and didn't seem to be in any hurry.

She fell in behind him at what she considered a safe distance, thinking of the men that she now was convinced had followed her and vowing to do a better job than they had. While waiting for a light to change at the corner of Park Avenue and Fifty-first Street, she looked over her shoulder and wondered whether the follower was being followed.

Greist went south on Park Avenue, past the barricaded entrance to the Waldorf Astoria, and took a left on Forty-eighth Street. Reed kept pace with him until he turned into the main entrance of the Inter-Continental Hotel. She quickened her pace until she reached the entrance, checked to make sure he wasn't lingering inside the door, and entered. Her heart tripped; Greist had stopped by the massive bird cage that dominated the lavish lobby. He was six feet from her. She turned and bent over as though searching in her purse. When she thought enough time had passed, she looked in the direction of the cage. He was gone. She quickly scanned the large, two-level lobby. The raised portion to her left was half-filled with men and women enjoying cocktails while a tuxedoed pianist played show tunes.

Annabel used the bird cage as a screen and looked through it. Greist had joined someone at a table, a woman wearing a black raincoat whom Annabel judged to be in her early sixties, with gray-blond hair cut short. Annabel couldn't see her full face because of the angle at which the woman sat, and she had absolutely no reason to assume anything, but only one thought came to mind: Mae Feldman.

She lingered a few seconds more, couldn't hear or read lips, and concentrated on remembering everything she could about the woman. Then she went back out to Forty-eighth Street, keeping her back to where Greist and his companion sat, and made tracks for the Plaza and a chance to get on the telephone.

TWENTY-TWO

MAC SMITH drove slowly along Route 50 to Annapolis. He wasn't at all certain whether Janet Ewald would be there, could only hope that she would. He'd tried to call Marcia Mims at the Ewald house but was told it was her day off, which he already knew. Would she be there, too? Again, all he could do was speculate.

He wondered how Annabel's second meeting with Herbert Greist had gone. Maybe it was still in progress. That was the first call he would make once he'd finished in Annapolis.

This time, he found a parking space close to the building that housed the store and Tommy's apartment. He looked up at the windows and saw that there was a light on—a positive sign. He got out of the car, locked it, and walked slowly toward the door, realizing that without Marcia and her key, he had no way of entering. He searched for a buzzer but found none, and rapped on the one small window in the exterior door. There was no reply.

Baloney, he thought as he crossed the street and looked up at the windows again. The light was low-wattage. He waited for ten minutes for some sign of life, a shadow, the movement of someone across the room. Nothing.

He decided to leave his car where it was and walked to Tommy's. The restaurant was as busy as it had been the previous night. Tommy spotted Smith as he walked through the door, immediately came over to him, put his hand on his arm, and guided him back outside.

"Something wrong?" Smith asked.

"I think so," said Tommy. "Marcia told me you were coming back tonight. She seemed uncertain whether you'd meet her here at the restaurant or at my apartment, and she decided to wait for you here."

"Where is she?" Smith asked.

"I don't know. She had a drink at the bar just before the rush began.

I was busy with paperwork in my office. When I came out, she was gone."

"Where did she go, to the apartment?"

"No. My bartender told me she received a phone call. She hung up and left."

"You haven't heard from her since?"

"No."

"What about the apartment, Tommy? Is . . ." He wondered whether Tommy knew that Janet Ewald was being hidden there by Marcia. He decided it didn't make any difference whether he knew or not. "Do you know whether Janet Ewald is still in the apartment? I swung by there and saw a light, but no one answered."

Tommy shook his head. "Marcia told me why she needed the apartment, but I haven't heard any more about Ms. Ewald. I don't know whether she's still there or not."

"Look," said Smith, "will you give me a key to the apartment so I can let myself in?"

"Sure." He handed the key to Smith.

"Thanks. Be back soon."

Smith returned to the small building, let himself in downstairs, and knocked on the door to the apartment. There was no answer. He tried it; it swung open easily. The light he'd seen came from an overhead fixture in the small bathroom.

He stood in the middle of the room and turned in a circle, his eyes taking in everything. There was no sign that anyone had *ever* been there. Everything was neat; a small suitcase he'd noticed the previous night, and had assumed belonged to Janet, was gone.

Then he looked at a table near the door. A manila envelope rested on it. He picked up the envelope and read what was written on it: "Mr. Smith. Take this and keep it safe. Please do not open what is in this envelope unless something happens to me. Thank you. Marcia Mims."

He left the apartment, got into his car, turned on the overhead light, and opened the envelope. Inside was a book with a blue leather cover. Stamped on it in gold leaf was DIARY. He put it back in the envelope, slid the envelope beneath the front seat, and drove back to Tommy's Crab Cake House.

"Anyone there?" Tommy asked.

"No." He handed Tommy the key and thanked him. "I'd like to talk to the bartender."

"Sure."

Smith introduced himself to Tommy's bartender and asked if he had any idea who'd called Marcia.

"No idea at all. It was a woman."

"You answered the phone?"

"Yes."

"What did the woman say?"

The bartender laughed and shrugged. "Just asked me if Marcia Mims was here. I told her to wait a minute, put down the phone, and told Marcia she had a phone call."

"Did Marcia seem upset when she got off the phone?"

"I never noticed. She was gone in a flash, left most of her drink sitting on the bar."

Smith thanked the bartender and Tommy, and drove back to Washington. He put his car in the garage, took the envelope from beneath the seat, and sat in his recliner in the study, the envelope on his lap. The temptation to open it and begin reading was strong, but he decided he'd be stronger. He placed the envelope beneath papers in the bottom right drawer of his desk and hoped there would never be reason to read it.

Then he sat looking at the drawer.

S E N A T O R Kenneth Ewald was winding up a speech in the ballroom of the Willard Hotel to a five-hundred-dollar-a-plate dinner of party movers-and-shakers. Always handsome, he was even more so in his tuxedo. Leslie, dressed in a simple but elegant white dinner dress, sat at his side and looked up adoringly. There was an unmistakable renewal of energy in his face and voice as he said, "This is a particularly happy day for Leslie and me. Recently, we've had a tremendous personal tragedy enter our lives. A talented and decent young woman was murdered in cold blood, a young woman who served me and the things I stand for so admirably as a member of my staff. Then, as you all know, our only son, Paul, was taken in and questioned about that brutal murder. You can imagine what that did to us as parents. That situation naturally had to take center stage in our lives, disrupting my run for the Democratic nomination. Leslie and I seriously considered dropping out, putting public service on the shelf, and devoting all our energies to helping our son. Fortunately, that wasn't necessary. Paul was released almost immediately because the police realized he had nothing to do with the murder."

There was long and sustained applause. Ewald waited until it had subsided before holding up his hands and saying, "Life, as we all know, seldom goes the way we would like it to go. Wilson Mizner said that life's a tough proposition, and the first hundred years are the hardest." He looked at Leslie. "We've lived our first hundred years this past week, and now that this terrible cloud has been lifted from our lives, are ready to devote our second hundred to winning the nomination in July, the White House in November, and to restoring this nation to one of equity for all, prosperity for all, and a return to the sort of values that the Democratic party has always stood tall and proud for. Thank you so much, and God bless every one of you." Everyone in the ballroom stood. The applause, cheers, and whistles lasted many minutes. Ken took Leslie's hand and drew her up next to him. They waved to the crowd, a preview, many thought, of what the scene would be at the Democratic National Convention in San Francisco in July.

Mac Smith, who'd been watching the news on TV, called Annabel at the Plaza. She told him of her second meeting with Greist, and that she'd followed him.

"What the hell did you do that for? Who do you think you are, Jessica Fletcher?"

"It was a whim, an impetuous act. Our talk was unsatisfactory. I'm glad I did."

"Why?"

"He went into the Inter-Continental Hotel and had a drink with a woman."

"So?"

"I think it was Mae Feldman."

"How would you know that? Have you ever seen a picture of her?"

"No, but the woman he was sitting with is exactly the way I picture Mae Feldman. Don't ask me to explain, Mac, I just have this feeling."

"Did you see them leave?" Smith asked.

"No, I didn't want to take the chance of being seen by him, so I came back here to the hotel."

Smith fell silent.

"Mac?"

"What?"

"Are you still there?"

"Yes, sorry, my mind wandered for a moment. Look, Annabel, I think you ought to get back here as quickly as possible."

"I intend to, first thing in the morning."

Smith glanced at a pendulum wall clock. There were no more shuttles between New York and Washington that night. He said, "All right, but grab the first shuttle in the morning. I'll meet you at the Watergate suite. I have a temp secretary coming in."

"Fine. Have you heard from Tony?"

"No, but I haven't checked the machine at the Watergate. I'll do that after we're through. Annabel, don't take any chances. Stay in the room tonight, and keep the door locked."

"Do you think I'm in danger?"

"I'm sure you aren't, but I'm becoming an advocate of the better-safe-than-sorry school."

He told her about having met Janet Ewald, and what had happened when he went back for their second meeting.

"Where do you think she's gone now?"

"I have no idea. Frankly, I'm more concerned about Marcia Mims." He filled her in on that story.

"Have you tried to call her?" Reed asked.

"No. I won't tonight. She's still on her day off, but if I can't reach her first thing in the morning, I'll start worrying."

"Well, Mac, we obviously have some pieces to fit together tomorrow."

"Yes, I'd say that. Okay, my dear, get some sleep. Thanks for getting involved for me. I love you."

"I love you too, Mac. Oh, by the way, I think I've been followed ever since I got to New York. Two men."

"Jesus, Annabel, why didn't you tell me earlier?"

"Because I keep forgetting about it. It happens, and then my mind gets on to other things and I just forget."

"Describe them to me."

She did, stressing the fact that they looked somewhat alike, but beyond that were without any unusual characteristics as far as she could see.

"Just blend into the background, huh? Double-lock the door, Annabel. I'll see you in the morning."

He called the Watergate answering machine. There was a long message from Tony Buffolino: "You owe me a bonus, Mac, a big one. I'm going out to dinner tomorrow night and to the opera with this fruitcake, Carla Zaretski. Whatta they call it, 'Beyond the call of duty'? That's what's happening here. Anyway, this Mandarin Oriental Hotel is some classy joint. They even give me slippers and a robe. *Ciao!*"

ANNABEL Reed got into *her* robe and turned on the television news on ABC. There was a promo for the appearance of Colonel Gilbert Morales on *Nightline* that night; she decided she would stay up to watch it. Then there was coverage of the activities of both Democratic candidates. The first item concerned Jody Backus, who'd spent the day in North Dakota, kissing babies and eating fried chicken. He was his usual jovial public self, and Reed had to admit he had a potent, albeit rough-hewn charm.

Next came footage of the Ewalds following the speech Ken had made. They stood together in the lobby of the Willard, he resplendent in his tuxedo, she lovely and silent as she stood at his side. They'd stopped to answer impromptu questions from reporters. The camera zoomed close on Leslie's face. A tiny tear came from one eye as she said, "Of course we knew that our son didn't kill anyone."

What the camera didn't show was the slender young Panamanian in a blue suit who stood in a corner of the lobby, far from the Ewalds. There was no expression on his face, no sign of the intensity with which he watched the scene across the lobby. As Senator and Leslie Ewald, accompanied by Ed Farmer, other aides, and Secret Service agents left the knot of reporters and headed toward the door, they passed close to the man Miguel, who'd flown back from New York late that afternoon.

TWENTY-THREE

I NEVER SAW such a view in my whole life," Tony Buffolino told Carla as they sat at a window table in the Top of the Mark. Outside, a setting sun stained San Francisco gold. The city's fog had begun to roll in over the Bay as if a curtain call; the Golden Gate Bridge was being wrapped in it, adding to its compelling beauty.

"Such beauty is always better when shared," she said. She'd started speaking with an accent that hadn't been there the previous day.

Buffolino observed her closely. She'd obviously gone to great lengths to get ready for the evening. Her red hair had been curled and redyed; less black showed at the roots. Her nails had been done, and her makeup was heavy enough to border on the outlandish. Green eye shadow flecked with gold sparkles covered broad, swollen eyelids, and the weight of long black false lashes threatened to pull her eyes closed at any moment. Her lipstick was as crimson as her nails, and she'd created too large a mouth with it. Pendulous gold-plated earrings hung from the lobes of her ears to her broad shoulders, and multiple strands of costume jewelry ringed her neck. The aqua caftan she wore swept the floor as she made her entrance into the Top of the Mark. Buffolino had been embarrassed that he was the one she sought, but reminded himself that he'd better shed such feelings. It promised to be a long night.

She'd ordered a perfect Manhattan. He ordered a screwdriver. They sipped their drinks and made small talk about the splendor of San Francisco, theirs to admire through the window.

"You got the tickets?" Buffolino asked.

"Yes, and with great difficulty, I might add."

"How come?"

"Because this is San Francisco. We love our opera here. The performance has been sold out for months."

"How'd you get tickets then?" he asked, not really caring.

"Friends, sir. This lady has friends."

"I bet you do. Good thing, too."

She placed her thick hands on top of his and looked deep into his eyes. "Strange, isn't it, how one person's misfortune can benefit another?"

"Yeah?"

"Poor Mae. Poor Andrea. Lucky Carla."

She squeezed his hands hard, and he forced a smile. "I know what you mean," he said. Heavy, cheap, and very sweet perfume wafted across the table. He freed his hands, sat back in his chair, raised his drink to his lips, stared out the window, and pretended to be seduced into silence by the view. Actually, he was thinking about life's little ironies.

He'd been headed for certain juvenile delinquent status as a teenager. Born to poor parents in an even poorer section of Brooklyn, he hung around with a bunch of wise guys. By the time he was sixteen, he'd been arrested twice, once for car theft, the second time for assault on a black man who'd wandered by mistake into the neighborhood. Then along came Father Benternagel, Brooklyn's boxing priest, who told the judge he'd take responsibility for "this kid who thinks he's tough."

Buffolino became a good amateur boxer, and made it to the finals in the New York Golden Gloves, losing to a southpaw from the Bronx who threw right jabs so fast, and so often, that Buffolino never saw them coming. It didn't matter that he lost, however, because two years in the gym and the Gloves with Father Benternagel had given him a different perspective on life, and what he wanted from it.

He even thought about college, but knew that wasn't to be. While his friends drifted into various criminal pursuits, Tony went in the other direction. He applied for the New York City Police Department, didn't stand a chance because of his juvenile record, realized he wanted to be a cop more than anything else in the world, and checked into other cities whose requirements weren't as stringent, who had more openings on their force, and who might not scrutinize his teenage years with as keen an eye as the NYPD had. Washington was it. He took the tests, passed, and lived in a boarding house during his training at the D.C. Police Academy.

He loved it; he wore his uniform with peacock pride, and devoted countless off-duty hours to representing the department in community activities. He didn't labor under any delusions. He knew he would never rise to management ranks within the department, but his promotion to detective and his assignment to the special narcotics squad represented the cap of his career.

Then, of course, there developed the acute need for money, and the selling out to Garcia, the Panamanian drug dealer; the expulsion from the force; the disgrace; the embarrassment; the countless nights buying sleep with bottles of booze; the lack of self-worth he felt and, worse, assumed everyone else felt about him. How many years since that fateful night in the Watergate? How many years of hiring out as a night watchman at local companies? How many years of avoiding contact with his children from both marriages because he couldn't stand the look in their eyes, couldn't deal with the scorn they must feel for him.

In a sense, Mac Smith represented another Father Benternagel, another "priest." Buffolino had argued long and hard with Smith about the disposition of his case. Smith had said he could make a deal with the local prosecutor: no criminal charges if Buffolino would accept departmental punishment. "No deal," he told Smith a hundred times. Finally, Smith had thrown up his hands and told him to find another lawyer, which Buffolino intended to do. But he knew down deep that Smith was right, that he was lucky to escape a jail term. He left his dream with his head bowed, and his belief in himself, and in mankind, on a par with his belief in Santa Claus and the tooth fairy.

Now things had come full circle again, even if temporarily. He was living better than he'd ever lived before. A thousand a week. A suite in the Watergate, where, if he could keep his mouth shut, he could entertain his ex-wives and children in a style that had to make a statement to them—Tony Buffolino was somebody again. He was needed by one of the top legal minds in the land, and was being paid accordingly. He had new clothes (Smith had seen only one of three suits he'd bought in the fancy men's shop downstairs at the Watergate). The frozen dinners and cans to which he'd become so accustomed had been replaced by beef Wellington, crab cocktail, chocolate mousse, and caviar. The cheap whiskey with which he used to lull himself to sleep had been replaced by top-shelf bottles, although because he didn't want to appear too greedy, he'd settled for the Watergate's own brand of liquor instead of the Beefeater, Stolichnaya, etc., that headed the room-service menu.

Here he was in San Francisco, staying in a fantastic hotel, money in his pocket, the jewel of a city spread out before him. . . .

He looked at Carla Zaretski, who seemed about to cry. This time, *he* joined hands and asked, "Hey, babe, what's the matter? How come so sad?"

She answered with regal dignity, "One who has lost a promising career in the opera is not destined to be happy." That prompted a fifteen-minute encore of the story of her failed operatic career, most of it going back to high school musicals. If she ever did have a portamento, it was gone by her first year of college.

When she was finished, Buffolino said, "Well, I'm ready for dinner. Got any ideas?"

"Yes, I have given it considerable thought. A man of your taste would be satisfied with nothing less than the best."

Even though Buffolino knew it was a silly thing for her to say, it puffed him up a little. "It's your city, my dear," he said.

"And it shall be yours," she said, standing and slowly turning so that those at adjacent tables would see her. She led him through the room, down to the lobby, and into a cab.

Minutes later, they entered a restaurant on Montgomery Street that immediately reminded Buffolino of every movie he'd ever seen in which the action took place in a Barbary Coast bordello. It was called Ernie's. Carla had told him during the short cab ride that it represented San Francisco's finest dining experience. Buffolino had his doubts, based on his theory that as opulence increased, so did prices, with a corresponding decrease in portions.

They swept in and were led to a table in the smoking section to accommodate Carla. The table was set with silver and crystal. Surrounding them were walls covered with mahogany paneling, red silk tapestries, and huge, gilt-edged mirrors. Carla stayed with Manhattans and chain-smoked as they studied the elaborate menu.

"What's good here?" Buffolino asked.

She took his hands across the table, something she would do with repeated frequency throughout the evening. "Allow me to order for the both of us, dear man."

She outdid even Buffolino at the Watergate. They dined on an hors d'oeuvre of preserved black turnips under foie gras in a port wine sauce; sliced loin of lamb with breast of rabbit garnished with eggplant and roasted garlic cloves; a salad of chilled slices of Maine lobster and squab with black truffles and vinaigrette spiked with Dijon mustard and green herbs; and, for dessert, a frothy lime soufflé flavored with a dash of acacia honey. He had been in the mood for a hamburger and fries, but had to admit everything tasted good, if a little operatic.

Over coffee and cognac, Buffolino made another attempt to bring the conversation around. "What a shame Mae isn't here to enjoy dinner and the opera with us," he said.

Carla, who had begun to show the effects of the wine, clutched her bosom. "Oh, my God, how true. Poor darling, she's had so much trouble in her life."

"Yeah, that's what Andrea told me. Funny, I never could get Andrea to talk about her father. It was like he didn't exist."

Carla's face turned serious as she again touched his hands. "Oh, yes, that is exactly what happened. He doesn't exist."

Buffolino laughed. "Some miracle," he said. "Second time. Does the Church know about it yet?"

She shook her finger at him as though he were a naughty boy in school who'd used a four-letter word. "It wasn't funny."

"Sorry, I—"

"Not what you said, dear man, but the circumstances surrounding Andrea's birth."

"Do you go back that far with Mae Feldman?"

"Yes. We were friends in college."

"You were friends back then, but you don't know who Andrea's father was?"

Carla sadly shook her head. "No, Mae refused to tell anyone. They weren't married, you know, and she didn't want the poor fellow to suffer the embarrassment of fathering a child out of wedlock."

"What about *her* embarrassment?" Buffolino asked.

"Mae, embarrassed?" She laughed. "Mae was never embarrassed about anything. She proudly carried that child through nine months, three days without a whimper, and brought her up as though Andrea had been born into a normal family."

Buffolino shook his head and finished his espresso. "I still don't understand how you could go nine months and never know anything about the man who knocked up your best friend."

"Nothing strange about that, dear man. I told you, Mae did not want to identify him. Oh, I know she met him in New York. He was . . ."

"Was what?"

"Was a young law student, I believe, passionate and impetuous. Mae was such a beautiful young woman. They fell head-over-heels in love. Then, as such things will happen, passion bred pregnancy. What time is it?"

Buffolino checked his watch and told her.

"Good Lord, we'll be late for the overture. Quickly, dear, pay the bill."

Buffolino had eaten in some fancy restaurants in his life, especially lately, but nothing equaled this one. The tip alone was bigger than his previous month's food bill. He used his VISA card, grumbled as he signed the receipt, and nodded curtly at everyone as they left the restaurant, severing all diplomatic relations.

"The War Memorial Opera House," Carla told the young taxi driver, "and please be quick about it."

She snuggled next to Tony in the backseat. He put his arm around her shoulders because he didn't know what else to do. She cooed in his ear, "You are so handsome. Many women must have told you that."

"Well, yeah, one or two." He thought of his two ex-wives and the women he'd dated since his second divorce, not counting the one-night flings that came with the territory of a cop. He was glad when the driver pulled up in front of the opera house and he could disengage from Madame Zaretski.

They were ushered to their seats just as the lights dimmed, and the orchestra began the opening bars of *Il Trovatore*.

So, that's Roseanna Gateaux, Buffolino thought as scene two began with the diva performing the role of Leonora. Great-looking woman, he said silently as, to his surprise, he slowly lost himself in the powerful and poignant music of the soprano's first aria.

At intermission, Carla insisted on having drinks at a small bar in the lobby. "You sure you want another?" Buffolino asked.

"From my father, I inherited an enhanced capacity for spirits," she said imperiously.

They stood off to the side observing the crowd. Most of the men wore tuxedos, the women formal dresses, although there was a contingent in jeans. One group in a corner dominated everyone's attention, a dozen people who were obviously being shielded from the rest of the crowd. "Who's the hero?" Buffolino asked a security guard.

"That's Senator Witmer."

Buffolino turned to Carla. "You know who he is?"

"Yes, he's one of our senators from California." She stood on the toes of her purple satin heels to get a better look at the senator.

"Your other senator is Ewald, the one Andrea worked for."

"Yes, I know."

"Did Andrea ever talk about the campaign, about Ewald?"

"Not to me, although she probably did with her mother. Mae was very interested in politics."

"They say Andrea had an affair with Ewald's son."

"Filthy lies, garbage," she snapped. "Andrea was a sweet girl, not the type to sleep around."

"Yeah, well, that's what they say. The son admits it."

"A liar, too, like his father. Fetch me another drink," she said from her tiptoe perch.

"Fetch you . . . ? You've had enough. Come on, let's get back to our seats."

She came down off her toes. "You darling man," she said, "caring about my health."

"Huh?"

"You are absolutely right. The time for drinking is after the performance. We shall go to Tosca and extend this glorious night."

Buffolino followed dejectedly behind her as she reentered the auditorium and slowly walked down the aisle, her caftan gliding silently over the carpeting, her head held unnecessarily high, looking left and right, a queen entering her castle. Enough of you, lady, Buffolino thought as he held his head low, eyes to the floor, and slipped into his seat with a sigh of relief.

"It was great," he said when they left the opera house. A cab took them to Columbus in the North Beach section. The Tosca Cafe was crowded, noisy, and festive, and it took some deft maneuvering to get a place at the bar, where Carla ordered cappuccino laced with brandy for both of them. An ancient jukebox played familiar arias, and individuals burst into song in every corner of the room. Buffolino nursed two cappuccinos, while Carla downed hers as though they were soft drinks.

An hour later, the evening took its final toll. Carla leaned heavily on the bar with one elbow, put her arm around Buffolino's neck, pulled him close, and said with a thick tongue, "The time for us to exit has come."

Buffolino helped her outside and directed the driver to take them to the public garage in which he'd parked his rented Lincoln. Once in it, Carla immediately fell asleep, leaving Buffolino to find Santiago Street on his own. He had better luck than he anticipated, parked in front of her house, and helped her inside, tripping over cats before allowing her to sink with great flourish onto the tattered chaise. He looked down into her blotched and weary face, makeup askew, one eyelash partially off, and, oddly, felt a profound sadness. She'd fallen asleep again, her mouth an open, crooked chasm, a series of snorts and snores coming from it. He was pleased the evening had ended this way—that there was no need to continue it. He debated attempting to get her into the bedroom, but thought better of it. "Sleep it off here, baby," he whispered as he slowly went to the front door, cast a final glance back, and returned to his car.

He sat behind the wheel and contemplated what he'd managed to learn that evening. It wasn't much, but in one way it was more than he'd planned on.

Staring at the adjoining house that was Mae Feldman's home, Buffolino was gripped with an overwhelming urge. First, he analyzed the situation: Carla Zaretski was passed out next door and likely to stay that way for a while. It was late; a few houses on the block had interior lights on, but not the ones on either side. He looked up and down the street, saw no one, started the engine, drove around the block, and parked a dozen houses removed from number 21.

He sat quietly again with the lights off until he was satisfied that no one was paying attention to him, got out of the car, pressed the driver's door closed, and casually walked up the street until arriving at the door marked 21B. He cast a final glance to the right and left before going around to the rear of the house, where a small, unkempt yard served both sides of the dwelling. There were two first-floor rear windows on Mae Feldman's side. Buffolino chose the one to his right, the one furthest from where Carla Zaretski slept. He tried to look inside, but the window was covered by heavy drapes. He surveyed the glass for signs of a security-system tape, saw none, placed his fingers beneath the top sash bar, and pushed. Nothing. He almost laughed aloud for thinking he'd be lucky enough to find it unlocked.

Squatting, he ran his hand over the ground until his fingers came to rest on a small rock. He wrapped his handkerchief around it and gently tapped against one of the panes. The second time, he hit it a little harder. His third attempt succeeded. The glass shattered, shards of it falling at his feet, the stillness of the night magnifying for him the sounds of the glass hitting the ground. He gingerly reached inside, turned the simple window lock, raised the window as high as it would go, and pulled himself over the sill.

He stood in blackness and waited until his eyes adjusted. Soon the outline of a bed was visible in a shaft of moonlight slicing through where the drapes had parted. The last thing he wanted to do was to turn on a lamp, but it hadn't occurred to him to pack a flashlight to go to the opera. He closed the drapes as tightly as he could, found a small table lamp on a dresser, and turned the switch. Perfect, he thought; the three-way bulb put out minimal brightness at its lowest setting. Now, everything in the room was visible.

He opened the door to a small closet and peered inside. A few pieces of clothing hung from the rod, most of it male, including two men's suits. An assortment of shoes was on the floor. Again, the majority of them were men's.

Buffolino pulled a jacket from one of the hangers and held it up in front of him. "Must be a damn gorilla," he mumbled. He replaced the jacket, ran his hand along the empty shelf at the top of the closet, and closed the door.

He got on his knees and looked under the bed for boxes. Nothing there. He quickly went through the dresser drawers and discovered that, like the closet, they contained a mixture of clothing, mostly male.

He quietly opened a door and stepped into the living room. He was reluctant to turn on a light that would be visible from the front of the house, but he didn't have a choice. Drapes were drawn across the front picture window; that would help. He turned on a floor lamp in a corner and quickly surveyed the room, which presented him with nothing of immediate interest.

An archway led to a small foyer. Buffolino passed through it and opened a closet door. There was just enough light from the living room for him to see a metal chest about eighteen inches wide, a foot deep, and fifteen or sixteen inches high, with a handle on either end. He slid the box toward him, and was surprised at how heavy it was—some sort of fireproof metal container. He returned to the living room and placed the box on a chair beneath the lamp. The box was locked. He reached in his pants pocket for a small pocket knife and tried to jimmy the lock. No luck. He thought for a moment, then decided to take the box with him, find a way to open it in the car, check its contents, and, if all still looked peaceful, return it to the house.

He'd just switched off the lamp when he heard a noise outside the front door. He stiffened and cocked his head. Someone was inserting a key in the lock. Buffolino quickly positioned himself just inside the door, drew his .22, and waited, watched, as the lock was released and the doorknob turned.

A man, small in stature, stepped into the foyer. He held a revolver in his hand. Buffolino struck, the weight of his right hand and weapon coming down squarely on the back of the man's neck. The intruder fell to the floor, and Buffolino leaped on top of him, twisted the arm that held the revolver and brought it up sharply behind the man's back, causing the revolver to fall, and the intruder to shout in pain.

Buffolino never saw the second person come through the door, only felt the thud of a heavy object against the base of his skull. He pitched forward, semiconscious, his .22 sliding across the tile foyer floor. He desperately reached for it, but the second man drove his foot into his temple. A sudden burst of brilliant white pinpoints of light preceded blackness.

H E was out for only a few minutes. He sensed that, got to his hands and knees, blinked against the pain in his head, and was aware that his revolver was gone.

He pulled himself to his feet and made a quick decision to leave the way he'd entered, through the back, reasoning that whoever had attacked him didn't know he'd come through a broken window in the rear. He passed through the living room, saw that the metal box was no longer where he'd left it, and cursed every step that sent a spasm through his skull. He entered the bedroom and listened at the window. It occurred to him how lucky he was. Whoever they were, they were armed. They could have shot him instead of just roughing him up. Small blessings. "Count 'em, Tony," he muttered as he placed his left leg through the window. Once that foot was secure outside, he dragged his right leg behind him, the one whose injury had almost prematurely ended his career as a cop. He'd hit the floor in the foyer pretty hard, and that knee ached.

Now he was outside, maybe not with what he'd gone in for, but he was out—and alive—aching knee and head be damned.

He placed his hands on the windowsill, drew a deep breath, and slowly exhaled. It was when all the breath was out of him that he became aware of someone behind him. He slowly turned to see the moon's rays reflecting off the barrel of a shotgun. "Hey, wait a minute," he started to say as the face belonging to the shotgun came into focus. Carla Zaretski stood there, the gun shaking in her hand, her face the same weary, swollen mess it had been when he'd brought her home.

"Carla, it's me, I—"

The shotgun discharged with a roar, the pellets from the shell tearing into the flesh of his right thigh from just below his crotch to his knee. Her second blast, which resulted from an uncontrollable spasm in her fingers, missed him and sprayed the wall with pellets. The force of the first shot blew his right leg out from under him and spun him around. He fell against the house and slid down it, a broad crimson smear tracing his descent. His only words before passing out were, "Not the knee, not the goddamn knee . . ."

F I F T E E N minutes later, two uniformed policemen and two paramedics placed Tony Buffolino on a stretcher after taking emergency measures to stop the bleeding. Carla Zaretski sobbed between swallows of straight rye from a tall kitchen glass. "I heard noise and went into the backyard," she said for the tenth time. "I saw the broken window and called the police. I didn't know who it was."

"Will he make it?" one of the cops asked a kneeling medic.

"Yeah, but he's lost more blood than the four of us own. Come on, let's move."

"You have any idea why he'd break in like this?" one of the cops asked Carla. "You live next door, right?"

"Yes. No, I don't know. Maybe it was . . ." Had he been after her in a fit of passion? That question comforted her long after Buffolino had been taken away and the police had completed their questioning.

TWENTY-FOUR

MAC SMITH and Annabel Reed sat together on the terrace outside the Watergate suite. Coffee and Danish pastries were on a table between them. Directly in front and below was the Potomac; the John F. Kennedy Center for the Performing Arts was visible to their left.

They'd just started discussing their recent experiences when a ringing phone interrupted them. They both started to get up, but Smith was quicker. Annabel listened from the terrace, heard him say, "Yes, this is Smith. I'm sorry, your name is . . . ? Dr. Thelen, Max Thelen? Yes, I can hear you better now, Dr. Thelen. You're with Moffitt Hospital? Yes, I understand, part of the University of California Medical Center. What can I do for you, Doctor?"

Annabel entered the room as the expression on Smith's face changed from simple interest to shock.

"He's alive, you say. He *is* expected to survive."

Smith listened to the caller's answer and said, "Yes, yes, I'm relieved to hear that. Please, Dr. Thelen, one moment." He put his hand over the mouthpiece and said to Annabel, "Tony's been shot. He lost a lot of blood. It was his leg. He's okay." He returned to his conversation with the doctor. "Do you have any details on who shot him? I see. Yes. Well, thank you, Doctor, thank you very much."

"Who shot him?" Annabel asked when he hung up.

"The doctor wasn't certain about that. Let me make a call."

Smith reached Joe Riga at MPD, told him what had happened to Buffolino, and asked if he could get any information from the San Francisco police.

"Yeah, I'll make a call, Mac. I'll get back to you."

Riga called fifteen minutes later and told Smith that Buffolino had broken into a home owned by one Carla Zaretski, who'd shot him as an intruder.

"He broke into *her* house? He told me he was taking her out to dinner and to the opera."

"Mac, I'm telling you what I got from a detective I know in Frisco. Here's the number, if you want to find out more. Hey, don't be so shocked. Tony's elevator doesn't always reach the top. Likable, maybe, but a whack job."

Smith poised to argue the point but didn't.

Mac and Annabel returned to the terrace and sat quietly. She asked him what he intended to do next.

"Well, Annie, there are now two people missing, Janet Ewald *and* Marcia Mims. I'm going to make some calls concerning Marcia. I also want to stop in at MPD and . . ."

"And what?"

"I've got to go to San Francisco. Can you come with me?"

"Yes, of course."

"What about the gallery?"

"I've already been drawn into this by your magnetic and persuasive personality, Mr. Smith, and I may as well stay in for the duration. I'll spend time with James at the gallery this afternoon. When do you want to leave?"

"I'm tied up tomorrow. How about Saturday?"

"Fine. I'll book us a flight. By the way, one of the men who I think was following me in New York was on my shuttle yesterday."

Smith turned to her and said sternly, "And you tell me this as an afterthought? I wonder if I'll ever get anybody on my side to speak out fully. Did you get a better look at him?"

"Yes. No long, jagged scars on the cheek, no shaved head. Looked like all the other businessmen on the flight."

They rode down together in the elevator and stood outside the main entrance to the hotel. "Do you know what I think I'll do this afternoon?" he said.

"What?"

"I think what I need is exercise. I'll hit the gym later this afternoon. Dinner tonight?"

"Sure. In or out?"

"In. A quiet evening at home with Nick and Nora Charles."

. . .

Smith's attempts to reach Marcia Mims were unsuccessful. He called the Ewald house and was told that Marcia had called in and said she would be taking a couple of additional days off. "Do you know where she's gone?" Smith asked. No.

He called Marcia's cousin Tommy, in Annapolis, and asked the same question. Tommy hadn't heard from her since she left the bar so suddenly.

When he couldn't reach Joe Riga, either, Smith decided to act on his plan to get in some exercise that afternoon. He wasn't devoted to physical activity, had never become one of what a friend termed "health Nazis," suddenly allergic people who sniff out smokers in restaurants like bounty hunters, drink only a little white wine despite serious cravings for gin, and run marathon miles each day in pursuit of eternal youth while turning their knees into centenarian joints. But because he had been an athlete, and because he did enjoy the mental clarity that usually followed physical activity, he did his best to work some form of it into his routine.

He'd been a member of the Yates Field House at Georgetown University for years, and even though he'd joined the faculty at George Washington University and had access to facilities there, he preferred to stick with familiar surroundings. He changed into shorts and a T-shirt in the club's locker room, and began a slow trot around the indoor running track. He was the only person on the track when he started, but by the time he'd gone halfway around, a familiar face came through the door, waved, and caught up to him. It was Rhonda Harrison. "Hello, Mac," she said. "Burning off major-league dinners?"

Smith laughed. "Always a need to do that, but this has nothing to do with calories." They jogged next to each other. "This is for the mind today," he said. "I need to clear it out."

"Same here," Rhonda said. "I don't know where I'm going to find the time, but my agent just got me a good fee to do a piece for *Washingtonian* on Andrea Feldman."

Smith stopped running, and Rhonda halted a few feet ahead. She turned to him. "You look spooked, Mac."

"That name does tend to get my attention these days."

She leaned against a railing and wiped beads of perspiration from her forehead. "Yes, I guess it should. I was going to call you in a day or two. I have a list of dozens of people to interview, and you're high up on it."

Smith gave her a friendly smile.

"And, Mac, don't tell me that you can't talk to me because you're defense counsel for Paul Ewald. He's out, which means you don't have a client anymore."

"True."

"Let me ask you a question."

"Shoot."

"I'm slanting the article along the lines of a young, attractive woman with a law degree hooks up with some political heavy hitters in Washington, and gets herself killed as a result. Her mother immediately disappears, doesn't even come forward to claim the body. The son of a leading candidate for the White House is the prime suspect. This young woman, who meets an unfortunate end, is killed with a weapon belonging to this potential president of our country. Still, no one knows who killed Andrea Feldman."

Smith shrugged. "Sounds like an interesting human-interest piece. I'm sure you'll do your usual bang-up job."

"Funny choice of words. I intend to. I've talked to Feldman's associates. Not many of them, Mac. She defined 'loner.' No buddies, no steady boyfriends, no family. If it weren't for the Ewald family paying to bury her out in San Francisco, she'd be planted in the District cemetery along with the tombs of the unknown winos and druggies. How come?"

"I'm listening, Rhonda, you're talking. Keep going."

"Damn," Rhonda said, laughing. "The more I talk about it, the better it gets. Andrea Feldman sleeps with Senator Ewald's son. Do you figure she was carrying information about Ewald out to his enemies— you know, pillow talk from Paul?"

"I wouldn't know." He hoped she would have the answer. Knowing what a good reporter she was, Smith wondered whether she'd uncovered anything about Andrea's affair with not only Paul Ewald, but with his father, too. He thought she might mention that next, but she didn't. Instead, she asked, "Do you have any idea where to find Andrea Feldman's mother?"

"No, I don't."

"I checked the birth records at Moffitt Hospital in San Francisco where Andrea was born. No father-of-record. A real mystery woman. Her last known address is in the Sunset district. I talked to her landlady, a flaky former opera singer who told me the mother left."

"Didn't know where she went?"

"Not according to her. The whole family is shrouded in mystery."

"Evidently."

They continued to jog, but without words. A man and a woman sprinted past them. Smith realized how long it had been since he'd done any running. He was getting winded quicker than usual. As they approached the door, Rhonda punched him on the arm and said with a grin, "That's it for me. See you around the quad, Mac. Can I call you in a few days about this?"

"Sure. Happy to talk to you again, Rhonda." He watched her disappear through the doors, did another lap, and headed for the gymnasium, where he lifted weights, did a series of stretching exercises that he knew he should have done before he started running, showered, dressed, and returned home. There he changed into a gray sweatshirt from his university, baggy khaki pants and Docksiders, and took Rufus for a long walk through the neighborhood.

He walked back into the house and made himself a cup of coffee. As he sat at the table, Rufus looked up with soft, watery eyes. Smith looked down into the dog's trusting face and said to him, "Doesn't make any sense to you, either, huh? Well, think about it. We'll talk more tonight." He went to his study and made notes until he realized Annabel would be there for dinner. He ran to a local market and bought the ingredients—pâté, swordfish, salad makings, new potatoes, and French bread—and made whatever preparations he could before she arrived.

AFTER they had consumed and saluted Smith's culinary gestures, they made a gesture of another sort at each other.

Now, an hour later, they sat together in bed, naked, watching a documentary on television.

"We'll take a ten o'clock shuttle," she said. "The noon flight to San Francisco out of Kennedy on Saturday was the only one open."

"That sounds fine. We pick up three hours going in that direction anyway."

The commercials ended, and they watched the next section of the documentary. When it was again time to move into a commercial break, Ted Koppel's face came on the screen and he announced his guest for that evening's *Nightline.*

Annabel asked whether he had watched Colonel Gilbert Morales Tuesday on the Koppel show.

"Some," he said. "I really didn't focus on it."

"He mounts a convincing argument," Annabel said.

"In substance or in style?"

"A little of both."

"I think he and his cause are frauds. The Manning White House makes continual public proclamations of the drug epidemic in this country, but they keep wrapping their arms around Morales, who, everybody knows, was one of the leading drug pushers in Central America."

"He *was* an ally."

"Allies like that we don't need."

"You are such a liberal, which, I must admit, is part of your charm. An old liberal. Hubert Humphrey found old liberals to be sad. I don't. I ended up in love with one."

Smith laughed. "I probably should have taken up with an eighteen-year-old Georgetown hippie instead of a middle-aged, relatively conservative beauty. We could have protested together."

"And died prematurely in bed. Think of the embarrassment to family and friends. Besides, you're dating yourself. They're not called 'hippies' anymore."

"That's one thing I'm damned enthusiastic about with Ken's campaign," he said.

"Dying in bed with young girls?"

"No, wench. If he *does* become president, I think he'll take quick and decisive steps to cut off all aid to that fraud Morales, as well as that charlatan evangelist Garrett Kane, who claims he's set up ministries in Panama. Bull."

"We promised ourselves we would never discuss politics, remember?"

"Sure, and for good reason." He looked over at her beautiful breasts above the comforter that covered her legs, reached to touch a pink tip, and growled.

Rufus raised his head from the floor at the sound, then put it back down.

"Mac, what are you doing?"

"Something apolitical."

"Are you suggesting twice in one night?"

"As you say, Annabel, you're in love with a liberal. I can't think of anything more liberal . . ."

Her eyes widened, and a wicked smile crossed her mouth. "And I'm not nearly as conservative as you think I am when it comes to matters of the flesh. I just thought that—"

"That this *old* liberal isn't capable of repeating a triumph? Remember FDR."

"So long ago. But."

She kicked the covers off, moved her leg over to straddle him, and looked down into his eyes. "On second thought, no buts."

After a moment, she said, "My God, Smith—do you think a third term is out of the question?"

TWENTY-FIVE

EARLY Saturday morning, Smith took Rufus to the local kennel, where the Dane was enthusiastically welcomed. "Don't worry about Rufus, Mr. Smith," the owner said, "just view it as him taking a nice vacation at a fancy dog hotel." The owner always said that when Smith delivered Rufus, but Smith always responded as though he were hearing it for the first time; he was very appreciative of the good care his friend received there.

Heavy weather had hit the East Coast overnight, delaying flights in and out of Washington and New York. They made their American Airlines flight from JFK to San Francisco with only minutes to spare.

"Did you talk to Ken or Leslie?" Annabel asked after they'd settled in their first-class seats and had been served Bloody Marys.

"Yes. I talked to Leslie yesterday. She kept thanking me for all I did for Paul, and I kept reminding her I didn't do anything."

"Maybe you did more than you think."

"In the meantime, we have this business with Greist to iron out."

"Well, Mr. Geist is probably nothing but a bumbling con man looking for a fast buck. Funny, but I'm anxious to meet Tony. I can't say he's my favorite person, based on the stories you've told."

"He's all right. What I want to hear from him is why the hell he was breaking into this Carla Zaretski's house after he'd taken her to dinner and the opera. His message on my machine indicated that she was a real—"

" 'Dog'? Don't use that word, Mac."

"I wouldn't dream of it. She was not the sort of female that particularly appealed to him. Better?"

"Much."

"So, I wonder why he was breaking into her house. Something must have developed during the evening that turned her into the girl of his dreams."

Annabel giggled. "You think he was breaking in to rape her?"

"No, just anxious to continue communing on a philosophical level. We'll find out soon enough."

After the flight to San Francisco, they got into a cab driven by a portly gentleman in his sixties with a swooping walrus mustache, a tweed jacket, and an Irish tweed cap. When everyone was settled inside, he turned to them, but failed to ask the expected "Where to?" Instead, he said, "And what political persuasion might you two be?"

Annabel and Smith looked at each other and stifled laughter. Smith said, "A Roosevelt Democrat."

"And you?" the driver asked Annabel.

"A conservative who has whatever it takes to make Roosevelt Democrats happy."

TWENTY-SIX

As MAC SMITH and Annabel Reed were winging their way west, Senator Jody Backus was finishing a speech to a group of supporters in the Antrim Lodge in Roscoe, New York, a little more than two hours from New York City and known as the trout capital of the world.

"Great speech, Senator," an aide said as the corpulent candidate for president climbed down from a platform at the end of the large dining room. A hundred people had paid twenty-five dollars each to break bread with him at lunch and to hear him call for a return to decency, family values, and morality in the media. He'd been warmly received. The "morality in media" issue had only recently been injected into his otherwise-standard canned speech.

He'd ended with, "And I'll tell you one more thing. When I'm president of these United States, you'll see a president with a total commitment to the environment. They don't call Roscoe the trout capital of the world for nothin', and I'll see to it that these beautiful waters, and these big, fat trout, are around for years to come." The crowd had erupted in applause. Backus added, "As a matter of fact, as soon as we break this up, I'm headin' for Zach Filler's lodge, where I'm intendin' to spend the rest of this day and tomorrow morning haulin' 'em in."

The limo, followed by a string of cars in which press rode, turned onto the quiet little main street of Roscoe and stopped in front of a sporting goods store. "Be back in a minute," Backus said as he pulled himself out of the limo. "Got to see what the local folks are catchin' them on these days." He disappeared into the store followed by an aide and Secret Service agents.

The luncheon, like the fishing trip itself, had been decided on at the last minute by Backus. An old friend from Georgia, Zach Filler, owned a small fishing lodge in the area, and Backus's staff knew their boss needed such days. They just wished he'd plan ahead a little better.

Usually, his press aides were able to turn these sudden deviations into something positive. Ewald might seem to have the nomination wrapped up, but Backus's boys were going to take him into the convention with strength. There would have to be some dealing. The staff had managed to bring in enough upstate New York Democrats for the luncheon, and made plans to take photographs of Backus fishing, which they would release to fishing magazines and sports pages. "Fly fishing's hot these days," one of them said. "Might as well sell the old man to those fanatics, too." When they announced their plans to Backus, he dampened their assiduity by telling them this was to be pure relaxation, with only a few close advisers and a single Secret Service agent accompanying him. One of the aides mounted an argument. Backus snapped, "Damn it to hell, I am sick and tired of people and press and pressing the flesh! I need a day with the fish, just me and some big, fat ol' trout." And when a senior aide questioned whether they should run the change of schedule through Backus's campaign braintrust, he erupted. "I don't need to clear nothing through nobody, and it's time people around here got to understand that! Jody Backus is his own man."

Lodge owner Zach Filler was waiting when the limousine and two accompanying vehicles pulled up to the main house. Backus was shown to the largest cabin on the grounds. It contained two bedrooms; Agent Jeroldson was assigned to the second.

"You really threw me a curve, you rascal," Filler told Backus as the senator settled into a rocking chair and accepted a glass of bourbon from his friend. A roaring fire took the chill off the room. There were bottles of bourbon, buckets of ice, and a large tray with cheeses, breads, cold shrimp, and smoked salmon and trout. "I had to shift some good regular customers around to fit you and your people in."

"And I appreciate it, Zach. Hope it wasn't too much of an imposition. The fish bitin'?"

"Yes, they are, mostly on black ants and nymphs."

"Damn it, Zach, the fella in the store said they were risin' to mayflies and caddis. I bought myself a whole bunch a' nice flies tied by Walt and Winny Dette." The Dettes, who lived in Roscoe, were considered among the world's leading dry-fly-tying experts.

Filler laughed. "Beauty . . . and what catches fish are in the eye of the beholder. Don't worry, Jody, I'll take care of you. You'll catch yourself a fish." Filler closely observed his old friend. Obviously, running for president took its toll. Backus looked considerably older, more fatigued, and less healthy than he had the last time they'd been together, a year ago in Georgia. He asked, "How is it going, Jody?"

Backus scowled at him and drew on his drink. "Could be better, Zach."

Filler asked whether Jody wanted another drink. "Not right away, Zach. I got some heavy thinking to do, and I'd better get on the phone. You heard any news today about my opponent, Senator Ewald?"

Filler laughed. "Can't say that I have, but that's why I bought this place. The rest of the world doesn't exist up here, which suits me fine."

Backus grunted and yawned. "I may have a visitor in the morning, Zach, a special one. I'd just as soon keep that between us."

"Absolutely. You ready for a good dinner? I brought in a fine Indian cook for you. I let my regular one go last week. Son of a bitch was stealing me blind, not money, but food, which comes down to the same thing."

"I figure I can put off dinner for a while." Backus tapped his large stomach and grinned, which pleased Filler. It was the first demonstration since he'd arrived that his friend was relaxing. "Look, Zach, anybody calls for me, I'm not available, hear? The others'll take calls. I got to get as far away as possible from them."

"I can understand that, Jody," Filler said, laughing. "I only keep a phone here for city guests who can't seem to be out of contact with their businesses. Some of them spend more time on the phone than on the stream. Don't know what they catch—but they can have it."

Backus closed his eyes.

"Let me get back and see how dinner's shaping up," Filler said. "There's five of you?"

"Right. I appreciate this, Zach. I feel better already."

"Always glad to help a good friend, Jody. I'll be back."

Backus sat alone in the cabin, the flames of the fire casting a ruddy, healthy glow over his round face. He'd shed his coat, tie, and shoes, and felt himself sink into the rocking chair's well-worn cane seat. Then, as though he'd suddenly forgotten something, he looked in the direction of the room assigned to Jeroldson and shouted, "Bobby, come out here."

Jeroldson, who'd been reclining on the bed reading a copy of *Service Star*, the Secret Service's employee publication, got up and stood in the doorway.

"Come, sit, Bobby, and let's talk while we got the chance."

The dour agent took a straight-back chair near the fireplace.

"Help yourself," said Backus, gesturing toward the platter of food.

"I'm not hungry."

"Then have yourself a drink."

"Not on duty."

Backus started to laugh, but it turned into a sputter. "You are some strange breed, Bobby," he said. "Duty? The only duty you have right now is to relax and talk to me. Go on now, have a drink. You don't like bourbon? Go on up to the house and tell Zach what it is you do want—gin, beer, moose piss, whatever."

"I'll have bourbon." Jeroldson poured a small amount of it into a glass filled with ice cubes, popped a shrimp in his mouth, and returned to his chair.

"Well, now, Mr. Bobby Jeroldson, tell me how the senator and Mr. Farmer felt when you were transferred over to me last week."

Jeroldson shrugged. "They didn't say anything."

"Seems to me the senator from California would be pleased. I heard he wasn't especially fond a' you."

The comment brought a small smile to Jeroldson's wooden face.

"You want to say the feelin's mutual, don't you?"

A shrug.

"All I can say, Bobby, is that you've done a fine job keeping this ol' boy up to date on what my friend and colleague Senator Ewald has been up to. I'm sincerely appreciative. I figure you're smart enough to know that whether it's me in the White House, or Vice-President Thornton, you've got yourself a fat job up on top of the Uniformed Division. Be a nice spot for you, Bobby, about a thousand men under you, respect, make a real name for yourself." He was referring to the Secret Service's special uniformed unit charged with protecting the White House, embassies, consulates, and chanceries. Although it had been the subject of considerable criticism because of its use of extensive manpower and excessive money to patrol Washington's safest streets and best neighborhoods—while the MPD had to deal with the city's worst crime areas—it had been considered a political sacred cow ever since Richard Nixon established it in 1969.

"I didn't do much."

"More than maybe you know, Bobby. Is he still sleepin' around with that opera star, Gateaux?"

"Yes."

Backus laughed. "Wonder if she's as good at shatterin' glasses in bed as she is on the stage."

"I don't think much about things like that," Jeroldson said.

Backus yawned and scratched his sizable belly through a gap in his shirt. "You see, Bobby, although Senator Ewald and I are colleagues in the Senate, we never seem to see eye-to-eye on certain things that I feel this country vitally needs. People like Senator Ewald, even though they might think they're patriotic, seem to be hell-bent on selling this country out to the Commies and their friends. I won't mince words with you. Havin' Ken Ewald in the White House could mean the end of this beautiful democracy of ours, and you have made a fine contribution to preserving this country I know you love as much as I do."

"Thank you." He said it with a lack of expression that matched his face. Jeroldson's evaluation report at the completion of his training at the Federal Law Enforcement Training Center in Brunswick, Georgia—where Backus first met him—and at the Secret Service's own academy in Beltsville, Maryland, had noted, "Agent Jeroldson possesses all the physical and mental attributes to become a useful agent. He is, however, a young man with unbending ideals and principles, which, perhaps, will have to be tempered if he is to develop into an agent with growth potential."

"I figured now that we're smack dab in the middle of the end of this campaign, it was better for you to be with me. Now, all you have to do is keep an eye on this fat ol' Georgia boy and make sure some crackpot doesn't mistake me for a moose."

"I'll make sure that doesn't happen, Senator."

"Good, good. Best you take a walk now, go on up to the main house and read a magazine. I'll let you know when to come back. Nice country up here, isn't it?"

"Beautiful."

"A little chilly. Keep the fire goin'."

After Backus had dined with Zach Filler on fresh bass, vegetables, and corn bread, the two friends took a walk. Backus wore old, wrinkled Sears work pants, a nubby green sweater over the dress shirt he'd worn that day, and a heavy black-and-red wool jacket.

They crossed a bridge, went up a lonely road, and stopped on a bridge from which they could see the famed trout streams of Roscoe. The night was crystal clear, and chilly. The black sky above was blistered with millions of bright white stars.

"Good dinner, Zach," Backus said, staring out at the stream.

"Joey's a good cook, when he's sober."

"Sometimes it's better not to be sober, Zach. Sometimes it's better for a man to miss what's going on around him."

"You feel that way these days?"

"Sometimes. My daddy always told me that when things get too complicated, all you've got to do is to stand back, give it some room, and it'll all clear up. He was right, only he wasn't dealing with the problems of keeping this country free. That's a little more complicated. You see, Zach, sometimes a man has to do things that are personally distasteful to him. He has to do those things because there is somethin' a lot bigger at stake, and in this case, it's the future security of these United States."

Filler, too, gazed out over the stream, where light from an almost full moon caught the ripples and sent them dancing. He said, "I've never pried, Jody, not where I'm not wanted, and I won't start now, but you look like a man with the weight of the world on his shoulders. If I can help . . ."

"You already have, Zach. Comin' up here is what my daddy said to do when things get rough."

"Ewald?"

"Yup."

"I could never understand how anybody could consider him for president, especially compared to you."

Backus let out a gruff laugh. "That, my old friend, is a gross understatement, and I won't pretend modesty. I have to hand it to Mr. Ewald, though, I really thought this country was finished with his kind of politics, and that I wouldn't have a hell of a lot of trouble whuppin' him in the primaries. The man proved me wrong. I gave it my best shot, Zach, and now that the handwriting is pretty much up there on the wall, I . . ." He shook his head. "Even though I'm a Democrat, I truly question what this country will be like if he ends up our president. Of course, I've got to go around sayin' I'll back him if he wins." He slowly turned and looked at Filler, who had been staring at him. "That a bad thing for me to be thinkin' and sayin'?"

"Not to me, Jody, but you're not the only one faced with that dilemma. Think of voters like me, who truly care about this country and sure as hell don't want the likes of California Ken Ewald in the White House."

"You understand, then."

"Of course I do, but all I have to do is vote. I wouldn't be in your shoes."

"I don't want to be in my shoes, either."

Filler didn't have any words for a few moments. Then he asked, "Do you think you can somehow still win the nomination?"

Backus's grin was illuminated by the moon. "Well, things have been better lately, Zach, only you never know. I know one thing."

"What's that?"

"I know that it's either goin' to be me or Raymond Thornton in the White House. Either way, this country will sail an even course."

Filler looked at his large friend with admiration in his eyes. "This country was built by people like you, Jody, and thank God we still have your breed."

THE next morning, another limousine arrived at Filler's lodge. Two men wearing chest waders, bulging fishing vests, peaked hats, and large polarized sunglasses stepped from it and immediately got into a Voyager minivan that was waiting for them. The driver, Secret Service agent Jeroldson, left the parking lot and drove the new visitors, along with Jody Backus, to a point on the stream where it curved, and where a deep trout pool existed. Backus and his visitors went down a gentle bank and stepped with care into the fast-flowing water, using wading staffs for support. They'd said nothing from the moment the men got into the van. Now, after they cast their flies into the water and stood silently for several minutes, Backus said, "I think we might be goin' a little too far."

The older of the two men who'd arrived that morning said agreeably, "I think everything is going just fine, Jody. Perfect, you might say."

"I don't know, there's a point where—"

"If there's a *point*, Senator, it's that we could come close as a fly is to a tippet to losing this country, to losing democracy all over the world."

"I couldn't live with that," said Backus.

"You won't have to. God is all-giving."

"God? Seems like a few of us mortals have done a speck more, of late."

The older man made another cast. As the line snapped forward after looping behind him, the hook on the small fly caught in the fabric of his hat. He removed his hat and glasses, and worked to disengage the barb.

Zach Filler, who'd strolled down to the stream and watched the action on it from a distance, narrowed his eyes and focused on the older man as he attempted to remove the hook. Filler hadn't had any idea who Senator Backus's visitors were, nor did he care. Now, nonetheless, he knew. There was no mistaking him—the flowing silver hair, the handsome tanned face, the smile. He'd been on television too many times to not be recognized as America's most famous television evangelist.

TWENTY-SEVEN

D R. THELEN, I'm Mackensie Smith. This is Ms. Reed."

"Oh, yes, Mr. Smith, Ms. Reed. You didn't waste time getting here."

"No, Mr. Buffolino is—"

"He's told me how close you are. You're partners, I understand."

"Partners? Well, it's more a matter of . . ." He could see Annie grinning. "Yes, we're partners. How is he?"

"Doing very well, considering the amount of blood he lost. His right thigh looks like it went through a meat grinder, but I'd say the prognosis is good. He'll heal nicely, won't lose too much leg function."

" 'Lose leg function'?" Annabel said. "We didn't realize it was so serious."

"Let's just say he won't be winning any medals for the high hurdles, but he won't need a cane, either," Thelen said. "He's lucky. That previous injury to his right knee was very severe. If he'd been hit *there* again . . . No, no, I think he'll do just fine."

"Can we see him?" Annabel asked.

"Of course. He's still under sedation, but he's fairly alert, sitting up, as a matter of fact. The woman who shot him, a Ms. Zaretski, is with him."

"She is . . . *with* him?"

"Yes." The doctor winked. "Been here almost every minute since he was brought in. An obvious accident. She thought he was a burglar."

"So I heard," Smith said.

"She was an opera star," Thelen said.

"Really?" Smith said. "Maybe if she thought he was a burglar, she thought she was an opera star."

Thelen laughed. "No, she's actually had quite a career. She told me all about it."

"I'm sure she has. We won't stay long."

Tony was dozing in a chair when they entered his room. His leg was bandaged from hip to foot. A dying old man was in the other bed, his eyes fluttering, his frail body hooked up to a variety of high-tech medical equipment.

Carla Zaretski sat next to Tony, holding his hand. When she was aware of Smith and Annabel, she looked up. "You must be Mr. Smith." She said to Buffolino, "Tony, your partner is here."

Buffolino opened his eyes and focused on Smith's face. "Mac." He freed his hand from Carla's grasp and reached up to Smith, who gripped it firmly. "How's it going, Tony?"

"Not bad. At least it wasn't the goddamn knee."

"Hello," Annabel said as Tony shifted his eyes to her.

"Well, the famous Annabel Reed." He smiled. "He drag you out here? How do you put up with this guy?" he asked. He started to laugh, which sent him into a painful coughing spell. When he regained control, he introduced Carla to them, and they chatted about Tony's condition. Smith asked, "Would you mind if I had a few words alone with him?" He indicated to Annabel with his eyes that she should accompany Carla out of the room.

Smith sat in Carla's chair. "I'm glad you're going to be okay, Tony. You're lucky she didn't aim a few inches higher."

"Or lower. The knee means more to me these days."

"Why were you breaking into her house?"

"I wasn't. She owns the house, but it's a two-family place. Mae Feldman rents one side from her." He grimaced in pain.

"Are you all right?" Smith asked. "I'll get a nurse."

"No, it's okay. I figured I might as well take a look inside Feldman's place, so I came through a back window."

"And she caught you."

"No. She was in her place sleeping off too much hooch. I found this locked box in a closet in Feldman's foyer and was going to take it out to the car when two guys came through the front. I didn't know there were two of them. The second one nailed me."

"Recognize them?"

"No. The first one had a piece. He was a little guy."

"Little guy? Very little?"

"Not big. I didn't see either of them good, Mac. Anyway, I come to and go back out the rear window, only the queen wakes up when she hears me getting it, figures somebody's rippin' off next door, grabs a freakin' shotgun, and does me. She didn't know who I was till it was too late. She's okay, a pain in the butt, but okay. Drinks too much."

Smith said, "I'll bet. Did the little guy and his partner take the box?"

"Yeah. When I come to, it was gone." He sounded angry.

"That's all right, Tony. The only thing you should be thinking about is getting better." Smith could see that Buffolino was drowsy. He asked, "Anything else in Mae Feldman's apartment? See anything interesting besides the box?"

"No, she must have a guy lives with her. Either that or she's a dyke. Most of the clothes are men's clothes, cheap stuff, cut funny. Maybe she lives with King Kong."

"King Kong?"

"Yeah, the sleeves on the jacket I looked at were funny, long, hung down. Know what I mean?"

"Yes, I think so." Smith thought of the description of Herbert Greist Annabel had given him when she returned from New York. He asked, "Does your friend out there know where Mae is?"

"No. She said she goes away a lot. I guess she really took off this time."

Smith frowned. "Tony, does Carla know that the men who beat you up also took a box from Feldman's side of the house?"

"Ask her."

"No, I'm not sure I want to do that. You say there was a lot of men's clothing?"

"Right, suits, shirts, underwear, shoes."

Smith looked over at the dying old man and hoped *he* wouldn't end up that way, frail, alone, tied to machines. "Tony, I would love to get back into Mae Feldman's side of that house."

"Shouldn't be hard. Carla will let you in."

"She will?"

"I don't see why not."

"I'd rather get in there without her knowing about it. Any ideas?"

Buffolino closed his eyes and moved his tongue over his dry lips. He opened his eyes and looked at Carla's purse on the floor next to Smith's chair. "Take her keys," he said.

Smith had to smile. He was not anxious to be arrested in San Francisco for illegal entry. It wouldn't look good when he returned to teaching law at the university. Still, the temptation was strong. "Tony, do you think she'll hang around here for the rest of the day?"

"Probably. That's one favor I want from you. Get the queen off my back, huh?"

"I'll do my best, but I want a favor from you, too. Keep her here for three or four hours. Make nice with her."

"You ask a lot for a grand a week, Mac."

"I'll give you a bonus. For war wounds, and double-time for Carla."

"Okay. Hey, another favor for me. Call my wife—wives—and let 'em know what happened to me, only don't make it sound too bad. And don't tell 'em about the queen out there. Maybe you could say I got gunned down by some mafioso, something glamorous, and tell 'em I'm still on the case and that they don't have to worry about money. Okay?"

"Of course. It's true. You are still on the case, and you don't have to worry about money. Anything else I can do for you in return for this great sacrifice you've made on my behalf with the lady out there?"

"Get me back to Washington. This is a nice place, and the doctors are great, but it's too far away, Mac, too far away."

"I'll arrange it. George Washington University has an excellent hospital and staff."

There was no further need for words. Tony looked at the closed door, reached over, slipped his hand into Carla's purse, and came out with a set of keys. He handed them to Smith.

"Here. Now you didn't take 'em."

Smith said, "We'll have these back in a few hours. Remember, keep your opera-singing friend happy *and here.* I'll check in with you later."

When the women returned, Smith asked Carla, "Will you be staying with my partner a while?"

"Yes, I could never leave this dear man alone in such strange and threatening surroundings."

"You're a very good person, Ms. Zaretski." It suddenly dawned on Smith: She was more than attracted—Carla had fallen in love with Tony. Tony deserved an even bigger bonus than Smith had planned. He kept his smile to himself.

"Well, Ms. Reed and I have some business to attend to," he said. "We'll be back later today."

"A pleasure to meet both of you," Carla said.

"The feeling is entirely mutual, Ms. Zaretski," Smith said as he took Annabel's elbow and guided her out of the room.

Downstairs, Smith handed Annabel the keys from Carla Zaretski's purse.

"What are these?"

"The keys to Carla's house. I assume one of them fits the door to the side Mae Feldman lives in. I want you to go there, Annabel, and take a good look through Feldman's side."

"Mac, where did you get these?"

"Tony took them from her purse. He's going to make sure she stays here until you get back."

"Oh, Mac, I don't think that I should be . . ."

"You have to."

"Why do I have to?"

"Because you're a breed of woman who will do anything for the man she loves. Grab a cab, look around out there, get back here as soon as you can, go up to Tony's room, figure out a way to get Carla out of it, and he'll replace the keys in her purse. Nobody will know the difference."

"Why don't we go together?"

"Because I have other things to do. We'll meet up at the hotel."

"All right, Mac, but I want you to know that behind that distinguished, pleasant facade lurks your real self."

"Which is?"

"A devoted second-story man and con artist." She kissed his cheek and went outside to where a line of cabs waited.

At the end of the day, Smith went to their hotel, the Raphael on Union Square, and ordered up a bucket of ice, bottles of vodka and scotch, and two club sandwiches. He stripped off his clothes, took a hot shower, turned on the television, and poured himself a drink. He took a halfhearted bite from one of the sandwiches, turned down the TV's volume, and dialed the telephone. One of the staff answered; a few moments later, Ewald was on the line.

"This is Mac. I'm calling from San Francisco."

"What are you doing out there?"

"Running down some leads."

"Leads to what?"

"To what seems to be an evolving scenario that gets more tangled with every step."

"I don't understand. Paul is home. The charges have been dropped. What scenario are you talking about?"

"I'll be back in Washington tomorrow night. We have to talk Monday morning."

"About what?"

"Do you know a New York attorney named Herbert Greist?"

"Never heard of him."

"Well, you're about to. Ken, this is not for the phone. I only called to let you know that I think we should talk as soon as possible."

Ewald's sigh was audible. "All right, but my schedule is really getting jammed. The polls are looking up again—and I want to keep them that way. Is there something I should be especially concerned about?"

"We can explore that when we get together. Say hello to Leslie."

Annabel arrived an hour later. "How'd it go?" Smith asked.

"Better than it went for you, I think. Are you drunk?"

"Don't be ridiculous."

He refilled his glass as she kicked off her shoes, discarded her suit jacket, and flopped on the bed. He handed her a drink.

"Mac, did you get the impression at the hospital that Madame Zaretski has fallen for our Tony?"

Smith laughed. "I plan to be best man at the wedding. What did you find at Mae Feldman's house?"

"Not much. There's a lot of male clothing in the closets."

"Yes, Tony told me that."

"As I was looking around, I kept thinking of what you'd told me about Andrea Feldman's apartment in Washington, sparse, looking as though it weren't really lived in. Her mother's place is the same. It's so Spartan, very little personal around."

"Like mother, like daughter. Did you notice anything unusual about the male clothing, particularly the suits?"

"I didn't look very closely at them. I felt them. Cheap fabric."

"You didn't pull out a jacket and look at it?"

"No, why would I do that?"

"I'm not saying you should have, but Tony did."

"He did? Why?"

"Because he's been an investigator a long time, I suppose. Remember the description you gave me of Herbert Greist?"

"Of course."

"You said his arms were especially long, and that one arm was longer than the other."

"That's right."

"Funny, Tony said the jacket he examined in Mae Feldman's apartment looked like it would fit King Kong."

She laughed. "Are you saying . . . ?"

"I'm suggesting that it's possible that Herbert Greist at least uses Mae Feldman's closets for winter storage."

"Or had a relationship with her that was a little closer than that."

"Exactly."

Annabel went into the bathroom, whistling on her way. Smith sat in the chair and observed her looking into the mirror and correcting a fault with her eyebrow that only she could see. Strange, he thought, that she would react in such a cavalier manner to the possibility he'd just raised about Greist.

She returned to the main room and changed channels on the television.

"Annabel, did you hear what I said?"

She looked at him and opened her eyes wide. "Yes, I heard you."

"And?"

"I think you'll need more tangible proof that the suits in the closet belong to Herbert Greist."

"Of course I need more tangible evidence, but don't you think it's . . ."

She got up, came to him, and touched him lightly on the nose with her index finger. Her smile was playful. "Would you like more tangible evidence?"

"Wait a minute, what are you holding back from me?"

She pulled something from her purse and handed it to Smith. "This was buried beneath clothing in one of the drawers."

Smith looked down at a photo of a man he judged to be in his early twenties. "Who is this?" he asked.

"Herbert Greist."

"This is Greist? This is a young man."

"Mae Feldman was obviously a young woman when she had Andrea. Sure, Greist is a lot older now, but this is him, Mac, the young Herbert Greist, Communist sympathizer, blackmailer, Mae Feldman's lover, and, probably, the father of a dead daughter named Andrea Feldman."

Smith scrutinized the photograph more carefully, looked at Annabel, and said, "You're sure this is Greist?"

"Yes. Young, old, it's his face."

Annabel started to remove her clothing in the center of the room.

"Good job, Annie."

"As good an investigator as Tony?"

Smith sighed. "Yes."

"I only did it because I am the breed of woman who will do anything for the man she loves."

"Enough," Smith said. "You got the keys back in Carla's purse?"

She looked sternly at him. "Of course. I also follow orders very well. By the way, Tony hopes we'll arrange to get him out of here and back to Washington."

"I've already put that in motion. I made some calls after you left the hospital."

She was now naked. "You are a beautiful breed of woman, Annabel Reed."

"Thank you."

He stood and removed what little clothing he wore, crossed the room, and embraced her.

"Hard feelings seem to have suddenly developed between us," she said.

He said into her ear, "We can't have that, can we?"

They resolved it shortly thereafter.

TWENTY-EIGHT

SMITH AND ANNABEL flew back to Washington on Sunday. He called Ken Ewald first thing Monday morning.

"I'm on my way to St. Louis for a fund-raising luncheon," Ewald said.

"I told you it was necessary we talk as soon as I got back," Smith said. "What time is your flight?"

"Eleven," Ewald said.

"I'll meet you at the airport," Smith said. "Get there early."

Ewald agreed, without enthusiasm. The Clipper Club at ten. My enthusiasm for all this is waning, too, Mac Smith thought. Too many lies, evasions, unanswered questions. I still think I should help this man, he still seems to want my advice, but he's also always off and running. In class this morning, there are probably unanswered questions and evasions, too, but those I could handle. . . .

As Smith was about to leave, his phone rang. It was an attorney named James Shevlin, who'd been with the FBI and with whom Smith had had dealings when he was in active practice.

"Pleasant surprise, Jim," Smith said.

"Yes, Mac, it's been a while. How've you been?"

"Fine, just fine. Busy, but . . ."

"Yes, I imagine, based on what I read in the papers and hear on television."

Smith laughed. "Well, it's winding down. Look, Jim, I've got to run out to an important meeting. Hate to be impolite."

"Any chance of getting together this afternoon?"

"Sure."

"Two o'clock, my office?"

"Sounds good to me."

Shevlin had been with the Bureau for sixteen years. Then, unexpectedly, he had resigned to open a private law practice in Washington. His resignation didn't make sense to most people; he had only a few years to go to retirement, and by resigning had presumably tossed it out the window.

Those more intimately familiar with the workings of the FBI, however—including Mac Smith—knew that Shevlin hadn't lost a thing by resigning. Although such moves were never confirmed, those in the know counted Shevlin among other agents who'd been "allowed" to resign, their pensions paid through a separate fund, in return for their continued cooperation with the Bureau. There were lawyers scattered across the country functioning in that capacity, just as there were accountants, also former agents, who fed financial information to the Bureau on candidates for tax-evasion charges.

Ewald was waiting in the Clipper Club with Ed Farmer, a Secret Service agent, and two senior advisers when Smith came through the door. "Can we talk alone?" Smith asked Ewald.

The others walked away.

"Ken, I have questions I'd like to have answered."

"Such as?" Ewald said flatly.

"I mentioned to you on the phone an attorney from New York named Herbert Greist."

Ewald shrugged. "I told you I never heard of him."

"That doesn't matter. Greist claims to be representing Andrea Feldman's mother, Mae Feldman. He says her mother wants to bring an action against you and the family for the loss of her daughter's civil rights."

"Preposterous. Paul has never been charged."

"Yes, that's true, but there's more to this. The fact is that Greist really doesn't want to bring a suit at all. That was his initial approach, when he suggested we discuss an out-of-court settlement. I sent Annabel to New York to meet with him, and she got a very different story. To put it bluntly, he's in the process of trying to blackmail you through me. He wants a half-million dollars."

Smith expected Ewald's face to reflect confusion and surprise. That's not what he got. Instead, Ewald sat back in his chair and slowly shook his head.

"Any idea what information he might have that would prompt him into such action?"

Ewald sat forward again. "No, no idea whatsoever."

"Ken, has Roseanna Gateaux ever mentioned Herbert Greist?"

"Why do you ask that?"

"Has she?"

"No."

"Annabel and I went to San Francisco to follow up on this. Actually, my investigator, Tony Buffolino, went out there first, and ended up in the hospital. That's a long story, and I won't get into it now. While we were out there, I made contact with an old friend who's involved with the Embarcadero Opera Company. It's small and struggling, but good. According to my information on Greist, he spent time in San Francisco. While he was there, he functioned in some legal capacity for Embarcadero. At the same time, Roseanna Gateaux was doing a considerable amount of fund-raising for the company. It seems to me that there is every possibility that they might have met under those circumstances."

"So what?"

"Well, you have had an intimate relationship with Roseanna Gateaux, and as we all know, pillow talk sometimes leads us to reveal things we wouldn't reveal under other conditions."

Ewald laughed; it was forced. "Mac, what the hell do you think I did, give Roseanna state secrets, the technical plans for SDI, the names of CIA agents? This is silly."

"It may be, Ken, but I have an obligation to you to tell you everything I know about this. Greist is serious. At least that's the way Annabel and I read him. Let me take another tack. How much do you know about Andrea Feldman's background?"

"Mac, I . . ."

"This is important, Ken. What did you know about her background?"

Ewald thought for a moment. "Very little."

"Do you have any idea who her father was?"

"No. Are you suggesting that . . . ?"

Smith shook his head. "Ken, I am suggesting nothing except that Greist must have *something* that he feels is of sufficient interest to you that you would pay to have it returned or forgotten."

"I have no idea what this Greist character thinks he has to sell about me, and I don't care." He looked at his watch. "I have to go. I appreciate what you've been doing, but, frankly, Greist sounds like an opportunistic crackpot to me."

"That may be," Smith said, "but he's been involved over the years with various Communist causes. The FBI and CIA have long dossiers on him."

Ewald stood and extended his hand. "Thanks, Mac. I know you're looking out for my best interests. It's just that I don't see much significance to any of this."

Smith scrutinized Ewald's face. Somehow, as convincing as his words sounded, Smith had the feeling there was more going on in his mind than a simple dismissal of Greist and his threats. Ewald, uncomfortable with Smith's hard stare, leaned close and said, "Mac, Roseanna and I may have slept together, but I assure you, the only words exchanged between us were the sort heard in bed between lovers, hardly the stuff national security is made of. We made love, not war."

Smith said, "I'm sure that's true, but do you think there's a possibility that the very fact that you slept with Roseanna Gateaux is what Greist knows, and is willing to hush up for a price?"

That hadn't occurred to Ewald. His face sagged, and his tone was somber. "I hope not, Mac. It would devastate Leslie."

Ed Farmer waved from across the room. "We have to go, Senator." Ewald said, "Sometimes Ed is a pain, but he's efficient." He started to walk away, but Smith grabbed his arm. "Ken, before you go. Did you have an affair with Andrea Feldman, too?"

"What the hell have you been doing, peeping through my windows?"

"No need to. There have been enough other people willing to do that. What about it, Ken? Did she have access to sensitive materials through you?"

"No."

"You did have an affair with her?"

"No, I did not. My son took care of any sexual servicing of Ms. Feldman."

Smith decided to press. He quickly told him about Tony Buffolino's evening with Mae Feldman's friend and landlady, about his being shot, and about a box being taken from Mae Feldman's home.

Ewald could not suppress the frustration and anger he felt. "What the hell does that have to do with me?" he asked in too loud a voice.

"I was hoping you could answer that."

"A locked box? Maybe it contained her will and cemetery deed."

"I hope that's all it contained. Look, Ken, I know you're busy, but everything I've laid out for you here could have ramifications for your candidacy, and you know it. I suggest you not dismiss it out-of-hand."

"Is that legal advice?"

"No, that's advice from a friend who cares about whether you make it to the White House."

A sadness came over Ewald's face. "I'm sorry, Mac. I guess I'm just on edge these days. Let's talk again when I get back."

"When will that be?"

"Tonight. I'll call you."

Smith watched Ewald join the group and start to leave the club, and was suddenly compelled to tell Ewald that he'd seen Janet. He caught up with them and said, "Ken, sorry, just one more private moment, please."

They moved to the side of the corridor. "I've seen Janet," Smith said.

"You did? When?"

"A few nights ago. She's disappeared again. She'd promised to meet me a second time, but she didn't show up. She says she's too frightened to come back."

Ewald guffawed.

"I just thought you ought to know. Safe trip."

SMITH showed up promptly at two o'clock at Jim Shevlin's law office. "How's your caseload?" Smith asked once they'd been seated and Shevlin had poured them coffee.

"Could be busier, but then I'd have to expand." Shevlin smiled. "I like being a one-man operation."

Smith smiled, too. When your major client—maybe the only one—was the FBI, you couldn't be anything *but* a one-man operation, unless your client sent you a cleared partner.

"So, what prompts you to invite me here?" Smith asked.

Shevlin lowered his voice and said, "Mac, what do you know about an attorney in New York named Herbert Greist?"

Smith told Shevlin what he'd learned from his friend in New York, Morgan Tubbs. Shevlin listened quietly, and the expression on his face led Smith to believe that Shevlin already knew everything he was saying. When he was done delivering his thumbnail on Greist, he asked, "What's your interest in him?"

Shevlin removed his glasses, rubbed his eyes, and placed the glasses back on his nose. "Mac, a more important question is, what's *your* interest in Herbert Greist?"

"Why do you assume I have any?"

Shevlin's voice lowered even more. "Mac, I really appreciate your coming here. I don't know whether you're aware that I maintain friendly ties with my former employer, have a few occasional contacts."

Nice understatement, Smith thought.

"Sometimes, when an important issue comes up, they'll ask me to do them a favor. It doesn't happen often, but I usually try to oblige."

I'm sure I would, too, under the circumstances, thought Smith. Did Shevlin realize that Smith knew that what he was saying was false, a boilerplate speech he'd probably made hundreds of times since leaving the Bureau and setting himself up as an unofficial link to that organization? Smith raised his eyebrows as though he were hearing something for the first time.

Shevlin hesitated, as though deciding whether to continue. Smith had no doubt that he would. He did. "This attorney, Greist, has had a long history of links with Soviet sympathizers, but then you already know that, according to what you just told me about him."

"Yes, I understand your former employer and the Central Intelligence Agency have been keeping tabs on him for some time."

"Exactly. Are you still the opera lover you were when you were in practice?"

"Yes. Why?"

"Well, I thought you might have run into Greist somewhere along the line. He was plugged into the opera crowd."

"Really?" Smith was glad he'd come; ideally, he would learn more than he'd be asked to give.

"Greist was involved with a group out in San Francisco called the Embarcadero Opera Company. My information is that he was general counsel to that group. Undoubtedly a fancied-up title."

"Undoubtedly. Jim, I don't know Greist personally, have never met him. I had occasion to check into his background concerning a threatened legal action but . . ."

"Mac, my contact at the Bureau, with whom I occasionally touch base, asked me how well I knew you. I told him we'd always had a friendly relationship. Right?"

"Right."

"So, my contact—"

"With whom you have only occasional contact."

Shevlin's smile started small, and ended up bursting across his face. "Yes, my contact felt that you might help us learn a little more about Mr. Greist."

"Help *us*?"

"Slip of the tongue. Help *them*."

"I have a feeling that my associate, Annabel Reed, and I have not been skipping through life these days unnoticed. Fair statement?"

A shrug.

"Annabel was recently in New York and noticed a few nondescript gentlemen exhibiting interest in her on the street. Now, I recognize that she is an extremely beautiful woman, and thousands of men have undoubtedly cast their eyes in her direction on many streets. But this was different. Have we been followed?"

"How would I know? I'm just a lawyer."

"And I'm just a college professor. Have I . . . have we been followed?"

"I think it's probably safe to assume that."

"And because my associate, this beautiful woman, made a visit to the law office of the distinguished Herbert Greist, these people with whom you have occasional contact were naturally interested."

"Sounds that way, doesn't it?"

"Why are you interested in whether Greist has a connection with opera?"

"I'm not. My friends are."

"Why don't your *friends* simply go talk to Greist?"

"They'd like to. In fact, they intended to do that yesterday, but they can't find him."

Another missing person, Smith thought. He said, "Annabel was with him last week."

"A week is a long time. Evidently, Mr. Greist has decided to abandon his law office on the West Side and to maintain an even lower profile. By the way, Mac, as long as we're having this friendly chat, can I toss another question at you?"

"I suppose so."

"You're pretty tight with the Ewald family, aren't you?"

"Yes, as everyone knows. We go back a long way."

"I really enjoyed that show put on for Senator Ewald the other night. Tragic what happened after it, the death of that young woman. I was very upset to hear it."

"You and a lot of other people."

"I admire many things about Senator Ewald, including the fact that he's a jazz lover. I am, too, you know."

"I wasn't aware of that."

"Oh, yes, I have an extensive record collection. One of the things I found interesting about the show was that all kinds of music were represented. Probably a good indication of Ewald's determination to appeal to a wide variety of voters. I assume you enjoyed Roseanna Gateaux, loving opera as you do."

Smith started to confirm that he had enjoyed the performance when it dawned on him that this portion of the conversation had nothing to do with the Kennedy Center gala for Ken Ewald. He decided to be direct. "Why are you mentioning Roseanna Gateaux? Do your *friends* have an interest in her, too?"

Shevlin laughed and stood. "No, of course not. Somebody brought up her name at lunch the other day."

"In what context?"

"I don't remember. Forget it. I don't even know why I asked. Thanks for dropping by, Mac, and please give my best to that beautiful woman who turns heads on city streets."

"I certainly will, and tell your *friends* they ought to go back to Surveillance 101."

TWENTY-NINE

SMITH MADE himself a drink when he got home, and spread leftover country pâté on stone crackers. He sat in his recliner and stared at his desk. Should he? He'd always prided himself on upholding agreements. A deal was a deal was a deal. No one had ever been burned by confiding in Mac Smith.

But he decided that this might be the time to violate his principles. Marcia Mims may have wanted him to open the diary only if something happened to her, but maybe something was happening to her and what was in it would preclude that *something* from a sad result. A weak rationalization, perhaps, but it would do.

He took the envelope from the desk drawer and returned to his chair. It wasn't one of those diaries with a lock, but he had trouble opening it—not because of any physical problem, but because of the guilt he felt. Guilt? He silently reprimanded himself for assigning something as decent as guilt to what he was about to do. He knew why his fingers fumbled: What kept him from immediately opening the diary was fear at what he might find.

Two hours later, he'd finished skimming the diary's pages. The phone hadn't rung once. Now, as he closed the cover, a succession of calls came.

The first was from Annabel. She was at the gallery, and wondered how his day had gone.

"Damned interesting. I caught up with Ken at the airport, and spent an hour with Jim Shevlin, ex—or almost-ex—FBI. And I've been sitting here for the past two hours reading a remarkable document."

"What document?"

"One I would like very much to share with you, but not over a telephone. Were you planning to come here tonight?"

"Sure, unless you want to go out for dinner."

"No, I think I'd rather stay here. Spend the night. I think we're in for a good long evening of reading and discussion."

"Fine. I'll swing by home and pack my bag. What's for dinner?"

"You. That's the main course. As for the rest, your choice. Bring something from the American Cafe."

He'd no sooner hung up when Rhonda Harrison called. She said she'd just left WRC and was calling from a booth. "Are you alone, Mac?"

"For the moment. Annabel is coming over."

"I really need to speak with you."

"About your article on Andrea Feldman?"

"Yes, but it won't be one-way. I have something you might be interested in."

Should be quite an evening, he thought. "Sure, come over any time. Annabel is bringing in dinner. I'll call and suggest she bring a third dish."

"No need for that, Mac."

"Time the two of you met anyway. I've been talking about you to her for years. She's bringing in from the American Cafe. Any favorites?"

"Oh, anything will do. Make it chicken tarragon with almonds on a croissant. I'll be there in an hour."

Another call, this one from Tony, still in his hospital room in San Francisco.

"Tony, how are you? How's the leg?"

"Good, Mac, yeah, really good. Feeling better every minute. I can't wait to get on that plane tomorrow."

"It will be good to see you. I've arranged for a car to meet your flight. Look for it. The driver will hold up a sign with your name on it."

"Make sure he spells it right, with an *o* instead of an *a.*"

"I'll do my best."

"Mac, I came up with something interesting out here."

"From the hospital?"

"Yeah, it's boring here. The old guy next to me died, and they haven't brought me a new roommate yet. I've been waiting for some dynamite chick to be brought in who's just had her tubes tied, but no luck so far. Mac, I got hold of that friend I mentioned at Wells Fargo Bank."

"And?"

"The old lady—Mae Feldman—did pretty good."

"You found her account?"

"Yeah, but it wasn't easy. My friend is in charge of a lot of accounts, including Mrs. Feldman's. What made it tough was that the account isn't just under her name."

"Whose name is it under?"

"My buddy."

"Which buddy?"

"Carla. Carla Zaretski. My friend, who shall remain nameless so that he doesn't end up a *former* Wells Fargo employee, told me that the account was opened a little more than a year ago, and that the deposits into it were pretty regular."

"If it's in Carla's name, how did Mae Feldman get to use it?"

"Because she's one of the signatures on the account. It was kind of a joint thing. But now it's cleaned out."

"How much was in it?"

"Two hundred thou."

Smith grunted. "Any connection between the account and Mae's daughter, Andrea?"

"I wouldn't know. At least, my friend didn't say anything."

"And you say the account was cleaned out?"

"Yup."

"Who did the cleaning, Carla Zaretski or Mae Feldman?"

"Ms. Zaretski. She took every cent out in cash."

"Cash. That's a lot of money to be carrying around. Have you seen her lately?"

"No, and that's kind of funny. She's been hanging around here like she was my mother. The nurses were ready to strangle her. A real pain in the ass. Then, yesterday, she says she has to run an errand and that's the last I see or hear from her."

Smith looked down at the blue diary in his lap. "Good job, Tony. I want you to do nothing now but concentrate on getting back here tomorrow. Forget about this case until you're settled here and we can talk. There's a lot happening on this end that I'll fill you in on."

"Great. Did you call my wives?"

"Damn it, no, I forgot. I'll do that right now. Give me their numbers."

After Buffolino got off the line, Smith tried both numbers, reached the second wife, Barbara, and told her Tony had been shot but was recovering nicely. She was sincerely upset and asked if there was anything she could do.

"No, I don't think so. I understand you and Tony and the kids were to have a party at the Watergate suite."

She sounded embarrassed. "Yes, but Tony and I had a fight and . . ."

"Don't bother to explain. All I want to say is that once Tony has recovered, we'll all have a party at that suite to celebrate."

"That's . . . that's a wonderful idea, Mr. Smith. Tony told me what a fine man you are and—"

Embarrassed himself, Smith mumbled something about having to take another call and got off the phone.

Now he had a decision to make. Should he show Marcia Mims's diary to Rhonda Harrison? It would only be fair, he told himself. She'd been open with him, and obviously was coming to the house that night to share even more information. Had the diary dealt only with Marcia and her family and the Ewald family, he wouldn't have considered it, but there were many provocative entries concerning Andrea Feldman, the subject of Rhonda's article for *Washingtonian*.

He was still grappling with that decision when his doorbell rang. He slid the diary into the middle drawer of his desk and greeted Rhonda at the door.

"Oh, my God," she said as Rufus stood on his hind legs, which put his head above hers.

"Get down, Rufus," Smith barked. "She's a beauty but not your type." The Dane reluctantly obeyed his master, but every muscle in his huge, powerful body twitched with the desire to continue greeting this new visitor.

"Come in, Rhonda, and make yourself comfortable. Annabel should be here soon."

"What a lovely house," Rhonda said as they moved through it.

"Yes, it's very comfortable, especially for one person, and it puts me within walking distance of the university, Kennedy Center, and the Foggy Bottom Cafe. Drink?"

"Sure. White wine?"

"You've got it."

Smith joined her with the drink he'd previously made for himself. "Well, you sounded as though you had some exciting revelations," he said.

"Yes, I might have, Mac. Do you remember a year or so ago when *Washingtonian* did an exposé on that San Diego–based group, the Democratic Action Front?"

"No, I don't think so, although I have heard of it. Holds itself out as a staunch anti-Communist organization, if I'm not mistaken."

"Yes, that's the one. The writer who did that investigation was Kyle Morris. He was from California and had wormed his way into DAF. He did a hell of a good investigative job, linked a lot of DAF's activities right back here to Washington, which was why the magazine commissioned the piece." She looked at him for a reaction. He didn't give her one. She continued, "Not long after the article was published, Kyle died."

"A young man?"

"Yes. The official report was that he was drunk and ran his car into a tree in California."

"Drinking and driving never did mix," Smith said, fighting off a fleeting, terrible image of the night his wife and son died on the Beltway.

"If you believe he'd been drinking."

"You don't?"

"They said so—but Kyle didn't drink. Besides, it struck more than a few people as strange that right after he does this exposé on DAF, he dies, like all those people who had something to say about the Kennedy assassination and ended up falling out of hotel windows or drowning."

"All right, let's say that this young man, Morris, paid the ultimate price for exposing the group. I'm sad to hear it. But why would that necessarily interest me?"

Rhonda sat back, sipped her wine, and smacked her lips. The look of a contented cat was painted on her pretty face. Her audience was now hanging on every word, and she seemed to be reveling in that moment of undivided attention.

Smith said, "I'm all ears, Rhonda."

She leaned forward. The smile was gone, and her eyes formed narrow slits. "Mac, Andrea Feldman was paid a lot of money by DAF."

Now it was Smith's turn to lean forward and to narrow his eyes. "By DAF? Andrea Feldman supposedly was a champion of liberal causes," he said. "That's why she went to work for Ken Ewald. Why would she be taking money from a right-wing organization?"

They sat silently and looked at each other. If their thoughts were printed out on paper, they would have read almost identically.

"She was being paid to spy on Ewald," he said.

"Has to be, right?"

"Not that it's set in stone, but it makes sense. The DAF organization supports the current administration."

"Sure. They've also contributed—undoubtedly under the table—to various campaigns of Senator Jody Backus, whose political persuasions have never been out of sync with theirs."

"I just learned from Tony Buffolino, my investigator, that Andrea Feldman's mother had a sizable account that was recently cleaned out."

Rhonda asked, "Did he come up with any evidence that the money came from the Democratic Action Front, and was paid to Andrea Feldman?"

"He didn't mention anything about that. No, in fact, I asked whether he knew the source of the money and he said he didn't. How did you come up with it?"

"I got pretty friendly with Kyle Morris when he was working on the piece. He shared a lot of things with me, especially the information he never used because he couldn't prove it to the point of satisfying his editors that they wouldn't be hit with a nasty libel suit."

Smith raised his eyebrows. "Are you telling me that you were told a year ago by this writer, Kyle Morris, that Andrea Feldman was being paid by them?"

"No, Mac, but Kyle did tell me that he knew DAF was an extension of the Garrett Kane Ministries. He couldn't prove it, but he knew it, said to me that there wasn't any doubt in his mind that Kane funded DAF."

"Which would mean that if Andrea Feldman was being paid by the DAF, the money really came from the Garrett Kane Ministries."

"Exactly."

"Back up a second, Rhonda. How did you come up with the information that Andrea was, in fact, receiving money from DAF?"

"Kyle Morris's sister lives in Washington. I got to know her, too. I called her yesterday, and we got together. She has everything of Kyle's, all the articles he'd written during his short life, his research, his notes, his tapes, and other materials an investigative journalist turns up. One of the things she had were two bank statements from DAF. Lord knows how he got hold of them. His sister didn't know. But there they were in a neatly labeled file folder."

"And?"

"And I browsed through them. There were two checks that had been issued to Andrea Feldman, endorsed over to her mother, and deposited in the Wells Fargo Bank of San Francisco."

There was the sound of a key in the front door. "Must be Annabel," Smith said, going to the hallway. "Hi, Mac," Annabel said as she stepped into the house, a large shopping bag from the American Cafe dangling from her arm.

He kissed her lightly on the lips and took the bag from her. Rufus tried to shove his nose into it, but Smith deftly swung the bag away from him and put it in the kitchen. As Annabel passed the entrance to the living room, she saw Rhonda Harrison, stepped into the room, and extended her hand. "He certainly has spoken of you a great deal, Ms. Harrison, and always in glowing terms. And, of course, I've been a fan of yours for a long time."

"Thank you," Rhonda said. "You're no stranger to me, either. He uses the same kind of terms when he talks about you."

Annabel looked at Smith. "Do you really?"

Smith said, "Usually, unless you've done something to upset me. Then . . ." He smiled. "Then I make sure I don't talk about you at all. Drink?"

"Love one. Make it out of real liquor and make it dark."

A few minutes later, the three of them sat in the living room.

"Annabel has been working on every aspect of this case with me, Rhonda." He told her about Annabel's meetings in New York with Herbert Greist, and then mentioned the photograph she'd found in Mae Feldman's house of Greist when he was a young man.

Smith enjoyed the wide-eyed expression on Rhonda's face. It's called getting even, he told himself. "Can you top this?" as a parlor game.

Rhonda asked questions about the Greist connection with Andrea Feldman, and Mac and Annabel answered them. Now, Smith made an instant decision. He would no longer choose what information to give her. She deserved better than that, and time was running out. They had to pool information. "Excuse me," he said. He returned carrying Marcia Mims's diary. "I received this from Ken Ewald's housekeeper, Marcia Mims," he said, handing it to Annabel.

Annabel asked, "Why did she give it to you?"

"I have no idea. We have to keep it confidential for now. I'd do a dramatic reading of the entire work, but I think that would bore everyone. I don't know how long you two want to sit around reading, but we have the night. I'll put the food on plates. Why don't you huddle on the couch and dip into the world of the rich, famous, and messed up?"

Smith served their food on a coffee table in front of them and took his plate to his study, where he reviewed shorthand notes he'd made while reading the diary. He checked in on them a few times. They'd hardly eaten anything.

A few hours later, Annabel had moved to a chair, leaving Rhonda alone on the couch to digest the final few pages.

"Well?" Smith asked when Rhonda had finished.

"I don't know what kind of upright president Ken Ewald will make," Rhonda said with forced lightness in her voice, "but he sure must be good horizontally. His bedside reputation isn't exaggerated."

Smith said, "Frankly, I don't think his reputation is deserved, although I suppose it depends on what church you go to. Janet Ewald was the one who first told me that she thought her father-in-law was having an affair with Andrea Feldman. Marcia confirmed it that night in Annapolis, although not with much conviction. Now, in the diary, she seems to make a more substantial case for it. If you read those sections carefully, however, you'll see that she deals from a certain base of supposition. The fact that Ken brought Andrea Feldman into the house on many occasions, and that she even remained there overnight on a few of them, doesn't prove they slept together. At least, it wouldn't hold up in court."

"It holds up with this juror," Annabel said. "Whether Ken Ewald and Andrea Feldman actually slept together or not isn't the issue. What is important is that Ken brought her into his inner circle, which meant she had access to a lot of information that would be of interest to his enemies, including his competitors for office."

"True," Smith muttered. "That means that there is the likelihood that Andrea Feldman was selling secrets out of the Ewald camp."

"Selling them to whom?" Rhonda asked.

"According to what you told me before Annabel arrived, Rhonda, she was being paid by the DAF, which, according to your sources, is funded by Garrett Kane Ministries. By extension, Colonel Morales and, possibly, Raymond Thornton could also be involved."

"What about Greist?" Annabel asked. "He claims to have something of great importance he wishes to sell to Ken Ewald, or at least is willing to hush up in return for a large payment."

"You'd have to nail down a link between Andrea Feldman and Greist," Rhonda said.

"I think we can do that," Smith said. He told them of the conversation he'd had with Tony Buffolino in the hospital in San Francisco. Buffolino had briefly filled him in on the content of his conversation with Carla Zaretski the night he was shot. She'd said that Andrea Feldman had been born out of wedlock to Mae Feldman, and that the father, whom Mae Feldman steadfastly refused to name, had been a young attorney in New York. That matched up with what Smith had learned from his friend Morgan Tubbs about Greist's beginnings. Then, too, there was the similarity between Greist's physical makeup, as described by Annabel, the size and shape of suits found in Mae Feldman's closet, and the photograph Annabel had pulled from a drawer in Mae Feldman's room.

"Herbert Greist was Andrea Feldman's father," Rhonda said.

"Looks that way to me," said Smith. "I'm not a gambler, but I'd put money on that."

Annabel sat up straight in her chair and became more animated. "If we follow through on this, Mac, it means that Andrea was selling secrets either to the DAF or to Herbert Greist."

"Or to both," Smith said.

"Why would she do that?" Rhonda asked.

"Maybe that's at the root of who killed her. Let's say she was supposed to deliver information to one of those two 'employers,' but delivered it to the other instead. That could get people pretty mad at her."

"The same information? If you're saying that she was selling inside information from the Ewald camp to the Soviet Union through Herbert Greist—and, bear in mind, we can't be positive that he is her father—what the Soviets would be interested in is hardly the same thing that would interest the DAF, Kane, and Morales."

"Maybe, maybe not," Smith said. "If I were a Soviet intelligence agent, I would find great use for information that might link DAF and Kane to the funding of Morales's troops in Panama. Don't forget that the Soviet Union is supporting the regime in power in Panama. If they could come up with something substantial that proved that DAF and Kane Ministries were funneling money illegally to Morales's troops, they could leak it to the Western press, which would, I'm sure you agree, put a hell of a lot of pressure on those people to stop."

Rhonda Harrison shook her head and said, "Somehow, from what I've learned about Andrea Feldman, which, I admit, isn't much, I have trouble accepting the scenario that she would deliberately sell information to the Soviet Union, even if her father is a Communist sympathizer."

"I tend to agree with you, Rhonda," Smith said. "Don't forget, there was a locked box in Mae Feldman's apartment that evidentally contained material sufficiently important to cause two men to break in and steal it."

"Maybe it was just money," Annabel said. "Tony said Mae Feldman had cleaned out the bank account."

"Carla Zaretski, to be more precise," Smith said.

"What if it wasn't money?" Rhonda asked. "What if it was material Andrea Feldman had stolen from Ken Ewald?"

"Certainly a possibility," Smith said. "Marcia Mims says in her diary that she observed Andrea removing papers from Ken's files."

"What would be unusual about that?" Annabel asked. "Andrea Feldman was a trusted member of the Ewald staff. It would be only natural for her to pull things out of files."

"That's something we'll have to ask Marcia when—and if—we see her again." Smith looked at Rhonda. "I agree with you, Rhonda. Seems unlikely that Andrea Feldman would sell secrets to an enemy of this country. She might have given whatever she stole from Ewald to her mother for safekeeping. In that case, Mae Feldman could have turned over that same material to Herbert Greist, which would have cut Andrea out of the picture as far as DAF and Kane are concerned. And by the way, let's not forget to include President Manning and Raymond Thornton when we mention Kane and Morales."

Annabel sat up even straighter now. "If Greist ended up with whatever it was Andrea stole, and was passing that on to a Soviet contact, that would be motivation enough for him to suddenly disappear as he has, and for the FBI to have a heightened interest in him beyond simple dossier-building. From what you've told me, Mac, Greist has always been nothing more than a Communist sympathizer, and, as far as I know, we haven't harassed Communist sympathizers since Joe McCarthy."

"At least not as overtly," Smith said glumly.

"Why didn't Marcia Mims just go to Ken Ewald and tell him what she'd observed about Andrea Feldman?" Rhonda asked. "I get the impression from what you've said about her that she's an extremely loyal and dedicated employee."

Annabel laughed. "That's probably true, except she keeps a diary filled with intimate details about her employer's extracurricular sexual life. Sounds to me as though she intended to write a book.

"Whatever her motivations," Smith said, "she certainly has been a keen observer. I was interested in her references in the diary to Ed Farmer."

"You mean how he picked Andrea Feldman up on the mornings after she'd stayed overnight at the house?" Rhonda asked.

"Yes," Smith replied. "She says she observed this from an upstairs window, and found it strange that Farmer did not drive through the gate and up to the front of the house, as he otherwise did. Each time he picked up Andrea, he waited outside on the street. Why?"

"Why was he picking her up, or why out on the street?" Annabel asked. "I certainly see nothing untoward about him picking her up. Ed Farmer is a young man with ambition, and people like that get called on to perform all sorts of services for their political masters, including covering up affairs. Besides, he and Andrea worked closely together. Maybe he just wanted to get her into work on time."

"Nothing unusual about him picking her up, Annabel, but why out in the street? According to Marcia, that broke his usual pattern."

Annabel slouched back in her chair. "Who has the answers?" she asked. "Marcia Mims has vanished. So has Janet Ewald. Andrea Feldman is dead. I suppose you could ask Ed Farmer about his habit of picking her up at the house."

"Yes, and I may do that," Smith said. "First, though, I want another conversation with Ken. I'll try to catch up with him tomorrow and put some of these questions to him."

"Want me with you?" Annabel asked.

"No, not necessary. By the way, Tony is returning on Thursday, and I would appreciate some help in seeing that he's settled. I made an appointment for him on Friday with Dr. Kroger at the university." He turned to Rhonda. "I made a last-minute decision to include you in on everything we've come up with, Rhonda, including Marcia Mims's diary. I know you've been very open with me." If Smith had expressed what he was thinking, he would have gone on to say that he'd lost his sense of propriety, maybe even lost his head. He'd breached a confidence by Marcia Mims and knew he should not have shown her diary to anyone, or even read it himself, despite his earlier rationalization. Was his involvement in this case beginning to undermine his character? Too late now, he told himself. To Rhonda, he said, "All I ask is that until we clear this up, you use whatever material that comes out of it for the article, and not to develop any fast-breaking stories for WRC. I realize that's putting a restraint on a good journalist and, Lord knows, I've stood up enough times in my career for the First Amendment. But can you live with that, Rhonda?"

She got up and placed her hand on his shoulder, looked into his eyes, and said, "Don't agonize over showing me the diary, Mac, and don't worry. You have my word that I won't do anything with what's been discussed here tonight until I get the go-ahead from you."

THIRTY

SMITH CALLED the Ewald house on Tuesday morning. "Hello, Leslie, it's Mac. Is Ken there?"

"No, he's not." She didn't sound happy. "He's in a series of meetings all day."

"I see. I am anxious to talk with him. Any idea when I might be able to catch him?"

"Well . . . he's meeting with party bigwigs at the Willard at four. They think the nomination's okay, or almost, but they also want peace with Backus. I'm meeting Ken at the Watergate at six to go over plans for the upcoming testimonial dinner."

"I see. Maybe I could steal a little of his time between meetings. Think you can arrange that?"

"I'll try. The Watergate meeting is in suite 1110. Why don't you stop by at five-thirty."

"I'll be there. Thanks."

AT four-thirty that afternoon, in one of the Willard Hotel's renovated suites, Ken Ewald sat in a meeting with the chairman of the Democratic party, Matt Blair, and Blair's staff.

"Ken, I think it's wonderful that things have been sorted out with your son," said Blair. "It must have been a difficult time for the family."

"Very difficult," Ewald said. "We're all thankful it's over."

"Frankly, you had us worried," Blair said. "Primary results aside, having that charge of murder hanging over your family's head would have . . . well, a lot of rethinking would have been necessary."

Ewald nodded. "Let's just say I'm glad rethinking won't be necessary. You've seen the latest poll we commissioned."

"Yes. Impressive. It was, of course, directed at those groups who are predisposed to support Ken Ewald."

Ewald laughed. "Has there ever been a candidate-sponsored poll that *wasn't* 'directed'?"

The secretary of the party, a former representative from Missouri, Jacqueline Koshner, said, "Senator, polls aside, we'd be less than honest if we didn't express certain concerns we have with your candidacy."

"My son? He's never been charged with anything."

"No, unless that flares up again between now and the convention. I'm talking about the irrefutable shift in this country toward a more conservative posture."

Ewald narrowed his eyes. "What I see is the pendulum swinging back."

"Maybe," Blair said, "but Jackie is right. If the pendulum has begun to return to center, it has, in our judgment, a long trip ahead of it. This is *now*, Ken. If you are the party's candidate—and it looks as though you have a good shot at it—we feel you'll need balance on the ticket."

"Jody?"

"Yes."

"Impossible. Oil and water."

"I prefer to see it as sweet and sour," said Jacqueline Koshner, "the palate being satisfied in all ways."

Ewald said lightly, "I hope you consider me the sweet in that recipe." His comment did not generate smiles. He said, "I will not run with Jody Backus."

Blair glanced at his staff, looked at Ewald, and said, "It's possible you won't run at all."

Ewald's anger was evident. "You aren't suggesting that the party . . . you . . . would attempt to deny me the nomination, are you?"

"Of course not. If the delegates give you the votes you need, you'll be our candidate. However, Ken, your candidacy is not without obvious problems. Jacqueline is right. We are still a country that for a long time has gone to the right of center, and that will be the case in November. We want the White House this time around, Ken, and we are not about to let it slip out of our grasp. This is the year. Manning has run his string, and Thornton represents only four more years of the same, or worse. You are extremely popular in some segments, unpopular in others. This thing with your son and the murder of one of your staff members, even though it seems to have been buried for the time being, hasn't helped. Do you . . . do you see any other such incidents looming between now and the convention?"

"Another murder that my son will be suspected of committing? No."

The expression on Blair's face said that he was not pleased with Ewald's flippancy. "I think all that's left to be said at this juncture is that if you win the nomination, the party will support you in every way. But also know that if you are our candidate for president, the choice of your running mate will not be yours to make unilaterally."

Ewald nodded and stood. "I'll be happy to confer on my choice of vice-president, but strike Jody from the list."

The others remained seated as Blair walked Ewald to the foyer. He slapped him on the arm. "Keep one thing in mind, Ken."

"I'm listening."

"Backus. Even though he lost to you in a majority of the primaries, he comes into San Francisco with a hell of a lot of clout. It may not be as easy for you as it appears at this moment."

"Nothing is ever easy, Jack."

"One last thing between friends."

"Shoot."

"Is there anything else, *anything* that might explode between now and the convention?"

"About me personally?"

"Yes."

"Do you know something I don't?"

"No, just . . ."

"Just what?"

"Just rumors. Things good at home?"

"Things are very good at home, Jack. Thanks for the time. I have to meet Leslie to plan the testimonial dinner for me. Looking forward to seeing you there."

"Yes, it should be a lovely evening. Thanks for coming by."

S M I T H arrived at the Watergate suite precisely at five-thirty and was surprised to find Ken there. He and Leslie were alone. "My good luck," Smith said, "to have both of you here at the same time."

Ewald shook Smith's hand. He was obviously not in a pleasant mood.

He spoke in short sentences, and the ready smile that endeared him to millions of voters across the country seemed to have been put on a shelf, at least for the moment.

"Look, I know you're terribly busy, Ken, and I wouldn't dream of getting in the way of your schedule, but I have some important information to share with you. In fact"—he looked at Leslie—"I think it's probably best shared with both of you."

Ewald perched on the arm of a stuffed chair and said, "Go ahead, what is this information?"

Smith filled a glass from a pitcher of orange juice, came to the center of the room, and said, "As I told you on the phone, Ken, we've been pursuing this Herbert Greist thing."

"Who's *we?*" Ewald asked gruffly.

"Various people I've brought into this, including Annabel, Tony Buffolino, my investigator, and a journalist who's been doing some pretty serious digging on her own." Smith's expression now matched Ewald's, made to seem all the more serious by dark stubble that had sprouted over the course of the day.

Leslie sat on the chair's other arm. "Go on, Mac, please."

Smith said, "I told Ken a little of this on my call from California, but let me fill you in quickly, Leslie." He told her about Tony having been shot in California, and that Tony had discovered a locked box in Mae Feldman's apartment but hadn't had a chance to ascertain its contents because of the intrusion of the two unidentified men. He said to Ewald, "We think that box might have contained material stolen from you."

Ewald looked nervously at his wife before saying, "You told me about this mysterious box, Mac, and I told you it couldn't have contained anything stolen from me."

Smith hesitated, then said, "What you told me, Ken, was that you never kept anything of significant interest in the house, at least from a national-security point of view."

"I said that because it's true."

Leslie asked, "Why are you asking this, Mac?"

"I'm just trying to put all the pieces together, Leslie. Let me continue. Ken, I assume you've told Leslie about the blackmail threat from Herbert Greist."

Ewald displayed his first smile, and directed it at his wife. "No, in the frenzy of everything I forgot to tell lots of people lots of things. Go ahead, Mac, fill her in."

Smith looked into Leslie's angry face and told her the salient facts about Greist and his threats. When he was done, she asked, "Who is this Greist? He sounds like a lowlife, a cheap blackmailer."

"Yes, he probably is those things, Leslie, but he also is probably Andrea Feldman's father."

Their mutual silence was palpable.

"How did you find that out?" Ken asked. Before Smith could answer, he added, "Can you prove it? What is this, speculation by this investigator you've hired, or some yellow journalism by this reporter? By the way, who is this journalist?"

"Rhonda Harrison, from WRC. She's not doing this for the station, however. She has an assignment from *Washingtonian* to do a piece on Feldman. She's good at her trade. Between Rhonda and Tony, they've discovered that Andrea had been receiving sizable amounts of money from an organization known as the Democratic Action Front."

Leslie's face registered a lack of recognition at the name. Ken's face was another matter. Smith waited for him to say something. Before he did, he walked to the window and looked outside. Rain had started to fall, and gusts of wind splashed it over the glass. He turned and said, "Okay, Mac, let's open this whole thing up. Not that that represents a decision on my part. You've already done it."

"Ken, what's this about?" Leslie asked.

Ken held up his hands and said, "Relax, Leslie, and you'll find out. Years ago, when I decided to make a run for president, I started building my base. That involved all the usual activities, lining up financial and political support around the country, seeking high visibility, taking stands on national issues beyond those I had taken before, the textbook approach to getting ready.

"I figured that my opponent would come out of the incumbent administration, which probably meant Raymond Thornton. Thornton would be tough, because the Manning administration has made everything seem hale and hearty in the country, manipulating economic statistics, calling tax raises something else, proclaiming a prosperity that, in reality, is built on a foundation of sand. I figured I ought to know everything I could about Thornton, and started digging." He laughed without mirth. "Funny, I used investigators, too."

"You did?" Leslie asked.

Smith looked at her. "You didn't know any of this, Leslie?"

She shook her head. "Not about investigators looking into Thornton's life." She asked her husband, "Did it result in anything worthwhile?"

"Yes, it certainly did. One of the investigators I hired was well connected in Southern California politics. He hooked up with a man named Stuart Lyme. Remember him?"

"Yes, I do," Smith said. "Stuart Lyme was a leading right-wing figure in California for years, a real back-room power player."

"You have a good memory, Mac," Ewald said.

"I also seem to remember that he died under mysterious circumstances, a fall from a window, something like that."

Ewald said, "He drowned off Baja. It happened shortly after Stuart had delivered to me, through this investigator, a report loaded with political explosives."

"Why would someone like Lyme, a dyed-in-the-wool conservative, work with you, help you out?"

"Because Stuart's son had been killed. The crime was never solved, probably because those in power didn't want it to be solved. Stuart knew his son had died at the hands of Garrett Kane."

"Kane?" Smith and Leslie said together.

"Yes. Not Kane himself, of course, but members of his inner sanctum. Stuart's son had become deeply involved in Kane's ministry. He eventually rose high enough in its structure to know what was really going on, and documented every scrap of it, including Kane's use of fronts through which to launder money, and to channel it to his pet causes, like Morales's activities in Panama. There were other fronts and causes, of course, but Panama and Morales have always been Kane's favorite.

"Lyme's son broke from Kane. I don't know why, but he did. He took the material with him. Kane eventually found out and ordered the son murdered. But before the killing could be carried out, Lyme's son had passed the material to his father.

"At first, Lyme didn't know what to do with the material. He knew that Kane was close to President Manning, and that Morales was being supported by the president and his national-security people but, as they say, blood runs thicker than water, and Lyme broke from them. That was when he decided to give me the material his son had given him. He had one request, that I use it to put Kane out of business. I've sat on it ever since."

"Why?" Smith asked. "If the material was that damaging, you could have used it to launch a Senate investigation."

Ewald's discomfort with the question was evident. He sat up a little straighter and said, "I decided to wait until I really needed it."

"Which was when you made your run for president."

"Yes. I didn't want to waste it in the Senate, where I was already comfortable and secure. I decided I'd use it against Thornton when the time was right."

"The material Lyme gave you implicates Thornton with Kane and Morales?" Leslie asked.

"In no uncertain terms," Ewald answered. "Everything was laid out—names, places, people, bank accounts, correspondence, the works. *That's* what was stolen from the house."

"Andrea Feldman?" Leslie asked.

Ewald shrugged. "I suppose so. Who else could it be? It all makes sense now, this business of Andrea receiving money from Kane through this phony organization—what's it called, Democratic Action Front?"

"Yes," Smith said.

Leslie asked, "When did you know it was missing, Ken?"

"A while ago."

"Why didn't you—"

Ewald cut her off by saying to Smith, "Sure, it all makes sense. Andrea stole it, and if this character Greist *is* her father, she gave it to him."

Smith shrugged. "Bear in mind, Ken, that Greist has been connected with Communist causes. I suppose it is possible that Andrea gave it to Greist for him to try and sell back to you, but we think it's more likely she stole it at DAF's behest. It might have ended up with Greist, but it probably wasn't Andrea's original intention to give it to him."

Ewald stood and paced the room.

"We have a theory, Ken," Smith said, "although we have no idea whether it holds water. We think Andrea might have stolen the material for Kane and Thornton, but left it with her mother for safekeeping. Her mother in turn brought in the father. They figured they could get big bucks out of you because you'd pay anything to get it back. Does that play?"

"I suppose," Ewald said. "Christ, all this would have to happen at such a crucial time."

"Well," said Smith, "at least you've confirmed that something tangible was stolen from your house." He was tempted to bring up Roseanna Gateaux. Jim Shevlin's mention of her had stayed with him. Why was the FBI interested in Gateaux? He decided he would raise the issue when he and Ewald were alone. Otherwise, it would only hurt Leslie and accomplish nothing. He said, "I know you're both terribly busy and I'll get out of your hair, but I would like something else cleared up for me. Paul indicated that he'd met Andrea at a party, and that she convinced him to put in a good word with you. Is that true?"

Ewald nodded. "It was obvious to me that Paul was infatuated with her, and that concerned me. I had reservations, but Ed Farmer tipped the scale in her favor."

"He did? He knew Andrea well enough to make such a judgment?"

"He seemed to. He told me that she would be a real asset to the campaign and urged me to hire her. I did."

"Paul must have been pleased," Smith said.

"Yes, too much so. I sensed something was going on between them long before Janet found out. I probably should have followed my gut instincts and not hired her, but with both Paul and Ed in her corner, I went with it."

He glanced anxiously at Leslie, who'd fixed him in a challenging stare. "Go on, Ken, finish the story for Mac," she said.

"What do you mean?"

"Tell Mac how Paul brought Andrea Feldman into the house and the campaign and how . . . how Daddy ended up sleeping with her."

Ewald leaped to his feet. "That's a lie, Leslie! I may have . . ."

Leslie laughed. "Little too quick with the tongue, Ken. What were you about to say, that you may have slept with others but not with her? Let's face it, Ken, your overactive glands have led this family into trouble it doesn't deserve. You had clear sailing to the White House, and look what's fallen on our son—suspicion of murder. And now you're being blackmailed because you couldn't control your libido."

She looked at Mac, who hadn't expected this eruption when he brought up Andrea's name again. He was distinctly and visibly uncomfortable. "Mac," she asked, "did you happen to see a confrontation I had with a young reporter a week or so ago?"

"The one who asked whether you would be the first divorced First Lady?"

"Yes. She nailed it—which is why I nailed her. We are not a happily married couple, and haven't been for quite a while. We are Ken and Barbie, but only for the voters. I suppose I really don't have to tell you this, Mac. You're astute enough, and have been around long enough, to have picked up on it."

Smith sighed and rubbed his eyes. "Whether I did or not, Leslie, doesn't seem to be terribly important. This really isn't my business."

"I disagree. I think it is very much your business. You have taken a leave from the university to help us, and if I remember correctly, the rule always was that your attorney must know everything."

"I'm no one's attorney, Leslie," Smith said. "I'm just a friend." He stood. "I have to leave, but there is another thing I would like to air before I do." He was happy to have something else to talk about other than their personal problems. "Lots of people presumably had reason to kill—or at least could rationalize killing—Andrea Feldman. If she were double-dealing Kane, he certainly wouldn't be a fan. Do you think she might have been murdered by someone at Kane's command, as you say Stuart Lyme's son was?"

"I wouldn't know," Ewald said, still glaring at his wife.

Smith took them both in slowly before asking, "Is there anyone within *your* circle—family, friends, household staff, campaign staff—who you think might have killed Andrea Feldman?"

"No," Leslie said without hesitation.

"Ken?" Smith asked.

"No, of course not. It was obviously someone connected with that madman Kane, maybe somebody from Morales's band of thugs, maybe even the Manning White House."

There was a knock at the door. Three members of the Watergate's catering staff had arrived for the meeting. "Come in, please," Leslie said pleasantly, a large and winning smile on her face, a triumph of muscle control.

"Thanks for your time," Smith said.

"Are you going home?" Leslie asked.

"No, I think I'll stop in the suite we've taken here in the Watergate. I have some details to take care of."

She stepped close to him and said, "I don't know why you're staying involved, but I am very glad you are." She kissed his cheek. He looked at Ken over her shoulder and saw a stone face. "I'm staying involved, Leslie, because I want to know what happened. Just that simple. I *need* to know what happened."

As Smith left the suite and waited for an elevator to take him to his floor, the young Panamanian sat alone in yet another suite in the Watergate, booked and paid for by the Reverend Garrett Kane. Earlier, Colonel Gilbert Morales had been there. Now, Miguel sat on the couch, a soft drink on the table in front of him. Around the glass were various pieces of metal. He picked up a few and began to assemble them. The Pachmayr Colt Model 1911 modular pistol had been delivered to him earlier in the day by one of Morales's aides. It had cost four thousand dollars, and could be configured to handle .45, .38 Super, or .9 mm ammunition. This model was set up for .38 Super.

He'd taken the sophisticated weapon apart and put it back together again a number of times. Each time it was fully assembled, he couldn't help but smile at the feel of it. It weighed only sixty-four ounces. The trigger had a light, crisp pull.

"*Bueno*," he said. As he slowly began to take it apart again. "*Guapo*. Beautiful, beautiful."

THIRTY-ONE

"**S**URE YOU'LL BE all right?" Annabel Reed asked Tony Buffolino after he'd settled into the Watergate suite late Thursday afternoon.

"Yeah, I'm fine. Where are you guys going, out to dinner?"

"No, I think we'll have dinner at my house, make it an early night," Smith said. "Are you sure you're well enough to stay here alone?"

"Hey, come on, take a look." Buffolino pushed himself up from the chair, slipped his crutches beneath his arms, and moved quickly—too quickly—across the vast living room, losing his balance near the kitchen table and grabbing it to keep from falling. Smith and Annabel started toward him, but he said, "No sweat, just have to go a little slower."

"Why don't you call one of your ex-wives and invite her up for dinner?" Smith said.

"That's not a bad idea. Yeah, maybe I'll do that."

"Well, good to see you back, Tony," Annabel said. "Don't forget you have a doctor's appointment tomorrow."

"I won't forget. You'll be by here in the morning?"

"No, I'd better put in some serious time at the gallery." Smith said he'd drop by first thing.

They were almost at the door when the phone next to Buffolino rang. "Hey, Joe, great to hear from you. How goes it? Yeah, great, I'm doin' fine. You heard about what happened to me in Frisco. You're where, downstairs? Sure, come on up. Love to see you."

He hung up and told them that Joe Riga had stopped by to see him.

"That's nice," Annabel said, pleased that he would have company. She didn't have much faith in his ability to coax his ex-wives there on such short notice.

"See you tomorrow," Smith said.

Minutes later, Buffolino and Joe Riga sat on the terrace, drinks in their hands. Washington was clear and balmy.

"How long you figure this will go on?" Riga asked.

"What, this case?"

"Yeah, and everything that goes with it. You've got a good deal here."

"You're telling me. This is the best gig I'll ever have in my life. They broke the mold when they made Mac Smith, believe me."

"Oh, I believe you, Tony. I always got along good with Mac. He was a tough defense attorney, but he played fair, gave the profession some class. You should see some of the whack jobs we deal with now. Tell me more about this crazy woman who shot you. You say she was Mae Feldman's landlady?"

"Yeah, old buddies. Feldman's probably as flaky as Madame Zaretski."

"Madame?"

"That's what I call her. She acts like a queen, only she ain't. She says she had this big opera career going till she lost her portamento."

"Her what? Who did it?"

Buffolino explained as though the term were old hat to him.

Riga said, "Oh, portamento. *That* portamento."

"Yeah, that one."

"So, Tony, things are good with you," Riga said.

"Yeah. You?"

"Nothing changes with me, Tony. The sun goes down, the honest citizens skip the city and the cockroaches come out. You pick up a bunch of the cockroaches, and the DA or a judge tells you to let 'em go. So you let the cockroaches go, the sun comes up and they sleep, the good people come back into the city, and sun goes down and it starts all over again."

Buffolino laughed. "Yeah, I guess nothin' does change."

"I heard how you pulled that old photo routine with Morse out at the Buccaneer Motel," Riga said. "What'd you show him, a picture of Mickey Mouse?"

"Van Johnson."

"Who's he?"

"An actor. Come on, Joe, you heard of Van Johnson."

"Nah, I don't go in much for the movies. Sometimes a good cop movie, something like that."

"How come you showed the old guy a picture of Paul Ewald?" Buffolino asked.

"Why not? She had a key to the motel in her purse, and Ewald was the prime suspect. We figured they might have been out there together, so I asked Glass in Rosslyn to run a photo by the owner."

"He lied, right?"

Riga screwed up his face. "No, he didn't lie. A cop shows him anything, he agrees. We could've shown him a picture of Hitler and he would have agreed Hitler shacked up there that night with the deceased."

Buffolino laughed. "You still looking close at Paul Ewald?"

Riga nodded.

"I don't think he done it."

"Well, that settles it then. We'll drop him from the list."

"Don't be a wise-ass with me, Joe. Hey, whatever happened to Garcia, that dirtbag who set me up?"

Riga shifted position in his chair. His brow furrowed. He touched Tony on the knee and said, "You know, Tony, I never had anything to do with that. It was IA all the way."

"I know that, Joe. You never did nothin' to me but good. What about Garcia? He went back to Panama, I heard."

"Right. After you took the fall, some of us decided that Mr. Garcia was a stud who shouldn't be left walking around. We put the arm on him and convinced him he ought to get out of the country, get out of the business. Between you and me, he left in a lot worse shape then you're in. Last I heard, he was still in Panama."

"Too good for him. Guys like that, even if you bust them up, keep the dough and live the good life, while we . . ."

Riga grabbed Tony's arm and shook it. "Hey, you look like you're doing pretty good. This ain't exactly skid row."

"No, but I'll be going back to skid row, Joe. This thing can't last long. Why should Smith hang in?"

Riga thought for a moment. "There is still the question of who murdered Andrea Feldman. Knowing Mac Smith, I figure he wants to be the one who finds out before he packs it in."

Riga's words seemed to buoy Tony's spirits, which had visibly sagged.

"Yeah, I bet you're right. Besides, you know what he told me before I went to Frisco?"

"What?"

"He told me that when this is over, he'd try to get me a good job. How about that?"

"That'd be nice," said Riga. "You know, Tony, I don't have much more time till I retire. Maybe he could help me out, too. Maybe you put in a word for me. Would you do that?"

Tony silently resented what Riga was asking. He wasn't proud of what he was feeling, but it was there. Just like Washington, he thought, everybody always looking out for themselves. He mumbled something unintelligible and sipped his drink.

After Riga left, Tony sat on the terrace until he fell asleep in the chair, his heavily bandaged leg propped on the table. Riga had made him another drink, and that empty glass joined others on the green Astroturf beneath his chair. He awoke at midnight to the sound of a low-flying commercial jetliner on its approach to National. He was drunk, but managed to make his way to the bedroom, where he flopped on the bed, fully clothed, and fell back into a fitful sleep.

RUFUS, the giant blue Dane, stretched out across the foot of Mac Smith's bed, forcing the human animals in it to retract their legs into the fetal position. Smith grumbled, got up, and went to the kitchen, where he turned on the coffee, squeezed fresh orange juice, retrieved the paper from the front steps, brushed his teeth, assured Rufus he'd be walked in short order, and climbed back into bed. "Coffee's ready in a minute."

Annabel stretched, cooed, and turned over. Smith smiled as he looked down at that mass of hair covering her pillow. He was filled with love, which soon blossomed into lust. Moving over her, he transmitted his feelings, but she said through a yawn, "Mac, be civilized. Go get the amaretto gop you call coffee."

He swung out of bed again, went to the kitchen, and returned with their breakfast on trays, flipping on the TV as he passed. "Breakfast is served."

"Oh, God, you are a brute," she said, pushing up against the headboard and running long fingers through her hair. "Turn off the TV. TV is for nighttime."

"Morning TV is important," he said. "The world might have blown up overnight."

"Good."

"You wouldn't say that if we were blown up with it."

"We weren't. We're here, in bed, with the world's biggest dog."

They watched the news before the entertainment portion of the Friday edition of the morning show resumed. As a young, pretty actress whom neither Mac nor Annabel knew chatted with the host about starring in her latest motion picture, Smith said, "I've been doing some thinking, Annie."

"About what?"

"About this whole adventure we've been on. I thought about it a lot last night. I think it's time to get out of it."

She was gripped with a set of immediate and conflicting feelings. On the one hand, she was relieved. On the other, she was disappointed. She said, "Why this sudden change of heart?"

"I don't know, I just wonder what's to be gained by hanging in. Leslie Ewald asked me last night why I was still involved, and I gave her one of those precious existential answers—you know, an I-want-to-climb-the-mountain-because-it's-there kind of thing. Who am I kidding? I realized last night that I've been staying with this because it makes me feel important. I don't need something outside of myself to feel important, never did. It's time to wind things down and get back to the life of the unimportant college professor."

"I wouldn't argue with you about that, Mac. Whatever you say is fine with me, and you know it." She kissed him gently on the lips. "Tony will take this hard," she said.

"I know. I told him I'd do my best to find him a job when this was over, a job where he's not expected to scale tall buildings. Maybe at the university. Besides, he's made some decent money already, and I'll see to it that he gets a healthy bonus out of what Leslie has paid me."

They watched television until Annabel asked, "Are you sure this is what you want to do?"

"No, I'm not sure, but a decision has to be made. As they say, any action is better than no action."

"Okay, then let's get the morning going," she said, jumping out of bed and touching her toes. "I have to get to the gallery, and you told Tony you'd be by to see him. Shall we have dinner out tonight to celebrate our return to the mundane?"

He started to say yes, but hesitated. She picked up on it; he wasn't sure whether he wanted to drop everything, and she could understand his ambivalence. She wouldn't press. Let the day go by and see what it brings.

THIRTY-TWO

HERBERT GREIST stood at the dirt-crusted window of a room
in a hotel on West Forty-seventh Street. He wore his black
suit pants and a sleeveless undershirt. His socks were light gray silk; a
large hole allowed one of his toes to protrude.

He looked at Mae, who was awake but still in bed. A succession of
noisy encounters in the next room between a prostitute and her Johns
had kept them awake most of the night. Mae was on her back, her eyes
fixed on the peeling ceiling. Greist picked up a cigar butt from a full
ashtray and, with some difficulty, lighted it and looked out to the street
again.

"It won't work," Mae said, only her lips moving.

"You never know," he said. "We asked too much. He doesn't want
this kind of thing spread around, not with running for president. A
hundred thousand, that's all. We can leave the country, go somewhere
safe and have enough to live on for a while."

Mae Feldman pushed herself up against the leatherette headboard
and said, "You always say things will work. You always say not to worry,
that you have it figured out. It doesn't work. It never works."

He slowly turned and fixed his eyes on her, the cigar firmly wedged
in the middle of his mouth. He removed it and said, "Things end.
Nothing is forever. We're still free, still with a chance. They don't
know where we are. We need money, that's all. We can get it from
Ewald."

"How? Call that attorney, Smith? Waste of time."

"I don't need advice from you. Look what you did to us."

"What did I do? All I did was put the money in a box, and somebody
stole it. That isn't my fault, Herbert. I didn't do anything wrong."

"You *always* do things wrong, Mae. You should have hidden the
money in different places, spread it out. That would have been the

smart thing to do. The files and papers, too. All in one place so they could pick it up and walk off. You're so stupid."

There was pleading in her voice. "I tried to do the right thing, Herbert. Don't be mad at me. I hate it when you're mad at me."

"That money and those files were ours."

"That money was blood money, our daughter's blood money."

"She's dead. She can't use the money."

Mae Feldman slumped back against the headboard and closed her eyes against the tears that seemed always to be forming.

Greist said, "We call Ewald direct. We call and tell him that if he doesn't hand us the money in cash, we go to the press, we tell them that he was screwing Roseanna and our daughter, too, for Christ's sake, who's now dead because of him. You don't think he'll pay a hundred thousand dollars to keep that quiet?"

She sat up in bed again and said, "Herbert, if we go to the press and tell them this, they'll quote us, run our pictures, and then the FBI will take us away for the rest of our lives, maybe even hang us for treason." Before, she'd been talking with sleepy slovenliness. Now that Mae was fully awake, her words had a sharper edge. "The one good thing that ever came out of my meeting you is dead. All she did was to come to me with information from Ewald. She left it with me so that it would be safe and so that she could secure her own future. What did you do when you heard about it? You said, 'Give it to me, and I'll make us rich.' How? Sell what Andrea worked so hard to get to your supposed friends, the losers you've hung with all your life? Get rich how, Herbert, by trying to blackmail a U.S. senator for a half-million dollars? Oh, my God, Herbert, you may be a lawyer, but that doesn't mean you're always smart."

He hurled the cigar at her. It bounced off the wall and fell to the threadbare rose-colored rug. "You'll set the place on fire," she said, leaning over and picking it up.

"Let it burn. Call him."

"Why should I call him? *You* call him, or get your tootsie to call him."

"You're sick, Mae."

"No, I am just tired of being used by you. I've loved you ever since the day I met you, and I have never done anything to hurt you. But you hurt me every day. You have that blond pig here in New York and you flaunt her, make sure I know you have other women."

"She's smart."

"Then go to her for money."

"She doesn't have any money."

She went to the bathroom. When she returned, she said defiantly, "Why should I call him? You're the lawyer, the negotiator, the one who is going to make everything work and everybody rich. Why should I call him, put my neck out, get linked up with you? As far as everybody knows, I don't even exist, because that's the way you wanted it."

"Shut up, just shut up and let me think," he said, turning once again to the window.

A n hour later, they left the hotel. She went first, stepped out onto Forty-seventh Street, and casually looked up and down the block. Few people were up this early on a Saturday morning. She gave him a motion with her head and he joined her. They walked half a block to a coffee shop and had Spanish omeletes, French fries, and coffee.

"Maybe we should just get on a plane and go," she said. "I have enough for tickets."

"No. Ewald is the one who should bankroll us. He owes. You're so sad about Andrea? She's dead because of him. Let him pay."

"You're talking about our daughter in these terms? You never cared about her. You left your sperm in me and walked away. I had her. I brought her up. She is my daughter, not ours. How dare you think you can—"

He reached across the grimy Formica table and gripped her wrists. "Don't push me more, Mae."

Fear flooded her eyes. She winced against the pain of his fingertips and pulled away, striking the back of her seat, causing people in the adjoining booth to turn and glare. He relaxed his grip and sat back. He now wore the black suit jacket, a soiled white shirt, and green tie. He brushed the lapels of his jacket. "I need a good cigar. You won't call Ewald? I will."

"And I am going to leave," she said. "You're crazy, don't you know that? We don't need money from Ewald or anyone else. Let's make our own way."

He grinned and picked a glob of green pepper from between two front teeth. "Suit yourself. You've always been a loser, Mae, and the only decent things you've ever had are what I gave you."

He stood at the side of the booth. She continued to sit, her fingers laced together as she tried to keep from crying. He was right. She'd never been anything, a pathetic and weak woman who failed at almost everything she did. Except, she thought, giving birth to and raising that beautiful young woman who went on to graduate from law school, and to work with powerful political figures. No one could ever take that away from her.

She looked up and watched him ogle a short, shapely Hispanic waitress who wiggled past them. She wanted to ask, she'd wanted to ask a thousand times since that night, whether he'd killed Andrea. Each time, she stopped herself because she reasoned that a father would not kill his own flesh and blood. No father would.

M A C Smith was about to head for the Yates Field House for some exercise when the phone rang. It was Ewald. "Catching you at a bad time, Mac?"

"No, I was going to the gym. That's always easy to put off. What's up?"

"Two things. First, I received a call from Herbert Greist."

"Greist called *you?* The FBI is looking for him."

"I know. He told me that he desperately needs a hundred thousand dollars. In return, he's promised not to . . ." Smith knew the sudden silence was Ewald making sure he wasn't being overheard. "He threatens to tell the public about Roseanna and me. He also claims I slept with his daughter."

"Andrea. Greist *is* her father. Where was he calling from?"

"He didn't say. He told me to give it some thought for an hour and that he would call back."

Smith leaned against the edge of his desk and sighed. "I wonder how Greist knows about your affair with Roseanna Gateaux," he said. "A few days ago, he was trying to sell back to you the information on

Garrett Kane that Andrea stole from your house. Now, he's not offering that, just a simple request for money to keep his mouth shut about Roseanna and Andrea." Ewald said nothing. "Okay, we'll try to figure that out later. You said there were two things. What's the second?"

"Marcia is gone. She came back after taking some days off, then disappeared again."

"Yes, I'm listening."

"Leslie was concerned about her this morning. We hadn't heard a peep from her. She went to Marcia's room and found that Marcia had packed a bag. One of the gardeners said he'd seen her leave the house early this morning. She was picked up by a cab."

"Ken, I think I'd better come over right away. Is that all right with you?"

"Yes, of course, but please continue to use discretion with this Roseanna thing. Leslie's out now, but she may return while you're here."

"You don't have to worry about that with me, Ken. I almost had the feeling that . . . I had the feeling during our conversation last night that Leslie might already know about Roseanna."

"Suspects, doesn't know for sure. No smoking handkerchief with lipstick on it."

"I'll be there as quickly as possible."

As Smith walked into Ewald's study, Ewald said, "You look like you're ready for the big game, Mac." Smith hadn't bothered to change out of his gray sweats and white sneakers. He wore a George Washington University windbreaker, and a rumpled tan rainhat that was a particular favorite. Ewald was dressed in a beautifully tailored Italian-cut gray suit, white shirt, and burgundy tie.

"Well, the saga continues," Ewald said as he carefully sat on a chair and made sure the crease in his trousers wasn't in danger of being crushed. "What do you think?"

"Let me find out first what *you* think, Ken. How do you feel about this?"

Ewald sat back and stretched his neck as though to work out a kink.

He said, "I just wish the bastard would go away so I could focus on the campaign. The convention is in front of us, the National Committee is on my neck. If it isn't one thing, it's another."

"Wishing Greist away won't do the job," Smith said. "Still, my instincts tell me he's bluffing. Think about it. He's being hunted by the FBI for traitorous acts. Someone like that isn't likely to go to the media to tell a story about a presidential candidate having slept with a woman other than his wife."

"I was thinking the same thing," said Ewald, seemingly relieved at Smith's corroboration.

"On the other hand," Smith said, "you never can predict what people like Greist will do. The chances are good that he's with Mae Feldman, Andrea's mother. She could be the one behind this desperate grab for money, and she may be willing to do anything. We've found out that Mae Feldman had a sizable bank account, and that it was closed down the other day by a close friend in San Francisco. I wonder why they're not getting money from *her*."

Ewald pressed his lips together in anger. "If Greist knows about my affair with Roseanna, that means he must know her, or someone who fed that information to him. That's cause for real concern, wouldn't you say?"

Ewald got up and paced. "Well, learned counsel, what do I do now?"

"Greist hasn't called again?"

"No. If he sticks to his promise to call within an hour, the phone should ring any minute."

"Obviously, Ken, you can't pay blackmail or runaway money to a fugitive from the FBI. It seems to me your only course of action is to turn him down and take your chances."

"Or try to reason with him."

Smith laughed. "Greist isn't the kind of creature you reason with. Annabel tried that on two occasions. Obviously, we should be on the phone right now to the FBI letting them know we might be able to help them find Greist and Mae Feldman. If you make a date with him to hand over money, that establishes where he is in New York. The Bureau can move in and arrest him."

Ewald walked across the room. As he stood at the window, and

Smith sat in a chair observing him, the phone rang. Ewald turned quickly. "Could be him."

"I'd like to listen in."

"Go upstairs to the small office on the second floor. It's—"

Smith stood, "Yes, I know where it is. Is it open?"

"Probably not. Here." He handed Smith a key.

The door to the study opened, and a secretary informed Ewald that he had a call from Mr. Greist.

Smith bounded up the stairs, opened the door, and entered the small office. He waited a moment to give Ewald time to pick up, then gently lifted the handset and heard their voices. As he listened, the reel of tape on the top shelf silently began to turn.

"Mr. Greist, you put me in a very difficult position," Ewald said.

"Yes, I know that, which is why I'm confident you will do what I say. Have you considered my offer?"

"Yes, I have. It goes against everything I stand for, but I am willing to meet your request in return for your total silence."

Greist's sigh of relief was audible. "Good. Here's what you do." He started to outline a meeting strategy when Ewald interrupted. "Mr. Greist, I have a few questions first."

"No idle talk here. I'm no fool. This call could be monitored. Here's the way it works, no questions asked."

"Go ahead."

"I want you to meet me tomorrow night in New York."

"Don't be ridiculous," Ewald said. "I'm not exactly an unfamiliar face. I'll send someone."

"Just as long as that someone has the money in cash."

"Don't worry, Mr. Greist, you will have your cash. Now, where and when?"

Greist gave him the address of a hotel in the theater district of Manhattan. Ewald's emissary was to come to room 7 at precisely nine o'clock Sunday night.

"You'll be in that room?" Ewald asked.

It was a low rumble of a laugh. "Don't take me for a fool, Senator. I won't be there for the same reason you won't be there. There will be someone waiting to accept the money."

"What assurances do I have that you will live up to your part of the bargain, Mr. Greist?"

"You don't, except that I have bigger things on my mind than tattling on you and your mistresses. I need the money. That's it."

"Fine, you'll have it."

The conversation ended, and Ewald and Smith met up once again in the downstairs study.

"What do you think?" Ewald asked.

"I think you handled it well. The question now is whether to bring in the FBI at this point and have them go to that room. If they do, you're going to have to tell them why you're being blackmailed by this cheap hustler. You may not want to do that."

"I'd give anything not to have to do that, but I don't see any choice. If I don't, I'm withholding information from the FBI. If I do . . . that could mean my affair with Roseanna getting out, maybe not to the public, but the Bureau would know."

"The FBI doesn't care about who you sleep with," Smith said.

"That's a little naive, isn't it, Mac?"

Smith smiled ruefully. "Yes, guess it is. The old FBI, Hoover's, would smack their lips. Even now, the Bureau works for whatever administration is in power. I suppose that kind of information would be of interest to Raymond Thornton."

"And/or to Jody Backus."

"Yes, to him, too."

"A rock and a hard place."

"Afraid so. Look, Ken, my advice is to let me handle things from this point forward."

"I can't let you do that, Mac. This is my mess. I made it."

"And I think I know how to get you out of it. I mean it, Ken, just get on with your campaign and let me handle it."

"That's a generous offer, Mac. What do you intend to do?"

"Leave it to me. There's no need for you to know everything. I'll keep you informed, especially if something might kick back on you. Fair enough?"

Ewald extended his hand. "Mac, you are a remarkable friend. I don't have any idea how to thank you properly."

"I don't need thanks, Ken. What I do need is to resolve this thing so I can get back to teaching law, something I miss a lot more than I thought I would. Don't tell Leslie about any of this. I also think it would be wise for you to . . ."

Leslie Ewald and Ed Farmer came into the study. "Looks like you've been out for a run," Leslie said to Smith.

"I'm just about to do that, Leslie. I was on my way to the gym and decided to stop in to see Ken." To Farmer, he said, "How are you, Ed? Things going well for the good guys?"

"Things are in good shape," Farmer said, "and should stay that way. As long as nothing stupid raises its ugly head between now and the convention."

"Let's hope that 'stupid' things are buried forever," Smith said. "Excuse me. I have to run, literally."

Smith left the house and sprinted until his breath gave out, and silently cursed a stitch in his side that slowed him to a walk. His mind told him he didn't have much time, but his body refused to cooperate. He cursed that, too, and the sages who said you were only as old as you thought. The bones and muscles always told the truth.

THIRTY-THREE

NOT LONG AGO, Washington's famed Akebono cherry trees, a gift in 1912 from Japan, had been in full bloom, attracting hundreds of thousands of tourists to witness their splendor. Now, the blossoms were gone, and this early Sunday morning at the Tidal Basin was quiet, except for a dozen joggers running their weekend route around the basin.

Smith stood in front of the Jefferson Memorial, dressed in his sweats, windbreaker, and squashed rainhat. The sky was a pristine blue; no rain forecast for that day.

A few minutes past seven, Jim Shevlin, dressed in running shorts and a sweatshirt, bounded up the stairs to Smith's side. He glanced up at the nineteen-foot bronze statue of Jefferson and said, "Good morning, Tom." Smith looked at him and said, "The same to you, Jim. Did I get you out too early?"

"For a Sunday morning, yes. Sunday mornings were made to sleep late. Anyway, you sounded like what you wanted to talk about was urgent, and I figured since you weren't suggesting breakfast, and insisted on meeting beneath the shadow of our third president, I'd better show. What's up?"

"We've had a run, let's take a walk."

They came down the steps of the rotunda and walked along the eastern edge of the basin, passing the Bureau of Engraving and Printing, and proceeding down along the treelined western edge of the water. Smith stopped abruptly and said, "Jim, I think I can deliver Herbert Greist to you."

Shevlin looked at him quizzically. "Deliver to me? Why would you say that?"

"Look, Jim, let's not play cloak-and-dagger. I don't have time. Let's just say that because of your previous employment with the FBI, you obviously know people within that organization who would be interested in knowing where Herbert Greist is. I thought I'd pass along the information to a fellow attorney as a favor, as a friend."

"As long as it's on that basis, proceed."

They moved on again, Smith talking as they walked. "I'm being blackmailed by Greist."

That stopped Shevlin in his tracks. *"You're* being blackmailed? What the hell for?"

"For nothing. Greist seems to think he has some deep, dark secret from my past that is worth money to me. He doesn't. Besides being an alleged Communist sympathizer and probable spy, he's a cheap hustler. The point is that I've agreed to pay him the money."

"Why would you do that?"

"So I can ascertain exactly where he is tonight and pass that information on to you, so that you can pass it on to your former employer."

"I see. You say tonight. Where?"

"New York. Actually, I'm not personally going to meet him. Let me back up a second. He's not going to be there, either. He's arranged to have a bagman waiting in a hotel in New York City. I'm sending Tony Buffolino with the money. I thought some of your friends back at the Bureau might enjoy accompanying him."

"Who the hell is Tony Buffolino?"

"An old friend of mine. He's—"

"That guy you defended, that foul-ball cop?"

"All in the past, Jim. Mr. Buffolino is now a respectable private investigator, and, I might add, a damn good one. Could we stop these diversions?"

"Go ahead."

By the time they had circumnavigated the basin and once again stood on the steps of the memorial, Smith had filled Shevlin in on what was to happen that night. "Interesting?" Smith asked.

"Very."

"Will you pass it along to your friends?"

"Yes, I think I will. Let's see, I seem to remember somebody who might be interested in getting involved in this little exercise this evening. Where will you be for the rest of the day?"

"Home until noon. Annabel, Tony, and I are flying to New York this afternoon. We'll be at the Waldorf."

"Okay, Mac. I, or someone from the Bureau, will get in touch with you either before you leave or in New York. Tell me, though, about this Buffolino. You really feel secure in sending him?"

"Yes. He's on crutches. Had an accident out in California about a week ago, but he's pretty good at getting around on them, at least good enough to get out of the way of another accident. Anything else you need to know?"

"Nope. Going for a run?"

"Yes, I'll jog back to the house. You?"

"Heading straight home for a good breakfast, a couple of hours with the papers, and a phone call or two, not necessarily in that order. Talk to you soon."

Annabel had packed and taken a cab to Smith's house. It was noon; Smith made salad. She sat at the kitchen table reading the papers while he put the dishes in the dishwasher. He said, "Do you know what's interesting about all of this, Annie? Greist is blackmailing Ewald in return for keeping quiet about his affair with Roseanna Gateaux. That tells me that neither he nor Mae Feldman have the stolen files on the Kane Ministries."

"You're right," she said. "Or he could be just looking for enough money to get out of the country—*with* the files—and use them later to go after bigger stakes."

Smith shook his head. "I don't think so. Those files have ended up in the hands of someone else, maybe the people who roughed up Tony and took the box from Mae Feldman's house."

"Who, in turn, undoubtedly turned them over to whomever they're working for," she said.

"Exactly. The point right now is that Greist doesn't have them."

Tony's cab arrived an hour later, and Smith helped him in with his small suitcase. The doctors at the university had redressed his wounds with a less cumbersome bandage; he was now able to wear his suit pants over it. To the surprise of Mac and Annabel, he was no longer on crutches. He had a cane.

"Are you steady enough on that?" Smith asked.

"Yeah, no problem."

"You look very distinguished," Annabel said. "A gentleman with his cane. Impressive."

"All you need is a bowler hat, and you'd be right at home in London," Smith said.

"I always wanted to go to London," Tony said. "Why don't you get somebody murdered, get us a British client, and send me there?"

Mac and Annabel looked at each other. There would be no new clients once this was over. They both knew it, but no sense dashing Tony's hopes.

Their three o'clock shuttle landed on time at La Guardia. Smith had arranged for a car to meet them, and they were driven to the Waldorf. New York City was so pleasant on Sunday, Smith thought, without the traffic jams and hordes on the streets. Very pleasant indeed. For five minutes. The rain began and was soon heavy; Annabel quietly hummed "April Showers" as the hired car pulled up in front of the hotel. They were taken to their rooms, which were across the hall from each other, and spent an hour in Tony's room going over plans for the evening.

"When do you figure they'll call?" Tony asked.

"The FBI? I don't know. They might not call us at all, just show up at the hotel without telling us. It really doesn't matter, although I would be more comfortable knowing their plans."

"Who do you figure will be in the room?" Tony asked.

"I have no idea, some crony, some gofer. Maybe even Mae Feldman."

"I'd like it to be Mae Feldman," Tony said. "Nothing I'd like more than to finally lay eyes on that woman. She damn near lost me my leg."

"Have you heard from Carla Zaretski?" Annabel asked.

"Yeah, she calls all the time. She keeps threatening to come to Washington, and I keep telling her I'm goin' out of town."

"Has she ever mentioned the money she took from Mae Feldman's bank account?"

"Nope, and I don't mention it. Should I have?"

Smith shook his head, "No, not yet."

An aluminum Samsonite camera case sat next to Tony's chair. Smith had taken it from his closet at home, removed the camera and accessories that were nestled into cutouts in the foam lining, and given it to Tony as the case he would use to carry the money. In it was a few thousand dollars Smith always kept in a safe at home. Annabel had arranged it in a layer to cover pieces of blank paper beneath. With luck, the person on the receiving end wouldn't dig too deeply.

"Where will you be?" Tony asked.

"Right here. Get this thing over with and come back as quickly as possible. Ready, Tony?"

Buffolino reached under his suit jacket and patted the bulge beneath his arm. He nodded. "Yeah, I'm ready. Any last-minute instructions?"

"Just protect your flanks," Smith said. Annabel kissed him on the cheek.

"Hey, I like that," Tony said. He looked at Smith warmly. "Don't worry, Mac, I respect you too much ever to make a move on your woman."

S H E had been in room 7 for the past two hours. She hadn't bothered to remove her raincoat because she was cold, and because she wanted an extra layer of protection while sitting in the dirty and only chair in the room, or on the edge of a bed covered with a soiled, torn bedspread. She smoked; an overflowing ashtray and half-filled empty coffee container held the stubbed-out results.

She checked her watch: eight o'clock. One hour to go. She'd considered leaving many times since arriving early in the afternoon, but knew she couldn't. Herbert would be furious. No telling what he would do to her. Because there was no phone in the room, she went down to the shabby lobby and called him from the pay phone. He snapped at her, "Why did you leave the room?"

"It's ours until—"

"Go back to the room, Mae. You never know. They might come early."

She hung up, went outside, and bought three packs of cigarettes and a cup of coffee to bring back with her.

When she heard the groan of the stairs fifteen minutes later, she knew someone was approaching the door. She'd been sitting on the edge of the bed; she tensed, stood, and went to the door, placed her ear against it. As she did, the person knocked, the sharp sound reverberating through her head. She pulled back. Another knock. She moved closer to the door and asked in a voice that broke, "Who is it?"

"It's Herbert," Greist said.

"Herbert?" Why was *he* here? They were to meet later, a few blocks away in a bar. "Herbert, is that really you?"

"Damn it, Mae, open the door."

She was both confused and relieved. Maybe he'd changed his mind and would replace her, or stay with her. That would be good. She hated being the one in that dingy room waiting to accept blackmail money.

Greist hit the door with his fist. "Open it, Mae."

She drew a deep breath and turned the knob. Greist carried a battered brown leather valise in his left hand. His right hand was in the pocket of his topcoat. "Thank God you're here," she said, standing back to allow him to enter.

He stepped into the room and closed the door behind him. "Herbert, I think we should leave," she said. "We don't need Ewald's money. We can find our own way, be together and not have to worry about—Oh, no." He'd brought his right hand out of his pocket. In it was a revolver. "Herbert, what are you doing? Why would you . . . ?" She began to retreat, her hands in front of her face, back and back until she bumped against the room's only window, which she'd opened to allow smoke to escape. "Dear man, please don't hurt me. We've shared so much, and there's so much to do together in the future if . . . if you don't . . . hurt . . . me." She whimpered like a puppy about to be hit with a rolled-up newspaper for soiling the rug, and cowered, shook, and said words to God.

Greist slowly crossed the room, the revolver still aimed at her face. When he was close to her, he raised his right arm and brought the full weight of the weapon against the side of her head. She fell to her knees; blood trickled from her left ear. He brought the weapon down on the top of her skull, and she pitched forward, her face landing on one of his shoes. He quickly replaced the revolver in his pocket, dropped the bag, and managed, with difficulty, to raise her up from the floor. She was unconscious. He leaned her against the window, and while holding her semi-erect by the front of her coat, opened the window with his other hand. The space outside was almost black, an air shaft, covered with years of the city's grit and grime. He slowly allowed her to sink back until her head and shoulders were out the window. Then he pushed her the rest of the way until she disappeared from view. Seconds later, the thud of her body hitting ground came back at him through the open window.

He looked down and saw her at the bottom of the shaft. Light from a first-floor window illuminated the body. She'd landed on her back, arms and legs akimbo. Her eyes were open, and there was what might be construed as a smile on her large red lips.

Greist picked up his bag and went to the door. He peered out onto the landing. There was no one there, and no sign of anyone coming up the stairs. He slowly closed the door, locked it, and sat in the room's only chair, waiting for the arrival of the money. He felt relief at what he'd just done. The woman was an albatross, always complaining, always second-guessing him. She'd lost the money and lost the files that were his ticket to retirement. Everything was gone now—everyone— his daughter and the mother of his only child, and that was good. It was better to be alone. Fewer problems, less worry. Now, all he had to do was accept the money, find a way to elude the FBI dragnet that had been cast for him, and get out, go to where he would be appreciated, maybe Cuba, or Panama, the Soviet Union itself, or Hungary, some- place where he and the money would go a long way.

A weary smile crossed his gray face. It would work now that they couldn't complicate his life. It was always someone else who caused trouble.

T o n y Buffolino said to the desk clerk, who'd just awakened from a nap, "I got to see somebody upstairs." The clerk shrugged and opened a magazine featuring naked couples. Tony cursed the lack of an elevator as he slowly went up the stairs, his leg throbbing with every step. When he reached the fourth-floor landing, he stared at the door to number 7, went to it, listened, then knocked. There was no response. He knocked again. Nothing. Had this all been a joke? Had whoever was there decided it might be a trap and left? Had Greist made that decision?

"Who is it?" a voice asked through the door.

"Tony Buffolino. I got something for you from the senator."

There was silence again.

Buffolino knocked. "Hey, open up. I got what you want, and I ain't gonna stand out in this hall much longer." Something smelled bad to Buffolino, and it wasn't the urine versus the cheap disinfectant that permeated the hotel. Why the delay in opening the door? This was to be a simple transaction. He pulled his .22 from beneath his arm and concealed it behind the aluminum Samsonite case.

Inside, Greist was going through his own set of concerns. It hadn't occurred to him until that moment that the person in the hallway might not be delivering money. It could be a trap, the FBI, the New York police. Ewald might have set him up. He put his mouth close to the door and said, "Identify yourself."

"For Christ's sake, I already told you my name is Tony Buffolino and I got the money you're waiting for. Password, Ewald. Five seconds, no more. Five seconds or you can go whistle."

A lock was undone, the handle was turned, and the door opened slowly. The gray man backed up to the center of the small room and stood at the foot of the bed. Tony stepped over the threshold. Greist held a leather bag in his left hand; his right hand was in his topcoat pocket.

"Here," Buffolino said, making a little move toward Greist with the aluminum case. "Here's your money."

Greist backed up further until he was almost to the window. "Put it on the bed," he said. "Just put it on the bed and get out."

"Yeah, sure, no sweat." Tony kept his eyes on Greist's right-hand coat pocket. You've got a piece in there, he thought. Because his weapon was already drawn and hidden behind the metal case, he wouldn't have a problem getting the drop on the man, whoever he was.

Buffolino slowly walked to the foot of the bed. He realized that the moment he tossed the case on it, his revolver would be exposed. That's okay, he told himself. Dump the case, hold him in place with the gun, and back out. No sweat. But then his eyes went to a red smear on the windowsill, to Greist's left. No question about it. Why would there be blood on the windowsill? Who was this guy? Had he killed someone else? Buffolino noticed that the window behind the man was fully open.

"I got a question for you," Buffolino said.

"No questions. Leave the money," Greist snapped, his right hand stirring.

"Somethin' ain't kosher here," Buffolino said. "Are you Greist?"

"I said no questions." The guy was obviously on the edge now. His hand started to come out of his pocket. Buffolino didn't hesitate. He tossed the metal case into Greist's chest. Buffolino's cane had been dangling from his left wrist. He grabbed the curved handle, held it out, and threw himself at Greist, the point of the cane catching him in the chest and driving him back and halfway out the window. Buffolino was instantly on top of him. He pressed the snout of his revolver tight against Greist's left temple. "You move that right hand, loser, and you're dead meat."

He yanked Greist up straight by the front of his coat and threw him against the wall, knocking a lamp to the floor. He rammed his revolver against the back of Greist's neck and said, "Okay, creep, you pull that right hand out real slow."

Greist did as he was told, his revolver dangling from his index finger. "Lay it on the table nice and easy," Buffolino said. "Do it my way, or I'm gonna leave a lot of you on this wall."

Greist lowered the weapon to the table and deposited it with a clunk.

"Nice, you take instructions real good," Buffolino said. "Turn around, slow, very slow."

Greist followed instructions and stood with his back to the wall, his arms raised above his head. There was a wild, frightened look on his face. Buffolino realized for the first time how old he was. At least he looked old, sickly, all gray and pasty, breath coming hard.

"What's your name?" Buffolino asked.

"This is wrong," Greist said. "Don't you know what you've done? I'll tell what I know about Senator Ewald."

"You know nothin'," Buffolino said. He nodded toward the windowsill. "Whose blood is that?"

"Blood?"

"Yeah, don't play dumb with me. You stay right here, don't move, don't even blink. You blink, you're a former human being." He slowly backed to the windowsill, his .22 leveled at Greist's chest. He ran a finger over the red blotch and examined what came off the sill.

"You don't understand," Greist said, trying to inject calm and reason into his voice. "We can make a deal. Believe me, I—"

"Shut up!" Buffolino leaned out the window, dividing his attention between Greist and the air shaft. He quickly looked down and saw the body at the bottom. He checked Greist and looked down again, longer this time. "Oh, damn it to hell," he said, "no." Looking up at him, with her heavily made-up eyes and garish red mouth formed into a twisted smile, was Carla.

"What'd you do that for?" he said to Greist.

"Please, listen to me. We can split the money you have. Give me half. Just give me a quarter of it, so I can leave. Take the rest. I won't say anything to anyone."

Buffolino came up close to Greist once again and shoved his revolver up under Greist's chin. Greist whimpered, whined, "No, please, don't."

"What the hell did you kill her for? What'd she ever do to you?"

"She was . . ." He had trouble speaking because of the iron pressure under his chin. "She was stupid. Let's talk. I know we can . . ."

Buffolino took a few steps back. His face was a mask of rage and frustration. What he did next was pure reflex, no thought directing the movement. He brought his cane up off the floor and smashed the end of it against the right side of Greist's face. Greist slowly slipped to his knees. He'd begun to cry.

"You cockroach. Come on, stop your bawlin' and get up."

Greist preceded Buffolino out of the room and they slowly made their way down the narrow stairs, Buffolino somehow carrying both cases and his cane in his left hand, his right hand steadying his revolver at the back of Greist's head. His leg throbbed, and he misstepped. Greist began to run. Buffolino found his balance and stumbled after him through the lobby. The desk clerk looked up from his magazine, and when he saw the gun in Buffolino's hand, threw up his magazine and ducked so that he was below the level of the counter. Greist made it through the front door.

Across the street, two men in raincoats came at him. Tony looked left and right; men dressed similarly closed in from the sides. Greist was surrounded and held. One pulled out a badge. "Simmons, FBI."

"Yeah, I knew you guys were coming. Tony Buffolino. This is the shyster Herbert Greist. There's a body at the bottom of an air shaft. Mr. Greist pushed a nice older woman out the window."

"You don't understand," Greist wailed. "It was an accident. She jumped."

"And hit her head on the windowsill going out," Buffolino said with disgust. Simmons, the leader of the group, dispatched two of his men to confirm what Tony had said. They returned and reported that there was, indeed, a dead woman at the bottom of the air shaft.

"So, here he is, your Commie spy. You don't mind if I leave him with you? I got to check in with my boss. And here's his bag. Empty, like him."

"You have to come with us," one of the agents said.

"No, let him go," said Simmons. "You're going to meet with Mackensie Smith at the Waldorf?" he asked.

"Yeah."

"We'll contact you there. Nice job."

"Yeah," Tony muttered. "Nice job." He looked at Greist. "I should've done you up there, creep. She was a nice lady—a little kookie maybe, but nice. You shouldn't've done that to her. She didn't deserve it."

He limped painfully up the street, the brushed aluminum Samsonite case in his left hand, the cane in his right, supporting his weight. A rare Sunday night in the rain yellow cab stopped at a corner and discharged a passenger. Tony slid into the backseat and laid his leg across it. "The Waldorf Astoria," he said painfully, "and don't step on it."

THIRTY-FOUR

SPECIAL AGENT SIMMONS came to the Waldorf the next morning and took a deposition from Buffolino. He thanked Smith for his help in setting up Herbert Greist, and told him they'd keep in touch.

The three of them caught an early shuttle to Washington. The hired car dropped Annabel off at her home, and took Smith and Buffolino to the Watergate.

"What's that you're humming?" Buffolino asked as he and Smith waited for the elevator.

Smith smiled. "I didn't realize I was humming anything. It's 'Celeste Aida' from Verdi's *Aida*."

"Sounds nice."

"Yes, it's a love song, one of my favorites."

"Yeah, nice. I was learnin' to like opera."

They stepped out on their floor. Directly in front of them was a large mirror over a marble-topped table. A bouquet of red and yellow fresh flowers dominated it. A young man, who'd been standing by the table, quickly turned his back to them and examined the flowers.

"That guy don't smell right to me," Buffolino said as they walked down the hall.

"I didn't notice," said Smith. "He might be part of the hotel security staff."

Smith called Ken Ewald at home and was told by a secretary he'd be back in two hours. He hung up and said to Tony, "With Greist out of the way, I'd say we're getting close to winding things up."

"Yeah, maybe, except we still got to find Janet Ewald."

"Yes, that's true, and Marcia Mims, too. Why don't you get on the phone and see what you can accomplish. I'm going back to the house. See you at four."

. . .

I N a motel room in Miami Beach, Florida, Janet Ewald sat alone. It was a small motel that catered to young people; signs outside heralded free drinks for women between 4:00 and 7:00 P.M., wet T-shirt contests on Wednesday nights, and chug-a-lug competitions every Friday. The fierce Florida sun threatened to burn through purple drapes Janet had drawn tightly across the window. The television set was on but without sound. A game show was in progress.

She sat in a purple vinyl chair, her arms tightly wrapped around herself; she was wearing a cardigan sweater because the blast of the air conditioner, even turned low, chilled her. She rocked forward and back. The chair was stationary; she created the rocking motion with her own body. She continued moving until a painful whine from deep inside came through her lips and nose and caused her to violently throw her head forward, then back against the chair.

She looked across the bed at a table and a white telephone. She'd reached for that phone many times since arriving at the motel the previous afternoon, had actually picked up the receiver on occasion, but never dialed.

Standing unsteadily, she went around the bed, sat on it, and read the instructions about how to dial. She was confused by them. She opened her purse, removed a small address book, slowly turned its pages until coming to the *C* section, and squinted at the handwritten number next to Geoffrey Collins's name. She dialed.

"Dr. Collins's office," his receptionist said.

The sound of a voice on the other end startled Janet.

"Hello, Dr. Collins's office."

"Hello. This is . . . this is Janet Ewald."

"Oh, Mrs. Ewald. Where are you calling from?"

The question threw her. Did the receptionist know she'd been missing? Could she trust her? Could she trust anyone?

"Mrs. Ewald?"

"Yes . . . is the doctor in?"

"Yes, he's in session, but . . . please hold on."

A few moments later, Collins came on the line. "Janet, how are you? Everyone has been worried about you."

"Yes, I know they have. Dr. Collins, I . . ."

"Are you all right?"

"Yes, no . . . Oh, Doctor, I just want to die."

"Why would you want to do that, Janet? You're young. Nothing can be so bad that we need death to resolve it."

"You don't understand. I know so much . . . I know things . . . I'm afraid."

"Where are you?"

"I'm in Florida."

Collins's laugh was professional. "I wish I were there. Is the weather good?"

"Yes, very nice . . ."

"Janet, will you come back, come directly to me? Surely, you're not afraid of me. I've always been your friend, and I'll make sure nothing happens to you."

She was silent.

"Janet. Are you there?"

"Yes. I know I should come back. I have to talk to someone. I talked to Mr. Smith, but then I got scared again and ran away."

"Mr. Smith?"

"Mackensie Smith, my father-in-law's friend."

"Oh, Mac Smith. Why don't you come back and let the two of us help you through this?"

"All right. I mean, I might."

"Here's what I suggest, Janet. Enjoy the sun, have a good rest tonight, and take a plane first thing tomorrow morning. Call now and make a reservation. When you get to Washington, come directly to my office. Call and let me know what time you'll be here."

"All right."

"Do you want me to call Mac Smith?"

"No, that's—yes, call him. I trust him. I trust you." She hung up.

SMITH returned to the Watergate at four and asked Buffolino, "How's the leg?"

"Pretty good. What are you up to tonight?"

"Annabel and I promised Ken Ewald that we'd attend a fund-raiser tonight at the Four Seasons Hotel. The arts crowd is throwing a party for him."

"Should be fun. I'll come along."

"No, you stay here and rest. After what you went through in New York, you could use a little relaxation."

"I don't know how to relax. Hey, Mac, let me ask you a straight question."

"What is it?"

"Are we gonna stay on this thing for a while? I mean, if this job is about to end, I'd better start making some plans."

"To be honest with you, Tony, I don't know how much longer we'll stay involved. Outside circumstances will determine that, I suppose. In the meantime, don't worry about it. You're still on the payroll, and I'll give you plenty of notice. Fair enough?"

Buffolino grinned. "You're always fair, Mac. Thanks."

Before leaving the suite, Smith dialed his answering machine at home. There was an urgent message from Dr. Geoffrey Collins. Smith returned the call.

"Good to hear your voice again, Mac," Collins said. "It's been a while."

"Good to hear you, too, Geof. I got your message. What's up?"

"I just got off the phone with Janet Ewald."

"You did? Where is she?"

"She said she was in Florida. I think I've convinced her to fly back here tomorrow morning and to come to my office. She mentioned she'd seen you, and when I asked whether she wanted me to call you, she said she did."

"This is good news, Geof. Do you think she'll actually show up?"

"I have no idea, but I would like you to be here if she does."

"Of course. Keep me informed, call anytime."

Smith said to Tony Buffolino, "That was the psychiatrist who's treated Janet Ewald. She called him from Florida and said she's coming back tomorrow. I'd just as soon she return of her own volition, but I don't have much faith in that. Can you put out some tracers in Florida? Let's assume she's in the Miami area, although she could be anywhere in the state."

"Sure. I got a friend in the airlines who owes me. They don't give out passenger manifests, but he's broken that rule for me a couple a' times. If she used her own name, I can get it. I'll give Joe Riga a call, too, and see if his pals can come up with something."

"Good. I'll check back in with you after the party."

Smith and Annabel went to a suite in the Georgetown Four Seasons where a cocktail reception for Ken and Leslie Ewald was in progress. This was a smaller gathering of a half-dozen movers-and-shakers in Washington's artistic community. A hundred lesser lights would be downstairs later.

"Any prepared remarks for me?" Ewald asked Ed Farmer.

"Prepared remarks for these people? All they want to do is shake your hand and hear you tell them how much their support means to you. Your Senate record on funding the arts makes you a hero to them. Just play hero." Smith smiled at Farmer's comment, although the campaign manager had delivered it, as usual, without any levity of tone. Farmer frowned at Smith and walked away.

Ewald and his entourage went downstairs to the larger affair where Smith and Annabel were introduced to a few people at the door, then drifted to a corner to watch Ewald work the room. Smith had considered telling Ken and Leslie about the possible return of Janet, but thought better of it. Wait for a quiet moment, when no one had to be onstage.

It was just another party until Ed Farmer captured the attention of most of the people by saying in a loud voice, "Ladies and gentlemen, I know the next president of the United States, Ken Ewald, would like to say a few words."

The whoops and hollers rose to a crescendo, and then died as Ewald said, "Ladies and gentlemen, I can say honestly to you that I've been to a lot of rubber-chicken-and-rice dinners. I've shared times like this with hundreds of thousands of people in many states, and will have to do the same in the months ahead, but never have I enjoyed an hour more than this." Applause. Ewald's hands held high in the air, Leslie beaming at his side. "As I stand here, what keeps running through my mind is the adage that many of you, especially in theater, live by. 'The show must go on.' This campaign—this *show* we are in the process of producing—has run into many out-of-town trials and tribulations. We've had to rewrite as we went, change scenes, juggle adversity—to say nothing of unexpected and unhappy surprises—but here we are ready for the convention, and I can tell you that *this* show is now ready for a long run, thanks to creative, caring people like you."

Smith looked at Annabel and smiled. "Prepared remarks?" he said. "He's better on his feet."

Ewald continued. "We took some battering a while back because of circumstances beyond our control. Now we have control again, and everyone in this room who cares about the cultural aspects of this society we share can rest assured that not only do I intend to win the Democratic nomination in July, I intend to become the next president of these United States. And as president, I will do everything in my power to help shift this society from one of hate and prejudice and misunderstanding to one in which the beautiful music can be heard once again, the magnificent words of our writers and poets can be heard, and the gentler aspirations that a society rich in culture fosters will be with us for at least four years and, hopefully, far into the future." He waited until the applause had ebbed, and concluded with, "This beautiful woman at my side has been my inspiration throughout the difficulties of this campaign. My main opponent is a gentleman with whom I've served for many years in the Senate. Senator Backus is a good man who loves this country as much as I do. The difference is that in an administration such as we now have in Washington, there is no room for beauty and culture, because most of the attention and most of the money are focused on destructive things. Don't misunderstand. We must have a strong and secure nation in order for the beautiful things to grow, to blossom, but there must be something else in a society if it is to be judged generations from now as one of compassion and love. Senator Backus represents an anachronistic view of how we take America and move it forward into the light, rather than into the shadows. What more can I say, except to say thank you from me and from Leslie and from every man and woman who has worked so hard to see their dreams—and your dreams—become reality once again. When November eighth is over, I promise you one thing . . . we will all gather again, only this time it will be in the White House, and we will raise a toast to the future of this free industrial, agricultural, commercial, *and* cultural giant . . . the United States of America!"

Many of those in the room tried to reach Ewald as he and Leslie made their way to the door, preceded by Farmer and Secret Service agents. Mac and Annabel didn't try to catch up with them. They lingered, watched, and, once the Ewalds and official followers were out of the room, made their own way to the lobby.

"What do you think?" she asked.

Smith shrugged. "I have my reservations about Ken, but I keep coming back to the conviction that he's a hell of a lot better than the alternative. Yes, I'd like to see him in the White House. I think some good things must come out of it."

When they returned to the Watergate suite, Buffolino told them that his airline friend found no passenger between Washington and Miami by the name of Janet Ewald. "Funny thing, though," he added. "Riga called me. His people have been checking manifests, too, and he said they ran across a passenger flying to Miami from D.C. by the name of Andrea Feldman."

Smith said, "The Andrea Feldman we know isn't taking trips anywhere these days."

"Yeah. Kind of spooky though, huh?"

"Try checking it through," Smith said.

Annabel turned on the TV. Buffolino said, "I think I'll go downstairs and get a drink. I'm getting cabin fever here."

Buffolino went to the lobby, which was bustling with well-dressed people—a typical Watergate crowd, he thought. There was a group of Japanese tourists, a familiar sight in every city in America. An aristocratic couple with regal bearing waited at the elevator, he in a tuxedo, she in a floor-length ball gown bursting with sequins. He then saw the same slender, nicely dressed Hispanic young man they'd seen on their floor earlier in the day. He thought of Smith's comment, that he was probably a member of hotel security, and decided Smith was right. He acted like a plainclothes security guy, his eyes taking in everything and everyone. Still, Tony didn't like it. Then again, all Hispanics made him uneasy since the night he'd been set up by Garcia. He had to admit that, and he did as he went to the bar and enjoyed a leisurely drink by himself. I hope this booze goes right to my thigh, he thought; it's killing me.

THIRTY-FIVE

MAC SMITH had never believed in the observation that the great leveling factor was putting on pants one leg at a time. For him, it was paying bills, and that unpleasant task, long neglected the past weeks, was what he focused on the next morning. It seemed a good chore to undertake while waiting for a phone call from Geof Collins about whether or not Janet Ewald had arrived.

Annabel called him from her gallery to see if he'd heard. "No. I think I'll call him," he said, looking up at the clock. It was noon.

"You'll let me know as soon as you find out anything."

"Of course. How are things this morning with your little stone friends?"

"My little friends are fine. I've missed them. They've gotten dusty, poor things. James is an asset, but I suspect he doesn't do windows, and I *know* he doesn't dust. Talk with you later."

Smith's call to Collins was disappointing. Not a word from Janet. "No idea where in Florida she called from?" Smith asked.

"None whatsoever, Mac. She's very fragile, very enigmatic. I'll be relieved when we do hear from her. *If* we do."

"You and a lot of other people. Mind if I call again in a couple of hours?"

"Not at all."

He was writing out a check against his monthly tab at the Foggy Bottom Cafe when the phone rang. It was Buffolino, who wanted to know what the plans were for the rest of the day.

"Frankly, Tony, I haven't made any. Annabel and I are going to the testimonial for Ken Ewald tonight at the Watergate." Smith laughed. "How do politicians stand it, one dinner after another, plaques that never get hung up on the wall, bone-crushing handshakes, fattening foods, and having to suffer fools always looking for something from you?"

"Takes a certain kind a' guy."

"Yes, it certainly does. Anyway, there is that dinner tonight we're going to. We'll stop up at the suite before."

The last of the bills paid, and after a lunch of two hard-boiled eggs, sliced tomatoes, Bermuda onion, and breadsticks, Smith headed for the Yates Field House for a workout. During the drive, he thought about the contest between Ewald and Backus for their party's nomination. He also admitted to himself for the first time that he'd begun to question Ewald's ability to lead the nation. Did his friend lack the necessary strength of character? Smith had never viewed it that way, preferring to chalk up any perceived weaknesses in Ewald as representing simple human frailty, a concept that was dear to Smith's heart. As he got older, he'd become more tolerant of his fellow man (and woman, of course), and of the human dilemma.

But running for president of the United States demanded less "humanity," didn't it, someone with fewer foibles than the pack? Ken Ewald was *very* human—good enough for a friend, but was that good enough to lead the greatest nation on earth? Smith puffed his cheeks and expelled the air in a burst. "Who knows?" he muttered. "Who knows anything?"

He thought of Backus, whose political views were anathema to him yet who seemed to possess those traits necessary, perhaps, to lead effectively. Ironic, he thought as he pulled into the parking lot, that his kind of human being might be the best qualification for the White House.

While Smith ran and lifted weights and thought about him, Senator Jody Backus reached Washington, Virginia, after slightly more than an hour's drive. There were few cars parked in front of the Inn at Little Washington, and they were what one would expect to see there—two Jags, two BMW's, and a Mercedes limousine.

He paused at the main entrance to the inn and looked back at the empty road. This was the first time since he'd announced his candidacy that there wasn't at least one other vehicle trailing behind, usually filled with Secret Service agents. He'd really had to put his foot down to get them off his tail today. Thank God for Jeroldson, who took the responsibility for letting him go off on his own for a couple of hours.

Backus knocked on the door of the largest suite in the ten-room inn.

It was opened by a young man who said, "Come in, Senator. We've been expecting you."

Backus had met this boy before and didn't like him. His name was Warner Jenco. A head of carefully arranged blond curls formed a helmet above his placid face. His suit, shirt, and tie were as bland as the rest of him.

Backus stood in the middle of the living room. "Where is he?" he asked.

"On the phone, Senator. He'll be with you in a minute."

"Tell him I don't have all day."

Jenco disappeared into a bedroom. Backus went to the window and looked out over the Blue Ridge Mountains; they might have been painted there for the visual entertainment of guests, who paid top dollar for the suite. A profound sadness came over him. The mountains reminded him of his home in Georgia, where as a boy he'd spent countless days roaming them. How long ago that seemed; he saw himself—a chubby, barefoot kid with the bottoms of his overalls rolled up—wading in a crystal-clear trout stream, a sort of Mark Twain–Norman Rockwell kid. Those were good days, when he was a good kid.

The moment of reflection calmed him. Now, as he paced the large room, waiting, his anger returned. Easy, he told himself. You'll have a heart attack. He took deep breaths. His face was red; he could feel his heart pumping in his large chest.

Just as he was about to go to the door and bang on it, it opened, and the Reverend Garrett Kane entered the living room. The smile that lighted up millions of television sets across America was in place as he said in his deep, cultured voice, "Jody, how good to see you." He closed the gap between them and extended his hand. Backus looked at it, and a sour expression crossed his face. Kane kept his hand extended, the smile never dimming. Backus finally took it, pumped once, let go.

"Please, sit down, Jody. Bourbon? I had it ordered up just for you, your favorite brand." He crossed to a small bar and held out a bottle for Backus's approval, like a wine steward presenting the evening's choice.

"Yeah, I'll have me some of that. I need a belt of something."

Kane carefully measured the drink with a shot glass, poured it over ice, and handed it to the senator, who had begun to perspire. "Turn on some AC," Backus said, downing the drink. "Hot as hell in here."

"I find it quite comfortable," Kane said, pulling up a straight-back chair. "Refill?"

"I'll get it myself." Backus poured directly from the bottle.

"Do you ever worry that you drink a tad too much, Jody?" Kane asked.

Backus looked at him with watery eyes. "What in hell business is that of yours?" He consumed half the drink, and added, "There's nothin' like men of the cloth who raise hell against sin, then go out and do all the sinnin' they damn well please." He sank into an oversized leather chair.

"I hate to see you this upset, Jody," Kane said. "No need to be upset about anything. It seems to me that things in general are very well in control, very well indeed."

"I don't see it that way, Garrett. I told you up at Zach Filler's lodge that I had a feelin' things had gone too far, and I'm here to tell you it's got to stop!"

Kane raised his head, an amused look on his face, the fingers of one hand gently touching his chin. It was a pose Backus had seen him adopt too many times before, a posture of superiority and scorn. Backus wanted to lunge at him, beat a fist into his smooth, tanned face, see his perfect white caps fall on the floor like little ice cubes.

"Jody, I only ask about your drinking habits because a man who drinks too much often finds his judgment clouded, his lips becoming unnecessarily loose. Do you understand me?"

"Look, drinking has nothing to do with this, and you know it. I didn't get to where I did with bad judgment and a mouth that flaps." He fixed Kane in a steely stare and, for the first time, saw the minister's cocky, arrogant expression change—not much, but enough to give Backus control. "What's happened here, it seems to me, is that like with a lot of good things, some people go too far, ruin it, turn somethin' good into somethin' bad, somethin' that starts to smell. I see it all the time. You could see it on the Iran-Contra committee. Riled the hell out of me that good people like North and Poindexter took a worthwhile project and turned it into somethin' stupid and illegal. I saw it when Nixon resigned in disgrace, and when Kennedy pulled his goddamn Bay of Pigs. Happens all the time in government, because people get swelled heads and think they know everything, think they are above everybody else. That's when good things go to hell in a handbasket, Garrett, and that's what I see happening here."

Kane had listened intently. When Backus's short speech was over and he returned to polishing off his drink, Kane pointedly looked at his watch. "Are you finished?" he asked.

"No, I don't think I am. I want your promise that the things I'm speaking of are goin' to stop. Listen closely to me, Garrett. If I don't get your promise, you lose this U.S. senator, and you need him."

"I think you might have it backward, Jody. The fact is, you need me more than I need you. That's probably hard for a man like you to accept, wheeling and dealing in the Senate for so many years, handing out favors, collecting your share, buying votes, and burying bodies." He strung out the last two words, said them with careful and precise emphasis. There was silence as they looked at each other.

Backus said, "You're the one with clouded judgment and loose lips, Reverend."

"And you're the one with the blood of a dead girl on your hands."

Backus rose to his full height and shouted, "Don't you say anything like that to me ever again, you hypocritical, sanctimonious bastard!"

Kane flinched at the power in Backus's voice. He quickly opened the bedroom door and said, "Come in here." Jenko and another young man stood in the doorway. Kane said to Backus, who still shook with rage, "I thought we might have the next president of the United States as a friend. You want to know the truth, Jody? You're a loser—a big, fat, drunken slob of a loser, who's going to end up shining Ewald's shoes and making speeches on his behalf. At least, that's what would be the case if I weren't here to think clearly, to understand what's at stake and to have the guts to stop it. Now, I suggest you leave and continue to go through the motions of seeking the Democratic nomination. It looks good that you do that, even though none of it makes any difference. Raymond Thornton will be the next president of the United States, and you will continue to slap backs and make promises in coatrooms until, one night, you've had too much to drink and run your car into a telephone pole. The nation will mourn the death of Senator Jody Backus." That famous smile suddenly lit up his face, and his eyes widened. "And I will be honored to officiate at the funeral. Get out!"

Backus started to say something, but the two young men came around to either side of Kane. Backus seemed unsure of what to do. He held up the glass that now contained only ice cubes, and for a second poised to hurl it at the Reverend Garrett Kane. Instead, he dropped it to the floor and slowly crossed the room, pausing at the door. He turned and said, "I've had a distinguished career as a United States senator. I may have played the political game rough at times, but I never lost sight of why. I love this country, Garrett, and I have given to it the best years of my life. You may think what you want of me, but if there is one thing this fat ol' Georgia politician is *not*, it's a party to assassination." He slammed the door behind him.

BACKUS had left for his meeting with Kane from his Senate office. Now, he drove directly home. His wife, Lorraine, was baking biscuits for dinner. "What are you doin' home so early?" she asked, her southern accent as thick as his. Lorraine Backus was a short, round woman whose reservoir of energy seemed never to run out. She was one of the most popular Senate wives in Washington.

Backus crossed the kitchen and kissed her on the cheek. "Those biscuits smell good," he said.

"Made them especially for you, Mr. Senator. You go take your shoes off and get comfortable, and I'll bring you a drink. I have some news for you."

Backus lumbered from the kitchen, heavy with a fatigue that threatened to pin him to the floor. He went to his study and did exactly as he was told, removed his shoes, slipped his feet into a pair of slippers, and sat in a favorite chair by a bow window. A window seat in front of the window was used as a ledge for many framed family photographs. Backus leaned forward and looked at them, as he often did. There was something wonderful about a family, something sustaining. Backus had two sons and two daughters, all grown and married, and five grandchildren. Nothing gave him more pleasure than being with his grandchildren. He'd taught them all how to fish. The youngest, Paula, had caught the biggest bass of the five; a picture taken on Jody's boat in

Georgia showed a proud Paula holding her catch, almost as big as she was. Behind her, and beaming from ear to ear, was Backus.

Lorraine Backus came into the study, handed her husband a glass of bourbon, and sat on a hassock at his feet. "Well, now, what brings you home at this hour?"

"I've got to do some serious thinkin', Lorri, and I got to do it fast. I figured I could think better here than someplace else. What's this news you have for me?"

"You are about to have yourself another fishing student."

"What in hell does that mean?"

"Winnie is expecting again. She called me just a couple of hours ago. Isn't that wonderful?"

Backus sat back and clasped his hands on his chest. Tears formed in his eyes. Few people knew that Jody Backus, all 260 rough-and-ready pounds of him, was capable of crying. He made sure he did it privately, but the tears were real in solitude.

"Jody, are you all right? You look very tired today, or very worried, or both."

He managed to smile, reached out and took one of her hands in both of his. "Just a little pooped, Lorri," he said. "I think it's time for you and me to get away, take a nice vacation, maybe go to Paris, where you've always been wantin' to go, then come back and spend a little time fishin' with the kids. That sound good to you?"

"Sounds wonderful."

"Sure does to me." He patted her hand and released it. "Now, you get back in that kitchen and make sure those biscuits don't burn. I need to be alone for a bit."

MAC Smith had just slipped on his tuxedo pants and was pulling the suspenders over his shoulders when the phone rang. Annabel, he assumed, whom he'd be picking up in a half hour. "Hi," he said.

"Mac, this is Tony."

"I thought it was Annabel. What's up?"

"Mac, I think you'd better get here right away."

"What's wrong?"

"We've got a couple of visitors."

"Who?"

"Two lovely ladies. One is named Janet Ewald, the other Marcia Mims."

"I'm on my way."

THIRTY-SIX

I WANT to apologize for all the trouble I've put you through, Mr. Smith," Janet Ewald said. She sat in the Watergate suite with Smith, Annabel, Tony Buffolino, and Marcia Mims.

"That isn't important, Janet, although I appreciate the sentiment. I'm just glad to see you here."

"Because of Marcia." She managed a weak smile at her friend before saying to Smith, "I was going to go to Dr. Collins's office, but Marcia. convinced me to come here. I called Dr. Collins and told him I was back. I'll call him again tomorrow and make an appointment. I think I could use it."

"What name were you traveling under?" Smith asked. He knew.

Janet glanced at Marcia before opening her purse and pulling out a VISA card. She handed it to Smith.

"Where did you get this?" he asked, passing it to Annabel.

"In Ken and Leslie's house."

Annabel said, "I assume—and please pardon me if I sound insensitive—I assume you found this because of Paul's affair with Andrea."

If Janet considered the comment insensitive, her face didn't say it. There was some strength there now as she said, "No. Mr. Farmer had that card. He left it in an unlocked desk drawer, and I just took it when the need arose."

"Ed Farmer? Why would he have it?" Smith asked.

"Because he and Andrea were close, *very* close."

"Are you saying that Ed Farmer had an affair with Andrea Feldman, *too*?" Annabel asked.

"I didn't say that," Janet said. "I said they were close, in a business sense. Mr. Farmer approved the credit cards for staff members. Andrea had a lot of them."

"What do you mean by a lot?" Smith asked.

"More than the others. Mr. Farmer gave her cards to department stores, house accounts at restaurants, American Express, VISA, MasterCard, all of them."

"He was the one who approved the use of them?" Annabel asked.

"Yes. He never questioned Andrea's charges."

"Go on," said Smith.

"I was in the house once when Andrea stayed overnight. She didn't know I was there. I'd been sick and decided to spend the weekend at my in-laws' house. I used the spare bedroom next to that small office on the second floor."

"Where was Paul?" Annabel asked.

"Away on business. I forget where. It doesn't matter. Sometimes when Paul is away and I'm not feeling well, I stay there to be close to Marcia."

Smith smiled at Marcia. "Go on, Janet, continue."

"That night, I heard them fighting. Andrea and Farmer. They were in the small office."

"Where was Senator Ewald?" Annabel asked.

"Out somewhere. I know he came back later because I heard him, but he wasn't there when the fight was going on."

"What were they fighting about?"

"About . . ." She looked at Marcia and suddenly went back into the shell that Smith recognized.

"Go ahead, honey, tell them," Marcia said, patting her arm. "Remember what we talked about, that you would come back and tell everything you know, get it over with."

"They were arguing about files that Mr. Farmer had stolen from Ken."

"That *Farmer* had stolen from Ken? We thought Andrea stole files."

"I think she did, along with him. I mean, I think what happened was that they did it together. I didn't pay much attention at first, and I didn't make any kind of notes, but when they really started yelling, I sat up and listened as closely as I could. She was threatening him. She said she was going to tell Ken what he'd done, and that he had better be good to her if he didn't want that to happen."

" 'Good to her'?" Annabel said. "Do you know what she meant by that?"

"No."

Smith asked, "Did you get any hint of why the files might have been taken, who they stole them for?"

"No. They kept talking about 'they,' but they never mentioned any names."

"Janet, there must have been something else said. Didn't they discuss why they'd done it, how they got started, who had the idea?"

Janet shook her head. "No, they didn't. I learned more from Paul than from what I heard that night."

"What did Paul tell you?"

"We were arguing one night about his affair with Andrea, and he told me that he hated her and was sorry he ever brought her into his father's life. He said she was no good, evil, cared only about money and her own success. He told me that files his father kept had been stolen, and he said she did it."

"I thought you said Farmer did it with her," Annabel said.

"Yes, that's what I heard that night, but Paul didn't know that."

"Didn't you tell him?" Smith asked.

Janet looked sheepishly at her lap. "No, I didn't. I wanted him to think it was all Andrea. I *wanted* him to hate her, so that he wouldn't see her again."

Smith took a walk around the room to stretch his legs—and his mind. When he took his chair again, he said, "You told me in Annapolis that your father-in-law had slept with Andrea." He looked at Marcia. "And you agreed with her, Marcia." He almost mentioned the diary, but didn't want to bring it up in Janet's presence.

Janet sat folded into herself, a blank expression on her face.

"Well, didn't you tell me that, Janet?"

"Yes, I did."

Smith waited for more. When it didn't come, he asked, "Were you lying to me?"

"Yes," she said in a low voice.

"Why?" Annabel asked.

"Because I've always hated him. I talked about it with Dr. Collins, and he said I loved Paul so much that I actually wanted to shift the blame to his father, to make it seem that the only Ewald who'd been with Andrea was him, not my husband. I know better, of course, always did, but I suppose I was playing some kind of game with myself." She sighed and stood, a person purged, rid of a poison. "I'm sorry," she said. "I know I've caused a great deal of trouble. I never meant to, but I suppose people like me always do."

Smith said, "I think you ought to stop considering yourself unworthy, Janet. You're a good person, and I'm glad we're all here."

He asked Marcia why she'd gone along with Janet's story about Ken Ewald having slept with Andrea Feldman. Her answer was, "I suspected he did, but never knew for sure. When Janet said he had slept with her, I believed her. I'm . . . sorry."

"You said you were afraid to come back," Smith said, "that something terrible would happen to you. Who are you afraid will do something to you?"

"Mr. Farmer."

"Afraid Ed Farmer will physically hurt you?"

"I don't know what he would do. I don't like him, don't trust him, never did. I think Paul's father made a big mistake in trusting him. And when Marcia told me about the tape and what happened the night Andrea was murdered, I knew I had to get away."

"Wait a minute," Annabel said, "are you suggesting that . . . Ed Farmer murdered Andrea?"

"Yes."

"What tape?" Smith asked. "What happened the night of the murder?"

"Here." Marcia pulled a reel of tape from her purse and handed it to Smith. "There's a tape recorder in the second-floor office that goes on automatically every time the phone is picked up. Mr. Farmer had it installed. This is the tape that was on the machine the night Ms. Feldman was killed."

Smith weighed the tape in his hands, asked, "What's on it?"

Marcia said, "The telephone conversation I had with Ms. Feldman. She'd called looking for Senator Ewald. I told her he wasn't there. She said to me that she would wait outside the Kennedy Center for exactly an hour, and that I was to tell him when he came home to meet her there. She said it was urgent. She sounded very angry, very upset."

"Did you give Senator Ewald the message?" Buffolino asked. It was the first thing he'd said since Smith and Annabel arrived.

"No, he didn't come home. He'd called from his office to say he had an appointment. I told Mrs. Ewald that, but I never had a chance to give him the message from Ms. Feldman."

"That was all?" Annabel said. "I don't understand why her conversation with you is so important."

"Because after I hung up on Ms. Feldman, I saw Mr. Farmer go into the upstairs office, and heard him listening to the conversation on tape."

"What did you do then?" Smith asked.

"*I* didn't do anything, but Mr. Farmer left the house immediately."

"To meet Andrea Feldman," Annabel said.

Janet Ewald just looked straight ahead.

"Marcia, why didn't you come forward with this, especially when Paul was taken in as a suspect?" Smith asked.

"I wasn't sure what to do. When Janet disappeared, I decided to wait to discuss it with her before doing anything else. I told her about it, and she told me about the fight she'd heard between Mr. Farmer and Ms. Feldman."

"And neither of you did anything," said Buffolino.

Both Janet and Marcia shook their heads. "We were afraid," Janet said.

"I didn't even write it in my diary," Marcia added.

Smith looked at his watch. "I want the two of you to stay here. Will you do that?"

"Yes, we will," Janet said.

"Forgive me for being skeptical, Janet," Smith said, "but you've promised me things before. I want you to trust me, to know that the advice I'm giving you is good, that you won't be hurt, and that you have nothing to fear. Annabel and I are going to be leaving shortly, but Tony will stay with you." He said to Buffolino, "I'd like to talk to you for a few minutes."

They went into the bedroom, where Smith told Buffolino not to let either woman out of his sight, and to do anything short of shooting them to keep them in the suite.

They returned to the living room. "Janet, Marcia, just relax," Smith said. "Order up room service if you'd like. Just let Tony know what you want. He knows the menu by heart. We'll be back."

"Is Mr. Farmer downstairs?" Janet asked.

"I assume so, but don't worry. Whether you're correct or not about him, I assure you he won't have the opportunity to do you any harm."

S M I T H and Annabel went to the cocktail party, spotted and cornered Leslie. "Leslie, we need additional seating tonight."

"Mac, I can't do that at this late date."

"It's important. I have special guests with me. Can you arrange for a separate table for us at the rear of the room?"

Leslie sighed. "I'll try. Who are these 'special' guests?"

"I wish to bring my investigator, Tony Buffolino, to the dinner. He'll be joined by your daughter-in-law, Janet, and your housekeeper, Marcia Mims."

The shock value of his words registered on her face. She composed herself quickly. "You can't do this to me, Mac. I mean, I'm delighted Janet is back, but having her at dinner under these circumstances will . . . well, I mean, everyone knows she's been missing. It will take away from Ken, from the focus of the dinner."

Smith smiled, although without complete sincerity. "Leslie, let me invoke the saying of Hollywood agents. Trust me. It's important that they be at the dinner."

She was angry, no doubt about that, but she backed off. She nodded. But her parting words were, "Please, don't allow anything to spoil this evening. We've worked so hard. How *is* Janet?"

"Fine. She wants very much to be part of this evening, part of this family again."

"I wish Paul were here."

"Why isn't he?"

"He's in Taiwan. An unnecessary trip. He's distancing himself from us. People! Families! Life would be so simple without them."

Smith half grinned. "And dreadfully empty. Thanks, Leslie."

W H E N Mac and Annabel returned to the suite, it was clear that Tony Buffolino hadn't wasted time in entertaining his guests. He'd ordered up shrimp cocktails, chicken liver pâté, an obscene mound of beluga caviar, spareribs, and an assortment of sandwiches. Janet seemed considerably more relaxed than when she'd arrived.

"Looks like you're taking good care of everyone," Smith said to Buffolino. "Expecting the Cabinet, too?"

"Just trying to be a good host," he said. "Help yourself. I think I overdid it."

"How are you feeling, Janet?" Annabel asked.

Janet managed a small, wan smile. "Better, thank you. He's funny." She looked at Buffolino.

"Yes, he can be amusing," said Smith.

"I was just tellin' 'em some of the old war stories from when I was on the force. That's one good thing about being a cop, huh, you always got a good story."

Unlike Janet, Marcia Mims was visibly on edge as she stood at a window and vacantly looked through it. "Marcia, could we talk for a minute?" Smith asked.

She followed him to the bedroom, where, the moment the door was closed, he asked, "Why did you give me your diary?"

"To protect myself," she answered.

"From what?"

"From the same things Janet is afraid of, the same people. Mr. Smith, because I've been with Senator Ewald and his family for many years, I know a great deal. I'm always there. I see, I hear. I never thought much about what that meant until Ms. Feldman was murdered. Then I knew it had to be because she knew something, too. I thought that if I gave the diary to someone else, people wouldn't have any reason to kill me. I could tell them you had it, knew everything. Does that make sense?"

Smith sat on the edge of the bed, his elbows on his knees, and rubbed his eyes. "From what you and Janet have told me, Marcia, it's very possible that Ed Farmer murdered Andrea Feldman. But there are others who had reason to kill her, powerful people, powerful organizations whose goals could be damaged by some of the things Senator Ewald has learned over the years and that he kept in his files. People like that stop at nothing, allow no one to get in their way. They justify what they do by claiming a 'greater good.'"

"Are you speaking of the DAF?"

"How do you know about that organization?" Smith asked.

Marcia took a deep breath. She walked across the room, leaned against a desk, and said, "I've made a mess of my life, Mr. Smith, and almost made a mess of everyone else's life around me. It's time to explain." She paused, then continued with what was obviously a difficult tale. "I tell you this for the same reason I gave you my diary. I think you're the only person I can really trust, aside from Janet and my cousin."

"Go ahead, I'm listening."

"Before I came to work for the Ewalds in California, I had lived a shabby life. I was many things, including a whore. I was a whore because it helped me survive. I used drugs when they weren't even common, except in the jazz musicians' world. I was married twice—no children, thank God—and I assaulted one of my husbands with a knife. He almost died, and I didn't care. The drugs saw to that." She drew in more oxygen to keep the fire going. "I reached the end, I suppose. I saw it that way, the end of my life. But I was lucky. A few good things happened to me, and I began to realize my life didn't have to end, that it could begin with something new, and decent, and clean."

"From the years I've known you, Marcia, I'd say that's exactly what did happen with your life. You know how respected you are by the Ewalds. They obviously place tremendous faith in you."

"Not deserved, I'm afraid."

"Why do you say that?"

"When I was so low, I naturally spent my time with others like me. Then I began meeting people in California who seemed to offer me the kind of support I needed. These were people who understood what it was like to be lonely and black and strung out in a strange place. One of the people who was so good to me was a man from Panama named Garcia."

"Garcia?"

"Yes, Hilton Garcia. Like the hotels."

The first name of the Garcia who'd set up Tony for his fall was Hilton. How many Hilton Garcias could there be?

"He was very kind to me. People said he was involved in drugs, but he never displayed that side to me, never offered any to me. He loaned me money, even found me an apartment. Then, one day, he disappeared, and I heard nothing from him again."

"Marcia, are you aware that the man in the next room, Tony Buffolino, was forced to resign from the police department because of a drug dealer named Hilton Garcia?"

She lowered, then opened her eyes. "Yes, I knew when I heard about that case that it must have been the same man. I was so uncomfortable in the other room with Mr. Buffolino. He doesn't know that I was friends with the man who hurt him."

Smith said, "I don't see how what you've told me so far would cause you to feel you've betrayed Senator Ewald."

"There is more, Mr. Smith. When I was hired by Mrs. Ewald in California, you can't imagine how happy I was, how joyous. It didn't mean that my past did not exist, but I *felt* different. All of a sudden, I was part of a regular and important *American* household, and I liked it. It made *me* feel important."

Smith felt considerable compassion for her. Marcia Mims was obviously an intelligent and decent woman who'd made some serious mistakes but had managed to rise above them. Certainly, nothing she'd said caused him to think less of her.

"One day—it was maybe a year, a year and a half ago—I got a call from a man who said that Hilton Garcia had suggested he contact me. His name was Miguel. He was Panamanian, too." She looked to Smith for a reaction; he gave her none. The name meant nothing to him.

"He seemed very nice, said he was alone in the United States and wondered if I would meet him for lunch. I remembered back to how I felt in California, and so we met on my next day off. He said he worked for a Colonel Gilbert Morales."

"That means he worked for a very controversial figure."

"Yes, I know that now, but I didn't know it then. I have read about Colonel Morales and the debate that surrounds him. Even though I work for a United States senator, I've never followed politics very closely. I don't know whether Colonel Morales's cause is the right one or not."

"I don't suppose it really matters, in a sense. What did this Miguel do for Colonel Morales?"

"He said he was an administrative assistant to him, that he was helping him return to power. He was very convincing, and during that lunch I did form an opinion of the colonel's goals. I started believing in them."

Smith looked at his watch. "Marcia, I'm going to have to get ready for Senator Ewald's dinner. Did you continue to see Miguel, become friends?"

"Yes. We met a number of times, maybe four, for lunch, dinner, or just a cup of coffee. Then . . ."

"Then what?"

"Then he said he wanted me to tell him things about Senator Ewald."

"What sort of things?"

"Things about conversations I might hear the senator having about Colonel Morales, telephone calls, people who met with Senator Ewald about Colonel Morales."

"He wanted you to *spy* on Senator Ewald."

"Yes."

"Anything else?"

"Yes. He asked me if I would look through any files Senator Ewald might keep in the house about Colonel Morales. He wanted me to make copies and give them to him."

"Did you?" Smith asked.

"No, I never gave him files, but I told him things about what went on in the house."

"Why did you do that to Senator Ewald? He's always been generous and good to you."

If Marcia were going to cry during this confession, it was now. Her lower lip trembled. She said, "I did it because Miguel knew everything about me from Hilton, about my whoring, what I did to my husband, the drugs. He threatened to destroy me with the Ewalds. I took that seriously. Can you understand that?"

Smith stood and put his hand on her shoulder. "Yes, Marcia, I understand it very well. The only important thing now is that you tell me the sort of information you gave Miguel that might have hurt Senator Ewald."

Her eyes were wet. "I never gave him much. I even lied, told him about things that never happened. I tried very hard not to hurt the senator, but at the same time did what I thought I had to do to protect myself." She almost smiled. "I became very good at that back in California, on the street."

Smith stepped back. "Have you been talking to Miguel recently? Has this been an ongoing relationship?"

"No. I mean, yes, we did talk recently. He stopped contacting me about six months ago. I was relieved, and assumed I would never hear from him again. Then he called me on Friday."

"This past Friday?"

"Yes. He wanted to know whether I knew Senator Ewald's plans for today."

"What did he mean, 'plans'?"

"Whether I had access to an itinerary, knew where the senator would be at every minute."

"Did you tell him what the senator's schedule was?"

"No, because I didn't know."

"Why do you think he wanted to know that, Marcia?"

"I have no idea. Well, I did think that . . ."

"You thought he possibly wanted to know those things because he intended to harm Senator Ewald. Is that what you were thinking?"

"Yes."

"You obviously know what this Miguel looks like."

"Of course."

"I'm glad you're coming to the dinner with us tonight."

"Mr. Smith, I couldn't do that. I'm the housekeeper. I . . ."

"You may become a housekeeper who saves a senator's life. Do you have any dressy clothes with you?" She was wearing a wrinkled lavender polyester pantsuit.

"Yes, I have a suitcase in the other room. I don't know if I have nice-enough clothes for a fancy dinner, but . . ."

Smith said, "Marcia, you are a very beautiful woman. You must know that. Remember it. Whatever you choose to wear will be just fine."

They arrived downstairs as the last guests from the cocktail party were entering the ballroom for dinner. Leslie Ewald stood at the ballroom door. She saw Smith and his group enter and went to them, stopping directly in front of Janet. She seemed to be struggling with what to say, then did the human thing that needs no words. She wrapped her arms around Janet and said, "I am very glad to see you, Janet. Welcome home."

"I'm sorry, Leslie," Janet said. "I've been a fool. I'm happy to be here."

"Come on. The catering staff here is marvelous. They've set up the table you asked for, Mac." She led them into the ballroom.

Their table had obviously been hastily set; the tablecloth and napkins were pink; the rest of the room was in red, white, and blue. "I did the best I could," Leslie said to Smith after they'd been seated.

"You did fine, Leslie, thank you. We can make do with pink."

Smith had instructed Marcia Mims to keep her eyes open for Miguel. He whispered it to her again as he excused himself and made his way to the front of the room, where he recognized a Secret Service agent, Robert Jeroldson. "May I speak with you for a moment?" Smith said.

Jeroldson scowled. Smith ignored his expression and said, "I'm Mackensie Smith, legal adviser to Senator Ewald. I have reason to believe that an attempt will be made on his life, either tonight or in the near future."

"Where did you get that?" Jeroldson asked.

"I really don't have the time, or the inclination, to explain." Smith now placed Jeroldson as the agent Ken Ewald didn't like. He asked, "Who's in charge of the Secret Service detail here tonight?"

"I am," said Jeroldson.

"Then listen to me. There is a young Panamanian named Miguel in the vicinity, probably in the hotel. My information is that he might be here to attempt an assassination of the senator. I haven't told Senator Ewald about this, nor do I intend to until the dinner is over." Smith pointed across the room to his table. "The black woman with me knows what Miguel looks like, and she's keeping her eyes peeled for him. I suggest you and your men stick especially close to the senator and his family until they're safely out of here. At that time, I'll get together with you and make a fuller report."

Smith didn't know whether Jeroldson resented being told what to do by someone outside his service or was simply a surly, unresponsive individual. Either way, Smith now shared Ewald's dislike for him. "Well?" Smith said.

"I'll discuss it with my superiors."

"I thought you were in charge."

"I have to call them. Excuse me." Jeroldson walked away from Smith and left the ballroom.

Dessert was served, and when it had been consumed the evening's MC stepped to the podium. "Ladies and gentlemen, please give a very warm reception to the next president of the United States, Senator Kenneth Ewald."

The room erupted into an ovation as Ewald came to the microphone. He held his hands high until the guests, most of whom were now standing, resumed their seats and quieted down.

"Ladies and gentlemen, you apparently think I'm okay, but *you* are wonderful!"

The applause started all over again, and most people jumped to their feet. Funny, Smith thought, how a simple declaration could trigger a reaction in a crowd. Politics. Strange game.

After the guests were again seated, Ewald began to speak spiritedly of his unbridled optimism for America, of the value of restraint in foreign affairs. He was well into it when Smith, whose back was to the main door to the ballroom, sensed that someone had entered. He turned and saw Jody Backus. Smith quietly left the table and went to where Backus was standing. "Senator Backus, Mac Smith," Smith whispered.

Backus acknowledged Smith's greeting but did not take his eyes off Ewald at the podium. The smell of liquor was heavy on his breath, but he wasn't drunk. Intense was more like it.

Why was he here? Smith wondered. What would bring Ewald's leading opponent to a fund-raiser? Smith slipped his hand in the crook of Backus's elbow and led him to the darkness against the rear wall. "What a surprise to see you, Senator. What brings you here?"

"Conscience."

"Conscience about what?" Smith asked in a whisper.

"About your friend up there, Mr. Ewald. I came up with some

information—it doesn't matter where I got it—that says to me that your friend might get himself killed. Lots a' people don't like him much, includin' me. The difference between them and me is that I believe in the system."

"We've been alerted to a possible threat on Ken's life tonight," Smith said. "I've primed the Secret Service, and I intend to tell Ken the minute his speech is over."

"That's good, Mac. You tell your friend up there to watch his ass. You know, I've played lots a' political games in my life, and nobody's ever been better at it. I've made lots of deals, sold out to lots of people because I believed the result was good for America. But every man has his limit, and I reached mine today. You know what I think?"

"What?"

"I think Mr. Ewald is goin' to be the next president of these United States. I don't like that idea much, and I've made no bones about it, but if he's the one the party and the people want, then I'll work my fat ol' Georgia butt off to help him, hear?"

"Yes, Senator, I hear," Smith said. "Please, join us at that table over there."

Smith took a chair that was against the wall and brought it to the table for Backus. Everyone at the table recognized him, but no one said anything. They were all tuned in to what Ken Ewald was saying at the front of the room.

When Ewald's speech ended, on a rare quiet note, and the room had again applauded at length, Smith said into Backus's ear, "Please, don't leave, Senator. I'll be right back." He skirted tables until reaching the dais where Ken and Leslie sat. Smith motioned for Ken to lean forward. "Ken, Jody Backus is sitting with me."

"What is he doing here?"

"I won't go into it now, but I believe, and so does he, that someone is about to make an attempt on your life tonight."

Ewald's face turned ashen.

"Ken," Smith continued, "I don't know what your plans are for the rest of the evening, but change them immediately. Take another route, leave this dinner early, and get to somewhere safe. I've told the Secret Service about it."

"Who?"

"All that later, when you and the family are safe. By the way, Janet is with me."

"Christ, is she involved with . . . ?"

"Ken, Janet is back because she wants to be. I'll see you later. Come to our suite upstairs, room 1117." He repeated it.

The band began a two-beat medley for dancing. Ewald, his face expressing his mixed emotions, turned and deftly handled the swarm of well-wishers flocking around the dais, each anxious to press important flesh.

Smith returned to his table. "What are your plans for the rest of the evening, Senator?"

"To tell Ken Ewald I think he'll make a fine president."

"I'm sure he'll be delighted to hear that, especially from you, but how about delivering that message up in our suite? I want him out of here as fast as possible. We can all go up together. I've told Ken about the possibility of an attempt on his life, and he's trying to wrap this up faster than usual."

"You know somethin', Mac Smith, Kenny-boy is right. You'd make a hell of an attorney general, maybe even chief of staff in his White House."

Smith's proclamation that he was committed to returning to teaching law was on the tip of his tongue, but he decided it was the wrong time and place to make it. He smiled, said, "We'll all be leaving in a minute."

"You say the Secret Service has been alerted?" Backus asked.

"Yes." Smith saw Jeroldson standing with a colleague and pointed to him. "He's in charge," Smith said to Backus.

"That don't necessarily mean anything, Mac."

"What do you mean?"

"He's . . . well, not to be trusted."

"I don't understand."

"Just believe me. We goin'?"

"Yes."

Smith told Tony Buffolino to stay as close as possible to Ewald, and to keep his eye on Marcia. If she showed any sign of recognition, he was to act.

"My piece is upstairs," Buffolino said.

"Then you'll have to do without it. I'll be with you every step of the way."

Smith took Janet's arm, and with the others from the table, including Jody Backus, melded into the flow of people surrounding Ken and Leslie Ewald, moved them through the large doors, crossed the room in which the cocktail party had been held, and entered the lobby. A large crowd was waiting. The sight of Ewald, who stood taller than most of those surrounding him, triggered applause. Smith glanced at Ewald; he was doing his best to smile, but there was unmistakable concern on his face. A wedge of Secret Service agents led the way, and slowly, gently but firmly, parted the crowd.

They were halfway across the lobby when Marcia Mims stiffened. "There he is, over there," she said.

Smith stood on his toes and looked in the direction she was pointing. It was the same slim young man he'd noticed waiting for an elevator and lingering in the hallway upstairs. Of course.

Tony Buffolino saw what was going on and asked Smith, "Who's that?"

"I think it's our man."

Buffolino moved quickly, his cane leading the way. "Excuse me, sorry," he said, pushing people aside. "Come on, come on," he said to those impeding his progress. "Move, Tony, move," he heard Smith say from behind.

Buffolino was no more than twenty feet from Miguel when he saw the slender Panamanian remove his hand from his jacket, the modular Pachmayr Colt in it. Tony glanced back, saw Ken and Leslie Ewald moving quickly as the agents opened up a straight path for them to the elevators—and directly toward Miguel.

"Hey, dirtbag!" Tony yelled as loud as he could. He shoved a matronly woman to the floor, pushed two men aside, and flung himself at Miguel, knocking up the arm with the weapon. A shot shattered dozens of small pieces of crystal dangling from a chandelier. Tony rammed the tip of his cane into Miguel's midsection. The Panamanian doubled over, and the revolver discharged again, this bullet kicking back up off the marble floor and passing through an agent's shoulder.

With his cane in both hands, Buffolino brought it down sharply across the back of Miguel's neck. He crumpled to the floor, and Tony held him there. The revolver had slid away, stopping at the feet of a hysterical woman. Secret Service agents and uniformed security guards stood over Tony as he pinned Miguel to the ground. Tony looked up. "How 'bout this guy? This guy wasn't goin' to vote for the next president of the United States."

THIRTY-SEVEN

THE ATMOSPHERE in the suite was charged with confusion and horror.

"Who was he?" Ewald asked Smith.

"His name is Miguel, Ken, and he works for Colonel Gilbert Morales."

Ewald looked at Smith. "Morales put a hit out on me?"

"It looks that way. He must have taken your speeches seriously, about trying to avoid returning tyrants to power. Even 'our' tyrants. We can thank Marcia for recognizing Miguel."

Ewald looked across the room to where Marcia stood with Leslie, Janet, and Tony Buffolino. He then spotted Jody Backus standing alone in the opposite corner, glass in hand. Ewald said to Smith, "I need some quick explaining, Mac. Let's go into the other room."

They started to make their way through a cluster of people when Ed Farmer stopped them, locked eyes with Smith, and said, "I want to talk to you."

"Yes, I'm sure you do," said Smith.

"What's going on?" Ewald asked.

"Ed and I will talk first, Ken," Smith said. "I don't think we'll be long."

Smith and Farmer entered the empty bedroom, and Smith closed the door. "I think I know what you want to say, Ed."

"Yes, I suppose you do, Mac. Interesting cast you assembled tonight. I can see we have the missing neurotic daughter-in-law with us, and the faithful minority housekeeper. They must be filling you with tantalizing stories."

"Tantalizing? That's tabloid talk. I prefer to think of what they've told me as useful, illuminating."

Farmer smiled. "Mac, obviously I'm going to need your help."

"For what?"

"To defend me, of course."

Smith looked steadily at the man. "For the murder of Andrea Feldman."

"I wouldn't use the word 'murder.' To me, murder is an act that accomplishes nothing more than the death of an individual. I did not *murder* Andrea Feldman."

"I've never been a fan of semantic games, but go ahead, Farmer, use your definition. You did *kill* her."

"Yes, but it certainly wasn't premeditated."

"You took Ken's gun with you when you went to meet her."

"Only because it was handy."

"Why take a gun at all if you didn't intend to use it?"

"For emphasis." He smiled again, which rankled Smith. "Andrea was bright enough, but sometimes didn't get the point. Do you know what I mean? She'd latch onto a way of thinking about something, and nothing, not even the most reasoned argument, could get her to see it differently."

"And she didn't see things your way when you met her outside the Kennedy Center."

"Exactly." The expression on Farmer's face seemed to indicate that he thought Smith not only understood what he was saying, but was sympathetic to it.

"What was it you were trying to get across to her?" Smith asked.

"That I was not somebody to threaten."

"What did she threaten you with, Farmer, that she would tell your boss, Senator Ewald, that you were selling him out?"

"Come on, Mac, nobody sells anybody out at this level of politics. You evaluate, read the tides, and take the boat that will get you there the fastest."

At least he hadn't used sports metaphors, Smith thought.

"Mac, Andrea was a slut, a user. She was capable of selling anyone out for personal gain. She called Ken's house after the gala that night. Ken wasn't there because he was shacked up with the opera singer. Marcia took the call. Andrea told Marcia to tell Ken to meet her behind the big German relief across from the Kennedy Center's main entrance."

"And you heard the conversation on the tape in the second-floor office."

"Yes. Who told you that?"

"It doesn't matter. What was Andrea going to tell Ken?"

"That I'd stolen sensitive files having to do with Morales and the Kane Ministries."

"Why would she say that? Did you steal them? My information is that *she* stole them."

"To be precise, Mac, I never physically took the files from the house, although I did make their contents known to certain people."

"What people? Garrett Kane?"

"No, the distinguished senator in the other room."

"Jody Backus?"

"Yes."

Smith stood and leaned on the back of a chair. "Why would you help Ken's major competitor for the nomination?"

"Ken Ewald won't win the White House," Farmer said.

"And you think Jody Backus can?"

Farmer shook his head. "No, Raymond Thornton will be our next president."

"So what did you have to gain by passing secrets along to Backus?"

"Assurance of a job. Backus might be a Democrat, but he's much more wired into the Manning administration and Raymond Thornton than anyone really knows."

Smith sighed. "Then the ideas that Ken Ewald stands for mean nothing to you."

"Ideas? Of course not. There are no ideas or ideals in politics. The only thing that matters is winning. Hanging in with blind faith and loyalty to a loser doesn't get you very far."

Smith felt, at once, disgust and pity. The young man with the bow tie, tweed jacket, and penny loafers was like so many young people in Smith's law classes, void of ideals, of dreams other than wealth and power; there were no causes that they would fight for unless there were tangible gains, nothing for which they would stand on a soapbox and preach, only a pragmatic sense of self. God help you, Mr. Farmer, God help us all, Smith thought. He said, "You brought me in here and said you might need my help. Do you really think I would defend you?"

"Why not? He's not going to win, which means you'll never become attorney general. I think you and I are very much alike, Mac. We're both good players in this game, and we're both dependent on how the voters see Ken Ewald versus Raymond Thornton. They'll go for Thornton. Trust me. There's nobody better at analyzing a political situation than me."

"That may be," Smith said, "but why did you have to kill her?"

"I didn't intend to. As I said before, I just wanted to emphasize my point. Funny, but it occurred to me just before I pulled the trigger that even if she told Ken Ewald what I'd done, it really shouldn't affect my future. But then the irony, the reality, of the situation became clear to me. There isn't a politician in this country who doesn't try to gain damaging information about opponents, and most of them are happy to pay for it. But the minute you're the one who sells it to them, they become self-righteous and brand you as a person who can't be trusted. What garbage, huh, Mac? I looked at Andrea that night and realized the difference. She'd sold out only for money. As far as I'm concerned, that's intolerable."

"You consider your own motives loftier?"

"Of course I do. Don't you see it that way?" He became uncharacteristically passionate. "I see wonderful things ahead for this country, and I see people like you and me helping to shape them. I can't do that standing at Ken Ewald's side when he gives his concession speech in November." A small smile crossed Farmer's lips, and Smith felt himself begin to tremble.

"When I saw Backus arrive tonight, saw Marcia Mims and Janet Ewald here, I knew you'd put it together. Was I wrong, Mac? You knew I was the one who killed Andrea."

"Not with any certainty, but yes, I knew."

"They'll have trouble proving it."

"I don't think so. I'll certainly testify to our conversation here tonight."

Farmer guffawed. "You can't."

"Why not?"

"Because you're my lawyer. Attorney-client privilege."

"I'm not your attorney, Farmer. You were willing to let Paul Ewald take the rap, weren't you?"

Farmer's eyes opened wide, and a smug expression crossed his face. "Of course. I really thought I was off the hook when they focused on Paul as the prime suspect. Seemed perfect. There he was having an affair with her, fighting with Janet all the time, disappearing the night of the murder, and having easy access to his father's gun. Then you came into the picture and the spotlight on Paul dimmed. You were one of the best criminal attorneys this city has ever seen, and I know you'll pull out all the stops for me. Believe me, Mac, someday I'll be in a position to return the favor."

Smith sprang from his chair, grabbed Farmer by the lapels, lifted him from the chair, and slid him across the desk into the wall. Farmer's glasses fell off, and his smile was replaced by an expression of terror.

"You slimy bastard, comparing me to you, sitting here calmly while you talk about all the good reasons you had for killing someone. Defend you? I'll do everything I can to see that you spend the rest of your pathetic life in jail." He released his grasp, opened the door, and stepped into the living room. Ken Ewald and Jody Backus were in the corner talking. People became aware of Smith and turned to him. Conversation dwindled, then stopped.

Smith motioned to Tony Buffolino to come to him. He said quietly, "Call the police and tell them we have Andrea Feldman's murderer."

Buffolino looked toward the open door to the bedroom. "Him? Joe Bow Tie?"

"Yes."

Farmer appeared in the doorway. He'd replaced his glasses and was straightening his tie. He smiled at Smith as he crossed the room to where Ewald and Backus stood. "Well, Senator Backus, telling your esteemed colleague how you tried to sell him out?"

Backus glowered at Farmer through watery eyes. He said to Ewald, "You've had yourself a Judas in your own house all along, Ken. You know what this weasel tried to do?"

Ewald look quizzically at Farmer.

"This little weasel tried to make a deal with me to sell secrets out of your campaign," Backus said. "How 'bout that?"

Smith joined them as Farmer said, "Don't listen to him, Ken. He'd do anything to make sure you never become president, including murder."

"What's he saying, Jody?"

Farmer continued, "Your good friend, the esteemed senator from Georgia here, arranged to have Andrea Feldman killed to cover up the fact that she was selling your files on Kane and Morales to him."

Backus was about to reach for Farmer when Smith stepped between them. He said to Ewald, "Ken, this will all be resolved and explained in short order. Let me just say that your trusted campaign manager Mr. Farmer is the one who murdered Andrea Feldman to cover his own tracks. The two of them, Andrea and Farmer, had been selling you out all along."

Ewald's face was sheer bewilderment. He shook his head and said, "I just don't understand what's gone on this evening."

"You don't know who your friends are, Ken," said Farmer. "I'm glad you'll never be president of this country. You've made too many messes in your life, and you won't have me anymore to clean up after you." He looked at Leslie Ewald, who'd come up to them. "Your whole family is pathetic," he said.

Farmer slowly turned and started for the door.

"Tony, don't let him leave," Smith said to Buffolino, who was on the phone with the MPD. Tony dropped the phone and started to get up, but Smith said, "No, don't bother. Let him go. He won't disappear." Or maybe he'll kill himself, Smith thought, not at all pleased at his casual acceptance of that possibility.

Smith looked at Leslie, who was obviously as confused as her husband. He said, "I think a lot of nasty things are behind you and Ken now." To Ken, he added, "I'll give you details another time. It's time for you to nail down the nomination, Ken, and for me to get back to teaching law."

Backus, whose glass was empty, slapped Ewald on the back, which brought a wince to Ewald's face. "It's been a tough campaign, Ken, and I bow to the better man. You've got my support one hundred percent, and you can count on it from this moment forward."

THIRTY-EIGHT

I HAVE NOTHING MORE to say today, except that I hope at least a few of you will occasionally take time away from your pursuit of fees and partnerships to do something with your legal education that benefits others." Smith surveyed the faces of the students in his advanced criminal-law class. It was the final day they would be together before graduation.

"Professor Smith."

"Yes?"

"Are you going to the convention in San Francisco?"

"Yes," Smith answered.

"Do you think Senator Ewald will be the Democratic nominee?"

"I would imagine so, now that Senator Backus has dropped out and has given his full support to Senator Ewald."

"If he wins in November, will you become his attorney general?"

"Why would that be of interest to you?" Smith asked.

"Well, sir, it would be . . ." She laughed nervously. "It would be a nice credential to have been taught by an attorney general of the United States."

"Frankly, Ms. Mencken, I don't see that as representing any particular advantage to a law student. People who become attorneys general are like some doctors who become chiefs of staff at their hospitals—and exhibit far more interest in politics than in healing the sick, or, in the case of your intended profession, in defending the unjustly accused or convicting the accurately accused. Not only that, they don't have time to practice their profession because they are always too busy running for office, one kind of office or another. If you must have surgery in the future, Ms. Mencken, I suggest you not seek the services of any medical chief of staff. Based on that thesis, it would be to your advantage that I *do not* become attorney general."

The red-faced young man next to her quickly raised his hand and said, "You've evaded the question, Professor Smith. Will you be the next attorney general if Senator Ewald becomes president?"

Smith smiled, slid his notes into his briefcase, and snapped it shut. He looked at the class and said, "Next November, I will be at this university teaching this course to other students. You will have graduated and begun your careers. I will be flattered if you drop in from time to time, or send me a brief note letting me know how you're progressing." He was about to end the class with his usual, "Good day, ladies and gentlemen." Instead, he waved to them and said, *"Ciao!"*

UNITED States Senator Kenneth Ewald had been receiving people all day in his suite at the Compton Court Hotel in San Francisco. The final roll call was that night. Things were looking good, although there had been a last-minute move to position a more conservative senator from Texas as a serious contender. But that ploy seemed designed as much for four years in the future as for the moment. The die-hard conservatives in the party determined to deny Ewald the nomination had been busy rallying elaborate support for the Texas legislator, but according to Ewald's new campaign manager, Paul Ewald, they were falling considerably short of their goal.

Still, Ken Ewald was worried, would be until the final votes were counted. He sat alone after a long meeting with leading delegates committed to him. A glass of club soda with a wedge of lime was at the table next to him. He looked at his watch: an hour before his next appointment. He had scheduled it that way. Ewald needed time to think, something he'd decided to do more of in the future.

Outside the closed door, in the living room, secretaries and staff members fielded phone calls. "No, the senator is unavailable at this moment." "Yes, he will be attending the meeting in two hours." "No, he has no intention of releasing a statement before tonight."

One of his secretaries, whose nerves were becoming frazzled from the pace of the day, answered a call with an abrupt, "Yes?"

"This is Roseanna Gateaux. Would it be possible for me to speak with Senator Ewald?"

The secretary placed her hand over the mouthpiece and said to a young aide next to her, "Roseanna Gateaux? Isn't that the opera singer?"

"Yeah. She's an old friend of the senator."

"She wants to speak with him."

The male aide shrugged. "He said not to disturb him, but I think I'd better with this one." He winked, went to the door, and knocked. Ewald told him to come in. "Senator, a Ms. Gateaux wishes to speak with you on the phone."

The mention of her name hit Ewald physically. He realized the aide was waiting for an answer. He said, "Put her through."

"Roseanna?" he said after the aide was gone.

"I know I shouldn't be calling you like this but . . ."

"It's all right." He didn't say he was aware that she was the one person capable of ruining his chances for the presidency, and ruining his marriage, which was, Lord knew, shaky enough.

"Ken, could I possibly see you for a few minutes? I promise it won't take me long to say what I have to say."

He wanted to say no, but he was afraid to. They hadn't had any contact since the events of a month ago, and he knew it had to be that way. Still, there was a part of him that thought it better to resolve problems face-to-face, and in this case to make it plain that there could never be a relationship again. He took into consideration the fact that he had scheduled this private time, and that Leslie would not be back for at least another two hours. "Yes," he said, "but I only have a few minutes. Where are you?"

"Downstairs in the hotel."

"All right, please come up."

His secretary ushered Roseanna into the room. Ewald was aware of a questioning look on the secretary's face and quickly dismissed her, saying, "It's okay. Five minutes."

"You look very good," Roseanna said, not moving from just inside the door.

"So do you. You do know, Roseanna, that this will be the last time we will ever be alone together. It has to be that way."

"I understand. I only came here to tell you that you need never worry about me, need never wake up in the middle of the night and wonder whether what we shared together will ever become public knowledge.

No kiss-and-tell books, no talk-show interviews, no articles in the *National Enquirer*."

He smiled. The smile represented relief at her words, as well as certain sadness at what they meant. "Come, sit," he said.

"No, I know you don't have the time, and—"

"Sit down, Roseanna, just for a minute."

They sat in armchairs that were side by side and looked at each other. She was the most inordinately beautiful woman he'd ever known, possessing a beauty so different from Leslie's; a difference that was, after all, part of the attraction.

She said, "You will become president."

"I don't know, Roseanna. I'm trying very hard to be, although I'm not sure I should."

"Why do you say that?"

"Because . . . because I'm not sure any longer that I'm the man to sit in such a position of power, of life and death."

Her hand poised in midair as though having a mind of its own, then decided to come down on top of his hand, lightly, fingertips only. Her eyes filled as she said, "I think this country will be very fortunate to have you leading it, and I consider *myself* very fortunate to have been able to touch you, to know you."

He was embarrassed, and looked away.

She stood. "Ken, what we had was very special to me. I know we will never have it again, and that is a sorrow. At the same time, I celebrate, rather than mourn, what I've lost. Good luck tonight. I'll be watching."

Before he could say anything, she went to the door, opened it and paused as though about to deliver an exit line, then went through it, and was gone.

M A C Smith, Annabel Reed, and Tony Buffolino had taken the afternoon to ride the cable car to Fisherman's Wharf, where they'd browsed the eclectic wares of sidewalk artisans, bought chocolate in Ghirardelli Square, eaten crab and calamari out of small paper bowls purchased from vendors along Jefferson Street, walked out of the famous Boudin Bakery with loaves of sourdough bread, and returned to the Raphael Hotel footsore and happy.

They sat in Buffolino's room and toasted their good day with champagne.

Eventually, the conversation got around to the events that had brought them together in this place. Buffolino asked Smith what he thought of Ed Farmer's chances in his trial. Farmer had pleaded not guilty, and had hired a top D.C. lawyer, Morris Jankowski.

"Jankowski is good," Smith said. "He'll find plenty of holes in the prosecution's case, including my testimony, which, I'm sure, Jankowski will paint as unimportant, create an atmosphere in which I had a personal grudge against Farmer, misunderstood what he was saying."

"Can you believe this about Greist?" Annabel said, picking up that day's San Francisco *Examiner* and tossing it back on a table. "Ridiculous!" Herbert Greist had suffered a fatal heart attack. The story in the *Examiner* was based on charges by a left-wing group that the Bureau might have killed him.

Smith laughed. "Tomorrow we'll read that a right-wing group is accusing the Communists of killing him to keep him quiet."

"Ya know, Greist looked like a guy with a bum ticker," Buffolino said.

"Anybody hear anything new about the Miguel person?" Annabel asked.

Buffolino said, "They'll never get him to admit any connection to Morales."

"Or to Kane," Smith said.

"Or to Backus," said Buffolino.

"Or to Thornton," Annabel said.

"Possibly because he didn't have a connection to any of them except Morales," Smith said.

"Getting soft in your old age," Annabel said.

"No, just getting less cynical as I enter into *middle age*. More champagne?" Smith asked. He refilled their glasses.

Buffolino asked, "Do you believe your buddy, Shevlin, about the box in Mae Feldman's house?"

Smith grunted, nodded. "Yes, I don't see any reason for him to lie to me. The FBI has wanted those files for a long time. They figured out where they might be and took them. They just also ended up with a couple of hundred thousand dollars in cash. What they didn't figure out was that Mae Feldman and Carla Zaretski were one and the same. Sorry you had to learn it under such nasty circumstances, Tony."

Buffolino scowled. "And I got cold-cocked in her house by a couple of Bureau guys." He looked up as though to commune with God. "Jesus, there I was with a box with all Ewald's files and all that cash." He laughed. "You never would have seen me again."

"I doubt that," Smith said. "You're a man of honor, Tony."

"Yeah, that's me, the honorable Anthony Buffolino." He raised his glass. "A toast to Mackensie Smith, who did good by me. I hope you know how much I appreciate everything, Mac."

"My pleasure." Smith had paid Tony a bonus, and arranged a security job for him at the university.

"A toast to you, Tony," said Annabel. "You're a lot nicer than what Mac said you'd be."

"Hey, Mac, what did you tell her? No matter. To you, Annabel, a real classy lady."

"Ready for an announcement?" Smith asked.

"What kind a' announcement?"

"We've decided to get married."

"No kidding?"

"Yes," Annabel said, giggling. "Isn't it wonderful? Two can live as cheaply as one, if you cut down on the takeout dinners. We're going to London on our honeymoon."

"Hey, congrats. If you have any problems, married-people problems, any questions, just ask me. I got experience."

"Up to being best man, Tony?" Smith asked.

"I thought I was all along." He stood and twirled his cane in the air. "London. I can't wait."

Mac and Annabel looked at each other.

"I'm goin' with you, right?"

"No," Smith said.

"No," Annabel said.

"No?"

"No," they said in unison.

"I guess you mean no."

"Yes, we mean no."

.   .   .

TONY Buffolino was invited to remain in San Francisco for a few days after the convention as the personal guest of Ken Ewald. He was put up in a penthouse suite at the Mark Hopkins, for, as Ewald said, "your heroism in the lobby of the Watergate Hotel on my behalf." Tony was delighted; he'd fallen madly in love with Alicia, a cocktail waitress at the Top of the Mark, and told Mac Smith that if he moved fast enough, there might be a double wedding.

Mac and Annabel shook their heads and flew back to Washington the day after the convention. Newspapers on their laps said it all: EWALD DEM CHOICE BY ACCLAMATION. BACKUS HIS VEEP. A large photograph of Ewald and Backus with their hands clasped and raised, their families at their sides, dominated the front pages.

"I'm proud of you," Annabel said, after their flight had taken off.

"For what?"

"For the way you turned Ken down when he asked you to manage his campaign, and to become attorney general."

"What else could I do with a redheaded honey badger standing within striking distance behind me?"

"For a second, I thought you might say yes."

"Not a chance. My brief moment in the political arena will last me a lifetime. Ken Ewald and Jody Backus. Strange bedfellows, as the saying goes."

"Incredible more than strange," Annabel said.

"I suppose so," said Smith. "I believe Ed Farmer when he says that it was Backus who made the deal with him to buy Ken's files on DAF, Morales, and Kane. But Ken doesn't believe it, which is just as well I suppose."

"Not if Backus sells him out in some way when he's the VP."

"I don't think that will happen, Annabel. This is politics, not real life. Hell, Germany and Japan tried to kill us in World War Two, and as a reward we've helped them kill us economically. No, Backus will be a loyal and useful VP, for whatever that's worth."

"Ken Ewald and Jody Backus, our next president and vice-president."

"Probably."

"Will we go to the inaugural? I'll need a new gown."

"We'll watch on TV. When it's over, we'll become not-so-strange bedfellows, and fool around a little."

"Yeah?"

"Yeah. Any objections?"

"Only one."

"What is it?"

"That we not have to wait until January twentieth. I propose we celebrate our own upcoming inaugural the minute we get back, provided that animal you call a dog will give us the bed."

"I miss Rufus already."

She growled. He laughed. And they clinked glasses, settled back, and fell asleep as if on schedule.

ABOUT THE AUTHOR

MARGARET TRUMAN is the author of eight successful mystery thrillers. Born in Independence, Missouri, she now lives with her husband, Clifton Daniel, in New York City. They have four sons and two grandchildren.